RAMSEY CAMPBELL

THE SEARCHING DEAD

The First Book of the
Three Births of Daoloth Trilogy

This is a **FLAME TREE PRESS** book

Text copyright © 2021 Ramsey Campbell

FLAME TREE PRESS
6 Melbray Mews, London, SW6 3NS, UK
flametreepress.com

US sales, distribution and warehouse:
Simon & Schuster
simonandschuster.biz

UK distribution and warehouse:
Marston Book Services Ltd
marston.co.uk

Publisher's Note: This is a work of fiction. Names, characters, places, and
incidents are a product of the author's imagination. Locales and public names
are sometimes used for atmospheric purposes. Any resemblance to actual
people, living or dead, or to businesses, companies, events, institutions, or
locales is completely coincidental.

Thanks to the Flame Tree Press team, including:
Taylor Bentley, Frances Bodiam, Federica Ciaravella, Don D'Auria,
Chris Herbert, Josie Karani, Molly Rosevear, Mike Spender,
Cat Taylor, Maria Tissot, Nick Wells, Gillian Whitaker.

The cover is created by Flame Tree Studio with
thanks to Nik Keevil and Shutterstock.com.
The font families used are Avenir and Bembo.

Flame Tree Press is an imprint of Flame Tree Publishing Ltd
flametreepublishing.com

A copy of the CIP data for this book is available from the British Library
and the Library of Congress.

3 5 7 9 8 6 4 2

HB ISBN: 978-1-78758-558-4
US PB ISBN: 978-1-78758-556-0
UK PB ISBN: 978-1-78758-557-7
ebook ISBN: 978-1-78758-559-1
Also available in FLAME TREE AUDIO

Printed and bound in Great Britain by Clays Ltd, Elcograf S.p.A.

RAMSEY CAMPBELL

THE SEARCHING DEAD

The First Book of the
Three Births of Daoloth Trilogy

FLAME TREE PRESS
London & New York

For Mat and Serena –
from the past and from a far land

What the dead behold, they may become.
Revelations of Glaaki, volume 9,
On the Uses of the Dead (Matterhorn Press, 1863?)

Some memories feel like a hook in the guts, but at least that means they're entirely mine. That's why I cling to every one that makes me wince – memories of loss, of humiliation, of doing things I should never have done, of failing to act as I should. They help to persuade me I'm still just myself and nobody else. Sometimes they succeed.

When I look back I see my life is littered with mistakes. I could easily feel it's composed of them. I often think the worst one was agreeing with my father that I was a thief. I only wanted to give him some peace, though I'd never stolen even the tiniest item. The mistake seems trivial compared with so much that has happened since, but then – like far too many people – I've seldom seen the larger context at the time. There's no use thinking I was just a child when I first heard hints of how the world would change. I might have noticed more if I hadn't been preoccupied with the changes that were taking place in my own small world.

CHAPTER ONE

1952: The Nocturnal Gardener

"Don't forget your cap, Dominic," my mother said, which was one reason why I overlooked so much that day.

I wasn't likely to forget it or the rest of my school uniform. The tie was helping the stiff shirt collar chafe my neck while the heels of the new shoes scraped the backs of my heels with every step I took. My parents had made me wear the outfit for our Sunday stroll in Stanley Park, parading me for everyone to admire when I would have liked to go unnoticed. While I didn't mind my first long trousers, I thought the cap and tie and blazer were unreasonably green, not much less bright than the trees shading the pavements on both sides of our road. Besides, the uniform felt as though the summer holidays had ended sooner than they should. My face was growing hot as the September afternoon, because my mother seemed to think I might let her and my father down, when he said "Best foot, son."

He could have been counselling speed because of the rain in the air, but I knew the issue was the lady who was hurrying under the railway bridge at the end of the road. "Coo-ee," Mrs Norris called and waved as well.

The bridge amplified her voice, not that it needed magnifying, and I felt as if everyone was competing to be first to our gate. We reached it before Mrs Norris did, but then politeness overtook my parents. "How are you, Mrs Norris?" my father said.

Though she was almost within arm's length, she matched his shout. "Well enough, Mr Sheldrake. Really quite well."

I was always amazed by how large a voice lived inside so small a person, presumably a product of her deafness. She was the neatest person I knew, and I used to think that was because there was so little of her to keep tidy, unlike my awkward gangling frame. I see her in her pale blue suit and white blouse fixed at the throat with an oval brooch not much less broad than her neck, fawn stockings with seams straight as plumb lines, her regimented greying curls mostly hidden by a domed hat as shiny white as the heads of the hatpins. By the time I'd taken all this in my mother would have been urging "Dominic."

I fumbled to raise my cap an inch and felt my face grow redder still. "Good afternoon," I mumbled, "Mrs Norris."

"Why, Dominic, you look like a real little gentleman." As I wished I could yank the cap down far enough to hide my face, she turned back to my parents. "He's a credit to you," she cried louder still.

"We try our best." When Mrs Norris cocked her head to catch the words my mother not much less than bellowed "He's our future."

I saw my father glance about in case they were disturbing any of the neighbours. "Should you be getting home, Mrs Norris? I think we're in for a storm."

Her small eyes brought a gleam to her concise assiduously powdered face. "Would you like to hear what's bucked me up?"

While he didn't sigh aloud, I saw his chest swell and deflate. It was left to my mother to say "Do come in for a cuppa."

"If you're certain you've enough."

This wasn't a sly insult, not in those last weeks of rationing, but it provoked my father to unlatch the rickety gate he kept promising to mend. "We've always some for visitors," he said without making sure she heard.

At least I wouldn't have to stand politely by while the adults chatted. As everyone crowded onto the path, beside which there was just sufficient room for my mother's three rosebushes, the trees along the road began to hiss and then to rattle their leaves. By the time we piled into the front hall the downpour was turning the pavements dark as tar. "Good heavens," Mrs Norris protested, "God must have it in for someone."

My father scowled at the irreverence, and I knew my mother would have sent me out to play except for the rain. "Find something to do in your room, Dominic," she said.

"I've got my book to read, or I might write."

"That's a good boy," Mrs Norris cried, planting her purple handbag on the tall but tiny table under the laden coatrack by the stairs so as to extract her purse. "And what do good boys get?"

Not only the question embarrassed me. I knew she was thinking of her late husband. Her eyes had begun to glint with moisture, and I yearned to look away as I mumbled "Dunno."

She snapped her purse open and fished out a coin. "Here's a pence for a good lad," she said as Mr Norris used to.

"What do—"

Before my mother could complete the shameful prompt I babbled "Thank you, Mrs Norris."

I earned my mother's frown all the same, having grabbed the penny in such haste I nearly dropped it. "Make yourself scarce now, son," my father said under his breath.

I didn't need urging. I hung my cap on the hook that bore my new raincoat and fled upstairs, past the framed mottoes on the wall. My mother's mother had stitched "Keep The Home Fires Burning", though I never knew if she'd done so after losing her husband to the first World War, and my father's was responsible for "Thou God See All", which used to confuse me by not being quite the phrase I'd been taught at school. As I reached my room my mother called "Don't forget your knees when you sit down."

She meant the trick I'd had to learn, tugging up my trousers to keep the creases sharp. I shut the bedroom door behind me – almost, at any rate. To close it properly you had to lift it on its loose hinges, another of the items my father kept undertaking to repair. I draped my blazer over the back of the chair opposite the bed and sat at the table, half of which was occupied by a Meccano bridge I'd built. Must I still feel guilty because I meant to listen, not to read or write? I made the halves of the bridge squeak up and down a few times, and fed the penny to my money box, a golliwog who raised his metal arm to drop the coin into his mouth, and then I gazed out at the graveyard.

My room had a view of Liverpool Cemetery – Anfield Cemetery, as it came to be known. Back then it never troubled me, not least because my parents obviously didn't think it should. I thought of it more as a park with stones and trees in, leading to the distant sight of the allotments where my mother had grown vegetables while my father was away at war. My sole uneasy moment had been the first time I'd heard the graves roar with an enormous wordless voice on a sunny Saturday afternoon – the sound of a crowd at a football match at Goodison Park beyond the graveyard. I should like to believe it made me dream of another immense voice, but I know better. No, I know far worse.

I heard the rising whistle of the kettle on the stove, and then china clinked downstairs, the best set that was reserved for guests. Either courtesy forbade conversation until tea was served or my parents weren't anxious to hear from their visitor. The rain had diminished to a drizzle, and a man was wheeling a pram along the nearest path. While I didn't find it odd that he'd brought a pram into the cemetery, it was unusual to see a man alone with one. His height was uncommon as well, and he kept stooping over the handle of the pram to address the occupant. As he passed my window I could see his long thin oval face so clearly that I saw he was talking about a mother. I leaned towards the window in case I could make out more words, and he met my eyes at once. He reared up to his full height, an action I found so daunting even at that distance that I nearly overturned the chair in my haste to hide. The next moment he returned his attention to the baby in the pram as if I meant nothing to him, and I was distracted by my mother's voice in the kitchen under my room. "Come and sit in the lounge, Mrs Norris."

I heard a discreet rattle of spoons against china as she carried the tray along the hall. Before anybody else spoke, the door of the front room shut tight. I thought I mightn't be able to hear unless I ventured closer, which would have meant owning up to eavesdropping if only to myself, but I didn't even need to strain my ears to hear Mrs Norris say "Thank you both for everything you've done for me."

The man and the pram were receding beyond trees that twitched with raindrops. "We've only done what neighbours should," my mother said.

"You'd be surprised how many that you thought were friends don't want to know you when you've had a loss."

"We've had a few in the family," my father said.

"That's why I wish you'd give our church a try sometime."

I imagined the frown that would be drawing his ruddy eyebrows together while he straightened his thick lips, an expression that made his broad big-nosed deceptively sleepy-eyed face look squarer still. "We've told you, Mrs Norris," he said, "there's only one church for us."

"I used to think that, even when I lost my parents. It was my Herbert convinced me to give the spirits a chance."

No doubt my mother was blinking more concern onto her roundish face. Her eyes always seemed enlarged by keenness, dwarfing her snub nose and compact mouth and dimpled chin. "We're glad if it brings you some comfort," she said.

"It's brought me much more. Nobody knows what our church can give them unless they find out for themselves."

"Mrs Norris," my father said, "we've already told you Catholics can't have anything to do with spiritualism."

"I wasn't thinking of you two just then. I meant a gentleman I brought into the church. Do you mind if I tell you about him?"

I barely heard my father say "I don't suppose it can do any harm."

"I was visiting my Herbert's grave out there at the back and I think the gentleman was looking for a relative. I don't like to pry, but he seemed a bit lost, so I did ask if anyone could help."

"What did he say to that?" my father said without sounding eager to know.

"He didn't seem too sure. I hope you won't think any less of me, but that's why I told him about our church."

"It isn't up to us to judge you, Mrs Norris."

Perhaps my mother found this unnecessarily gruff. "He joined, did he?"

"He did, and he's done so much more. It's as if he's been waiting for the inspiration all his life. For a start he's taught us how to bring our graves alive."

"I don't know if I like the sound of that," my father said.

"It's nothing bad. It reminds us how life goes on, not just on the other side. All we do is plant flowers there, or herbs bring you even closer."

"Closer," my father said like a denial.

"To our lost ones, except I shouldn't call them that. They aren't lost to us at all."

"We know we'll meet our family again," my father said, "but we aren't meant to in this life."

"You mustn't think me cheeky, but I can promise you you're wrong."

Though the silence felt as if my parents were willing it to end the discussion, my mother was apparently compelled to say "Will you have another cup?"

"I've had sufficient, thank you. Shall I tell you why you're mistaken?"

My father had been driven to the limit of civility. "Suit yourself, Mrs Norris."

"Because I've spoken to my Herbert and he's spoken back to me."

My father cleared his throat with such force that he hardly needed to add a remark. "Don't they put on that kind of a show quite a lot at your church?"

"Desmond." As an additional rebuke my mother said "Some people don't think it's a show."

"Mary, I'm trying to be nice."

"Don't fret on my behalf, Mrs Sheldrake. I know Mr Sheldrake is a convert to your faith just like I am to mine. We're meant to be the best defenders, aren't we, Mr Sheldrake?" When my father gave no response that I could hear, Mrs Norris said "I'm not talking about the sort of medium you know."

"We don't know any," my father said, "and I'm afraid we'll be staying that way."

Just the same, my mother said "What sort then, Mrs Norris?"

"He doesn't speak for anybody's loved ones." Without lowering her voice Mrs Norris managed to convey respectful awe as she said "He brings them to us."

"And just how does he work that?" my father demanded.

"Because coming to our church showed him his gift. That's what he says himself. You believe in not wasting your talents, don't you? It's in our Bible too, you know."

"I think Desmond was asking what happens," my mother said before he could speak.

"I told you, we hear from the people we went there to hear."

"You all do," my father said like some kind of question.

"Not all just yet. I was one of the first," Mrs Norris admitted with pride. "He says I guided him."

"No," my father said, "I'm asking if you all hear them."

"That would be wonderful, wouldn't it? Then people would have to believe. They wouldn't need any faith." All this might have been postponing the answer. "Just the people they belong to hear them," Mrs Norris said.

"If it helps you I'm glad for you," my mother said.

"I haven't made you understand yet. I don't just hear my Herbert, I can feel him there. He comes to me when I need him."

"I expect you have to be alone for that, do you?"

"It's when I'm feeling lonely, yes. Mostly in the night." Mrs Norris seemed to take a hint, perhaps an intentional one. "You'll be wanting to see Dominic is ready for his new school," she said. "Thank you for putting up with me and my palaver."

When I heard the front door shut I grabbed a magazine in case anybody came upstairs and suspected me of having listened. The *Hotspur* was a boys' paper, not a mere comic, and so had my parents' approval. "You're too old to look at pictures," my mother had been telling me for years. I did my best to concentrate on a heroic tale while I wondered what a visit from Mr Norris might be like. Even if he was as benign as ever, the notion of wakening to find him by the bed or even of waiting in the dark for him didn't take my fancy.

Since he'd been in the graveyard by our house for weeks, I preferred not to think how he might feel.

The words on the page piled up like rubble among my thoughts, and I was still attempting to read when my father switched on the radiogram in the lounge. 'Sing Something Simple' was the signature tune a chorus began singing, which meant it was Sunday teatime. "We'll sing the old songs like you used to do...." All the songs dated from before I was born, and some might have been older than my parents. We'd had dinner at midday – sliced ham with salad from our allotment – and the evening treat was my mother's invention, boiled potato sandwiches with the last of the margarine that the bucket of water in the larder had only just held back from turning rancid. To drink we had orange juice, diluted close to tastelessness. My father left the doors of both rooms open to let the songs drift in, and they took the place of conversation until I risked asking "What did Mrs Norris say?"

"Just some grown-up things," my mother said. "They wouldn't interest you, Dominic."

"Was she talking about Mr Norris?"

Before my mother could reply my father flapped the napkin that he called a serviette and wiped his mouth hard. "Do you care more about him than your own family, Dominic?"

I didn't know if he meant my own parents or his, who had died when I was a toddler, my grandfather surviving the loss of his wife by just a few months. If my father had them in mind, I'd had years to grow fonder of Mr Norris. I was about to lie, though it would have made me feel as guilty as the reason, when my mother murmured "Desmond, maybe he's worried about tomorrow."

"There's no call for anyone to feel that way about it. It's meant to be the best school." Nevertheless my father relented. "Forget about the other business, son," he said. "Nobody was saying anything about him."

"That's right, Dominic. We were just talking about her church."

So my parents told lies. As I got ready for bed, having been sent upstairs for an even earlier bedtime than usual, the insight left me feeling more grown-up than thoughts of the new school did. It didn't help me pray when I knelt at the foot of the bed. I'd prayed for Mr Norris every night I was away on holiday with my parents, and I'd looked forward to telling him my adventures, which he'd asked for in the voice that in the space of weeks had grown as thin and pale and determined as him. I'd hoped my reminiscences would lend him new life if not cure him somehow – the railway journey to the Yorkshire coast, the stuttering of pistons and the busy clatter of the wheels, the salty smell of smoke as it billowed past the dwarfish aperture at the top of the third-class window, a tang like an omen of the seaside; the dogged race with luggage across stations to change trains as a blurred voice broadcast indistinct instructions; seagulls flocking on fish at Whitby like a greedy screeching blizzard; the sea view from our cliff hotel in Scarborough, where the distant flat horizon let me glimpse the vastness of the world; coach tours across the moors where hawks fell like arrows from the sky and signposts bore names that have stayed lively in my mind: Highcliff Nab, Ugglebarnby, Hutton-le-Hole, Falling Foss... I stored up all this and much more to revive Mr Norris, but when I went round to his house on my first day back I saw every curtain was drawn to shut out the sunny morning. I knew this denoted an event it was impolite to convey in plain words, and I knuckled my tears away as I ran almost blindly home.

I felt as if my prayers had failed, or I had. I did my best to believe in the ones I mumbled on the night before starting at the new school. Though the prospect made me feel apprehensively excited, I slept before the sun went down. Hours later I wakened in the dark. The barking of a dog had roused me, and now another one started to yap. I tried to ignore them, but curiosity sent me out of bed. I stumbled to the window and eased up the sash. As I craned across the corner of the table and out of the window, a breeze set the leaves of the trees in the graveyard swarming and then fumbled at my face.

The dogs were in the back yards of two houses down the road, near the allotments. The only activity I could see was the scurrying of a few fallen leaves across the grass between the graves. The dogs were as noisy as ever, but I was about to close the window when a movement drew my attention towards the allotments. For a moment I imagined one of the stone figures in the dimness beneath the trees had come to life. No, someone had stooped to pick up some item. No doubt a gardener was collecting vegetables, even if it seemed an odd hour for the task. The figure straightened up with its prize, and I didn't want to be caught watching. I inched the sash down, shutting out some of the canine clamour, and went back to bed. I was almost asleep when a thought overtook me, after which I found it hard to sleep. There was a hedge between the cemetery and the allotments, which meant the figure couldn't have been where I'd thought I saw it. It had been in the graveyard.

CHAPTER TWO

The First Day

It was saying goodbye at the end of my road that made me feel how much my life had changed. "See you sometime," Bobby said, and marched across the tram tracks as soon as the policeman on point duty beckoned all the children who were waiting at the kerb.

Just then I didn't understand how much of her performance was bravado. I thought her attitude went with her broad straight shoulders, not to mention her prominent chin and long nose, which she was fond of pointing at anyone who disagreed with her – she only had to raise her face an inch to make it haughty, a trick she'd learned from her mother. "Well," I said to Jim with some bravado of my own, "now we're the Tremendous Two."

We'd walked to school with Bobby for years, but that wasn't what I had in mind. Originally our crew, which we'd called a gang because that was the word you used, had been the Faithful Five. The name was my idea, derived from books by Gnid Blyton – at least, that was how I used to read Enid's signature that was printed on every cover. We were a benign bunch, whose most daring exploits included braving the police station to hand in a wallet we'd found in the park and tracking down a lost dog that took all of us to capture it, leaving Bobby with a bite for which she'd had to have a jab. Then Paddy and Sean's family had moved to Dublin, reducing us to the Tremendous Three, and now I felt as if we'd lost another member – felt that the dual carriageway, on the far side of which Bobby was talking to girls in the same grey uniform at the bus stop, might as well have been as wide as the Irish Sea. "That's us," Jim agreed, though he didn't sound anxious to linger over the subject, perhaps in case any of the boys around us overheard. "Hey, here's a tram."

The route was one of the last in Liverpool. I'd liked trams more than buses ever since I could remember – the metallic squeal of wheels on the tracks, the peremptory clang of the bell, the crackle and spark of the pulley on the wire. In those days we wouldn't have dared to cross to the tracks until the policeman signalled that we could, and we reached the stop in the middle of the dual carriageway with just seconds to spare. We rode on the top deck as far as Queens Drive, and couldn't resist tipping back the wooden seat to face the wrong way before we clattered downstairs. Now there was nothing to distract us from the prospect of the day, and the bus stop at the crossroads was crowded with boys in the green Holy Ghost Grammar uniform.

All of them were older than us, and quite a few let us know with disparaging glances. "Here's a pair of tiddlers," someone remarked, and another said "More like a fat frog and a shrimp." Since Jim ignored this, I did my best, though the colour of my face must have given me away. We were so inexperienced that when a bus drew up we assumed everyone would board in some sort of order, but even when we managed to gain a foothold on the platform, several boys tried to shove us aside. "Watch out, fatso," the first of them told Jim.

"I wouldn't say that to him," I said with relish.

I ought to have restrained myself, I think now. I could have been setting him up for a fight, even if the bus driver would have intervened – in those days adults often did. Jim might have been plump, but underneath was solid muscle, and most of his ample width wasn't fat. He grasped the metal pole at the corner of the platform and used his entire back to propel the boy against his friends, who staggered backwards like a slapstick routine, barely managing to stay on their feet. "That's shown them," I muttered to Jim.

His foe's face had turned mottled wherever acne left some room. "We'll get you," he said.

It was a standard threat meant to leave us feeling vulnerable. "Go to bed," Jim retorted, since wishing him to hell was stronger language than we were supposed to use, and his adversary elbowed his way along the downstairs aisle to glare at a smaller boy until he gave his seat up.

We'd forgotten about him by the time the bus reached the school. I didn't understand why, having piled off the platform, everyone immediately quietened down, and then I saw a priest waiting just inside the school gates. Both tall gateposts bore a stone dove, a holy symbol somewhat undermined by the dungy whitish crown a rival bird had planted on the left-hand sculpture. I thought it best not to look at Jim in case we made each other laugh, a reaction I could see the priest was unlikely to appreciate. He was the youngest priest I'd ever seen, which might have been why he was keeping his face as severe as his black robe and the celluloid collar that hemmed in his neck. I didn't grasp my mistake until I heard a boy so old he didn't have to wear a cap say "Good morning, Brother O'Toole." All the boys with caps raised them while saying "Good morning, sir," and I was nervous of stumbling over the ritual. I was glad that Jim performed it first, but the man I'd taken for a priest was unimpressed. "First day," he said as if this wasn't much of an excuse. "Name?"

"Jim Bailey, sir."

"Bailey. Make sure your tie is knotted properly in future." Brother O'Toole was already scrutinising me as though he wouldn't be satisfied until he found a fault. "Your name, boy," he said, plainly expecting not to have to ask.

"Dominic Sheldrake, sir."

"Sheldrake." His tone made it clear that I shouldn't have included my first name. "You'll need to learn to speak up at Holy Ghost," he said. "You won't be staying quiet in class."

"No, sir," I blurted, fearing silence wasn't allowed.

"Cut along, both of you. You've much to learn about how to conduct yourselves here, and the sooner you start the better."

I was afraid that some of the parade of boys doffing caps might have observed my humiliation. I felt half my age and acutely out of place, feelings aggravated by the sight of the school towards which everyone was trooping. The elongated two-storey red-brick building was enormously larger than Bobby's and our old school – as wide, I thought, as a street was long. The daunting prospect made the gravel underfoot feel like a penance, and I wasn't halfway along the drive when my feet began to ache so much that I ventured onto the extensive lawn. At once Brother O'Toole's thin sharp voice cut through the gnashing of gravel. "Sheldrake, keep to the path."

My face was still blazing by the time Jim and I reached the school. The broad central doors were for masters, one of whom was striding in while his black gown flapped back from his shoulders, and the pupils had a side entrance half the size. Beyond it coat hooks bristled on the walls of an extensive alcove at the near end of a corridor. A determinedly dour-faced boy who I gathered was a prefect showed us the back of his hand to indicate the nearest hooks. "New boys hang there," he said as if daring us to misunderstand.

The day was so cloudlessly hot that it could almost have been mocking our incarceration, and we'd left our coats at home. Since there were only a few empty hooks, Jim hung his cap over mine. "Best pals, are you?" the prefect said.

"We're good ones," Jim admitted, and I mumbled "That's us."

"So long as that's the most you are. We don't want any pansies here."

Anger overcame my shyness, and I returned his stare. "We've never met one up till now."

Beyond a pair of fire doors the corridor led past a flight of bare stone stairs and met us with smells of the school – floor polish, chalk dust, boyish sweat and the cloth of a multitude of uniforms. The passage overlooked an empty schoolyard and then a playing field bracketed by football posts, while internal windows hid classrooms behind frosted glass. A large vague murmur let us know that the double doors at the end of the corridor belonged to an assembly hall.

It was two storeys high and full of several hundred boys, who sat on backless benches fixed to the uncarpeted wooden floor. Sunlight slanted through windows more than halfway up the wall, and I couldn't help finding their inaccessibility reminiscent of a prison. Prefects stood at the corners of the hall, and the nearest crooked a jerky finger at us. "New boys sit in front," he called. "Get a move on. Don't run."

We'd only just sat down at the far end of the bench closest to the stage when the general murmur was wiped out by the rustle and shuffle of a mass of boys rising to their feet. Teachers were emerging onstage through a doorway at the back. The monks came first, followed by the masters in their gowns, which barely fluttered with the pace of the procession. Several dozen men lined up in front of chairs at the rear of the stage before a final monk strode to the front. "Good morning, boys," he said in a high voice that I could have thought was being strangled by his collar.

"Good morning, headmaster."

Jim and I had been seconds late in standing up, and now our response lagged behind the chorus. Mine was so belated that the silence isolated the last syllable, which sounded unintentionally derisive. "For you new boys," he said and fixed me with a glance, "I am Brother Trainer."

That's what I heard, which suggested the threat of being trained like an animal. I didn't realise until I saw his name in *The Good Spirit*, the school magazine, that it was Treanor. "Once I was like every one of you," he said.

Apparently he'd been a pupil at the school. Had he really felt as nervous as I did, and made to feel smaller by everything he encountered? Just then I was preoccupied with how he'd grown to look. His head was a little too large for his body, and tapered from a high broad shiny forehead towards a small triangular chin, aggravating the resemblance to a balloon pumped out of his round collar. "See that you make full use of your years at this school," he said. "Every one of you is worthy of the Holy Ghost, or you would not be here."

Perhaps he didn't just mean the Eleven-plus, the examination we'd all had to sit to qualify for admission, but he brought it to mind. These days even the assumptions it implied about the children it was testing seem impossibly remote: the decimals and fractions and the other calculations the Arithmetic paper expected us to master before we reached our teens, the parsing of sentences and correction of grammar in general English, the close reading of extracts that Comprehension required, the numerical puzzles and mixed-up sentences that made up General Intelligence and Knowledge, the infrequent opportunities for creativity afforded by Essays and Compositions... Back then I was haunted by a sentence for correction in which I'd failed to see any mistake: *The bishop and another fellow then entered the hall.* Years later I learned you were supposed to refer to the bishop and another gentleman, a distinction I found finicky even then, but I was still trying to solve the problem as Brother Treanor said "Your years at Holy Ghost will give you gifts for life. One gift is hope. One gift is faith. One gift is truth."

In that case I've kept just one of them. He had a good deal more to say, though nothing I recall now, before he led the school in prayer. "I believe in God" – I joined in without faltering, since the words of the Apostles' Creed were so familiar that I hardly heard them. "Viriliter contendere," he said after the amen, a phrase that persisted in bemusing me when the staff and all the boys apart from our year repeated it at the top of their united voice. "That is our motto," he informed us, "the first words you will translate in your Latin class. And now you are excused from singing the school song on your first day, but be sure you are all ears. You must know it when we assemble tomorrow."

"Come, Holy Spirit, fill our souls
And keep us straight and true.
Come fill our minds with faith and truth
Which both shine forth from You..."

It had been composed by a former choirmaster at the school, and felt as if the past had found a voice. It referred to striving like a man – the meaning of the Latin motto – and to eagerness for knowledge, and victory on the field, whether at sports or in battle. I did my best to store up every word, though I was diverted by how Brother Treanor marked each beat with an almost imperceptible nod, bobbing his head more than ever like a balloon. Two lines in particular stay with me, and I wonder whether even then I should have noticed some reaction from one member of the staff:

"We learn from men who went before,

And are the men to come."

A stentorian reprise of the first verse brought the song to an end, and Brother Treanor delivered a last nod. "New boys remain seated while you are assigned," he said.

Each year was divided into three classes – Alpha, Beta, Gamma – and we'd had to sit a second test to determine which we would be in. We perched on the bench, whose absence of a back was making my spine ache, while the veteran boys and all the staff except two monks and a lay master filed out of the hall. The master was the tallest of the three, and actually appeared to gain stature as he came down the steps from the stage. "Here are the Alphas," he said, producing a page from inside his tweed jacket."Listen for your name."

I was afraid Jim and I might be separated, especially when the teacher said "Mr Bailey." The sentence about the bishop was troubling me, suggesting that I could have done less well than Jim at the Holy Ghost examination. The alphabet snagged on several names that began with Mac or Mc or M before it came anywhere near me, but at last the master said "Mr Sheldrake." Though I'd started to dislike the sound of my name shorn of the one I identified with, I felt flattered by his way with it. "Here, sir," I said and stuck my hand up. He stooped in my direction to acknowledge me, just as he had with the others, and at last I recognised him.

Shouldn't I have done so earlier? Even now I'm not sure whether it was simply that you often don't recognise someone when you meet them in a context different from how you first saw them. Having finished off his list with Mr Yates, he gestured us all to stand. "Please follow me, gentlemen," he said.

He led the way to the nearest classroom and held the door open while we all filed in to select our desks. I sat next to Jim, though I would have retreated to the back if he hadn't taken a seat in the middle of the room. The teacher closed the door, shutting out the sound of someone scraping painfully at a violin, and picked up a stick of chalk from the trough at the foot of the blackboard on the wall. "I'm Mr Noble," he said, writing the name with a series of flourishes over an incomprehensibly blurred trace of an earlier message, and ending with a shrill full stop. "I shall be your form master. Come to me with any problems, gentlemen. Let's work together to make this a rewarding year for all," he said, and I felt I was going to like him. I didn't even think he realised I had watched him push the pram through the graveyard.

CHAPTER THREE
A Glimpse in a Field

Is the resilience of youth a blessing or a curse? I suppose it's both. Most children accept their life, since it's the only one they experience for themselves. It took me just a few days to grow used to attending the Holy Ghost, and then with the intolerance of all my years I wondered how my younger self could have had a problem. Once you learned the layout of the school it was entirely manageable and by no means as immense as it had seemed. Within a week the schoolyard was as familiar as my own back garden, and before long the playing field was too. Soon many of the teachers were part of my life as well, and their quirks in particular.

Some were harmless, and some we pretended were. Mr Askew lived up to his name, since he'd been shot in the leg at Dunkirk, and introduced himself by telling us "I'm taking you for English" as if he hoped we'd hear a pun. Mr Clement always said "Bon jour, mes amis" and stayed in the language for the first five minutes of each French lesson, timing himself with a gold watch he fished out of his waistcoat. Brother Monrahan clapped his pudgy hands whenever a mathematics problem was solved, urging "Add that up. Five more marks for another easy answer." Brother Titmuss often said "Pardon the flatulence" when we trooped to the laboratory to be met by a sulphurous stench, but he didn't welcome any laughter, and his voice would rise to a whinny if anyone botched an experiment. Mr McIntosh would complain "Eheu" several times in the course of every Latin lesson, and would inform us yet again how vital the language was before setting us exercises out of a textbook as a prelude to subsiding into boozy torpor at his desk. For Religious Knowledge we had Brother Mayle, who would drape a languid arm around the shoulders of whichever boy he'd singled out and murmur "If you know your apostles you won't go wrong." Sometimes we saw him strolling past the gymnasium, where at the end of the period Mr Jensen delighted in subjecting the class to all the excesses the communal showers could produce. Brother Stimson regularly counselled "Reach for beauty" to his art classes, which Jim and I chose as the alternative to music, but he closed his eyes tight and emitted a stuttering sigh when confronted with most of the results his advice produced. Mr Bushell would cover the blackboard with maps at the start of each geography lesson and stub a blunt finger on some location that whoever he called out would have to identify at once, or else the board and then the boy would be hit with a strap. This was an implement most of the Holy Ghost staff had a use for, though some favoured more eccentric methods: Brother Mayle liked tugging sinners up on tiptoe by a tuft of hair, while if an error roused Mr McIntosh he was liable to thump the offender's head with the blackboard duster, scattering a dandruff of chalk. Brother Treanor proved to be obsessed with the exact words of the school song, so that if he thought he heard anybody singing "And we're the men to come" he would make the entire school repeat every verse while he prowled the aisles, strap at the ready. The only man who never used the strap was Mr Noble, which was one reason why Form One Alpha liked him.

Another was how he talked to us, like young men rather than faintly contemptible inferiors or receptacles to be crammed with unquestioned information. Whenever he was on yard duty he would engage some of us in conversation, not least about ourselves and our families. I was still a little disconcerted by his trait of ducking his upper body towards whoever he was about to address – because it reminded me of my first sight of him, I supposed, although I hadn't seen him in the cemetery since. We were all fond of his history lessons, which were always engrossing and, when he showed us caricatures of historical figures, amusing too. I thought him audacious for telling us which newspapers printed cartoons of Macmillan and other dignitaries of our time. Not just the pictures but the subjects seemed to make him laugh, an attitude I found excitingly subversive, though I think I wondered if he valued anybody very much. All the same, nobody betrayed any doubts about him until Paul Joyce asked him about the war.

It would have been late in the year, because the afternoon was already growing dark. Mr Noble's was the final lesson, preceded by an English class. Whenever he taught Shakespeare Mr Askew spent the last few minutes in performing a soliloquy from memory, limping up and down the classroom with his gown cast over his arm. The gloom lent more conviction to his speech about the dagger, and I could almost have imagined that I saw it leading him into the dark. The school bell blotted out most of his line about the wicked dreams that rose from the dead half of the world, but once the shrilling ceased he recommenced with witchcraft and its sacrifices and continued to the end. "It is a knell that summons thee to heaven, or to hell," he said, throwing up a hand as though to signify the recent interruption. With him we were never sure if we were meant to laugh, but a few of us risked a titter, and he looked ready to react until Mr Noble loomed on the frosted pane of the classroom door. "Yes, yes," Mr Askew muttered, limping to let him in. "They're yours and I wish you joy of them."

He snatched the door open so abruptly that Mr Noble's smile of greeting faltered. For an instant he resembled a boy who'd been caught spying, the way I'd felt at my bedroom window. "Take your time, Mr Askew," he murmured.

Perhaps he hadn't meant to draw attention to his colleague's disability, but it was clear that Mr Askew didn't welcome the indulgence. He lurched out of the classroom, only to stumble over the sill. Mr Noble caught his elbow, an action that earned him a scowl the twilight failed to hide. "Q," Mr Askew said, a thanks so truncated it was pinched to barely a syllable.

"Do switch the light on, Mr Shea." Once Henry Shea had done so, Mr Noble gazed at us as though to ascertain how much we'd observed. "Learn to make allowances, gentlemen," he said. "They'll help you get on."

I couldn't decide whether he was talking about success or sociability if not both, but Paul Joyce wasn't concerned with that question. "The Krauts gave it to him, didn't they, sir?" he said.

"Let's leave slang outside the gates, Mr Joyce. But yes, Mr Askew was injured in the last war."

"Weren't you, sir? My dad lost an eye."

"As you told me, and I hope you passed on my condolences."

"Sir, he said ta very much. He wanted to know where you fought, sir."

"I'm afraid you will have to tell him I didn't participate."

Someone sniffed or drew an expressive breath, and the general silence said quite a lot more, but I wasn't so sure how I was entitled to feel. While my father had returned intact from the war, he never spoke about it except to thank God more than once that it was over. "Why not?" Joyce said, adding less than swiftly "Sir."

"The dead outnumber us by many billions, Mr Joyce. I can see no point in adding to them without a pressing reason."

"Sir," Frank Nolan said, "don't you think what they were doing to the Jews was one?"

"We weren't aware of the camps when I joined up, Mr Nolan."

"Sir." Joyce looked as if someone, possibly himself, had tricked him. "I thought you said..."

"My apologies, gentlemen. Always take care with your words. I should have said I didn't fight. I was with the ambulances. At the front, if anyone would like to know."

"What was it like, sir?" Shea among others was eager to hear.

"I imagine Mr Joyce and his father would say it hardly matters how it was for me."

As Joyce looked abashed Shea said "What about the casualties, sir?"

"Some we patched up and they either came home to their families or went back into the field. And some we could do nothing with. Let me tell you, gentlemen, quite a few wished they weren't alive."

"That's a sin against the Holy Ghost," Brian O'Shaughnessy protested. "Isn't it, sir?"

"Unless they were ready to see what leaving their bodies could show them."

I doubt that any of us found this notion less than odd. Perhaps Nolan meant to bring the discussion back into familiar territory by saying "My dad says there won't be any more wars."

"He has visions of the future, does he? Why does he think that, Mr Nolan?"

"When everybody's got the bomb they'll be too afraid to start a war in case they blow the world up."

Something like amusement flickered in the teacher's large dark eyes and twitched his thin pale lips. "Unless someone does and the dead claim the world."

His odd way of thinking silenced us until Joyce said "Those men you were talking about must have helped us win, mustn't they, sir?"

"You'd like to think they were of use. I just wish some of them had had the proper rites."

Aware of failing to contribute, I blurted "Sir, my dad says if people could see where it happened they wouldn't want any more wars."

"The devastation, I suppose he means. The dead land, except we all know nothing ever really dies." A gleam had surfaced in the teacher's eyes.

"Thank you for the inspiration, Mr Sheldrake," he said. "What do the rest of you think?"

Nobody argued against the idea, and several boys supported it, though I thought some of them might have been anxious to ingratiate themselves with him. "Well then," Mr Noble said, "what are you saying we should do?"

While he often encouraged debate like that, I don't believe any of us had a proposal in mind. It was Jim who said "There are school trips in the holidays, aren't there, sir?"

"You're suggesting visiting the battlefields. I can certainly put it to the headmaster. It's related to history, after all."

I saw Jim was pleased with himself, and at the time I thought I should be, except for a sense that the teacher had directed things somehow – that he'd guided us to a conclusion that was already in his head. The following week he told the class that Brother Treanor had authorised him to organise a tour of sites of both World Wars in France. "I think it's only right that anybody here who wants to go should take priority," Mr Noble said, "since it was your idea."

In that case, I was provoked to think, I ought to be first in the queue. I wasn't quite so confident once I heard the price of the trip, and by the time I reached home in the icy twilight I didn't know if I should even raise the subject. My mother emerged from the kitchen, her chapped hands gloved in soapsuds from using the washboard. "Is something wrong at school?"

"It's fine. I am." Since this only made her widen her eyes by raising her brows while she turned her small mouth downwards, I had to say "Just Mr Noble wants us to go to France for history."

"That sounds like a treat." All the same, or perhaps because of it, she said "You'll have to ask your father."

A few minutes later he and a fierce smell of coffee came home. You caught the aroma if you even walked past the store where he worked, Cooper's on Church Street downtown. As soon as he'd removed his overcoat and loosened the knot of his tie we had dinner, sprouts and potatoes and a pair of sausages each. We were still at the table, where my parents were smoking after-dinner cigarettes – Du Maurier out of an elegant red box – when my mother said "Dominic wants to ask you something, Desmond."

"Mr Noble wants the class to go on a history trip to France."

"And what's the cost of that, son?"

"It's a lot," I said to prepare myself for disappointment. "Fifty guineas."

"That's a bit ferocious," my father said but didn't flinch. "Will it help you at school?"

"It might." While I didn't feel justified in making more of a claim, I did add "He's taking everyone because I told him you thought people ought to go and see."

My father glanced at my mother, who met him with a hopeful look, before saying "All right, sign yourself up and let us know what's needed. There won't be much to spend our money on for a while yet."

I was so excited that I found it hard to sleep that night, and when tiredness overtook me I couldn't be bothered to leave my bed to see why the dogs along the road were barking. In the morning I was almost too impatient to wait for Jim in case Mr Noble didn't save us places on the French trip after all. We were at the school and making for the assembly hall when I caught sight of Mr Noble beyond the schoolyard. "Let's tell him we'll be going," I said.

We were crossing the yard when I realised he wasn't alone at the edge of the playing field. While his companion was hidden by the wall – one of the smaller boys, presumably – Mr Noble kept stooping towards them. He had his back to us, and I heard him murmuring. We were almost at the wall when I caught some words, which made me falter. "Leave me now," he was urging. "Go back. Not here."

Jim told me later that he heard none of this, which was why he kept on. At the sound of his footsteps Mr Noble reared up, twisting around. I didn't see his face, because I was distracted by a movement beyond the gap that led onto the field. "Mr Bailey, Mr Sheldrake," he said more harshly than I'd ever heard him speak. "Why aren't you in the hall?"

I was too daunted to respond, but Jim said "Sir, we just wanted to tell you we can go to France."

"I'll be seeing you all in class after lunch," Mr Noble said on the way to resuming his usual mildness. "No, I shouldn't rebuke your enthusiasm. You're the first to join the merry band. I didn't realise I had an audience, that's all. I hope you won't think your form master has a screw loose."

I was beside Jim at the gap by now, and saw that the teacher was by himself. "No, sir," I thought it best to say.

"Don't sound quite so dubious, Mr Sheldrake. Do you know what I was sending packing? Nothing but a dog that took a shine to me on my way here. I can't see it any more, can you? I expect it's nearly home. You two head for the hall now and I'll be along directly."

As soon as we were out of earshot I whispered to Jim "What did you see?"

"Nothing. What did you?"

"Nothing either," I said, because the truth wasn't sufficiently clear to let me say anything else. I supposed I'd seen the shadow of the dog Mr Noble had mentioned, a dark vague shape slithering away across the turf. I assumed there must have been a breeze at ground level beyond the wall, because as the shape darted out of sight, the short grass through which it was passing had stirred, almost too imperceptibly for me to think it had. I glanced back at Mr Noble as we left the yard. He was still in the same place beneath the pale unbroken clouds, and as he ducked forward again I wondered if the dog had strayed back to him.

CHAPTER FOUR

The Same Man

On Christmas Eve my mother sent me to fetch the turkey from the butcher's. Usually my father bore the prize home, but he was out at work. I managed to feel like the man of the family as far as the corner of our road, where I had to rest the cumbersome lump on an equally frosty garden wall. Carrying it by the handles of the plastic bag only made them dig into my fingers through the gloves my mother insisted I wear, while clutching it in my arms let a chill indistinguishable from an ache seep through my duffle coat and settle on my chest. All the way along our road I had to keep planting my burden on walls, beyond which many of the front rooms exhibited Christmas trees. Although every tree was decorated, very few had lights. They reminded me how Mr Noble had offended Brian O'Shaughnessy by suggesting that the festive trees were older than Christianity – I'd had a sense that the teacher might have said more if he hadn't been wary of going too far.

By the time I reached our gate I was pricking with wintry sweat. I had to pin the obdurate bird against my chest while I fumbled with the latch before stumbling along the path to clank the clumsy knocker on its anvil. My mother didn't hurry to answer the door, but the moment she saw me she speeded up like a comedy film, grabbing the bagful of bird and dashing to the kitchen with it before bustling back to me as I struggled to drag off a glove. "You must be frozen," she cried. "Come by the fire."

She'd lit the one in the front room, where Christmas cards drooped like bunting above the mantelpiece. She moved the fireguard along the hearth and tonged chunks of coal out of the scuttle to drop them into the dull pink heart of the fire. I watched them smoulder and start flaming, and couldn't help thinking of hell. The fiery version I'd originally been taught was receding into memory, having been supplanted by the vision Mr Noble had proposed when he returned to discussing the war. Paul Joyce had asked him where he thought the villains of the piece had ended up, but I wasn't sure if the teacher had answered the question. He'd suggested that some people might be condemned to eternal terror, having lost their minds as a result of losing their bodies, a fate that would be worse than any physical hell. In any case, how could flames harm you if you were a disembodied soul? Perhaps those had simply been a way of terrifying the mediaeval faithful with a notion of hell they could grasp. O'Shaughnessy hadn't liked that much, but I was excited by the questioning of beliefs we'd been encouraged to embrace, though I was wary of telling my parents about it in case they took against the teacher. I was musing on all this when my mother came back from the kitchen, and I guessed from the stains on her apron that she'd been rooting inside the turkey for its giblets. "When you're ready, Dominic, would you do one more little thing for me?"

"Shall I get something from the allotment?"

"You can later if you like, but just run round to Mrs Norris's. If she's on her own, ask her over for a mince pie."

I retrieved my coat and tugged my gloves on and braved the icy day again, where the emptily blue sky seemed to let the sunlight escape straight back into space. Beyond the point where Bobby's street met mine at a fork, the road led under the railway bridge to Cherry Lane, where Mrs Norris lived opposite that side of the graveyard. As I made for her house a train raced over the bridge and then across the stone arch at the nearest cemetery entrance. The arch was so deep it was virtually a tunnel, and I heard the iron gates send a tremulous echo into the stony dimness.

I hadn't seen Mrs Norris for weeks. The narrow front yard of her little house was filled by three red clay pots of flowers beside the stubby path. I'd thought she cared as much for the flowers as my mother did for her roses, but several were hanging down their heads on withered stems, as if they were ashamed to keep company with the weeds that were invading the circles of earth. Both of the small bay windows were uncurtained now – at least, the middle pane on each floor was clear. I was reaching for the knocker, where I saw greenish spots on the long brass tongue, when the Norris dog started to bark. "What is it now, Winston?" Mrs Norris pleaded somewhere in the house.

Her tone disconcerted me so much that I tapped TT in Morse on the knocker, a message only Jim and Bobby would have understood. "It's Dominic," I called, though my parents disapproved of shouting.

Winston's was the only answer until Mrs Norris inched the door open just wide enough to show her face. It looked drawn into itself, wary of letting out too much. A trace of lipstick had strayed past the left-hand corner of her mouth, and her face was so heavily powdered that tan crumbs had lodged in the furrows of her forehead. "Dominic. You're a good boy," she added, though I couldn't have said why, and stepped back. "You can come in," she said as if someone had suggested otherwise. "Be quick before he runs off."

As I shut the door she reminded Winston who I was, and he gave a yap that sounded more like recognition than the clamour he'd been making. He was a long-haired mastiff, and strands of his grey hair stuck to the jacket and skirt of the blue suit Mrs Norris was wearing. She and the dog and the bicycle her husband used to ride weren't leaving me much space in the portion of the hall ahead of the stairs, and I had a sense that Mrs Norris wasn't sure which room to take me in. "Come along, then," she said as though the indecision was my doing, and led the way into the front room.

A smoky fire was sputtering behind the sooty fireguard on the tiled hearth. Open cards were pinned like butterflies to most of the wall above the fireplace, and some weren't Christmas cards but messages of condolence. The room smelled of used cigarettes – several half-smoked broken ones had gathered in an ashtray on a small squat table – and of the dog. His basket nestled against a sofa, half of which was occupied by an open photograph album. "Sit down, don't be shy," Mrs Norris said.

Of course this made me shyer. As she sat beside the album and Winston lay down in his basket I perched on the edge of an armchair, poising myself to escape. "My mum's made mince pies. She says come and have one."

"That's thoughtful, but I'd better not if you could tell her, Dominic. If I leave the dog he'll disturb the neighbours."

I wondered when he'd started doing that, since I'd often seen her out by herself, not least visiting the cemetery. "I know Mrs Sheldrake doesn't like dogs in the house," she said, "and he'll only let the street know if I leave him outside."

"I could take him for a double you eh el kay," I said so as not to rouse him with the word, "if you like."

"You're a good boy and we've always said so." I assumed this brought Mr Norris to mind, since she paused while her gaze retreated inwards. "Just apologise for me to your mother," she said. "Say I have to stay in for the postman."

I could have thought she'd taken time to find a further excuse to remain in the house. "Your parents could come here if they liked," she said.

"My dad's at work."

"Oh, I see," Mrs Norris said as if she suspected my mother of waiting until he was out of the way. "Perhaps another day, then," she said, though without much faith.

I was about to make my escape – however muffled the fire was, the room felt oppressively warm – when Mrs Norris picked up the photograph album. "That's my Herbert," she said.

It was a snap of Mr Norris some years younger than I'd ever known him, in an army uniform. He looked determined, and not just to smile. Once I'd mumbled an acknowledgment Mrs Norris turned the page while still holding the album towards me. "There he is again," she said.

She was showing me another photograph of him in the same uniform – more recent, with a thinner face and a faraway look in his eyes that suggested he was searching for some aspect of the past – but I was distracted by Winston's behaviour. The dog was watching the hall through the doorway, and now he raised his head as if some activity out there had prompted him. At once I wondered if Mrs Norris hadn't been talking about the album, an idea that made me blurt "Do you still hear him?"

She lowered the album and cradled it on her lap while she held my gaze with hers. "I never told you about that," she said as though she had to reassure herself. "You heard me talking to your parents."

"I wasn't spying," I protested.

"No need to shout at me, Dominic. Everybody thinks there is." She shook her head, dislodging a wry grimace. "I can understand how you might have heard," she said.

"Does Mr Norris?"

Perhaps I'd lowered my voice too much, because she frowned. "What are you saying?"

"Mr Norris. Does he talk like that?"

"He only has to whisper. That's how close he comes." When her mouth struggled to fix on a shape I was afraid she was going to show more emotion than I could cope with, but she wiped it with the back of her hand as though to rid it of a taste. Almost too low for me to hear she said "I don't like how he feels, though."

Winston had turned his head towards the elongated shadow that lay

low behind the sofa. I was both anxious and reluctant to ask "Where is
he now?"

"Perhaps he's here. I don't know till he lets me know. He hides in
things, Dominic."

She hadn't looked away from me, and I could have thought she was
nervous of glancing around the room. I didn't know how to take her
remark, which I would rather not have heard at all. Might the doors of
the sideboard creep open to reveal Mr Norris packed inside, twisted into
some grotesque shape to fit the space? Or was the cushion sagging on the
empty armchair about to shift into some version of his face? "I'd better go,"
I muttered and stood up just as awkwardly. "Mum wants me to fetch things
from the allotment."

"I'm sorry if I scared you. You know he'd never harm you, don't you?
Wouldn't you like to see more of him before you go?"

Of course she meant the album, but I was nervous of another meaning.
"I will next time," I promised, though it felt a good deal like a lie.
"Merry Christmas."

"You be sure and have one, and your parents too." She closed the album
so gradually that she might have been laying the images to rest, unless she
was wishing she had stayed content with her memories. As I edged towards
the door she murmured "I'm almost sorry I met him."

My dismay must have been apparent, because she raised her voice. "Not
my Herbert, Dominic. Never him."

"Who, then?"

"Mr Noble, I was meaning."

Of course we could have known two different people with that name,
but my world was too small to admit the possibility. "Who?" I said in a bid
for disbelief.

"Christian Noble," Mrs Norris said and looked wary. "I thought you
heard me talking to your parents. He's the gentleman who has done so
much for our church."

"You never said his name." Now I had to ask "What's he like?"

"He's very tall. You could say he's imposing."

I think I was still hoping to be proved wrong as I said "What does
he do?"

"I don't think your father would want me telling you about
that, Dominic."

"No." I was growing desperate for the truth. "Mr Noble, does he have another job?"

"That isn't a job. It's his mission." Mrs Norris sounded offended enough to make this her entire answer, but I saw her taking pity on my age. "I believe he's a teacher," she said.

I remembered seeing him for the first time. As I'd watched him push the pram through the graveyard, Mrs Norris had been ready to tell my parents about him. It made me feel events had converged on me, as if I'd been singled out somehow. I wanted to be alone to ponder what I'd learned. "I ought to go," I said, which felt like renewing my confinement in the oppressive almost airless room.

"Yes, you've said." Mrs Norris sighed and laid the album next to her on the sofa. "Stay," she added twice as loud.

In a moment, though an unpleasantly prolonged one, I realised she was talking not to me but to Winston. The dog had lifted his head when his mistress stood up, and now it sank between his paws as if he felt no less imprisoned than I had. From the hall I saw him watching the elongated shadow like a trench behind the sofa. "Don't forget your pence," Mrs Norris said.

She took her purse out of her handbag on the post at the foot of the banisters and produced a bright two-shilling piece. "That's from both of us," she said, "for Christmas."

"Thank you very much indeed." This would have made my parents proud of how they were bringing me up, but then on an impulse I called "Thank you, Mr Norris."

Mrs Norris parted her lips, which emitted a dry sound like a shriveled word. I felt as if I were taking a breath on her behalf to let her say "Did you hear him?"

I heard a soft restless sound in the front room and hoped it was only the dog. "No," I blurted, bruising my fingers on the latch in my haste to leave the house.

I didn't slow down much until I reached home, only to realise that I hadn't prepared anything to tell my mother. She was wielding brush and dustpan in the hall, and stared past me as I opened the front door – I could almost have imagined she saw someone at my back. "Is Mrs Norris on her way?" she said.

"She can't bring Winston and she doesn't want to leave him at home."

"You could have taken him out for her if you'd let me know. Another time you can. Now fetch me some potatoes, please. The best ones for Christmas."

The entrance to the allotments was on the main road, past a row of five shops. The bacon slicer in the butcher's gave a huge metallic squeal – no, a passing tram did, together with a crackling flash. Whenever I unlatched the wooden gate and crossed the field divided into plots of vegetables, I felt as if the countryside that used to be there had ambitions to return. I thought gardeners might have been collecting Christmas produce, but I was alone in the allotments. I found a trowel and a frayed brown canvas bag in the communal shed and made my way around the grid of narrow earthy paths to our plot, which was near the graveyard hedge. I dug up half a dozen hulking spuds and dropped them in the bag, and was stooping to retrieve it when I faltered. I'd seen someone else in that position round here, and at last I realised who.

As the memory came into focus I saw that he'd bent to pick whatever had been growing on the grave exactly as I'd seen him stoop towards the pram and lean towards boys he was addressing, me included. Leaving the bag of potatoes on the path, I went to peer over the hedge. Where exactly had Mr Noble been standing? If I couldn't detect that I would be letting the Tremendous Three down. When I'd watched him from my window he had been just beyond a statue, which meant that the grave was just in front of it now – in front of the Mother of God, whose marble arm was lifted in a blessing that had vanished along with her hand, so that she appeared to be displaying an injury she might have suffered on a battlefield. The grave I'd located was marked with a family headstone, the most recent date on which was 1952. The family name wasn't Noble. That didn't appear on the gravestone at all.

The grave was spread with gravel inside a rectangular stone border. A granite vase full of flowers stood in front of the headstone, and a few inches of the far end of the gravelled plot were green. While I didn't know why this should matter, I strained my eyes until I made out that the growth was clover. As I stared at the tiny leaves they appeared to stir like a nest of torpid insects. No doubt my vision was the problem, since the grass around the grave didn't shift. I grabbed the lumpy sack, and as I hurried home I heard carollers making their way from house to house.

"Somebody's hungry," my mother said when she saw the contents of the sack, so that I thought she was saying I'd dug up too much until she added "That's all right, it's not a sin. We aren't planting for anyone else."

As a toddler I'd been aware that we contributed much of our produce, a duty that my mother often told me was helping soldiers such as my father. "Does it matter where you grow things?" I was inspired to ask.

"It depends on the soil. Why are you asking?"

If I mentioned how I'd seen Mr Noble at the grave she was bound to tell my father. Given his view of Mrs Norris's beliefs, he would certainly condemn Mr Noble's behaviour. He might even move me to a different school, leaving behind friends I'd made there, not to mention Jim. "Just wondered," I said.

"I've been working like a nigger all day," my father declared as soon as he came in, not a usage that would have raised an eyebrow in even the politest company back then. "I think we can open that sherry, love. It's as good as Christmas."

He won a tussle with the cork as my mother took the coat he'd draped over a kitchen chair into the hall to hang it up. He filled two waspish glasses to the brim while my mother protested about having to sip from hers before she could pick it up, and then my parents clinked them against my tumbler of tart squash. "Here's to better years," my father said. "How's the day been treating you?"

"I've got on with everything, and Dominic's been a help."

"You know I'm watching out for items that will save you work. Go shopping in the New Year, that's the drill," my father said. "I hope you know what a pearl we've got, son. What have you been doing for her?"

"You won't need to go to the allotment, Desmond," my mother said. "And he went to ask Mrs Norris to keep me company, but what was her excuse, Dominic?"

"Winston might have upset someone. Mum says I can take him for walks."

"Good on you, son, but I'll tell you what, Mary, you don't need to wait till I'm out of the way to invite her. She knows where I stand and that should be the end of it. Besides, it's Christmas."

"You can take him if Mrs Norris says so, Dominic. You still haven't told me how she is."

"A bit lonely, I think."

"I don't want that being my fault, Mary. Maybe I should go round and invite her myself."

"I should think she'd appreciate it," my mother said without looking away from me. "Is that all, Dominic?"

I'd been taught that reading thoughts was God's trick, but my mother seemed proficient at it too. "I think," I admitted, "she may be a bit frightened as well."

"Her church can't have helped her much," my father said, "with all their mumble jumble."

If the last phrase was a joke intended to placate my mother, it didn't work. "I thought you'd finished talking about that," she said.

"I'll be mum if it'll keep the peace," my father said and winked at me. "Two mums in the house."

"Did Mrs Norris say why she was worried, Dominic?"

It seemed safe to risk a little of the truth. "She thinks Mr Norris is hiding."

My father's affability vanished as if he'd poured it back into the bottle. "Hiding how?"

"Somewhere in her house. Maybe everywhere."

"She told you that." My father doubled his outrage by informing my mother "She said all that to him."

"No, dad." I could only try to make amends for having said too much. "I just thought I heard her talking to Mr Norris."

My father stared at me, but he lacked my mother's skill for judging when I'd been stingy with the truth. "You can forget about the dog. I don't want you anywhere near that house."

Disappointment not far from a sense of betrayal made me blurt "You don't believe Mrs Norris, do you, dad?"

"Of course I don't, and your mother doesn't. Mr Norris is in purgatory, where we all hope to go."

I wasn't sure I did, but I said "Then I don't believe her either."

"I hope you never did, son."

"That's what I meant. I don't think she's very well."

"All this nonsense she's involved with could have driven her potty," my father conceded, mostly to my mother. "You'd have to be deluded to get mixed up with it in the first place."

"Shouldn't someone keep an eye on her, dad? I can. You said we do what neighbours are supposed to."

When he frowned I thought he'd realised that I'd eavesdropped on their conversation, but he only said "I don't know if it should be you, son."

"I told her I'd walk Winston, and you say I should always keep my word."

"They've taught him how to argue at this school, don't you think, love?" I wasn't sure how favourably he viewed this until he said "You use all your brain if it gets you on, Dominic. We want you in a better job than mine."

None of this was an answer, but I'd learned not to insist. Having lingered over a sip of sherry, he said "We'll see about you and the dog after Christmas."

"I can't believe he'll come to any harm, Desmond, when it's Mrs Norris."

"He'll need to tell us anything at all that's wrong. That isn't snitching, son. It's looking after someone who may want it even if she doesn't know she does."

"I will, then," I said, but I was vowing not to report anything that might turn my father against Mrs Norris, and not only her. His reaction had shown me how much more hostile he would be to Mr Noble if he learned the teacher was responsible for her beliefs. That was when I pledged not to let my parents know the medium she'd mentioned was my teacher or to tell them any number of the things he said. Looking back, I can only attempt to believe that if I'd told them at the time it would have made no difference to the world.

CHAPTER FIVE

Meeting the Family

That Christmas Day the entire country fell silent while the new queen made her first broadcast to the nation, or so my parents led me to believe. It felt to me like yet another of the rituals adults insisted upon. The routine with my school cap had begun to put me in mind of how some people used to have to touch their forelock. Half the time I hardly seemed to have a chance to sit down before I had to stand up – whenever a lady entered the room or a teacher did, or repeatedly in church for no purpose I could grasp, or at the end of a film show, when they put on the National Anthem. Even then some filmgoers remained seated however much my parents and other patrons frowned at them, which helped to convince me that the practice was meaningless, and were the other customs any more meaningful? Now I feel almost nostalgic for them – for rites that don't alter the world.

"I am speaking to you from my own home, where I am spending Christmas with my family; and let me say at once how I hope that your children are enjoying themselves as much as mine are..." My mother smiled at me to ensure I appreciated the queen's wish, but it left me impatient to enjoy my presents, to read a new book or play table soccer with my father or try to win more marbles with the ones I'd been given in a bag. Now the queen was talking about families, but I didn't think hers or her home would be much like ours, and I'd begun to suspect her of reading from a script, not least because she sounded even more unnaturally precise than the announcers on the radio or most of the people in films. When she said we were all part of a bigger family – the British Empire – my father agreed with a weighty nod. I was more taken with "that courageous spirit of adventure that is the finest quality of youth" and wondered how soon the Tremendous Three might find a new mission. The queen wanted everyone to "build a truer knowledge of ourselves", but she could never have predicted what this would come to mean. She or her scriptwriter thought that "the tremendous forces of science" could be used for "the betterment of man's lot upon this earth", and I recalled that scientists had just discovered the secret of creation, though the Big Bang was one of the increasing number of issues I felt wary of discussing with my parents. The queen rounded off her speech by anticipating her coronation and asking us to pray for her on that occasion. When my father sat back in his armchair by the fire and clasped his fingers together I thought he was going to propose an immediate prayer, but he was only miming satisfaction. "The country's in good hands," he said.

My mother murmured an assent, but I recalled a discussion in the classroom. "One of the boys at school doesn't think we should be ruled by a woman."

"He hadn't better let his mother hear him say that. We don't mean you either, Mary," my father said with a wink, and then he grew more serious. "Who does he want in charge, a Greek? It's not long since we saw the Jerries off. Let the British rule the British, and we can run a lot of other people too."

The festive sherry was talking, and not too coherently either. "He said it was in the Bible," I told him.

"So is it? You should know if he does."

"I think it is."

"Maybe you should read the Bible a bit more and your space books a bit less." My father gave them – the interplanetary novels that were my favourite presents that year – an imprecise blink. "If it's in the Bible it has to be right," he said and appeared to grapple with a contradiction before he said triumphantly "But that tells us to respect the monarch."

I wondered how this would have fared in the classroom, where O'Shaughnessy had reminded Mr Noble "It says a woman shouldn't have authority over a man."

"Have you had your nose in one of the apostles, Mr O'Shaughnessy? Perhaps we shouldn't take quite everything they wrote as gospel."

While O'Shaughnessy looked shocked, I suspected that I wasn't alone in feeling some exhilaration. "It's the word of God, sir," he protested.

"Perhaps what you read is more like –" I could have thought Mr Noble rejected the first word that came to mind. "Let's call it a commentary," he said with a smile too faint to betray any meaning. "And I don't know if you realise the queen is the defender of the faith."

"Not our faith, sir."

"They really aren't so different if you look at them in perspective. Beliefs keep on developing, you know. Evolving, if you like," Mr Noble said, and his smile grew almost reminiscent. "You'd be surprised what you would find if you traced them to their source."

In a tone close to a challenge O'Shaughnessy said "You'd find Almighty God."

"I wonder how you would cope with the revelation." I was hoping Mr Noble was about to say more on the subject, but he seemed to remember where and who he was. "Don't start dismissing women," he said, and not just to O'Shaughnessy. "They're how we're made or we wouldn't be here."

"I still don't think she ought to be the ruler, sir."

"Let me tell you a secret, Mr O'Shaughnessy, and the rest of you as well. Whoever's on the throne won't matter much. You'll learn it's just a symbol. There's no power there to affect your lives."

I had a vague idea that he was talking about politics, and I knew some of my classmates wouldn't be too happy if he started preaching any kind of radicalism. Instead he murmured mostly to himself "There are greater powers to come."

Any of us other than O'Shaughnessy might have been embarrassed to ask "Do you mean Jesus, sir?"

"The second coming." The teacher's gaze had grown distant, but now it reverted to us. "A return, Mr O'Shaughnessy," he said, "such as the world has never seen."

I saw O'Shaughnessy take this for confirmation, but even then I wasn't sure that Mr Noble had endorsed his belief. I kept the rest of the discussion from my parents, and soon my father heaved himself out of his chair. "I'll give you a game of footy," he said. "A real one if you like."

I fancy he was trying to work off some Christmas clumber. We'd hardly started kicking the ball outside the house, where the entire street boasted just a few cars, when boys and their fathers came out to expand the game. On Boxing Day most of us had a return match, having regained our excess weight, and in other ways too that day resembled a rerun of Christmas. The third day wasn't so traditionally defined, and my mother sent me to invite Mrs Norris over and take Winston for a walk.

At first I couldn't make out how her house had changed. I was at the gate when I saw both the bay windows were uncurtained. I thought she'd pulled the curtains down to let in all the light she could, and then I realised they were bunched thin at the very edges of the outer panes. A framed photograph lay face down on top of the album on the sofa, and now I wonder how often Mrs Norris may have used it to cling to a memory. Otherwise the room was empty; even Winston's basket was. I lifted the knocker on the front door, only to appreciate how ominous the two slow blows that were the code of the Tremendous Three might sound to Mrs Norris. Instead I tapped "We Wish You a Merry Christmas". The dull echoes made the house sound hollow and roused Winston to bark. "Who's that?" Mrs Norris cried, and then she pleaded "Don't scare them."

I had a nervous fancy that she might not be talking to the dog. "I'm coming," she called, and a door shut, muffling Winston's barks. "I'm coming now. Don't go away."

Was she desperate for company? She'd repeated her appeal by the time she opened the door. "Oh, Dominic, it's you," she said.

She wasn't bothering to hide her disappointment. No doubt she was hoping for someone who might have made her feel safe – the insurance man, perhaps, or the rent collector, in fact any adult at all. I wondered if she'd slept in her blue suit, which looked not much less rumpled than the blanket in Winston's basket always was. Some of her greying curls had started to unravel. I thought she meant to improve on her welcome by asking "Did you have a lovely Christmas?"

"It was good, thanks." I could see no way to avoid enquiring "How was yours?"

"I wasn't on my own." As I tried to think that she was talking about visitors or even merely Winston, she said "What can we do for you, Dominic?"

Sometimes people referred to themselves plurally even if they weren't the monarch, and I wanted to believe she had. "My mum and dad say come and see them," I said, "and I can look after Winston."

"Look after him." Some notion – perhaps the thought of leaving me in her house – made her eyes flutter in their sockets. "Take him for a walk, you mean," she was anxious to confirm.

"You said I could."

"There's a good boy," Mrs Norris said, and I tried not to feel she was commenting to someone besides me. "Wait and I'll fetch him."

As she made for the kitchen I caught sight of her husband's overcoat on a hook opposite the stairs. It looked emptied, but not quite vacant enough.

It was buttoned from the collar to nearly the hem, and the chest seemed to be partly inflated, as if it had taken a breath. Were the dangling sleeves not as flat as they should be, as if they contained limbs, however thin? When Mrs Norris passed the coat without a glance I was afraid of seeing fingers grope out of the cuffs while her husband's face swelled out of the collar. She opened the kitchen door, and as pallid December light spilled into the hall I stifled a cry with my hand, because the coat had stirred wakefully on the hook. Had a draught shifted it, or had only shadows moved? It was displaying its innocence now, flattening itself against the wall like a creature determined not to be noticed, and it stayed quiescent while Mrs Norris led the dog on his leash along the hall. "See who's here to take you in the park," she said. "You behave yourself for Dominic."

She halted just short of the threshold, relinquishing the leash as though it were a lifeline. Before I reached the gate she closed the front door, and I heard her start to talk. Though she'd lowered her voice, I thought she said "Just be there. Don't come close." I might have lingered to hear more if I hadn't been afraid she would see me from the front room. Winston had lifted his ears, but timidly. When I said "Walkies" they wavered higher.

I was setting out for the park when a passing car made him flinch, nearly tripping me up. When had he started reacting to traffic like that? While we were unlikely to encounter much of it along Cherry Lane, there would be more on Walton Lane, the main road I'd meant to follow to the park. Usually I wouldn't have taken a dog in a graveyard, but now the short cut seemed to be the best route.

Winston insisted on cocking his leg against the edge of the arch at the nearest entrance to the cemetery. I glanced around for fear we'd been caught desecrating the place, but couldn't see anyone watching. I didn't know how he might behave if a train thundered over the arch while we were underneath, and I urged him through it almost at a run. Beyond it a broad straight path led to a chapel. Just a few people were tending graves beneath the wide pale sky. I was glad the nearest graves and trees beside the path were too distant for Winston to reach, even when he strained at the lead. We reached the chapel without too many struggles on the way, and I was turning along a path that would take us to a gate opposite the park when I saw someone ahead.

He was pushing a pram, and I recognised him from the back as soon as he stooped in his usual fashion to address the child. Now that the chapel wasn't in the way I could hear him. "What can you see, Tiny Tina?" he was saying. "What can you see?"

I only just managed to suffocate a giggle of embarrassment, and would have liked to retreat behind the chapel. I was trying to coax Winston out of sight when Mr Noble said "What can you hear, Tiny Tina? What can you hear?"

I could hear nothing apart from his voice and the rubbery murmur of pram wheels, but Winston pricked up his ears, the way he had when Mrs Norris began talking in her supposedly empty house. A small high voice came out of the pram. "Dem," it said.

"Not dem, Tiny Tina, them. The, the, the. Say them."

"Dhem."

"That's very good. That's excellent. Them, them, them. Now can you tell me what they're called?"

I strained my ears for an answer. Curiosity made me follow, willing the dog to stay as quiet as I was. "No need to be afraid, Tiny Tina," Mr Noble said.

"Fray."

"A, a, a. Frayed, frayed, frayed. We'll never be the ones who are afraid."

"Frayed."

"That's the smile your daddy likes to see. You know you can be proud, don't you? Proud not to be afraid. Now can you talk to them?"

"Lo."

"Lo and behold, and people will. What else are you going to say? Speak and more will come."

I wanted to believe he was talking about language, telling his daughter that words would bring more words, but I'd begun to suspect that he was training her to perform like him at the spiritualist church, though surely not until she was much older. "Lo," she said again.

"Not just hello. If you can see them tell them. Tell them what you see and hear."

I felt as if I were being urged to do so. Mr Noble's repetitions had started to feel hypnotic if not ritualistic. I was peering about at the graves when Tina said "Like face."

"You like a face, do you? No, you mean it's like a face. Where is it, Tiny Tina? Show your daddy where."

As I stared around me my gaze snagged on an evergreen bush among the graves to the left of the path. The bush was overgrown with ivy, and I wondered if the bush itself had grown around a monument – a shape that was caged by the twigs. If it had a face, I was unable to make out how much of the shape the features occupied, but the object was taller than me. I had to think that the shadows of the twigs were making it appear to be composed of a multitude of filaments. I strained my eyes to grasp its shape, which seemed to make the filaments creep forwards, as if its substance was rising to the surface of the bush. Before I could distinguish anything further Winston let out an unhappy bark. Mr Noble rose to his full daunting height but didn't immediately turn. The time he took felt ominous, though perhaps he was simply preparing an expression. "Why, it's Mr Sheldrake," he said as though he was just as politely surprised as his look. "How long have you been there?"

"Only just now, sir."

This was so precisely true that it did duty as a lie. I was growing up fast, though in ways my parents wouldn't have approved of. I glanced at the bush to see that it was nothing but a shrub. I put my odd glimpse down to a change in the light, since there was no monument inside the bush or behind it either. "Well," Mr Noble said, "I don't think you've met the little watcher."

For a mortified moment I thought he meant me, and then I gathered he was referring to his daughter. "Tina," he said, "this is Mr Sheldrake."

I knew adults were expected to enthuse over the occupants of prams, but this was the first time I'd felt invited. As I stepped forward I had to tug at Winston's lead to make him follow. I almost faltered too, because the girl in the pram was gazing straight at me. Though her head was done up in a pink woollen hood, this didn't lessen her resemblance to her father; it simply made the long thin smooth oval face look like a miniature vignette of his. Her eyes were practically black, and I could have thought they were even keener than her father's. "Ache," she said.

I wondered if Mr Noble was about to take my name apart and reiterate the bits, not to mention whether I'd be able to suppress my mirth if he did, but he only said "Mr Sheldrake, my daughter Tina."

I couldn't help feeling that he should have started with this introduction, since I was so much older. Was it yet another case of giving females special treatment? One reason Bobby belonged to the Tremendous Three was that she never wanted to be treated like a girl. Perhaps resentment made me incautious, and I said "Why is she a watcher, sir?"

"Because young eyes are the best. Young ears as well. In fact, every sense. You might try extending yours, Mr Sheldrake."

This seemed to be my cue to ask "What was she watching, sir?"

Mr Noble turned to the pram, and I had the unsettling fancy that he and the infant exchanged a look. His pause led me to expect him to say a good deal more than "Birds."

"Birds, sir?"

"That's what I said, Mr Sheldrake. Creatures of the air. You may even have heard me encouraging the little one to strike up a conversation with them."

All that I'd overheard let me dare to ask "Which birds, sir?"

As he swung his head around to hold me with his gaze the pram came to rest, and Tina started to wave her arms almost vigorously enough to dislodge her pink mittens. "Star thing," she cried.

"Hear that, Mr Sheldrake. You recognise the starling, surely. It's among our commonest birds."

I might have wondered if Tina had meant something else until I heard a succession of rattles and equally harsh squeaks from a treetop. "There it is," I said and pointed to establish that I wasn't guessing.

"Well spotted, Mr Sheldrake," the teacher said, though I wasn't sure how ironically. "What else can you find? Can you beat my daughter at the game?"

I hadn't realised we were playing one, and I didn't feel entirely comfortable with doing so in a graveyard. Besides, the challenge felt like a pressure for my senses to grow more acute than I might care for. I could have imagined that the place had begun to tug at them, if less substantially than Winston was tugging at the lead. The graveyard had started to remind me of one of those puzzles where you had to find shapes hidden in a picture. I was looking not much less than desperately for a mundane sight to report to Mr Noble when Tina said a word, and I saw movement at once.

She hadn't meant a spirit, I tried to tell myself. Just the same, the activity was in front of a headstone, in the midst of a ragged patchwork rug composed of dead leaves. A brownish object was fumbling among them, though surely not from beneath the earth. Surely their rustling wouldn't grow louder as more of the restless presence groped into view. "I'm afraid she triumphs," Mr Noble said. "Can't you even see a sparrow, Mr Sheldrake?"

Of course, I thought, that was what she'd named, however precocious it proved her to be. The object rummaging among the leaves was indeed a sparrow. "What can you tell us about sparrows, Mr Sheldrake?" the teacher said.

I felt as if I'd been singled out in class and had no answer worth standing up for. "It's a common bird, sir."

"I'd have thought the Holy Ghost would give us more than that." As I concluded that he meant the school he said "What does the Bible say? God's supposed to care for every one of them. He must have a lot on his mind, you might think."

I had a sense that Mr Noble was going further than he would have dared in class. I was feeling special, close to conspiratorial, when he said "What do they find to eat here, do you suppose?"

"They'll be insects, sir."

"Worms, I shouldn't wonder. What do you imagine those feed on?" Before I could respond – I would have tried so as to save his daughter from thinking of an answer – he murmured "Maybe you have to dine on something of the kind if you want to take to the air." He was gazing ahead, surely at the gate, not at the pram. "I think we've seen what's to be seen," he said. "Your dog must have scared them off, Mr Sheldrake."

I would have said that Winston wasn't mine if I hadn't realised Mr Noble might have asked whose he was. I followed the teacher through the gate and saw a lorry bearing down on us. "Sit, Winston," I said.

"If only everything were so obedient," Mr Noble said as the dog squatted by the kerb. "What a lot of traffic there's starting to be, Tina. By the time you're my age you'll hardly be able to cross the road."

Before I could remember to be shy I said "I write about the future sometimes, sir."

"You have visions of what's to come, do you?" When he gazed into the pram I thought he might have been reflecting that Tina was his future, though his eyes had grown so dark that they could have been contemplating the depths of outer space. "Well, Mr Sheldrake," he said, "what do you write?"

"Just stories, sir. Some of them are about what might happen."

"I'd be interested to read those. Perhaps you ought to show them to Brother Bentley for the magazine as well."

He wheeled the pram across the road and into the park, and once we were well past the gates I let Winston off the lead. As he dashed away to chase a flock of pigeons off a wide expanse of grass – "Pidgin," Tina seemed to cry, as if she was describing her own language – I decided this was my excuse to leave Mr Noble behind. I was about to make my farewells when I saw a woman striding towards him.

Her face was so broad, and the features were so substantial, that it resembled an exaggeration of a face. Framing it used up most of her headscarf, barely leaving enough material for a knot. Several uncertainly auburn strands of hair had escaped from the scarf to cross the deep lines of her forehead. Despite her bulk she looked somehow depleted, drained of energy if nothing else. Perhaps this was why she was close to breathless with determination, repeatedly squaring her shoulders as she approached. "Christian?" she called.

I might have answered yes, however automatically, but she meant Mr Noble. I saw him ready his expression – a moderate smile with a hint of surprise – before turning to face her. "Why, whatever brings you out, dear?" he said. "Don't you think you may catch cold?"

She was bundled up in a heavy overcoat that was a little too big even for her, and I supposed that her condition left her vulnerable to the wintry chill, though this had lessened since we'd crossed the road. "Where did you take her?" she demanded in a voice that was regaining breath. "Who has she been talking to now?"

"Why, to Mr Sheldrake. Isn't that so, Mr Sheldrake?"

Up to this point she'd seemed to regard me as no more than a distraction she was determined to ignore, but now she peered so hard at me that her frown clenched her face. "This is Mr Sheldrake, dear. One of my Holy Ghost men," Mr Noble said. "Mr Sheldrake, this is Tina's mother Bernadette."

Since I had no cap to raise I held out a tentative hand, which Mrs Noble gave a look that made it droop. "I asked," she told her husband, "where you've been."

"Don't embarrass Mr Sheldrake, dear. You can see where we are."

"And where were you before that?" Mrs Noble lurched towards the pram as if she meant to seize it from him. "Where did he take you, Tina?"

I could tell that unlike him, Mrs Noble didn't expect their daughter to respond. I might even have thought she was nervous of hearing an answer, because she swung around to face me. "You've been with them, have you, Sheldrake?"

I felt not just interrogated but scrutinised, and not only by her. I could have thought that Tina's gaze was rivalling her father's, which made me realise how little she looked like her mother. "That's right, Mrs Noble," I said.

"And what have you been doing with them?"

"Just walking the dog," I said and brandished the lead, which brought Winston back at a run.

"You know what I mean," she said like a teacher displaying the last of her patience. "Where have you all been?"

"Like Mr Noble said, in the park."

"And where before that?"

I felt as if her stare was shrivelling my vocabulary. "I just said."

She kept up the stare as though it could probe out the truth, and then it succumbed to weariness. "I understand," she said. "You can't say too much or you might find yourself in trouble at school."

This hadn't occurred to me – as much as anything, the way she used my surname had made me side with Mr Noble – and he said "I hope Mr Sheldrake will never have a reason to think me so vindictive."

His wife was still watching me, but as she parted her bitten lips Winston began barking for attention. "I think we'd better head for the happy home, dear," Mr Noble said. "We don't want Tina's ears hurt, do we? You know how sensitive they are."

She gave him a look that refused to admit defeat. "Then let me have the pram."

"By all means, dear. She's yours as well as mine. You shouldn't feel left out. You ought to tell me if you do."

Some if not all of this seemed to enrage Mrs Noble so much that it choked off her words. She clutched the handle of the pram before her husband let go, and I thought she came close to wrenching it out of his hands. As she wheeled the pram away at speed Mr Noble marched after her. He was overtaking her with ease when he glanced back to give me a single blank-faced nod.

I called Winston, who'd wandered off to chase birds out of a bush, and hooked the lead to his collar. Once the Nobles turned a bend in the path I followed them, and reached the gate on the corner of Walton Lane in time to spy them at a house on that road, Mrs Noble backing the pram over the doorstep while her husband lifted the front wheels off a terse garden path. The sight struck me as oddly mundane after the encounter I'd just had.

An entrance to the cemetery faced the exit from the park. As I took Winston home I noticed that only the opposite side of Walton Lane was built up. The graveyard overlooked the rows of houses interrupted by side streets, or would have except for a thick spiky hedge. I was being one of the Tremendous Three, playing the investigator. Sometimes I wish it had stayed a pretence.

The festive rhythm on the knocker brought Mrs Norris to her door. She looked confused, as if I'd woken her. "Thank Dominic for your walk," she said, and Winston held up a paw for me to shake. "And thank your parents for the invitation, Dominic."

"Didn't you go round?"

"Something kept me here, would you please tell them. But you can take Winston whenever you like, can't he?"

I hoped she was addressing the last phrase to the dog. His ears pricked up none too eagerly as she shut the door, and then she began to talk. I wasn't sure whether she was speaking to Winston, and I wasn't anxious to overhear, since I had to report to my parents. I was barely home and hanging up my coat when my father came into the hall to complain "Did your Mrs Norris get lost on the way?"

"She had to stay in her house, dad."

"Is she still up to those tricks?" He might have been interrogating me in her stead by demanding "Are we going to be told why?"

"I think she needs to talk to someone."

"I think she does too." Presumably this was clear enough not to need elucidation, and he said "Anything else we should know about?"

Since I'd sneaked my previous answer past him, I felt confident at keeping secrets. "No, dad," I said, and perhaps it would ultimately have made no difference if I'd kept less to myself. Just the same, now I know that year was the beginning of the end of so much that we took for life.

CHAPTER SIX

1953: The Creeping Future

Every Friday morning before lessons Brother Treanor gave a talk to the assembled school. Generally it warned us of the latest perils of the world, and always led to prayers, often for the victims of events – the family murdered by terrorists in Kenya, the hundreds of people drowned in the North Sea flood, a disaster apparently designed to remind us that God's plan was too large for us to grasp. By contrast, Derek Bentley's execution somehow demonstrated that British justice came from God. We prayed that the hydrogen bomb stayed out of the hands of our enemies or, if they got hold of it, that God would send us the means to destroy their weapon. Brother Treanor's fiercest prayer was aimed at Crick and Watson, who he believed were venturing too close to the sacred secret of creation, along with the scientists he held responsible for putting the Big Bang into our heads. He wasn't much less passionate about forbidding us to watch *From Here to Eternity* – "a filthy film of a filthy book," he proclaimed, emphasising the adjective with vigorous nods of his oversized head – before it had even been released. One especially spectacular performance involved a horror comic found in a fourth-former's desk. "Never forget the Americans are our friends," Brother Treanor told us all, "but remember also that their influence can be pernicious," and once he'd lectured us about the evils of comic books and Hollywood and jazz he spent some minutes tearing each page of the offending publication into the smallest shreds he could produce, after which their owner had to collect every fragment from the stage and bear them away in a waste bin.

I wasn't far from knowing how the boy must have felt. Of all the aspects of my encounter with the Noble family, I was most impressed with Mr Noble's interest in my writing, and so I brought 'The Tremendous Three in Space' to show him. I waited until the end of the Monday lesson before lunch. A discussion of the Light Brigade had led to an argument about the inevitability of war, during which the teacher suggested that some people were born to die for the benefit of others, perhaps of a very few. I wondered if he regretted having said so, because he seemed preoccupied when I approached his desk. "Mr Sheldrake?" he said, though not at once. "Are you bringing me a problem?"

"Sir, you wanted to see this."

"Did I? Why was that?" He didn't bother sitting at his desk while he leafed through the exercise book. "Ah, I recall," he said and gazed at me as though to ascertain how much I remembered. "This is your future, is it, Mr Sheldrake?"

"It's just a story, sir."

"I believe I recommended letting Brother Bentley see it for the magazine."

I was seeking confidence by asking "What do you think he'll think of it, sir?"

"I can't speak for our religious brethren." As if to leave this admission behind, he declared "I should hope he's in favour of creation."

This helped me approach the editor, a fat monk whose expansive mottled face wore a constant disappointed look. "Write your form and your form master on it" was how he greeted my submission when I found him in the dining hall that lunchtime. "Neatly, Sheldrake."

At least this didn't feel like a rejection. I wanted him to see the story I was proudest of, where the Tremendous Three discovered that a neighbour who worked late in his allotment was building a space rocket in his outsize shed. He was a spy as well, and took Bobby prisoner when he caught her writing notes about him on her pocket typewriter. She might have been shot into space, never to return, if she hadn't managed to alert Dom and Jim with a photograph she sent from the phone she'd hidden in her shoe. The boys were in time to stow away but not to release her, and once they'd survived being crushed by the take-off all three took over the controls. After flying around the moon they returned to earth to find that Dom's dog Winston had trapped the Russian spy in the wreckage of the shed. I went to bed imagining how the tale would look in actual print, and when Brother Bentley beckoned to me next day in the corridor I went eagerly to him, though his habitual expression hadn't changed. "What do you mean by it, Sheldrake?" he said.

"I'm not sure what you mean, sir."

"That's what I asked you, boy." Having given me time to suffer from the reminder, Brother Bentley said "This nonsense you imagine is appropriate for our magazine."

I felt my face grow suffused, and more so when I realised all the passing boys could hear. "Sir, I didn't think—"

"That's painfully apparent. What in heaven's name possessed you to perpetrate such rubbish? Do you honestly believe there will ever come a time when most people own a telephone, never mind one they can carry about with them?"

"Sir, I did read—"

"I won't ask what your parents permit you to read, assuming they do. Just you make sure it comes nowhere near the Holy Ghost," Brother Bentley said. "A telephone that transmits pictures, by everything that's holy. Don't you even know the difference between a television and a telephone?"

I was so thrown by his reaction that it felt like a defence to say "We haven't got any at home."

"Sir." Once he'd extracted a slavish echo, he homed in on my worst outrage. "And people flying to the moon," he scoffed. "The Astronomer Royal himself says that's balderdash. Do you consider yourself to be more of an authority on the subject than one of our leading scientists, Sheldrake?"

"Sir, it's just a story."

"Stories ought to tell some kind of truth or they have no business being told. I suggest you look to your Bible for an example before writing anything further."

As he grasped the book in both hands my innards shrivelled. I was afraid he meant to treat my tales the way Brother Treanor had dealt on the stage with the copy of *Witches Tales*. Perhaps he simply meant to dismay me, because he thrust the book at me. "Be thankful I'm not confiscating this," he said. "Never bring it to the Holy Ghost again."

I almost dropped the book in my haste to keep it safe. I was stowing it in my satchel when he said "At least you were right about the Godless neighbour."

I was shamefully eager to learn "How, sir?"

"I suspect there are far too many of his sort lying low amongst us. It is our duty to keep watch for them."

This sounded like a call for the Tremendous Three, but I wouldn't have asked what he thought of them even if he hadn't turned away with a sombre flurry of his robe. I was wishing I could hide my reddened face while I fumbled my coat off the hook in the corridor when Jim gave me a sympathetic grimace, having overheard. "Miserable old," he said, but fell short of another word.

I saw Mr Noble leaving the school and hurried to catch up with him. "What's the calamity, Mr Sheldrake?" he said, rather more than glancing at my face.

"Brother Bentley doesn't like my story, sir."

"I'm sorry if that's the case. I did say I couldn't speak for him."

"I mean he really hates it. He thinks I oughtn't to have written it."

"I can't see what you'd have me do about that, Mr Sheldrake."

I felt so betrayed that I let out the only protest I could think of. "He said I had to put your name on it, sir."

"My name." He halted so abruptly that Jim bumped into me. "How is he saying I'm involved?"

"You're our form master."

"Ah, I understand," Mr Noble said, laughing as if he ought to have seen the joke sooner. "He didn't mean I gave you visions of the future. You carry on telling your tales, Mr Sheldrake. I can't see what harm they could do."

I felt patronised, reduced to less than my age. I made for the gates, hardly caring if Jim kept up. At the stop I struggled onto a bus in the midst of a mob of boys, and Jim fought his way along the aisle to join me. "What's your story about?" he said.

"You can read it if you like."

He couldn't then, since we were standing, not to mention staggering whenever the bus pulled up at a stop. The driver seemed determined to treat us all like skittles, perhaps in retaliation for the way we'd piled onto his bus. After Jim and I caught a tram at the crossroads we were able to sit down. "Can I see your story now?" he said at once.

His eagerness heartened me, and felt like loyalty as well. Our stop was in sight by the time he finished reading, and he handed me the book as he stood up to tug the cord that rang the bell. "Did you like it?" I was surprised to have to ask.

He didn't turn to me until we'd left the tram. His close-set features made his face looked squashed before the corners of his large mouth turned up towards a frown. "Why did you have to put us in it?" he said.

"Because it's about the Tremendous Three."

"Okay," Jim said, a word forbidden by the Holy Ghost or at least the school, "but why have you got to use our names?"

"Because that's who we are."

"I wish you hadn't, Dom. You don't want everybody laughing at us, do you?"

"You think my blasted story's that much poo."

This was stronger language than I'd ever previously used – I'd have been afraid to let my parents hear me saying damn or hell – but just then I didn't care if the policeman who was gesturing us to cross the road arrested me for it. "I didn't mean that, Dom," Jim protested as he hastened after me. "I'm just glad it won't be in the magazine for everyone to read."

This felt like even more of a betrayal than Mr Noble had perpetrated. I was about to stalk home, leaving Jim behind, when Bobby stepped down from a bus that had drawn up on our side of the road. "Bobby," Jim called. "Come and look at this."

"You come here if you want me to see anything."

She sounded like the girl we knew, and despite her school uniform she looked like it too. One kneesock was around her ankle, and a pigtail was well on the way to unravelling. As we went to her she yanked a strip of plaster off her wrist, revealing several reddish scratches punctuated with scabs, and dropped the plaster among the used tickets in a bin. "What have you been falling off, Bobs?" Jim said.

I wouldn't have been surprised if the marks were souvenirs of a climb up a tree or over a wall, but Bobby raised her big-eyed face to point her nose and chin at him. "I had a fight with a girl."

"Who won?" I said, only because I was sure I didn't need to ask.

"Me." In case this wasn't sufficiently forceful she added "It didn't need a plaster, only my mum said."

"What did you tell her?" Jim was eager to hear.

"What happened. Why wouldn't I? Her and dad say I've got to stand up for myself."

"What was the girl doing to you?"

"She kept calling me Hanger."

Jim began to laugh, but a look from Bobby stopped him. "Why?" he said.

"You'd better not think she was right, Jim Bailey. Nobody calls me that now." With an even fiercer look Bobby said "She kept telling everyone I looked like I'd left the hanger in my blazer."

I thought it best to look away from her broad straight shoulders and concentrate on the angry dots and dashes on her wrist. I've no idea where Jim found to look until she said "What did you want me to see?"

"Show her, Dom."

"I don't know if I want to."

Was I being coy or shy? Whichever, it still makes me wince. "Go on, Dom," Bobby said. "I showed you my scars."

"It's nothing. It's just a story I wrote."

"It's a story about us," Jim said.

By now my disinclination was more of a performance, and I lingered over rummaging in my satchel. "You won't like it," I said once I felt unable to delay producing the exercise book any longer. "He thinks it's putrid."

"I never said that," Jim protested. "I don't want boys calling us things like that girl called her, that's all."

Bobby handled the book with a delicacy bordering on reverence, qualities she'd never previously displayed. She dawdled over the title page, which I'd painstakingly inscribed in letters imitating print: *Tales of the Tremendous Three by Dominic Sheldrake, aged ten and eleven.* She leafed through the book as we made for her road, and then she halted. "Are these all about us?"

While I wasn't certain of her tone, I could only admit "Yes."

"Can I have a lend of it to read?"

"You can borrow it," Jim said. "I mean, you can if Dom says."

"All right, Mr Clever. We can't all go to grammar school," Bobby said, punching his arm hard enough to make him flinch. "I can speak better than you if I want to. My dad says more girls would pass if the perishing exams weren't fixed."

Jim smirked but dodged out of reach of another punch. "Why would anyone be doing that?"

"To keep girls down. My mum says they won't be able to much longer, not when all the women worked so hard in the war."

Jim glanced at me. "Her mum and dad sound like what Bent was talking about."

In a tone that threatened worse than a punch Bobby said "And what's that like?"

"Just someone in one of my stories." When this failed to placate her I said "Someone who doesn't like how the country's run."

"They don't. My dad's in a union and my mum won't stand up for the queen." As Jim opened his mouth to condemn at least one of these offences Bobby said "So can I take this home? I'll take care of it, I promise."

"If you want," I said, hoping my indifference hid my desire for praise, and watched her slip the book like a fragile treasure into her satchel.

Jim and I left her at the end of her road next to ours. I wondered if it was my book that made her raise a fist and shake it slowly twice in the code we'd lost the habit of using – the sign of the Tremendous Three, the silent Morse of its initials. We responded with the gesture, but as we headed home Jim muttered "My dad says he'd arrest anyone who insulted the queen."

I might have asked if his father belonged to the police union, but I was too busy enjoying Bobby's esteem for my opus. Just then the book and her opinion seemed as important as anything else in the world. I still have the book, as if it even slightly mattered. I have a copy of another book from that year, and I wish it mattered just as little. However suspicious of the future Brother Bentley was, he could never have foreseen where that other book would lead.

CHAPTER SEVEN

A Voice from the Past

Brother Treanor marked the Easter week with accounts of the agonies of Christ that were as gruesome as any horror comic. Every sin we committed added to Christ's sufferings, he told us: arguing with prefects, smoking while we were in uniform or staining the school's reputation in any other way, eating meat on Fridays or being otherwise unholy on a holy day, not attending church on any day of obligation or letting our attention stray while we were there, failing to pray with sufficient fervour, entertaining impure thoughts, coveting more than the share God had allotted us, neglecting to honour authority... By now I was worrying about Bobby's parents and their views, but besides daunting me with a sense that practically anything I did might be sinful, the headmaster was disturbing my concept of time. I took my doubts to the classroom, and felt sufficiently at ease with Mr Noble to ask "Sir, how can what we do hurt Christ when he's already been crucified?"

Mr Noble raised his eyebrows, but his widened eyes kept their expression dark. "Perhaps you should put that to the headmaster."

"It's not supposed to be how time works, is it, sir? If we do something now it may change the future, but it can't go back into the past."

"You disappoint me, Mr Sheldrake. You're meant to be the science fiction man," he said, and no longer just to me. "See it as symbolic if you like."

"How do you mean, sir?" O'Shaughnessy said.

"Some things can reach back." For a moment Mr Noble seemed to be gazing at someone who wasn't in the room, and then his darkened gaze returned to us. "Perhaps your tradition symbolises that, Mr O'Shaughnessy," he said.

"It isn't only mine, it's everybody's here. It's yours as well, sir."

"I appreciate the reminder. If you have any further questions on the subject you had better address them to the brethren."

This was aimed at me as well, and felt like a rebuke I couldn't quite interpret. If he was blaming me for having raised the issue, I didn't think my doubts had been resolved. In one more day the school would break up for Easter, but since Brother Treanor had already dealt with the crucifixion at grisly length, I wondered what he could have kept in store for Thursday morning – possibly the resurrection? Perhaps good deeds could reach back to help Christ emerge from his tomb, and I hoped the headmaster might offer us this reassurance.

On Thursday it was clear at once that he wasn't going to give his ordinary sort of talk. A solitary chair had been placed at the front of the stage where he customarily stood, and his march onstage was less forthright than usual, while his stance beside the lone chair wasn't far from deferential. "Today we are honoured to be visited by an old boy of the school," he said. "He's here to speak to the boys who will be visiting the battlefields, but his words will benefit you all. Please stand up for a hero of the Great War. Mr Noble?"

As we all stood up with a shuffling rumble like awkwardness rendered audible, Mr Noble moved away from his chair on the stage. I was wondering how he could be related to an event so far in the past – it might have been another demonstration of the unreliable nature of time – when he vanished through the door beside the row of chairs. "This way, father," he said, though not at once.

A series of wooden thumps preceded the man who eventually limped onstage. If Mr Noble hadn't called him father I wouldn't have known they were kin. Even at his full height the stooping man would have been inches shorter than his son, and his flat squarish snub-nosed loose-lipped face could have had very little in common with the teacher's even before it grew wrinkled and grey. Half of his uneven steps were emphasised by thuds of a stick, on which he leaned while he lowered himself by halting degrees onto the isolated chair. When Mr Noble offered to support him, the old man grimaced, shaking his head until his son retreated. "Mr Jack Noble," Brother Treanor said and swept a deferential hand towards him.

As he and the teachers sat down we all did, and the old man hitched himself forward with his stick to peer in a generalised way at us. "You boys don't know how lucky you are," he said. "I expect you'd like to hear about the war."

His voice was stronger than the rest of him appeared to be. We murmured assent, which sounded as though nobody wanted to be singled out by saying an actual word. "Life in the trenches, is that the favourite?" the old man said. "The lice and the rats and the food we ate if they didn't get to it first? Or do you want how I lost my toe?"

He held up his right foot, exposing the eroded heel of the shoe, and squinted over it at us. "One of you pipe up for pity's sake," he urged. "It's worse than talking to the dead."

For an instant I glimpsed his son's resemblance to him, though only because they both looked as if they thought he'd said too much. Then a boy some rows behind me called "Yes please, sir."

Brother Treanor jerked his head up. "Please remember to raise your hand if you wish to speak."

"No call for that. My boy's the only teacher in the family. It's the toe you're after, is it, lad?"

As the headmaster subsided while his gaze did the opposite the boy said "Yes please."

"I was luckier than some of my pals. If the water kept getting over the tops of your boots you could think about kissing your legs goodbye. Trench foot, they called it, but it was trench leg half the time. How many of you chaps change your socks three times a day?" When the only response was a leaden silence the old man said "Three times was recommended, but most of us had to make do with twice. At least the medics chopped my rotten toe off before it got to any more of me."

I suspect I wasn't alone in wondering how much we were meant to laugh at his inky humour, if at all. Most of the teachers looked monolithically respectful, and I thought Brother Treanor was trying hardest. "You'd think you'd be scared of getting shelled most of all," Mr Noble's father said, "and some of the lads never stopped even after they came home, but some of us ended up dreading the rain just as much. It didn't only rot you, it could get into your food till it wasn't fit even for the likes of us, and I've seen soldiers buried when a trench collapsed with all the rain."

If it was a memory that made him pause, it let Brother Treanor say "Mr Noble is telling you how brave the soldiers had to be."

"We didn't feel brave. We just got on with it because we had to, those of us who managed. You'd be surprised what you can get used to if you're stuck without a choice, but I never got used to the lice." The old man peered at us as though searching for an infestation. "I don't mean the kind some of you may have," he said. "You'd know it if you had trench lice. Once they took a liking to you they were yours for the duration, and it didn't matter how much you washed your clothes or yourself, that's if you had the facilities. And I can see some spotty faces but trust me, you're pinups compared with how we looked after the lice had been feeding on us."

Brother Treanor looked ready to direct the lecture, but he hadn't spoken when the old man said "The rats were the real devils, though. They'd steal the food out of your pockets given half the chance, and you'd wake up with them on you when you were trying to catch up on your sleep. Shelling didn't see them off, and gas didn't either. I used to think if we were all killed off, the rats could take over. Maybe they're the future of the world, or something else that isn't us."

I saw his son and Brother Treanor react to this. Mr Noble's gaze grew so distant that it left all expression behind, while the headmaster opened his mouth in dissent and looked close to speaking up. "Some of them were bigger than your head," the old man told us. "We didn't like to wonder what things like that fed on. Once I saw a rat come out of a dead man's mouth and take the lower jaw with it."

As the headmaster took an audible breath the old man used his stick to point at someone in the middle of the hall. "I said no need to stick your hand up. We've had a war to stop the likes of that. What's your question, lad?"

"Did you kill anyone, sir?"

"I thought I had once. Heard him scream a lot, and then he stopped. I'd have put him out of his misery sooner, only the officers were telling us not to waste ammunition. And then I kept hearing him whenever I tried to sleep. It's my belief that if you're mixed up in someone's death you may have a job getting rid of them once they're dead."

This time his son as well as Brother Treanor looked near to speaking, but the old man hitched himself around in his chair to face the headmaster. "Sorry if I'm not what you ordered," he said. "I don't want your boys going off to see the pretty battlefields and just thinking how sad it was, that's all. If enough people know what it was really like, maybe they won't be anxious to repeat it. Maybe there won't be so many dead."

"Pray continue, Mr Noble. I'm sure everything you have to tell us will be discussed in class."

"There's one battlefield I hope they won't be visiting." Having lingered over saying so – I couldn't see who he was looking at – the old man inched himself around to face us. "I won't tell you where it is or what it's called," he said. "Maybe it's not marked. I hope it's somewhere nobody goes anywhere near."

A boy behind me spoke for all of us. "Why, sir?"

"Because I don't believe it can have changed that much. How can I put it so you'll understand?" The old man clutched at his stick, though he appeared to be seated securely enough. "It felt," he said as if he was trying to restrain a memory, "hungry for the dead."

I began to raise my hand before remembering I needn't. "What does that mean, sir?"

"I'll tell you what happened and you can decide for yourselves," Mr Noble's father said, taking a firmer grip on the stick. "We were well used to digging up the countryside as soon as we stopped anywhere, and to start with that place looked like more of the same, just a field in the middle of nowhere much. There were a few bits of a big old building of some kind or other, but you could hardly tell which bits had been part of it and which were just lumps of rock. One of us thought it might have been a church, because he dug up something he said was a gargoyle, only it was a lot uglier than any gargoyle I've ever seen on any church. It didn't have hands or a face, just a lot of stuff like grubs where they ought to have been. The lad who found it chucked it in the middle of the field and said he wished he could have buried it. And I'll tell you now, I wished I'd dug somewhere else than I did. Because when I stuck my spade in I felt I'd woken something up."

I was so eager to hear more that I forgot to keep my hand down. "What, sir?"

"Something that wanted us dead, that was waiting for someone like us." The old man sighed, a noise like losing faith in language. "It doesn't sound too likely when I say it now, does it? It didn't seem too likely there either, in a field with the sun shining on us for a change and so many birds singing in the trees you couldn't have counted them. I asked my pals if they felt anything like I did, and not a one had. Maybe I was chosen somehow." He shook his head as if to expel some unwelcome item and said "I never asked them if they noticed what happened while I was digging. The birds stopped singing one by one, and we never heard any there again."

"Perhaps hearing you men digging drove them away," Brother Treanor said.

"You'd like to think so, wouldn't you? I know I would. Only just then I felt every time I dug the spade in it'd touch whatever was waiting under there."

I could hardly wait to ask "Did you see it, sir?"

"Not then and maybe never. Felt it, though." The old man ignored Brother Treanor, who had parted his lips with a noise like a tut pinched thin. "We hadn't dug in long when they started shelling us," old Mr Noble said. "And every time a man was killed I felt that thing under the ground come more alive. It felt like it was creeping closer to the surface, and I had to stand there and wait till it came."

Brother Treanor cleared his throat, a shrill harsh sound. "I think perhaps—"

"There's not much more, and then we'll get to better things." Just the same, the old man looked as if those might be some way off. "You wouldn't believe I could sleep, but I did," he told us. "You do if you're too tired to stay awake. And that's when I thought I saw what was under the earth."

"Sir" – by now I'd quite forgotten any shyness – "what was it like?"

"Like the gargoyle, only bigger. Bigger than a man as well, but I somehow knew it used to be one. And I was right, it was coming to the surface underneath me, seeping up like the water in the trenches could under your feet. It got hold of my hands, and it felt like meat somebody had tried to keep cold but it had gone off, too soft is what I'm saying. Then I think I woke up."

Though Brother Treanor's cough was shriller still, it failed to daunt me. "Don't you know, sir?"

"I must have, mustn't I? I'm here." The old man twisted his head towards Brother Treanor. "You'll be glad to hear that's all of that," he said and faced us. "It turned out the other side retreated overnight, so we moved on. But I couldn't feel whatever was under the trench any more. Maybe it was satisfied somehow and went back where it came from. I don't know where else it could have gone."

As Brother Treanor made a throaty noise, not so much a dry cough as an omen of one, old Mr Noble said "I promised you better memories, didn't I? Here's the best one. The next time I went home was like going to heaven. Tea that didn't taste of vegetables because it wasn't brewed in the same vat, and meat that didn't come out of a tin, and bread instead of biscuits. And then it wasn't too long after I went back to the front that they signed the armistice, and us who were left went home for good, and I got the best news of all. We had a baby on the way, and all of you can see him if you look."

I imagine every boy's eye went to his son – certainly mine did – and several of his colleagues glanced at him. No wonder he looked uncomfortable, though I had an odd notion that he hadn't only just begun. His father hardly helped by adding "Me and his mother treasured him even more because he nearly died. He was born at Easter, but then he stopped breathing, and the doctors didn't know if they could save him. One of them told us they'd never seen a newborn that was so determined to live."

Brother Treanor gazed along the line of teachers at the subject of the speech and appeared to share some of his discomfort. "Mr Noble," the headmaster said to the old man, "this isn't really about the war."

"I'll get back to it," old Mr Noble said and told us tales of carnage for most of half an hour. At least some were sufficiently heroic that Brother Treanor's eventual thanks for the talk didn't sound too insincere. All the same, I suspect that the old man's anecdote about his son had lodged in more minds than mine, so that nobody was anxious to start a discussion once Mr Noble led us to the classroom. I might have been speaking for quite a few people when I said "Sir, are we going where your dad had his dream?"

"Why should you imagine I should want to go there, Sheldrake?" In a moment he regained control of himself. "Forgive me, Mr Sheldrake. My mind was elsewhere," he said. "We won't be paying it a visit, no. As my father mentioned, it's unidentified."

I think most of the class took this on trust, but I'd seen more of the truth. As he lost control I'd remembered that the school trip had been his idea, even if he'd made it sound like mine. If he hadn't been so thoughtless that he'd used my naked name I might have let the insight go, but now I was sure he had something to hide. He meant to find the place where his father had sensed some kind of life beneath the earth.

CHAPTER EIGHT

The Fleeing Trees

France welcomed us with a smell of fish. We'd have called it a stink, and some of us did while others greeted it with groans, since several hours across the Channel had left many of us seasick. More than one port official seemed amused by our state, and the drivers of the coaches that picked us up didn't help by slewing the vehicles around every bend of an hour's worth of country roads and puffing on the foulest cigarettes we'd ever smelled. Jim and I were in the lead coach, together with the rest of our form and Mr Clement's. At least the French master was able to address the driver in his own language, provoking imprecations every time the coach had to halt for someone else to jump off and throw up. Before we reached the hostel where we were to spend the night, several of the boys were praying for journey's end. Jim and I kept each other in our seats by swapping the most repulsive jokes we could think of, though some of Jim's made me have to swallow very hard indeed.

Most of us did without dinner. Even Jim did, despite the bulk he had to maintain. We went up to the dormitory as soon as we could. Once Mr Noble had led us in a token prayer I lay wondering if all the beds seemed to rock from side to side like mine, but I hadn't time to be surprised by how fast I fell asleep. In the morning I felt ready for more than breakfast, especially when it proved to be the Continental kind, which struck me as not too different from rationing. Jim did his best to make up for missing dinner, and would have had yet another helping if Mr Clement hadn't produced his pocket watch to confront everyone with the hour.

I was eager for adventure now – for my first real trip without my parents. Even having to wear the Holy Ghost uniform didn't detract from the excitement too much. When Mr Noble handed out boiled sweets on the coach to help us travel, it felt like celebrating how confectionery was no longer rationed at home. "En route," Mr Clement urged the driver, earning a scowl almost as black as the tobacco in the cigarette that lolled out of the driver's mouth.

For days the convoy of three coaches travelled across France, stopping each night at a hostel. During the days we visited wartime sites. More than once we saw bombed buildings that had been left as memorials, which put me in mind of entire blitzed districts of Liverpool. Once the coaches slowed alongside a meadow where an old woman was bending effortfully down to lay a single poppy on the grass. Elsewhere we trudged through battleground museums while morose guides lectured us in approximate English. We were impressed most by a field where unmarked crosses stretched to the horizon, as if the throng of unidentified dead were erasing the landscape. I wondered if this might be the hungry place Mr Noble's father had told us about, which I'd been looking out for ever since we left the seaport. It wasn't, and when our tour brought us to it I didn't know at first it was the site.

We'd lunched in the garden of a hotel, where the six teachers had shared a bottle of wine. Some of the older boys looked envious, though not of Mr Clement's meal of snails and brains. Most of us had soup and a casserole that was filling enough even for Jim once he'd finished gnawing bits of rabbit off the bone. Sunlight like the sound of water rendered visible glittered on a nearby stream, and everybody was relaxed when we went back to the coaches. No doubt this was why Jim asked Mr Noble "Have you had your birthday yet, sir?"

"It isn't every Easter, Mr Bailey, only the first one. I'll be celebrating next week, and then I'll have done better than Jesus."

This caused quite a silence, and Mr Clement seemed not to know where to look. "Forgive me, gentlemen," Mr Noble said. "I only meant to say I'll have lived longer than your saviour."

"He's yours too, sir," O'Shaughnessy protested.

"As much as he's yours, true enough." While the coach groaned up a slope Mr Noble said "I wasn't really meaning to connect his years with mine. It's a traditional enough number."

"How is it, sir?" I felt inspired to ask.

"Locally it's the number of life, isn't it, Mr Clement? The one the doctor has you say while he's sounding your lungs. It's the number of beads the Mohammedans have, and one of their preachers believes everyone will be that age in heaven. It's how many times God's name appears in Genesis, and the sum of the bones of your spine, Mr Sheldrake. It's what the letters of the word Amen add up to, and you might try adding up the miracles they say Christ performed."

I had a sense that he was gradually venturing towards some information, which was why I didn't prompt him. "Come to that," he said as if he didn't care who heard, "if you want to go all the way back—"

I don't know how many people thought Shea had interrupted him. Having laboured to the top of the slope, the coach was speeding alongside a large field. All the trees on the near edge leaned so precipitously away from the field that several looked close to toppling into the road. Branches kept scraping the roof of the coach, an assault that seemed to goad the driver into putting on more speed. "Why are the trees like that, sir?" Shea said.

Mr Noble turned to look once he'd gazed at the hedge on the opposite side of the road. "It must show the direction of the prevailing wind, Mr Shea."

"Not just these ones. The trees all round the field. That can't be the wind, can it, sir?"

I peered between the contorted trunks and saw that the field was entirely bordered by trees, every one of which stooped away from it. "Was it a battlefield, sir?" Joyce said. "Did a bomb do that?"

"It doesn't look much like a battlefield to me, Mr Joyce, and I can't imagine what size of bomb you have in mind."

I was reflecting that most of the sites we'd seen no longer looked like battlefields when Mr Clement said "Perhaps it's something in the earth."

"I can't think what that could be either," Mr Noble said, and at once I knew he could. He'd pretended not to notice the field until Shea drew his attention to it, and now he was trying to persuade us it wasn't worth lingering over. "It must have been a hurricane, of course," he said. "Maybe several. I wouldn't be surprised if they're a feature of the region."

I suspected that the question Mr Clement asked the driver was about this, but he didn't elicit much of a response. A last branch made a feeble bid to snag the roof, and a few minutes later our coach led the procession of vehicles into a courtyard in front of a hostel. Mr Clement led his form off first, and I moved to sit opposite Mr Noble. "Sir, what else were you going to say about that number?"

He stared at me as if I'd tried to catch him out. "Let's just say," he said louder than I thought was necessary, "that it's significant to people whose beliefs Mr O'Shaughnessy wouldn't approve of."

In fact I hadn't especially wanted to know. I was making sure I was the first of our form off the coach. As I'd hoped, the hostel was set out like some of the others we'd stayed in, with each form in a separate dormitory overseen by the form master. Now that I was in the lead it was easy to bag the bed next to Mr Noble's, which was by the only door, and hold the bed on the far side of mine for Jim. We all unpacked our bags yet again and stowed our belongings in tin lockers, and then I tried to find an opportunity to talk to Jim, which didn't come until it was time for dinner. As we trooped into the dining hall, a long room that trestle tables laid with utensils and jugs of water didn't render much less bare, I grabbed Jim's elbow to let our classmates pass. "What's up?" he protested. "Don't make me miss my dinner."

"I want to tell you something while they can't hear," I muttered. "Did you realise what that place with all the bent trees was?"

"Was it where Nobbly's dad told us about?"

"You bet it was. And you know what else, I'll bet it's why he brought us here."

Jim looked as if he felt each of the boys who were hurrying into the hall was denying him his dinner, but he couldn't resist murmuring "Why?"

"You watch, he'll go there when everyone's asleep." Lower still I said "We've got to follow him."

Jim glanced towards the dining hall again. "What for?"

"I've found out stuff about him. I'll tell you later. Don't you want to see what's there and what he does? Remember we're the Tremendous Two."

This time when he glanced away from me Jim looked anxious to make sure nobody had overheard, especially my last words. "Dunno," he barely pronounced.

"Jim, he's got to be going or he'd have let on that he knows what it is. I bet he goes tonight. I don't want to go by myself, but I will."

"How much do you bet?"

I couldn't afford to be miserly. "Sixpence."

"Go on then." Perhaps it was the extravagance – a whole week's pocket money – or the imminence of dinner that persuaded Jim. "Only if I go," he said at once, "I haven't got to pay."

I thought his presence would be worth it, though I felt he'd played a sly trick. "It's a deal," I said, echoing a film if not a few of them, and followed him into the dining hall.

We wouldn't have missed dinner. Brother Mayle was delaying grace while he waited for the two empty places on a bench to be occupied, and sent us a reproachful shake of the head. "Enter Banquo and Duncan," Mr Noble remarked to Mr Askew, prompting a quick grin or at any rate a grimace. Some of the other teachers seemed to find the comment inappropriate, and Brother Mayle might have been trying to drive it away with the prayer.

A stout unsmiling moustached woman in a shapeless overall ladled out a dinner that might well have used more grace. A soup with an oily surface reminiscent of a stagnant pond stared back at us with the dead eyes of fish, some of which bared their teeth. "Dine with a will, gentlemen," Mr Noble urged. "They would have been glad of it in the field." Once the remains of fish were stranded at the bottom we had to return the bowls to our host while she inflicted a portion of a casserole from a vat on each of us. Even Jim poked at more of his helping than he ate, though he made up for it with half of mine. "If everyone's replete," Mr Noble said at last, "we've come a long way and we've a long way to travel tomorrow," and I realised everyone except Jim and me would take him to be ensuring the boys caught up on their sleep.

Jim and I were soon out of the communal bathroom, where Brother Mayle kept up an avuncular look as he watched boys undress, and then we scrambled into our low cramped beds. When everyone was back in the dormitory at last, Mr Noble switched off the bare bulbs that hung above the uncarpeted aisles between the twin ranks of beds. "Good night, gentlemen," he said. "Dream well."

Before long I found his last words not just odd but ominous. I was lying on my side with my face towards Mr Noble's bed. I heard the mattress creak as he lay down, and he murmured a few words that I didn't think were a prayer. I narrowed my eyes, and once they adjusted to the dark I made out his dim silhouette. He was prone on his back with his fists gripping the blanket on either side of him. While I couldn't distinguish his expression, I wasn't far from fancying that he was anxious to keep himself there, or was he just waiting to be certain everybody was asleep? I don't know how long I watched him before my eyelids gave up the battle for alertness, but as soon as they sank shut I felt I was about to dream. I was nervous of glimpsing what his father had seen in the trench, and my eyes wavered open at once. Mr Noble hadn't moved, and I was able to see that he wasn't trying to sleep. He was gazing up at the dark – at least that far – and his eyes looked darker still.

I tried to stay as awake as he was, but my body had other ideas. Whenever my eyes closed I strove to open them at once, not least because of the threat of the dream. More than once the dark inside my eyelids appeared to grow restless, writhing in search of a shape to take. I thought they never closed for more than a few seconds at a time, after which I had another sight of Mr Noble's unchanged silhouette. Perhaps this lulled me into carelessness, because yet another sleepy glance showed me an empty bed.

As I lurched upright, crumpling the scrawny pillow and thumping my shoulders against the wall that served as a headboard, I saw the door creep shut a last inch. Mr Noble had made as little noise in sneaking out of bed, despite the creaky mattress. If I'd had any doubts about his intentions, I hadn't now. I slid out of bed and grabbed Jim's arm. "Jim," I whispered, "quick."

His eyes struggled open, and his voice sounded just as effortful. "Wad you one?"

"Quiet." I nearly laid a finger on his lips, except that wasn't how boys behaved. "He's gone," I hissed. "He's going to that field."

"Howdah no?"

"Because he just crept out." At the far end of the dormitory a boy moaned as though he didn't like a dream, and I was afraid of waking people up. "We bet, remember," I murmured urgently.

"All rye, uncommon," Jim mumbled, which he clarified by sprawling out of bed.

At least our clothes were within reach, since we'd all been told to lay them under the mattresses. As we dressed, another boy made an uneasy sound in his sleep, and I had the irrational notion that he was dreaming what I'd striven not to dream. I was heading for the door when Jim nudged me and demonstrated how to make a supine shape under the blankets with a pillow and a bundle of pyjamas. No doubt this was how the Tremendous Two ought to cover their tracks, and so I copied him, although the result looked a good deal less convincing than stories made it sound. I could only hope that nobody would give the contents of the beds a second look. Once I'd finished easing the door open Jim took even longer to close it behind us, which gave me time to try and think of an excuse in case a teacher came out of any of the dormitories along the hall. I hadn't thought of anything I could have said with any confidence when Jim muttered "Go" in my ear.

The wooden stairs were warped. I'd noticed earlier how loudly some of them squeaked, but if Mr Noble had made so little noise on his way downstairs, surely we could. I did my best by walking on the edge against the bare brick wall, but more than one tread made a muted protest, and complained louder about Jim. All the same, I thought we reached the downstairs corridor without disturbing anyone, and we were halfway to the outer door when a woman in the room we'd just passed called out a question in French.

I was so thrown that I opened my mouth. I might even have given her some desperate answer if the rest of my brain hadn't overtaken my response. In a moment a man shouted to her from the room we had yet to pass. Even if she hadn't asked who was in the corridor – her words had been too fast for me to translate – I was afraid the man would go to her and see us. I was glancing about wildly for somewhere we could hide when the woman grunted, apparently expressing some form of satisfaction, since that was the end of the dialogue. Before I felt safe to move, Jim leaned over my shoulder. "Go," he said with such vigour he spat in my ear.

The outer door had a massive latch. As I eased the bar up it scraped against the socket, and I froze until I had to take a breath, having heard no reaction along the corridor. The door was so heavy that I was afraid it would catch against the stone threshold, but when it lumbered towards me it stayed just clear of the step. I held the latch up until Jim followed me outside, and then I inched it into place, having wrestled the door shut. As we paced across the courtyard I glanced back to see that all the dormitories at the front of the building were dark, while the only window that was lit downstairs was curtained tight. Nevertheless I didn't feel safe from being seen until we were out of sight beyond the courtyard wall.

High above us the moon was just past full. It blackened all the trees along the silent road and iced the upper surfaces of branches white. The nearest leaves looked crystallised by luminous pallor. The surface of the road glistened so much like fresh tar that I almost expected my shoes to stick to it. A wakeful magpie chittered in a tree, a brittle icy sound, but the fluttering of wings among the leaves couldn't distract me. Hundreds of yards ahead, a man was vanishing around a bend towards the field we'd seen.

As soon as he was past the bend we hurried after him. Despite trying not to make a noise we startled the magpie, which flapped across the road like an abstract of the monochrome midnight and sailed down to rest in a meadow. The moonlight turned even our green blazers black, so that I could have fancied we were characters in a black and white film, a heroic duo pursuing a respected citizen who nobody else realised wasn't what he seemed to be. I was about to share the fantasy with Jim when he murmured "So what were you going to say about Nobbly?"

"He brings the dead to people. I think he wants to find out who's in that field."

"Are you having me on?" Jim peered at me as if he wished there were more light on my face. "How do you mean, brings the dead?"

"He did for Mrs Norris who lives past the bridge. He brought her husband back."

Jim made a sound on the way to a skeptical laugh. "Who says?"

"She does, and I've heard her talking to him."

Jim added the rest of the laugh. "Big deal. Have you heard him, though?"

"I feel as if he's in her house."

"That'll just be her making you think he is. All it means is she's mad," Jim said and stared at the bend we were striding towards. "Anyway, what's that got to do with Nobbly? Did he drive her off her rocker?"

"It's not just her. She told my mum and dad he's brought lots back for people. She's a spiritualist and he's some kind of medium, and he goes to their church."

Jim halted as though his shadow had snagged his feet. "Then what's he doing at our school?"

"He can be, can't he?" I was disconcerted by Jim's outrage. "Brother Treanor said everybody's welcome so long as they believe in God."

"If you think Nobbly does. Some of the things he says, you'd wonder. Maybe he's one of the lot Bent said you should watch out for. Fifth column, my dad says they're called, only he says it should be filth."

"Mr Noble's not like that. He's just got his own beliefs."

"My dad says that lot have and that's why they're dangerous." At least we were walking again, and now Jim said "Get a move on or we'll lose him."

The pursuit felt less like an adventure than it had. "You won't tell anyone about him, will you?" I pleaded.

Jim glanced at me but didn't slow his march. "Why not?"

"Suppose he has to leave the school, then we won't be able to watch like Bent said."

Jim was silent except for the footsteps he was muffling as much as he could. I was wondering if it would be inadvisable to remind him of the Tremendous Two when he said "Let's see what he does."

I wasn't sure if Jim meant now or in the future, or how he would react to it. From the bend we saw that the road was deserted all the way to the next turn. The moon was gliding higher, shrivelling our shadows. I felt silenced by the night and diminished by it too. While I was relieved not to be on my own, Jim's eagerness to reach the field had begun to outstrip mine. The isolated sound of our minimised footsteps made me realise that since we'd startled the magpie I hadn't seen or heard a sign of life. At the time I mightn't have been able to articulate my impression that the moon had deadened the countryside, or something even older had. To the left of the bend ahead trees stooped towards the road as if the night were crouching in wait for us, and I knew they were at the corner of the field we were bound for. I was wondering how close we could venture without alerting Mr Noble, and about to suggest slowing down in case he heard us on the road, when I saw a flurry of movement ahead.

It was beneath the bent trees, which made it harder to distinguish. Half a dozen dark shapes, small but of various sizes, were scurrying across the road. They'd emerged from the field we were heading for, and now they vanished through the hedge opposite with a shrill rustle of undergrowth. They infected Jim with their haste, and I was hurrying after him when the last of the animals blundered towards us along the middle of the road.

We could tell from its progress that it was virtually blind. I saw its pink nose twitching in a black bewildered face, but I didn't know if this meant it had scented us. In a moment it veered aside and shuffled rapidly onto the right-hand verge, where it disappeared into the earth, leaving a mound of upturned soil and uprooted grass. It had halted Jim, and I grabbed his arm to keep him where he was. "Wasn't that a mole?"

"Could've been. I've never seen one."

"I'm sure it was, but they shouldn't do that, should they?"

"Dunno," Jim said and took an impatient pace forward, freeing his arm. "Do what?"

"If it was scared of us it should have hidden where it was, don't you see? Something else scared it out of that field, and the rest of them."

"Yes, Nobbly did, and I want to see what he's up to. Aren't you coming? It was your idea."

I couldn't bear the notion that Jim was more adventurous than me.

I wasn't so sure he was braver, since he appeared not to think there was anything to brave. I wouldn't have been able to convey my apprehension, even if my breaths might have by turning as pale as the moon because of the chill that had gathered around us. "We mustn't make any more noise," I whispered, "or he'll hear."

Jim made for the bend as fast as he could while planting his feet softly on the road. He reminded me of a comedian miming stealth, but I wasn't inclined to laugh. I was doing my best to imitate him when I heard a sound ahead – a sharp creak of wood. It came from a tree at the edge of the field, but it wasn't sufficiently high up to have been made by a branch or even, I thought, by the trunk. I'd just had an unnerving notion when another sound distracted me: a voice.

It was Mr Noble, who was somewhere on the field. His voice was distant enough that his words were incomprehensible, and so we risked running to the bend. Before we reached the corner of the field we saw him through the trees. He was on his knees with his back to us in the middle of the field, which was scattered with uneven overgrown mounds. I suspect they were all that remained of a ruin. Like the rest of the field, the vegetation that covered them was drained of colour, presumably by the moonlight, though had there been a hint of this depletion even in the daytime? As Jim and I each found a tree to hide behind, the notion I'd had earlier made me peer at the edge of the field. I was disturbed to see something like evidence – faint furrows leading to the roots, marks so nearly obscured by grass that I wasn't sure I was seeing them. Could they really suggest that in the process of growth the trees had tried to edge out of the field, as though fleeing like the animals at their own lethargic pace? I was about to draw Jim's attention to the marks when Mr Noble raised his voice. "Is he praying?" Jim muttered.

It didn't sound like any prayer I'd heard. The voice rose and fell as though, having reached for its goal, it kept recoiling. Perhaps it was a kind of chant, but so unlike the ones we heard in church and school that I could almost have imagined I was listening to someone wholly unfamiliar. I still couldn't distinguish a word, and so I dodged to the next tree and then to its neighbour. From behind the third tree I saw that Mr Noble wasn't as prayerful as he'd looked. Though his head was bowed and his shoulders drooped, his hands weren't clasped. He appeared to have dug them into the earth. At once I thought of the bird I'd seen in the cemetery at home, pecking at the soil in search of food. I was recalling how Mr Noble had greeted the sight when Jim dodged past me to hide behind the tree beyond mine. "What's he got?" he demanded.

Mr Noble's head reared up, and I was afraid he'd heard until I saw that the teacher was gazing at the moon. His stance made his words more audible, though I couldn't judge whether he'd raised his head in some form of ecstasy or as part of a convulsive attempt to drag himself free of the earth. "Father," he cried, and was still speaking as Jim said "What's he saying about his dad?"

Mr Noble lurched backwards and sprang to his feet, twisting to face us. As he stooped in our direction, that rapid habitual movement put me in mind of a snake. When he jerked his hands towards us at arms' length while the night used his shrunken shadow to imitate the gesture, I was sure he'd seen us. I don't know how long he stood like that, his black eyes glinting in his whitened face – long enough for my lungs to begin throbbing with my held breath. At last he turned away, and Jim dashed past me before I'd even thought of moving. "Come on while he's not looking," he whispered.

As I darted after him on tiptoe I glanced across the field. Mr Noble was extending his hands towards the second corner, and I guessed this was some kind of ritual. I would have pointed it out to Jim, but he was already too far along the road to see it, let alone for me to speak to him. I could only follow him while I tried to understand what I'd heard Mr Noble say. Who did he mean had "really won"? I was happier to concentrate on this than on the glimpse I'd seemed to have as he stood up. Surely he hadn't been digging for worms, but perhaps he'd found two fistfuls just the same. They hadn't been fingers, I told myself, even if they'd appeared to clasp his before they writhed their pallid way back underground. I didn't want to think they had anything to do with how Mr Noble had started to behave, scattering earth from his hands like a benediction or a seed at corner after corner of the field.

CHAPTER NINE

The Dreams

As Jim and I took the other front seat on the upper deck of the bus, Bobby said "What did you bring me back from France?"

Jim looked at me, and then I looked at him. "I thought you got her something," Jim said.

"I thought you were going to."

Since I was sitting in the aisle seat, I got the punch on the arm. While I was expecting it, though it felt even more vigorous than usual, I didn't expect her to say "Shows how much you both care."

She sounded more like a girl than I was used to. "We had other things on our minds, Bobs, that's all."

My parents often used that excuse to each other. Sometimes it seemed to placate the recipient, but Bobby said "More important things than me."

I'd heard my mother retort along those lines. I felt as if we were playing adults, unless it meant they sometimes behaved like children – far too frequently, I'd begun to think. "They were important, Bobs," I pleaded.

"I'll bet they were to you."

"Look, you decide how important they were," I protested, having lowered my voice. "The teacher who took us to France, we know things about him the school doesn't know."

Jim nudged me almost as hard as Bobby's punch had been. "Thought you said we couldn't tell anyone."

"Bobby isn't anyone, she's us. She's—"

"Okay, I get it," Jim said and crouched over his knees. "No need to say."

"What are you saying I am?" Bobby said in a tone like the threat of a punch.

"I just mean we're the Tremendous Three," I told her. "Only Jim doesn't like me saying."

"I don't mind," Bobby said as Jim crouched lower. "No need to let my friends hear, though, okay?"

This didn't sound much like support to me. Perhaps Bobby sensed my disappointment, because she said "And I liked your stories about us. I hope you write some more."

Her praise was at least as awkward for me to receive as she seemed to have found it to utter. I looked away towards a blitzed street we were passing, where the jagged scraps of housefronts backed by a mass of rubble put me in mind of a set on a stage. "Thanks," I mumbled while my face grew hotter still.

"I'll give you your book when we go home," Bobby said and shuffled closer along her seat. "So are you going to tell me about your teacher?"

I glanced back through all the smoke that loitered in the aisle. Apart from us, almost everybody upstairs had a cigarette, even the passengers who weren't much older than us. No doubt some of them had been recommended to smoke by their doctor. The nearest people, a pair of headscarved women leaning together to chat, were three rows behind us, but I flattened a hand alongside my mouth before murmuring to Bobby "Why he got the school to take us all to France, it wasn't what he said."

Bobby made a face she usually saved for lemon drops, even the thought of them now that we could buy them. "Did he interfere with someone?"

"That's Brother Mayle," Jim said, "except he didn't either. He just likes watching everybody in the shower."

"We've got a teacher like that too."

"You've got to let him see you in the shower?" Jim demanded in outrage not quite unmixed with envy. "You ought to report him."

"No, stupe, she's a woman." As Jim remained outraged or at any rate incredulous Bobby said "Some of the girls are in love with her, but I'm not. I'll never be in love with anyone."

Jim returned to his defensive crouch as my face rediscovered its heat. Since neither of us knew how to reply if we'd wanted to, it was Bobby who relieved the silence. "What did your teacher do, then?"

"It isn't mostly what he does," Jim said, "it's what he thinks. He's a spiritualist and he goes to their church."

"What's wrong with that? We've got a Muslim and a Buddhist at our school. My dad says once you start telling people what to think you're on the way to a dictatorship."

To head off the argument she could have provoked I said "But your school knows about those girls, doesn't it? Why do you think ours doesn't know about him?"

"How do you know it doesn't?"

"Because he never lets on what he is," Jim said. "Only maybe he's trying to turn us all that way with some of the things he says."

"Sounds like one of Dom's stories."

"Well," Jim said more resentfully than I appreciated, "it's the truth. We don't tell lies at our school."

"It's not just what he says," I said to forestall yet another disagreement. "He does things too."

Bobby gave me a look to make it clear that I'd better earn her attention. "What sort of things?"

"He's supposed to bring the dead back for the people at his church to talk to. Really talk like you and me are now."

"I wouldn't mind talking to my dad's mum. I used to like her."

"We'll all see everyone like her," Jim protested, "when God brings us back together."

"My dad says religion—"

I suspected how she meant to go on, and interrupted before she could provoke Jim. "We haven't told you what our teacher did in France."

"Go on then, tell."

The bus had reached the crest of Everton Brow, from which streets sloped down towards the distant river. On its bank a pair of giant stone birds were tethered to their perches as if they would otherwise take flight, and I couldn't help thinking of Mr Noble in the cemetery – of the idea that flight was somehow associated with the dead. It made me oddly nervous of saying "He sneaked out one night and went off to a battlefield."

"How do you know where he went?"

"Because we trailed him," Jim said.

"Well, I wish I'd been there. What did you see?"

"It was somewhere his dad fought in the first war. We thought he might have been praying for the men who were killed there, but I don't think he was." Having said all this, I was still reluctant to add "He brought something out of the ground."

"I saw it too."

Jim's intervention came as a relief. "Tell her what you saw," I said.

"There'd been some kind of church there. His dad talked to us at school and told us. Nobbly dug up a bit of some old statue, only don't ask us why. Maybe he wanted a souvenir of where his dad was in the war."

I felt not just betrayed but abandoned. "You didn't say you saw that then."

"It's what it must have been, though."

"Why didn't he want anyone to know where he was going, then?"

"Maybe he decided it ought to stay there. Just because he's a spiritualist doesn't have to mean he hasn't got any respect."

I was growing desperate not to be left alone with my experience. "What about the dream we had?"

"I've stopped thinking about it. It was just a dream."

"You're never scared to remember it, Jim," Bobby said.

"Don't be thick," Jim said with enough resentment to suggest she wasn't wholly wrong. "It was a man in that field with worms eating his face. Happy now?"

"You didn't say you dreamed that," I objected. "You said they were his face."

"Who gives a monkey's? We only dreamed it because Nobbly's dad said he did."

"Nobbly." Once she'd giggled at this Bobby said "What did you think you saw, Dom?"

"Something like Jim said. I don't want to argue any more."

It was rather that recalling what I'd seen and dreamed made me feel as if the object in the moonlit field was reaching to take hold of my mind. "Your teacher doesn't sound much like a spiritualist," Bobby said.

"Then maybe he's something else," Jim said. "That's another reason to watch him."

"Maybe it's a job for the Tremendous Three," Bobby said.

We'd never said that to one another, but the trio in my stories often did. I felt both flattered and uneasy about the proposal. "Jim means watch him at the school," I said, only to be thrown by feeling I was trying to protect her. I was quite relieved when she responded with a token punch.

The bus was downtown now. We might have left it at Lime Street and watched Professor Codman's Punch and Judy show opposite the railway station, but we were too old to join the crowd of noisy children. Instead we stayed on board all the way to the terminus, where we caught the overhead railway to Garston for the view the journey gave us of the river. Once we were back at the Pier Head we climbed up James Street into the town. The Saturday streets were full of shoppers liberated by the relaxation of rationing, and there were even cars among the trams and buses. Our first stop was at a music store, where we convinced the shop assistant that we might buy records if she put them on for us. We crowded into the listening booth in time to hear Jim's selection, the Stargazers telling us that birds with broken wings couldn't fly, though in the past they'd flown up to the sky. I was reminded of Mr Noble and the graveyard yet again, and Bobby's choice of record didn't lighten my thoughts. While I wasn't old enough to find the doggie in the window childish, it brought Winston to mind, and the idea of somebody needing a dog because they'd been left alone evoked far too much about Mrs Norris and her situation. I chose 'Wonderful Copenhagen' because Bobby liked Danny Kaye, though perhaps I was simply anxious to be done; we only asked for Top Ten hits in shops, and it was the first that came into my head. I was quite glad when the assistant lost patience and sent us out of the shop. At least now we were bound for the cinema.

Through the hordes that were close to spilling off the pavements on both sides of Church Street we heard cries of "Lost city higgo" – the call of the man who sold the *Liverpool Echo* from an upturned box outside Woolworth's. The Kardomah Coffee House greeted us with a polite scent of ground beans, nowhere near as harsh as the smell of coffee that assaulted you across the road at Cooper's. Next to the House of Bewlay, where dozens of tobacco pipes mouthed roundly at the window, was the Tatler News Theatre, which changed its programme of cartoons and comedies each week. Usually on Saturdays we went to one of the big cinemas, but that day they were showing films we either wouldn't have been let into or didn't want to see. We bought a tub of ice cream each, and an usherette with a flashlight showed us to seats in the smoky auditorium.

I want to remember everything I can, but I'm not sure what we watched that afternoon, even though we sat through the hour's worth of films several times. I think the adverts welcomed us as we sat down – perhaps the false teeth marching to the song of an almost military male voice choir:

"Oh won't you try this experiment
And clean your dentures with Steradent?
Then your teeth will gleam
Every time you beam

Which will mean you'll always show merriment..."

Some titles come to mind, and perhaps we saw those films then. *A Chipper Chappie* has Chaplin donning a dress suit that fell off the back of a van and passing himself off as a toff at a formal dinner. In *Hovering Husbands* Laurel and Hardy struggle to master a balloon that eventually raises them helplessly heavenwards, leaving their wives to find a gun and shoot them down. *Acme Jack*, the salesman who sells the coyote a series of disastrously faulty items, proves to be the Road Runner. I do recall that we watched *In the Tweet Bye and Bye*, in which Sylvester succeeds in swallowing the canary, only to be haunted by Tweetie's spirit and eventually carried off to an afterlife peopled by demonic birds. In the end it turns out to be a dream, though Tweetie's rather than Sylvester's. This didn't reassure me much, while Jim's and Bobby's mirth at all the films simply left me feeling isolated with my thoughts. I could almost have felt that the entire audience was chortling at the images in my head.

Both Jim and I had dreamed of a man rising like a snake out of the earth. I'd fought to stay awake even once Mr Noble had crept into the dormitory, most of an hour after we'd regained our beds, because I'd felt nervous of closing my eyes. The dream might have been lying in wait for me, and at once I'd seen the swollen fleshy filaments that the figure had for hands and face begin to writhe as if they were groping for another shape to take. Perhaps the nightmare had its roots in the talk old Mr Noble had given, but I didn't think this was its only source. When I lurched awake, stifling a cry, I remembered what I was increasingly certain I'd seen in the moonlit field – the boneless fingers worming up to clutch at Mr Noble's, not reaching out of the earth so much using it to take shape. I had an awful sense that this meant the substance stuck to Mr Noble's hands had been fragments of the fingers, which had been the benison he'd scattered to the four corners of the world.

CHAPTER TEN

The Unexpected Guests

I did my best to enjoy every minute of the coronation. It was on television, after all – the first television I'd ever watched. Many of the neighbours had rented a set for the occasion, and those who hadn't were the guests of somebody who had. I might have liked to have gone somewhere other than next door, a cluttered house with a piercing smell of disinfectant, where the Quiggin sisters told me virtually in chorus to wipe my feet as soon as I stepped over the threshold. We were there in good time to watch both sisters struggle to adjust the reception of the set, which was tuned to a dogged broadcast of the test card, while they offered each other advice or at any rate criticism. Eventually my father took a turn at wandering about with the aerial, and when the sisters grudgingly agreed that planting it among the china dogs on the mantelpiece brought the least befogged image, everybody settled down to wait for the picture to change. The adults sipped cups of tea flecked with curdled milk while I was let off with a glass of water. When at last the test card gave way to a view of Westminster Abbey, my father raised a cheer that I suspected mightn't have been simply patriotic.

While the television was no wider than my chest, a magnifying screen stood in front. I felt as if I were watching activity under a microscope, observing the antics of a form of life quite unlike myself. The unctuous commentary distanced me further, describing the gold of the royal coach that looked silver at best, enthusing about the stained-glass windows and their myriad colours that I saw were as black and white as a moonlit field. The sight of doll-sized figures enacting ritual movements so slowly that I thought they must be weighed down by their robes only made me wonder how Bobby's father might be greeting the spectacle. I don't know how many hours it took me to grasp that the ceremony would be even more protracted than the service we had to sit and stand and kneel through every Easter. I risked giggling at one of the choruses of coughs the congregation almost ritualistically produced, making full use of the acoustic of the venue, but the reproachful look my parents sent me quelled my mirth, though I found it unfair that the grownups weren't as silent as they apparently expected me to remain. My mother and the sisters made sounds like the one the doctor had me imitate when he inspected my open mouth, and my father added the occasional appreciative manly grunt. The loudest sighs came not when the celebrant lowered the crown onto Elizabeth's head – I was put in mind of a scientist warily wielding an element prone to explode – but as she and her prince took communion together. It struck me that my mother had let out just such a sigh when the prince resurrected Snow White in the Disney film.

The queen had been crowned for just a few minutes when I heard noises outside the house. The street was closed off for a party to celebrate the coronation, and it sounded as if the festivities had begun. When I betrayed signs of restlessness my parents renewed their disappointed look. Once we'd sat through several minutes of a parade of horsemen topped with furry helmets as tall as their heads, however, my father stood up. "Thank you so much. That was lovely," my mother told the sisters, and my father said "Very nice."

The party hadn't started after all. People were still carrying plates of sandwiches and jugs of lemonade out of their houses to the trestle tables that occupied the middle of the road. Everyone was dressed for Sunday, and the aisle of trees along the road reminded me of a church, since some of the leafy branches came close to meeting overhead. The trees were hosting a contest of birdsong, but I couldn't help remembering the silent trees around the moonlit field in France.

My parents fetched our contribution from the house – a plate piled with fish paste sandwiches, their crusts cut off in the service of good breeding and fed to the birds, and a strawberry jelly that quivered to enact my mother's fear that it hadn't set enough. The end tables in our street and the next one met at the junction near the railway bridge, and when we found seats there Jim's family and then Bobby's came to join us. Some of the parents hadn't previously met, and I thought the introductions and handshakes felt like an unspoken truce. When paper crowns were handed out, Bobby jammed hers on her head as if to cover up the pink ribbon she'd obviously been compelled to wear.

We were demolishing my mother's dessert before it drooped too much in the June heat when I saw that Mr Parkin – Bobby's father – was impatient to speak. He was a wiry fellow not much bigger than his daughter or his wife, with a face that looked as though he'd tugged it thin by thrusting it through some inhospitable medium, dragging his eyes permanently wide and sharp. Bobby's mother kept playing the peacemaker, laying a hand on his arm to restrain some remark. Several people had left their front-room windows open so that we could hear the coronation commentary and various attendant sounds, all of which engaged Mr Parkin's attention more than the talk of summer holidays and which items had reappeared in the shops. When the chat reached a lull he jerked a thumb over his shoulder to indicate the broadcast. "There's one good thing come out of today, any rate."

It was obvious where Jim inherited his size from. Both his parents looked not merely rounded but padded, a protection against any unpleasantness they might encounter. While their faces were placid, I thought this was simply how they would prefer to be, and now both of them blinked, hinting at lines on their foreheads. "A lot more than one, Mr Parkin," Mrs Bailey said.

"Bill," Mr Parkin said, not entirely like an invitation. "What do you reckon we should all be cheering for?"

"Being ruled by someone who believes in God," my father said, "to start with."

"We all like being some woman's subject, do we?" Mr Parkin said without asking. "I'm just here for the party food, me."

"We like seeing all our neighbours," his wife tried to remind him, "don't we, Bill."

Another burst of music swelled out of the houses to compete with the birdsong in the trees, and Mr Parkin jerked his thumb again. "I'm saying it's a good thing we got to see what's going on for once. Maybe having televisions will help people wake up to the truth. Looks like the powers that be can't stop some getting through."

"Which truth is that?" Jim's father said, and shortly "Bill."

"How much all that's costing us. Us commoners have only just come off rationing but that was in the coffers all along. They've got plenty to spend when they want to remind us we're subjects and we need to know our place."

"Some of us enjoyed the spectacle," his wife said.

I suppose she was hoping to placate him, but she provoked not only him. "Someone has to lead the country," Jim's mother said, "and set an example."

"I don't need anyone to show me how to behave," Bobby's father retorted. "Specially not somebody we didn't even vote for."

"What would you rather have?" my mother said with an attempt at mildness. "A president like Mr Eisenhower?"

"Not him or his crony Nixon neither. I don't want us getting any more like the Yanks. We tag along after them too much of the time as it is. They treat their workers even worse than our lot do, and the rest of the masses as well."

"At least they're showing us how to deal with infiltrators," Jim's father said. "In fact that's too big a word for it. Traitors will do."

"Hey, that's comical. Watch out you don't cut yourself being so sharp." With even less evidence of amusement Mr Parkin said "Who are you talking about, Kevin?"

"I thought you'd have heard of Senator McCarthy, Bill."

"I've heard all about the— I won't say the word in front of ladies and children. See, I don't need to be taught how to behave after all."

Before anybody could respond Mr Parkin said "Know what they used to call him in the air force? Low-Blow Joe. He's still going in for those, but now he's doing it to his own people."

"The ones he's after aren't his people," my father said, "and I wouldn't like to think they're anybody's here."

"They're just trying to live their lives like real Christians would if they went back to the basics."

"Excuse me, Mr Parkin," Jim's mother said, "but communists don't believe in God."

"You can believe in both if nobody's stopping you," Mr Parkin said and turned on Jim's father. "I'm as much a Catholic as you'll ever be, but fellers like your friend the senator ought to make us ashamed we are."

Somewhere in the distance I heard a dog barking and a woman calling to it. I hoped this might distract our parents, but Jim's father wasn't to be diverted. "So what else are you, Bill?" he said.

Before anybody else could speak Bobby said "There's a teacher at Jim and Dom's school who's like that."

Of course she intended to protect her father. Too late I realised that we hadn't told her to keep what we'd said about Mr Noble to herself. "Like what?" Mr Bailey demanded.

"He's more than one thing. He thinks you can bring back the dead."

"That's up to God," Bobby's father said as if he was demonstrating his religiousness.

"She means he's a spiritualist, dad," Jim was anxious to establish.

"He's misguided, then. Still, that crowd are harmless enough," Jim's father said, and then he frowned at Jim and me. "Has he been teaching you boys about it?"

I thought it wise to be the one who answered. "He's never said anything about it at school."

"Then how do you know about him?" my father said.

"I heard about someone with his name and then I realised it was him."

"What name?"

I felt trapped and ineffectual. "Mr Noble," my father repeated once I'd finished mumbling. "That's what you said."

"Yes, Mr Mumble."

"I'll be having a good look at him at the parents' evening and maybe you'll want to as well, Kevin," my father said and stared towards the railway bridge.

I'd been hearing the dog for a few minutes now. If it hadn't been for all the talk I might have realised sooner why the barking had grown hollow and enlarged: because it was under the arch that led into the graveyard. Now it was smaller although closer, and in a moment Winston appeared under the bridge. As that amplified his barks I heard Mrs Norris calling if not crying out to him. She'd hardly lurched into sight beneath the bridge, where her footsteps sounded as if they were tripping over their echoes, when Winston fled towards us. At that distance he looked like a welcome distraction. "Winston," I called, clapping my hands as well.

The dog hesitated and then ran to me, trailing his lead. His eyes were flickering from side to side, and I had the uneasy notion that they were bigger than they used to be. His tongue was hanging out, and he was dribbling so copiously that all three mothers in our party made sounds of distaste. I captured his lead, though he almost snatched it out of reach by flinching, and coaxed him to me so that I could pat his head. "Be careful of him, Dominic," my mother said. "He doesn't look too happy."

"He knows me, mum," I said and raised my voice. "I've got him, Mrs Norris."

Though Winston jerked at the lead, I didn't think he was too eager to rejoin her, and I sensed how my parents and our neighbours were suppressing their reactions to her appearance. Despite being held by several pins, her hat was barely even perched on her dishevelled curls, and the blue suit I'd seen her in too many times was greyish with Winston's hairs. As she emerged from under the bridge she blinked hard at the trestle tables. "It's that day, isn't it?" she said and made a noise vaguely related to a laugh. "I'd have brought something if someone had reminded me. I've had such a lot on my mind."

Jim and I and all the nearby men stood up as she stumbled towards us, though Bobby's father took his time. At least Jim and I had no caps to raise, and I didn't think we needed to lift our paper crowns. As Mrs Norris made for the place I'd vacated, Winston dodged behind me, tugging at the lead. "Will you take him round the table, Dominic?" Mrs Norris said. "Maybe if he can't see me he'll calm down."

Nobody appeared to understand this any more than I did. Just the same, once I'd led Winston to the far side of the table I managed to persuade him to lie down, though he kept his ears high. Having sat down, Mrs Norris gave her immediate neighbours a flimsy smile and fumbled at her hatpins, which didn't leave her hat any less precarious. "Here's a plate and a cup, Mrs Norris," my mother urged. "You have whatever you like."

As Mrs Norris laid a solitary sandwich in the middle of her plate my father filled her coronation mug with lemonade, and I couldn't help thinking of the tea parties that girls unlike Bobby staged for their dolls. Mrs Norris and my parents were playing a different kind of game – a pretence that only the street party mattered or needed to matter. Bobby's father didn't seem to want to play, since he said "Today doesn't mean that much to you, then."

Perhaps he was looking for someone who shared his attitude, but Mrs Norris said "My Herbert isn't letting me think about much except him."

"Who's he when he's at home?"

"Just my husband," Mrs Norris said as if she hoped this was the case.

"Is he a bit of a handful, Mrs Norris?" Jim's mother said, glancing at my mother to share the wifely joke.

My mother was prefacing her answer with a dismayed look when Mrs Norris admitted "He's dead."

"Oh, I'm so sorry. Please forgive me. I didn't know," Mrs Bailey said and went so far as to pat her arm.

"You shouldn't get the wrong idea. He's dead but he's not gone."

"Oh." This sounded as though Mrs Bailey might have added that she saw, but she plainly didn't quite. "You mean he's," she said.

"Mr Noble brought him back to me."

"Noble." My father had been keeping the conversation at a distance, but now he leaned towards her with a sharp look at me and Jim. "He's not a teacher, is he?"

"He's taught us a lot at the church. He says those who've gone before us can see more of the truth of things, and they can bring some to anyone who can bear to know."

"No," my father said as if he hadn't time to argue, "does he teach at a school?"

"That's his job. Why, do you know him?"

"We're going to," my father said like an ominous promise.

"I know I told you before Christmas you ought to go and see him, but I don't think I would now."

"Why's that, Mrs Norris?"

I'd started to wish my father would leave her alone. She was growing uneasy, repetitively brushing at the lapel of her faded jacket, and appeared to be infecting Winston with her nervousness, since his ears had begun to twitch. "I'm sorry he chose me. I'm sorry I found him," Mrs Norris said, and with something like defiance "It isn't only me who wishes they'd never met him."

Although he looked vindicated, my father said "You're still not saying why."

"Maybe he can't help what happens. Maybe it's how people like my Herbert end up," Mrs Norris said and raised her voice as Winston started barking. "Can you keep him off?"

"Dominic," my mother said, "just take the dog for a little walk. See if your friends would like to go with you."

"Not the dog," Mrs Norris said, adding a shrill sound that came nowhere near a laugh. "My Herbert. Can't someone keep him off me for a while?"

She was swiping at her jacket more wildly now, flailing at her shoulder as if to dislodge some object none of us could see. "Dominic," my mother called over the incessant barking, "will you and your friends do as you're told."

As Jim and Bobby stood up like contestants at awkwardness, Mrs Norris lurched to her feet, flinging her chair away with such force that it tripped over the kerb and fell on its back on the grass verge. "He shouldn't feel like that," she cried. "I don't know what's done it. He's making me afraid like him."

She began to dodge about beneath the nearest tree, staying in its shadow. She was flapping at herself with both hands now, and I thought she looked desperate to ward off some kind of intrusion she was terrified to touch. My parents hurried to her, and my father reached for her arm. "Come in the house, Mrs Norris," my mother said.

I'm sure she was being solicitous, but I felt as if she was anxious to shut away the spectacle for the sake of the neighbourhood. Did I see my father's hand recoil for a moment from touching Mrs Norris? As he grasped her arm I was distracted by an odd sound – a microscopic clattering. It came from the tree, and I could have fancied that I glimpsed parts of the bark growing surreptitiously restless, an activity that swarmed up the trunk as if some form of life had taken refuge behind or among the scales of wood. I told myself I was seeing the shadows of leaves, and in seconds the movements vanished into the foliage. Winston had fallen silent as my parents ushered Mrs Norris towards our house, but he renewed his clamour when a bird flew away from the treetop with a screech that sounded close to articulate, not as birdlike as I would have preferred. "Take him right away, Dominic," my mother said.

As Jim's parents followed mine, Bobby's father stood up. "I'll go and phone the quack. She needs some help, your friend."

Mrs Norris gave him a bewildered blink as he headed for the main road and the nearest phone box. "I'm all right now," she protested, contradicting herself by repeating it several times. Jim's mother and mine coaxed her into the house while our fathers lingered in the garden, and Bobby's mother did her best to be involved by taking Mrs Norris her festive mug. As Jim and Bobby and I made for the railway bridge with the suddenly subdued dog I heard my father telling Jim's "I hope you don't still think it's nothing. We need to think what we should do about their teacher."

CHAPTER ELEVEN

The Prints

I don't think any of us said much while we were out with the dog. I kept him away from the main roads, where the traffic might have unnerved him, but I didn't venture near the graveyard either. People at street parties made sympathetic noises at the sight of us walking the dog, and quite a few invited us to join them. Jim looked tempted, but Bobby was committed to our mission, such as it was. We didn't need to tell one another that we were anxious to find out what was happening to Mrs Norris, and in less than half an hour we turned back.

Ambulances rarely used their sirens in those days. You might think they were showing respect for the sick. When we reached the bridge we saw an ambulance parked just beyond it, as close to our street as the party tables would allow. Two men in white were guiding Mrs Norris to the open back doors, while my parents and Jim's followed them at the pace of a funeral procession, miming concern on behalf of all the neighbours. The moment they saw us Jim's father and mine gestured us away, but Mrs Norris called "Dominic, will you come here a minute?" My father threw his hands wide and his responsibility away, and I gave Jim the lead to hold while I hurried under the bridge.

Somebody had brushed most of the dog hairs off Mrs Norris's suit. She looked calmer or at any rate more somnolent, though her eyes were fluttering a little. I suspect she had been given a tranquilliser. "Thank you for catching him," she said. "There's a good boy."

She appeared to be trying to grasp a thought, and I hoped she wasn't about to embarrass me in front of everyone by paying me a penny. My face had grown hotter than the summer afternoon by the time she said "Will you take him home?"

"How can Dominic get in?" my father objected. "If you give him your key he'll have to give it back."

I suppose he didn't like the notion of my visiting her in the kind of hospital he thought she might end up in, but she said "Mrs Brough next door has my spare one."

"Pardon me, but what are you expecting him to do with your dog?"

"Just put him in the house, Dominic. Mrs Brough will see to him. She always does when Herbert and I are away."

"As long as you're sure," my father said, though she was plainly uncertain about a good deal. As the men helped her into the ambulance he called "I hope you'll be home soon."

The driver's colleague stayed with her. The ambulance veered back and forth between the pavements several times before it was able to turn towards the bridge. Jim and Bobby had joined us, and as the ambulance sped away at last I said "Who's coming with me to her house?"

"I will," my mother said.

I hadn't meant an adult, but her presence might be reassuring, even if I preferred not to admit that to myself. I was about to prompt Bobby and Jim – I wanted them to see whatever might be at the Norris house – when my mother said "The rest of you can go back to the party. We shouldn't be long."

Jim headed for the table readily enough, and Bobby tramped after him. Jim's parents lingered as if they wanted a word with mine, but presumably I was the hindrance. Once they left us alone I took the chance to murmur "Dad?"

"No point in worrying about the lady, son. She'll be looked after however she needs to be."

This wasn't the whole of my concern. "Why didn't you want to touch her?"

"Who says I didn't?"

His vehemence disconcerted me so much that I wished I didn't have to answer. "I just thought you looked as if you didn't like to."

"I've never heard such rubbish. I've no reason to be scared of catching what she's got. I didn't look like that, did I, Mary? I know what's true and it'll take a lot more than the likes of her to make me start doubting it. Just you make sure you don't pick up that sort of thing from this teacher of yours, son. Tell me and your mother if he starts saying anything he shouldn't."

"Come along, Dominic," my mother said, though only when it was clear that he'd finished.

As soon as we were past the bridge, which would have amplified my voice, I said "Dad looked like that, didn't he, mum?"

"Mrs Norris isn't quite right in her head just now, son. It'll be losing her husband and all the things your teacher told her, but some people don't like being near anyone who's in that kind of state."

I took her to be trying to defend my father. I wasn't sure if she'd seen him flinch from touching Mrs Norris, but I could think of nothing more to say as I followed her to the Norris house. While Cherry Lane was clear of tables, a party was in progress round the corner. My mother was opening the gate, which was liberally spattered with bird droppings that put me in mind of panic, when a large woman in a politely floral dress left the nearest table. "Excuse me," she said, "is that the Norris dog?"

"Yes, it's Winston," my mother said.

"Mrs Norris isn't in just now. I live next door," the woman said with limited enthusiasm.

"Are you Mrs Brough? Mrs Norris says you look after him."

"I want nothing to do with that noisy creature. We've been kept awake half the night these last weeks, what with her shouting and him."

My curiosity outstripped my shyness. "Was she shouting at Winston?"

"Tell me who else she'd be talking to." Though the woman couldn't quite ignore me, she directed the remark at my mother. "And she answers herself too," she complained. "She just puts on a voice as well."

Before I could ask the question to which I was afraid I already knew the answer, my mother said "So aren't you Mrs Brough?"

"I thought I'd made that obvious. You still want her, do you?" When my mother confirmed it the woman marched back to the party. "Mrs Brough," she called, "you're wanted at yours."

The woman who plodded to find us was a head shorter than her neighbour but outdid her in width. "How can I help?" she said, and less eagerly "Is that Winston?"

"It's him right enough," my mother said, which the dog corroborated with a yap. "Mrs Norris has been taken off to hospital."

"The poor thing. Do they know what's the matter?"

"I think she may be having a bit of a breakdown."

"That would explain it." Before I could bring myself to ask what it explained, the woman said "Tell her she'll be in our prayers."

"I will if I see her." My mother was making it plain that she thought

Mrs Brough should as well. "She told us you look after Winston," she said.

"I'll have to. Can you leave him inside for now?" Mrs Brough said, reaching in her handbag. "I'll let you in."

"Will he be all right on his own?"

"Once he's in his basket with his bone he's never any trouble." All the same, Mrs Brough paused on the way to adding "I'm sure he'll behave now there's nobody to disturb him."

I wondered if she should just mean Mrs Norris. She waddled up the path, past the three clay pots full of weeds and dead flowers, and used both small hands to twist the key in the tarnished lock. "I'll come and see you later, Winston," she said, stooping to pat him as she retreated past the gate. "Shut the door of his room and give the front one a good slam on your way out, Mrs... "

"Sheldrake."

"She's talked about you, Mrs Sheldrake. You're the only one round here who'll listen to some of the things she keeps saying. Are you from her church?"

"I'm afraid we aren't," my mother said with no regret at all.

"Well then, you're a true Christian."

Perhaps Mrs Brough was eager to return to the party, since she waddled away at speed. As I followed my mother up the splintered weedy path I saw that every door along the hall was wide open, as well as all those visible up the stairs, and yet I felt that some kind of darkness was lying in wait beyond the front door. The bicycle propped against the wall at the foot of the stairs was home to several spiders now. The buttoned overcoat still hung by its gaping neck from the hook on the wall, and I told myself that nothing was poised to crawl out of the collar or the sleeves, though the coat looked less empty than dormant. "Do you know where the dog goes?" my mother said.

"He lives in the front, mum."

She strode into the front room but halted on the threshold. "Dominic."

It wasn't a rebuke, just an expression of dismay. I could only wonder which aspect of the room had distressed her most, unless its entire state had. The right-hand curtain was heaped beneath the window, presumably having been torn off its rings by a bid to let more light in. Photographs were strewn across the sofa from one of the albums precariously stacked on its arm, while the butts piled at least an inch high in the overflowing ashtray on the squat table looked grey with dust as well as ash. I saw my mother frown at the cards pinned to the wall above the mantelpiece, expressions of condolence from nearly a year ago and greetings from last Christmas. She retrieved a card that lay among the ashes on the hearth and, having shaken it over the cold grey mass in the fireplace, stood the faded Santa on the mantel. "I'll come round and give her a hand when she's home," she said mostly to herself. "I shouldn't interfere when she isn't here to see."

I wondered if my mother didn't want to be by herself in the house. Certainly she sounded urgent when she said "Bone, Winston. Bone."

She lifted the chewed rubber object in the basket with the toe of her shoe, and the dog ambled to it readily enough once I'd unclipped his lead. As soon as he curled up in the basket my mother headed for the hall. "Good boy. Stay," she said, and I was hurrying after her when I faltered. "Mum, what's this?"

Was she reluctant to turn around? She looked impatient when she did. "Mrs Norris must have been looking at memories, Dominic."

"I know they're her photos. I mean what's happened to that one."

I saw my mother expecting me to pick it up and show her, but I didn't want to touch it. With a breath that sounded like a declaration of an effort, or else relinquishing a word she might have uttered, she tramped to the sofa and peered at the topmost of the scattered photographs. "It's Mr Norris before you knew him."

"I know that, mum, but what are those?"

She squinted at the marks at the edge of the photograph, which showed the smiling Mr Norris in his army uniform. "They'll be where Mrs Norris was holding it," she said. "It shows how much it must mean to her."

She made for the hall at once, but I lingered for a last glance. I supposed the marks could have been left by a pair of thumbs, though they seemed too large not just for Mrs Norris but for her husband. If she'd been overcome by emotion while gazing at the photograph, perhaps that could even explain why the marks were as indented as they appeared to be – so vigorously embossed on the glossy cardboard that the whorls of fingerprints were faintly visible – except that the prints weren't merely blurred; in fact, they weren't blurred enough. They looked as though the fingers that had made them were composed of a multitude of filaments that were trying to form the prints. While I couldn't put it into words then, the marks suggested a desperate attempt to cling to the photograph and what it showed. I fled into the hall, where I hung the lead over the end of the banister. "Be good, Winston," I called, and as I closed the door I felt as if I might be shutting not just him in the room.

When my mother slammed the front door I was afraid this would disturb him, but he didn't start to bark until she'd shut the gate, and then gave only a token yap. It sounded like the way he'd greeted Mrs Brough, but undermined by a nervous whine. "Hurry up, Dominic. We've done what you promised," my mother said and made for the railway bridge. I was tempted to go to the front window, but told myself I might rouse Winston. As I ran after my mother I was able to believe that all the voices I could hear were in the street or on television, not in the Norris house. The blurred one must belong to a broadcaster on a set that was drifting off the station, even if it sounded as though it was struggling to shape itself into a voice – as though it didn't have much of a mouth.

CHAPTER TWELVE

The Confrontation

"Well, I don't think much of his Latin man."

I was following my parents away from Mr McIntosh's form room. "Mum," I muttered.

"I'm sorry but I don't, Dominic. I'm just glad he isn't taking you for anything important."

The teacher's lecture about Latin hadn't impressed her, then. Perhaps she'd been preoccupied with his beery smell. He'd spent several minutes in demonstrating to my parents how Latin hid in words they used before he conceded my progress was adequate. "Maybe he'll need it," my father said now, "if he goes to university."

It took me a few moments to grasp that he was talking about me, envisaging a future I couldn't imagine, though years later it caught up with me. So did the insight that my parents must have been as nervous that evening as I was. I just wanted them to be proud of me and not to embarrass me, but they had Mr Noble on their minds. I should have known that when they left him until last, but I was busy being satisfied with how most of the evening had gone. Brother Titmuss praised my enquiring mind – "he likes finding out how the world is put together." Mr Jensen proved to be content with my sporting abilities and in particular my sporting attitude, and took time to share my father's zeal for the Everton team, which put me in mind of the crowd I sometimes heard across the graveyard. Brother Monrahan enthused about my mathematical skills, which emboldened me to say red-faced that I wouldn't have been so good except for him. Mr Clement said my French was passable but suggested that I could have learned more in France, which reminded me how much I'd learned that hardly anybody knew. Mr Bushell felt I needed to work on my sense of how geography dictated ways a place was used, and even this brought the moonlit field to mind. Brother Mayle was happy with my knowledge of the Bible and hoped I would model my life on it, a principle that made me feel uncomfortable, close to hypocritical. Brother Stimson said I wasn't yet an artist and advised me to focus more on beauty, to find it wherever I could; I wonder if he's still looking, dead as he is. Mr Askew declared that I was more eloquent on paper than in class but allowed this might be characteristic of writers. "I hear Sheldrake has written some fiction," he said. "I understand it may not be for our magazine, but that's not to say he shouldn't keep it up." Of all the comments I heard at the parents' evening this was the one I valued most, and I was letting it repeat itself inside my head when we came in sight of Mr Noble's room.

Jim and his parents were standing in the corridor. "We let someone else go ahead," his father murmured as we joined them. "We said we'd all go in together."

Jim stared at me, and I saw he knew as little of the plan as I did. "Will he see us all at once?" my mother doubted aloud.

"He's letting people wait in his room. We want to be there so we can all hear what's said."

Mr Bailey was making for the form room when my father caught his arm. "Who wants to go first?"

"Maybe you should. You know the woman he sent off her rocker."

It was clear that our mothers hadn't been kept informed either. "You aren't going to make a scene at their school," Mrs Bailey protested.

"We've just got a few questions to ask," Mr Bailey said. "We'll be polite."

Mr Noble looked away from the family seated in front of his desk as we all trooped into the room. "Two more of my eager band," he said. "Do find yourselves seats. We shouldn't be long now."

In some way he struck me as more eager than he'd said Jim and I were. Once the Joyces proved to have no queries he told them he looked forward to seeing them next year and straightened up to end the interview. He said nothing further until the door shut behind them, and then he inclined his upper body towards us. "Who's first for the inquisition?"

"We are," my father said, squeezing out from behind Henry Shea's desk.

"Mr and Mrs Sheldrake." Mr Noble reached across his desk to shake hands with both of them at once, which looked to me like some kind of secret sign if not a reminiscence of a seance. "You can be proud of your son," he said and glanced past them. "Mr Bailey, Mrs Bailey, I'll tell you the same."

As we sat on a trio of folding chairs in front of him my mother said "You think Dominic's doing well, then."

"Both of them are. You enjoy grasping the past, don't you, gentlemen?"

When Jim mumbled an assent I did as well, but I couldn't avoid thinking of the glimpse I'd seemed to have in the moonlit field – the objects that had clutched at Mr Noble's hands. "They're hungry for knowledge," Mr Noble said, "and that's the sort of mind we need to shape."

"So long as it's the right kind of knowledge," Jim's father said.

"The approved variety, of course." As if to leave no time for anyone to suspect him of sarcasm Mr Noble said "Brother Titmuss tells me they have questing minds. Their like is the hope of the world."

This appeared to throw my parents, as I imagine it did Jim's. None of them had responded when Mr Noble said "I've had no complaints as their form master. If nobody has any questions, may I take it you're as satisfied as I am?"

"No panic, is there?" Jim's father said. "We haven't had our interview yet."

"None at all if you'd like an individual session." All the same, Mr Noble didn't pause before saying "As long as you were all together I thought I'd made it clear that my remarks apply to both your sons."

I thought he was ensuring that I didn't bring up my encounter with him and his family. He couldn't have realised that I wouldn't have dared to. I sensed at the very least impatience as he said "Now I see some visitors are waiting in the corridor."

"Let them wait," Mr Bailey said. "We did and we weren't complaining. We've got a few questions we'd like you to answer."

"By all means ask them," Mr Noble said and sat up straight enough to be miming readiness.

Perhaps his apparent enthusiasm left the parents less sure of themselves. I could see mine growing awkward now that it was time to confront him. I suppose they were realising how impolite they might have to be, and in front of us boys as well. It was Jim's father who broke the silence. "Are you starting, Des?"

My father hunched forward on his chair. "Mr Noble, we think you know one of our neighbours."

"Besides Mr Bailey's parents, would that be?"

"Yes," my father said as if he couldn't tell how sly the answer was, "as well as them."

"Do you know the name?"

"Of course we do. It's Mrs Norris."

"Not the most uncommon name."

"She lives in Cherry Lane." When Mr Noble turned his empty hands up, my father said "She lost her husband last year."

"The dead are multiplying as we speak. Perhaps we should be glad that where they go is infinite." As my father looked more confused than gladdened, Mr Noble said "Supposing I should know the lady, what did you want to establish?"

"She's had to be taken into hospital for her nerves."

"I hope she's helped, but I'm not sure what you're expecting of me."

I thought Mr Noble was challenging him to be impolite. I could see the social rules were inhibiting my father, but Mr Bailey said "Hang on, Des. Jim, get the door. No need to have those hanging round out there."

Surely the presence of more people would make it harder to confront Mr Noble, and he seemed happy to let Jim call the newcomers in. "Mr O'Shaughnessy," the teacher said. "Mr and Mrs O'Shaughnessy. We shouldn't keep you much longer."

By the time they found seats my father looked more constrained than ever. I think he might have been close to abandoning the interrogation if Jim's father hadn't said "Mr Noble, are you a Christian?"

The teacher raised his head a little higher, and his eyebrows too. "Isn't everybody in this room?"

"We're asking you."

"Forgive me, has there been some prior discussion?"

Perhaps Mr O'Shaughnessy took this to be aimed at his family as well, because he said "We don't know anything about it."

"I'd just like to be clear about who may be speaking for whom."

I couldn't help feeling this might be some kind of threat to me and Jim. I don't know if my father felt as much, but he said "Aren't you going to answer the question?"

"I must say I thought I had."

"We aren't all as clever as you, Mr Noble," Jim's mother said, "but some of us don't think you did."

I saw a glint in the teacher's eyes, which I thought was contempt – a sense that he was playing with inferior opponents – but I'd barely glimpsed it when his look grew neutral. "Then let me tell you plainly, since it appears to concern you," he said. "Of course I believe."

Though my father looked embarrassed, he wasn't giving up. "In what?"

"In the three persons." With a flicker of a smile Mr Noble said "I hope that's true for everybody here."

"You know it has to be," Jim's father said, which broadened Mr Noble's smile. "You aren't a spiritualist, then."

"Aren't they meant to believe in God? I rather think they may as much as you do."

"Not in our way, and their kind aren't welcome here." This was addressed to Peter O'Shaughnessy's parents as well, and when they murmured in agreement Mr Bailey said "So what's the answer to the question, Mr Noble?"

"I give you my word I'm not a spiritualist. I can swear to it if you like."

"You don't go to their church," my father said.

"Why would I when I don't share their faith?" Mr Noble kept his eyes on my father for some moments before gazing past him. "If there's been a misunderstanding I hope I've put your minds at rest," he said. "Now if I may return to the purpose of the evening, I have other parents to see."

This abashed my father into silence, but not Jim's. "So it's another man called Noble who's a teacher," he said, "who told our neighbour he could bring her husband back."

"I believe you've summed it up as well as I could, Mr Bailey."

"You won't mind if we check who he is, then." Mr Noble only gazed at him, even when Jim's father said "I know who'll be able to check. Your headmaster."

"If you feel you must go to such lengths you can't be expecting me to prevent you."

Was this another undefined threat? I'd grown so nervous that I might have spoken if I could have thought of anything to dare to say. Instead it was Mr O'Shaughnessy who protested "Can somebody tell me what all this is about?"

"The lady who lives near us, she's a spiritualist," my mother said and turned to him. "She met a Mr Noble in the graveyard by us and took him to their church. He convinced some of them he could raise the dead but now she doesn't like what she thinks he brought back. I shouldn't be saying all this in front of the children, but it's affected her mind so much that she's had to go into hospital."

I was growing red-faced with resentment of being called a child when Mrs O'Shaughnessy said "If it's affecting minds we're talking about, I'd like to know what gave our Peter nightmares."

Mr Noble widened his eyes. "Are you saying anybody here did, Mrs O'Shaughnessy?"

His gaze failed to daunt her, and perhaps it provoked her. "I'm saying it started when you took the boys to France."

"Mam," Peter mumbled. "They weren't that bad. They were only dreams."

"They were bad enough to wake us when you got home," his father said. "Just you tell your teacher what they were about."

Indistinctly enough to be trying to hide his words Peter said "A wormy man."

"Don't be sounding like a baby, you. You can speak better than that when we've sent you to this school."

"It was a man that was all worms and caterpillars, things like them. I thought he was a puddle when he came up out of the ground, and then he got a face on him like a bunch of maggots and tried to get my hand. That's all I kept dreaming before I woke up."

"That's babyish as well," his father said before redirecting his disfavour at the teacher. "That's how going off with you left him."

While Peter was speaking I thought I glimpsed a hint of recognition in Mr Noble's eyes, but he'd suppressed it now. "I really can't imagine how you think I could have been responsible."

"You were meant to be responsible for all your boys, weren't you? We trusted you with them." In a voice like an omen of anger Mr O'Shaughnessy said "We heard you even slept with them."

I wasn't sure how close this came to an accusation, but Mr Noble met it with a look that dared him to be clearer. "I was in charge of a dormitory, as were my colleagues," the teacher said. "The boys knew they could come to me with any problems, but I can assure you your son never made me aware of anything unwelcome."

"It wasn't only me," O'Shaughnessy blurted. "Lots of the others had dreams too."

"You never told us that," his mother complained, slapping the side of his head.

"Ow, mam, I forgot. I've stopped having the dreams, so I don't want to remember."

"I should think you'd feel that's sensible," Mr Noble told Peter's parents. "Now if we could move on—"

"We haven't got to catch the last tram, have we? Let's just put on the brakes." As the teacher's face absorbed the smile it had started to offer, Peter's mother said "How about you two? Did you have nightmares over there?"

I couldn't see Jim without looking over my shoulder, and I didn't want to be the first to speak. Seconds passed before he admitted "I dreamt something like that too."

"I did as well," I said at once.

As our parents made it plain that we should have told them, Peter's mother said "Did you stop when you came home?"

I had, and Jim proved to have as well. "What have you got to say about that, Mr Noble?" she said.

"I'm afraid I may be able to explain."

"Then you go right ahead."

"Do you think you might have been dreaming about my father's story, gentlemen? Perhaps you haven't bothered telling your parents about that either."

"We don't know anything about it," Mr O'Shaughnessy warned whoever should be blamed.

"My father was invited to address the school to prepare the gentlemen for their French experience, but I don't think one of his memories sat too well with the headmaster."

"What one was that?" my father said.

Mr Noble hesitated as if to select his words. "Let's just say he told everyone about a battlefield he thought was, how shall I put it, eager for the battle. And you'll remember, gentlemen, he described a dream he had there. I think you'll agree that he made it so vivid it's no surprise if you had it too."

As I gave in to an uncertain dishonest nod, Jim's father said "And what about you, Mr Noble?"

I saw this catch the teacher unawares. For a moment he seemed not to know how to answer. "You could say I experienced something like a dream," he said.

I didn't quite dare to speak, but Jim did. "We went where your dad told us about, didn't we, sir?"

"We may have driven past it, Mr Bailey."

"How did he know?" my mother said. "Did you tell them?"

"I did not," Mr Noble said and fixed Jim with a look that did its best to stay blank. "What's the solution, Mr Bailey? I should like to hear it too."

Jim mumbled and had to be prompted by his mother. Even more reluctantly he said "Must've been the dream."

I felt he'd let me down, which drove me past my shyness. "It was the trees as well, wasn't it, Jim?"

As Mr Noble's eyes withdrew any expression they might have shown, Jim's mother said "Which were those?"

I was hoping Jim would answer, but he left it to me. "There was a field all the trees were leaning out of," I said. "Leaning all round it, not just off one side. Mr Noble said there must have been a hurricane. Wasn't that the place your dad meant, sir?"

"I'm sorry if you weren't prepared to accept my explanation, Mr Sheldrake," the teacher said and seemed to find another thought more useful. "I shouldn't decry your son's imagination," he told my parents. "He may need it for his tales."

I wasn't sure how they took this, because I felt too defeated and embarrassed to look at them. "I apologise if my father gave your sons his dream," Mr Noble said. "I would just mention that it was the headmaster who invited him to talk to them."

"So you're blaming him as well," Jim's father said. "That's another reason we should have a word with him."

"Would you care to do so now?"

This might have been a challenge or a dismissal, and Mr Bailey took it as both. "Are we done here, Des?" he said.

My father turned to Peter's parents. "If you want a chat about anything you can ring me at Cooper's where I work."

"There's a thought," Jim's father said. "We know some of the other parents too."

I was acutely embarrassed by how they were letting Mr Noble know they intended to discuss him. Perhaps my mother felt that way, because she murmured "Thank you for all that you've done for our boys, Mr Noble."

At the very least this was polite, but he appeared to think it was a gibe, and perhaps that made him reckless. "It's a pity you've so little time for beliefs other than your own," he said as my father opened the door. "You may learn better."

Jim's father looked ready to argue, but his wife urged him out of the room. He didn't speak until we were well along the corridor. "Do you know what struck me most in there? You can't trust a word he says."

"Shall we save it for later?" his wife said.

I gathered that she didn't want Jim and me to hear, but Jim's father was eager to share his observation. "If he's the man who goes to that lady's church," he said, "he won't even let on he's a spiritualist. If he isn't one I'd like to know what he is and why he goes."

Jim looked as uncomfortable as I felt. "What are you going to do, dad?" he said.

"Nothing you two need to know about or worry about either, so keep your mouths shut about it till it's done."

I was more worried how Mr Noble might treat us the next time we saw him. In the morning my eyes kept being drawn to him on the stage in the assembly hall, but I could never catch him watching me or Jim, despite a persistent impression that he'd just looked away from us. "I hope last night was rewarding for you, gentlemen," he said at the start of our first period with him, and precisely because he wasn't looking at us two I felt that the remark was meant to have an ominous significance for us. After that any question he asked me or Jim in class seemed to conceal some meaning that his neutral tone denied, not least since they were all about history – about reaching into the past. I was constantly nervous that he might raise the subject of the French trip and the things we'd said, but he didn't for the whole of the rest of the term.

I didn't feel ignored so much as secretly observed. I wondered what Jim's parents and mine might be doing, if they hadn't already carried out their plan. During the summer holidays I did once ask my mother, but she only said "Mr Bailey had him right. He isn't what he wants people to think." When I tried to enquire further she said "Just make sure you stay away from him, Dominic." I didn't understand how that would be practicable until I realised we would have a different form master when we moved up a school year. It was only when we returned to Holy Ghost in September that I learned Mr Noble was no longer at the school.

CHAPTER THIRTEEN

1954: The Hidden Book

That year it was a film magazine we all watched being torn to bits, as Brother Treanor made its owner shred it page by page. My memory suggests that it was quite a serious journal, and the fourth-former protested that he'd brought it into school to show Brother Stimson, but his demurral only stoked the headmaster's rage. The magazine never had a chance, given that the cover displayed Burt Lancaster and Deborah Kerr in their swimwear, embracing supine on the beach. I suspect Brother Treanor was even more infuriated by the Oscars that *From Here to Eternity* had received – best actress, best actor, best film. No doubt this confirmed his sense of the ungodliness of the world.

Other news would have as well. When Lord Montagu of Beaulieu and his friends were jailed for gay behaviour, Brother Treanor railed at length against "unwholesome and unhealthy friendships", citing the diseases with which God would smite us. When the saucy seaside postcards of Donald McGill earned him a prosecution for obscenity, the headmaster took the chance to lecture us about impure thoughts and the temptations females represented. At least Roger Bannister's four-minute mile let Brother Treanor exhort us to strive for our goals, and now I recall the argument Jim and I had with Bobby later that month when Diane Leather broke the women's record for the distance, Bobby complaining that the athlete hadn't been granted half the publicity her male counterpart enjoyed, Jim insisting this was fair when she'd taken five minutes to conquer the mile, a contention that earned him half a dozen vicious punches on the arm. The event Brother Treanor hailed most fervently was Eisenhower's revision of the Pledge of Allegiance, adding "under God". "Let us pray this sets other nations an example," the headmaster said, "let us pray it shapes the future of the world," and set about leading the school in a prayer to which we only had to say

Amen. I saw Brother Bentley mouthing all the words like a barely tardy echo, and his Amen was the most heartfelt of all.

He was our form master now, and also our history teacher. He still edited the magazine, and I was glad he seemed to have forgotten the story I'd shown him. He taught history with a religious bias that outdid even the headmaster's zeal. Everything was part of God's plan, which wasn't to be queried. If anybody raised an awkward question, Brother Bentley's fat face would grow yet more mottled while his standard disappointed look turned sourer. "The devil's put that in your head," he would rebuke the questioner. "Nobody but Satan wants to question God." I remember feeling that God had left Satan quite a few awkward questions to ask, and I was tempted to raise some of them – whose side God had supported in the carnage Mr Noble's father had described to us, for instance, or why God had stood by while the Nazis did their work. Although shyness kept me mum, such thoughts had begun to feel less like temptation than ideas I shouldn't avoid having. If the school and its concept of God were opposed to them, perhaps this might even be the fault of the school.

The way some of my classmates acted, competing to impress the staff with beliefs the school approved of, didn't assuage my doubts. After Brother Treanor warned us about gayness, Henry Shea brought up the subject in Brother Bentley's class. "We wouldn't have things like that here at our school, would we, sir?"

I wondered how many of us had watched Brother Mayle while the headmaster condemned forbidden relationships – the teacher had looked as innocent as a virgin if not a virgin birth – but Brother Bentley seemed to see no contradiction. "I profoundly hope not, Shea."

"Or people who don't believe in God like us," O'Shaughnessy contributed. "They're not welcome either, are they, sir?"

I was trying not to feel referred to when Brother Bentley said "They should not be welcome in your lives."

"We helped get rid of one," O'Shaughnessy said. "Me and Bailey and Sheldrake did."

"We will not speak of that here." As O'Shaughnessy looked abashed Brother Bentley said "I will just say the three of you are to be commended for your vigilance. Others might do well to follow your example."

I wasn't quite the rebel I'd begun to hope I might be. I didn't simply welcome the praise, even though it left me red-faced; I craved more from the teacher who had dismissed my tale of the Tremendous Three. I suspect that was one reason why I behaved as I did about the secret book.

I saw it first on a sunlit day in June – the Holy Ghost sports day. Clouds far larger than the sports field were wandering across the sky, fraying at the edges and changing shape so gradually that it was impossible to catch them in the act. Their shadows drifted over the competitors and the cheering spectators, though Jim and I and the rest of the runners were denied any shade while we dashed five hundred yards. We'd showered and rejoined our parents, and were watching a prefect vault over a progressively elevated bar, when a man limped around the corner of the school and peered towards the field. It was Mr Noble's father.

He had a book under one arm. At that distance I could make out only that its cover was black. He took a lopsided step towards the field, supporting himself with his stick, before glancing down at the book and then at the crowd. Some misgiving made him limp rapidly towards the nearest entrance to the school. Moments later the door shut behind him with a reticent thud.

Presumably everyone else was too intent on the pole vault to notice the old man, but I saw him limping at speed along the corridor that led to the gymnasium. As he disappeared beyond the last of the windows on the corridor I could only wonder where he was bound for. The gymnasium windows were too high to see through, but he reappeared almost at once. I watched him lurch back along the corridor to fling the door open. He wasn't bothering to mute it now, and he no longer had the book.

I glanced at Jim to find he'd only just become aware of the old man. So had quite a few others, not least members of staff, more than one of whom stepped out of the crowd until Brother Treanor gestured them back. He strode across the field, his robe flapping louder than a crow's wings, and met Mr Noble's father halfway across the schoolyard. "Mr Noble," he said barely audibly. "What brings you to us now?"

"I'm hoping you can help," the old man said in very little of the voice with which he'd addressed all of us. "I don't know anybody else who can."

The headmaster glanced towards the field, where he must have seen far too many people watching. Even the boys in charge of the vaulting bar had paused at their task. "We'll talk in my office," Brother Treanor said and took the old man's arm to usher him towards the school.

I was convinced they would be discussing Mr Noble, and eager to hear what was said. It might have been a job for the Tremendous Two if we wouldn't have drawn more attention than me by myself. What would Dom have done in a tale? The moment inspiration came I hid my hands behind my back and groped to unstrap the wristwatch my patents had given me for my thirteenth birthday last month. As I slipped the watch into my trousers pocket I said "I've just got to go back to the gym."

"You don't need to go right this minute," my mother murmured. "You'll have people thinking you don't care about your school events."

"Mum, I left my watch."

She shook her head as though to rouse a thought. "Weren't you just wearing it, son?"

I saw Jim listening and glanced hastily away from him. "Before I got changed for the race," I said with all the conviction I could feign.

"It'll be safe till your sports are over, won't it? There aren't going to be any thieves here."

"I don't like leaving it," I said, feeling desperately childish. "You and dad gave it me."

From the side of my eye I saw Jim start to edge towards us, and was worried that by trying to help he might ruin my plan. I was striving to think how to stop him when my father said "Let him go if it means so much to him, Mary. Just hurry back, son."

I felt ashamed of deceiving them and of using their gift as the ruse, but I dashed away without looking back, especially at Jim. I was across the schoolyard and letting myself into the silent corridor when I realised that if anybody challenged me I had no excuse to be where I meant to go. While I lingered to think one up, Mr Noble's father might be telling Brother Treanor what was troubling him. Surely everybody else was on the field, and nobody would follow me to find out why I'd come into the school. Just the same, my heart and my breaths seemed to have entered some kind of race as I turned left along the corridor, away from the gym.

I couldn't hear the headmaster or the visitor. No doubt they were in Brother Treanor's office. Before I reached the bend that led there I had to quiet a pair of fire doors, which even when I eased them shut produced a thud at least as noisy as my heartbeat. Advancing to the bend involved holding my breath, and when I saw that the corridor beyond another set of fire doors was deserted I was unable to restrain a gasp, so loud that I was terrified it must have alerted the headmaster. I was hesitating when I heard Mr Noble's father. I couldn't distinguish any words, which frustrated me so much that I sprinted on tiptoe to the doors, a move that felt like being compelled to enact a cartoon.

As I inched the right-hand door ajar I heard the old man again. "He'd have to listen to you," he was protesting. "You were his head." While his voice was raised in entreaty, Brother Treanor seemed to have lowered his to compensate or in a bid to calm his visitor, since I couldn't make out the response. To understand him I would have to venture past the doors, where there would be nothing between me and the office except the deserted corridor. Although the Tremendous Three would have braved it in a tale – even in reality, I liked to think – it was too daunting for me on my own. Instead I leaned against the door to hold it slightly open while I kept out of sight beside the small square window in the top half. I strained my ears and heard my eager troubled pulse, and then Mr Noble's father. "He won't take any notice of the head where he is now. He thinks he knows better than the lot of us."

In that case surely his son wouldn't heed Brother Treanor, and perhaps this occurred to the headmaster. Whatever he murmured failed to pacify his listener. "He's gone further," the old man protested. "I don't know what he's started. I told you he's got more people with him." Even when I leaned closer to the gap between the doors I heard only his words. "Someone needs to find out what he's up to in that church... I'm past doing that and his wife's too scared. She can't even stop him taking their daughter... The man who fixed things up for him can't realise Christian's using all of them. He puts things in your head, but just what he wants you to know..." Each time the old man faltered the headmaster murmured in response, which plainly didn't help. "The world would be better off without him," the old man cried at last. "We should never have had him. His poor mother, rest her soul, at least she can't see what he's like."

This shocked even me, and without managing to distinguish any of his words I could hear it distressed the headmaster. I'd begun to grow uncomfortable with eavesdropping, not least because it brought me very little that I understood. What about the book the old man had been carrying? I assumed he'd meant to show it to Brother Treanor, in which case why had he hidden it instead? I could only think he'd been afraid to let too many people know he had it. How much longer might I have before someone came to find me? The idea brought me so close to panic that I almost let the fire door bump its twin as I stepped away from it. I blocked it with my elbow just in time and, having eased it shut, performed another cartoonish sprint along the corridor.

Once I was past the door to the schoolyard I felt a little safer. At least now I was in the area where I'd told my parents I would be. I dashed past the classroom our form had this year and shoved open one of the twin doors leading to the lobby of the gymnasium. Except for those doors and the pair to the gymnasium itself, all four walls were occupied by lockers stacked just higher than my head. There was nowhere in the gymnasium to hide a book, and I didn't think Mr Noble's father would even have had time to go in. The book must be hidden in a locker, but which? How long might I have before he brought the headmaster?

I was turning to the lockers – so many of them were closed that the sight took me to the edge of despair – when I noticed something lodged behind the nearest set, a strip of black material squeezed between the wall and the backs of the lockers at rather less than an arm's length from the side. I hardly dared to hope that I knew what it was, but when I slid my hand behind the lockers it was easy to retrieve. I suppose the old man's arm couldn't struggle very far through the painfully narrow gap he would have found, because the strip of material was indeed the spine of the book. He must have been desperate to use the first hiding place he could think of. The featureless black leather covers of the book were scuffed and scratched by his attempt to hide it, and the pages had been dragged away from the spine on their strip of black linen. As the volume fell onto my chest it felt big and heavy enough for a stone lid. I cradled it in my arms and let it sprawl open wherever it would.

I recognised the handwriting at once. In the previous school year I'd frequently seen it on the blackboard and at the end, not to mention sometimes in the margin, of my history homework. On the board it was chalky white, while the comments on homework were in red ink, but now the extravagantly looping script was as black as the cover of the book. I read the first few sentences on the left-hand page, and they were enough.

He whom my father roused beneath the field was within me before I was born, and what may have been reborn through him? How far may we reach towards the primal source? Not only the past seeks to take hold of the world. The future yearns for incarnation, and the more remote the future, the more power it may draw from the accretion of time beyond man's grasp of that truth...

Though I understood very little of this, I felt capable of deciphering it all if I tried hard enough. The prospect of bringing my mind to bear felt as if the words in the book were fingering the inside of my skull. Instead I shut the book, which I'd guessed was Mr Noble's journal. As soon as I saw through the pane in the door that the corridor was still deserted I made for the Form Two Alpha classroom. I was so certain of the course I meant to take that I might have fancied the book was as anxious to be hidden as I was to keep it safe until I could read it all. I would never have been able to smuggle it unnoticed out of the school that day, and so I hid it under the books in my desk. As I hurried out of the room I had such a sense of a job well done that I almost forgot to strap my watch on before I left the school.

When I stepped out of the building I was met by a chorus of groans, the kind that might have greeted the appearance of a villain or at any rate a profound disappointment. I was close to taking it personally until I saw that a sprinter had tripped on the field. The distraction let me dash across the schoolyard while Mr Jensen helped the injured boy up, having established that his ankle was only twisted, and ushered him to his parents with some bluff words of praise. I thought I'd managed to return unobserved, but my mother didn't let that happen. "Where on earth have you been all this time, Dominic?" she cried in a voice apparently meant to be muted. "I don't know who'll have been wondering where you'd got to."

"I couldn't find my watch, mum." I felt my face grow red, and had to hope my parents would think she was embarrassing me, but I couldn't look at Jim. "I only just did," I protested, displaying my wrist as if it were evidence.

I saw her readying another reprimand when Brother Treanor came out of the school by himself and strode in a flurry of his robe towards the field. He must have let Mr Noble's father out of the front of the school. If the old man tried to retrieve the book he would have to show himself, since the front door would be locked, but I didn't think he would return. Perhaps taking the book away from his son was enough for him. I no longer minded the lecture my mother was continuing to deliver – I even felt my face revert to the afternoon temperature – because the book was safe.

The sports day ended with a half-mile race and the presentation of trophies, instantly repossessed for displaying in a glass case outside the assembly hall. As the spectators headed for the gates, Jim joined me to mutter "Did you follow them?"

I wasn't ready to mention Mr Noble's book. "Yes," I whispered.

"Then what? Give."

"Couldn't hear much. Wasn't close enough." I saw his frustration and murmured "I think Mr Noble's dad is scared of him. He wanted Brother Treanor to stop him doing something, but I don't know what."

"Maybe we ought to find out."

Our parents looked back to determine what we were up to, which brought the discussion to an end, leaving me alone with the lines I'd read in Mr Noble's book. They felt as if they were enticing me to read more – as if the book was hungry to be read. They kept repeating themselves in my mind like an attempt to compel me to interpret them. That night I lost sleep over worrying that somebody might find the book before I could take it away from the school. Once – it must have been when sleep caught up with me at last – I mistook my skull for a huge dark place where the words from the book were taking more of a shape, groping inside my cranium like the legs of a great restless spider.

All day at school I was aware of the book in my desk. I had to force myself to hear the teachers above the mental clamour of its words, the ones I'd read and the horde I imagined were waiting for me to read them. Whenever I opened the desk I saw the book, which the rest of the contents couldn't entirely hide, and grew afraid all over again that someone would ask what it was. Brother Bentley did as I struggled to fit it into my satchel at the end of the last class. "Have you more of your fictions in there, Sheldrake?"

I tried to lie as little as I had to. "Sir," I said.

He kept his discontented look while he sauntered towards me. "Is there anything I ought to read?"

I couldn't tell whether he meant to disapprove or was hoping for the opposite. "No, sir," I said in any case.

This didn't halt his advance, and his expression drooped still further. I had an unhappy sense that I'd made him determined to examine the book. He was raising his hands to take it from me while I strove to thrust it into the satchel. I had the wholly absurd idea that if I succeeded before he reached me, he would let it go. Just in time I had a desperate inspiration. "Sir, it isn't finished."

"Perhaps I had better see it when it is." Even this didn't stop him, and he came so close that I could smell the black cloth of his robe, a thin desiccated odour. "I should like to see whether you have followed my advice," he said and moved away at last, only to turn his renewed disappointment on me. "If it is unsuitable it should not be brought into the school."

Jim overtook me in the corridor. "Is he going to like it when he reads it? I hope you haven't put our names in again."

"I haven't," I said, which felt like a slyer trick than I'd played on Brother Bentley. For a moment I wanted to tell Jim about the book, but something prevented me – perhaps some aspect of the book itself. After all, I was still a child, and I wanted to keep my prize for my own at least until I'd had a chance to read it by myself. If I'd shown it to an adult at once, would that have made any difference? Could it have averted anything? None of us will ever know.

CHAPTER FOURTEEN

A Father's Words

When did I grasp that my parents were not the source of me but merely the medium through which I came into the world? Perhaps when I learned that the world they saw was not mine; that I was aware of presences they were incapable of perceiving. Some truths I knew before I had words for them, until they found words for themselves. In my cradle I saw how the stars were reaching for me out of darkness as remote as the time from which their light came. Even as an infant I had a sense of the nature of time which the masses never glimpse; of how the pincers of the future and the past close on the moment, for they are the twin halves of a single process. Or is the moment which the masses mistake for existence simply the closure of the circle which they misperceive as past and future? Soon even they may be unable to avoid the truth.

Early in my life I learned to keep my insights from my parents. To start with they found them precocious, much like my rapid grasp of language and of reading. I was eager for every skill which would help me take hold of the world. At first my parents were proud to show me off, inviting the neighbours to watch me read the Bible when I was three years old. Tina, I think you may be younger still when you read this, and how young may the third of us be?

I still recall my father's grotesquely engorged face when he thought I had insulted his father. I had done no more than state the truth which I was beginning to appreciate: that the old man, like all my parents' relatives, was unrelated to me in any way which mattered. My father struck me to the floor, which made my mother scream, and despite the pain of the blow to my head I felt as if they had been enacting a charade, a set of clichés of behaviour. I had begun to see how banal most human activity is; how it seems designed to dull the minds of the masses, to blind them to truths beyond their encompassing.

After that I played the human game, despite its horrid tedium. With me you will have no need, Tina. I had few friends except for books, and no wish for them. I suspect that the children at school and in the neighbourhood avoided me because, in their limited fashion, they sensed more about my nature than adults could let themselves suspect. I was content to impress my teachers at school, though I had to restrain myself from correcting their errors. In the great perspective those were less than negligible, and I concentrated on not drawing unwelcome attention to myself.

When did I grow aware of being chosen? Perhaps as the source set about speaking within me, not in words but in revelations which language can only confine. Once I glimpsed the face behind the sky, while the noonday sun blinded everyone about me to its galactic vastness, and on another day I sensed how the world resembles a fruit full of worms which once were men. Perhaps that vision was my first step towards our goal.

A succession of funerals helped set me on our course. Grandparent after grandparent gave up the ghost, as the ignorant were wont to term it, more accurately than they could know. Each funeral showed me how the dead were being misused; abandoned when they still had qualities to offer. The rites were as ponderously solemn as the plodding of the horses which drew the hearse, and far more ineffectual. Every open grave I had to stand beside was a gateway to knowledge which nobody other than I appeared to realise was there to be tapped. As mourners dropped earth on the coffin it sounded very much like knocking on a door, and I imagined how terrified the priest and his little congregation would be if any opened in the earth. Each cemetery ceremony let me sense the dormant dead everywhere around the latest grave, though my impressions fell short of grasping their state.

I was nine when I set out to discover what was being wasted in the graves. I could see that my father was touched by my visiting his mother's, not least because he rightly thought I had disliked her. He saw me across the road from our house — still ours, Tina — and watched me as far as the cemetery entrance. How much was the source attempting to convey to me about the necessary method? My ideas were imprecise, and I thought the bouquet which I laid on my grandmother's grave might help to entice her out of the dark beneath the sunlight. Wherever this inkling of the true rite came from, I failed to interpret it correctly, and once I was sure that nobody else was nearby I began to call her name. When this had no effect I tried envisioning her as she must be, boxed and supine, and then urging her to rise to the surface in that form. I held that in my mind until twilight settled on the graveyard. Then I felt my mind catch hold of something more solid than the vision, and the plot of earth began to stir, quivering the flowers that leaned against the headstone. Perhaps this was simply a distortion of the air, because a colourless shape, less substantial than water but denser than mist, was seeping out of the grave. It was nearly the length of the mound and not much less wide, and was struggling to take more of a shape: unmatched limbs, undivided wads for hands, a head without features or hair. All at *once it gave up the effort and drained back into the earth. I tried to retrieve it with my mind, and instantly my grandmother's face stretched up out of the mound. It had no colour, and resembled a thin flat mask no broader than the gravestone but as tall as I am now, Tina. Perhaps all this was why or partly why it was howling like a tortured beast. I imagine only I would have been able to see or hear it, but it brought me to the brink of panic, not least for fear that somebody might blame me for its presence. I fought to let go with my mind, but even when I succeeded, the elongated face took some time to sink with a series of shudders into the earth. I heard its subterranean howls of outrage as I bolted from the graveyard; indeed, all the way to our house. Even I was too young to welcome the encounter, and I avoided inviting its like again until not long before you were born, Tina. The Bible holds a few truths for those who can sift them. The prophet must live out the allotted span of years before he can come into his inheritance...*

None of this persuaded me that someone ought to see the book. Even Mr Noble's words to his daughter struck me as more embarrassing than disturbing. When at last I concluded that I should show the journal to an adult, I almost took it downstairs to my parents until I realised they were bound to confiscate it. By this stage I was far too fascinated to give it up, and then I saw I didn't have to – not in any important sense. I spent more than a week's pocket money on exercise books, and then I devoted night after night to copying the journal.

I let my parents think I was busy with homework or writing a new tale. I knew this was the kind of unspoken lie the Holy Ghost staff found especially pernicious, but their influence was losing its power over me. As I copied Mr Noble's secrets I heard fragments of the radio programmes my parents had on: Arthur Askey calling "Hello playmates," Rawicz and Landauer tinkling their pianos, the comically camp cries of Frankie Howerd, a song by Vera Lynn on *The Music Goes Round*, singers adding vocals to the band of Henry Hall or evoking nostalgia in *Those Were The Days*... Perhaps all this distracted me from the material I was transcribing. Certainly I copied some of it almost automatically while its meaning stayed aloof, though I could easily have fancied that the words themselves were eager for a second home.

I passed decades in the wilderness of ordinary mundane life. I played the schoolboy and his elder self and then took the role of teacher. I found the minds of my pupils no smaller than those of their seniors, and occasionally not quite so imprisoned within themselves, but there was little chance of expanding them except along the dully hide-bound lines the school approved. Telling them truths might have exposed me, and I could only bide my time, or more precisely live in that sense of the insignificance of time which I inherited from the source. Tina, let me confess that in those days I was no more aware of my own true nature than of my purpose.

Then came the opportunity of the new war. My father persuaded me not to fight, perhaps because he had brought terror home from his own battlefield experience. He may even have been directed along the right path, unbeknown to him, since my years with the ambulance corps let me spend more time with the dying than involvement in the conflict might have afforded me. I had heard the view expressed that war was a waste of life, but soon I came to see that it was a waste of death. I remembered my grandmother's face above her grave, and wondered if, far from protesting her retrieval from the unknown dark, her howls had been a comment on the state in which she found herself. How much might she have been able to convey about the territories to which death gave admission? Every dying man whom I encountered in the war was a fresh cause of frustration, so close to answering questions which I could scarcely formulate and yet denied to me by the banal presence of my fellow Nightingales. I returned from the war determined to bring my insights to life.

I had seen a further truth. However slow the process of enlightenment might appear to the masses, and even to myself while I had yet to gain my nature, it had no need of time as man perceives the medium. From observing how many of the war dead never enjoyed a floral tribute I deduced why flowers were important to the dead, or had been before the upstart religions misrepresented an ancient practice, one of a multitude of distorted truths. You are my second person, Tina, and we shall bring forth the third. In the old days flowers were never gifts which the living gave the dead; rather were they signs which the dead presented to the living, although even in that era so close to our own primal state, perhaps only the chosen could survive the rite.

I thought myself equal to it, and when the last of my grandparents died I took the opportunity to test myself. The school where I played pedagogue was closed for the summer, and my parents were sojourning at the seaside for a week. I had already planted a herb on my paternal grandfather's grave under cover of laying a wreath. I brought home the product of the grave, where the swiftness of its growth suggested how eager its roots had been to reach deep into the earth, urged by the essence of the tenant of the coffin. As I lay on my bed, chewing as a shaman chews his drug, I felt as if I were adopting my grandfather's posture, the better to share his experience.

Tina, I was not as ready as I wanted to believe. With my eyes closed I had the impression of occupying a lightless place whose dimensions were as indefinable as my own had become. I was unsure not just of my identity but of the extent to which I myself was the indefinite darkness. When I attempted to take hold of the impression I felt a shapeless presence start to blunder about inside my skull, fumbling as though desperate to clutch at my substance without the benefit of any members that would serve as hands. Worse still, I had a sense that my mind was about to migrate to the place from which the intruder had come; to leave my body and expand in a helpless bid to grasp the boundaries of the dark, beyond which I might waken a vast form infinitely more inhuman than the invader of my skull. My mind recoiled, and I rushed to the lavatory to vomit up not just the herb but, if I could, the vision. For many nights it threatened to rise up from my slumber.

You may be forgiven, Tina, if you struggle to believe what I have to tell you now; that my mission of discovery was revived by encountering your mother. Otherwise she need not concern us. Previously I had found no use for her kind, but the time for your birth was approaching, and so I sought a suitable candidate without knowing why I did. Sometimes our source withholds its purpose from me until it is achieved. When I chose her your mother was a fellow teacher, but now she is your mother. I still recall the moment when I was brought to see you newly born, and I believe you do. As our eyes met we recognised each other, aspects of a single being, while your mother was no more than an aid to your birth, like the staff around us at the hospital.

Your arrival was an omen of imminence. My yearning to learn from the dead returned with renewed strength, and your presence gave me the courage. What other forces may have been at work the day I met the Norris widow in the graveyard? Some versions of the future are no less determined to be born than you were, and wield events to bring about their goal. I was attempting to sense which graves contained tenants whose identities had survived the onslaught of the dark when the woman approached me to proselytise on behalf of her church. I had heard of its like, but only now did it occur to me that the adherents of such a belief might act as buffers between me and the dead.

I observed some of the mediums at the next service. Frequently they are dismissed as charlatans or worse. Not long after I was born, one Sidney Mosley wrote a book which attacked the famous Arthur Conan Doyle for his faith in spiritualism, wakened by his observations of the battlefield. In fact Doyle had a modicum of our instincts and intelligence, however timid his exploration of the afterlife may have been, while Mosley made a popular mistake, which is to dismiss the dead on the basis of the imprecision of their messages. Tina, those messages are merely attempts by the dead to cling to their memories and regain some sense of themselves. That their communications are so often vague to the point of impersonality demonstrates how difficult it is to maintain that sense of self in the great dark.

When I proposed to members of the congregation that I could restore their lost ones in a way the mediums could not, many were as skeptical as their detractors are about their church. Having introduced me to their faith, the Norris widow felt compelled to test my offer and persuaded several of her friends to follow suit. One baulked at consuming the produce of her late husband's grave, but the rest found my proposal palatable enough; some declared that the act itself brought them closer to their dead. Soon those creatures became their companions, and I saw why I had been inspired to use their church: because the bereaved helped the dead to recover their personalities, simply by perceiving them as they used to be.

At first I was able to wield those restored personalities by partaking of the yield of their graves. As I sent them farther into the infinite void which knows neither space nor time but which is the secret essence of the universe, however, so they began to return transformed by their exploration. Perhaps the nature of the place which they investigate is closer to the primal instant of creation, before life was restricted to whichever single form each example took, but I have also concluded that the very act of perception compels the explorer to reflect, however imperfectly and reluctantly, that which is perceived. Even observing this in the imprecisely mimicked form which the dead bring back is capable of shaking the foundations of the lesser mind.

Tina, I believe that together we shall be stronger than even I have been. My visit to the field in France whence I originated has revealed to me how many secrets we have yet to learn. He who lies beneath the field has gained strength from them, though centuries of searching for them has left him monstrously transformed. You need not fear him, Tina. He is but an emblem of the revelations we shall experience. When I took his transmuted hand he conveyed hints of some of them to me, so that I beheld why the moon grins, and saw beyond it to the galaxy which a restless tract of the cosmos wears for a mask. Together with these glimpses a word came into my mind: Daoloth, which is the name of that which rends the veils men call reality. So much I subsequently learned from a set of volumes which even the librarians have recognised is not meant for the mundane eye. In the field from which

my essence came, my true father yielded up a portion of his substance to be
scattered to the points of the compass in that most ancient ritual which some
surviving traditions imperfectly reproduce. What gifts may he bestow upon
you, Tina? My instincts have yet to reveal when the two of us should visit
him. May it be soon...

At times I'd come close to forgetting who had written this, since it was
so unlike how Mr Noble spoke. I wouldn't learn until much later that many
writers don't speak the way they write – that writing lets their true selves
speak. The paragraph about the field in France brought his behaviour all too
vividly to mind, however, and I felt anxious for his daughter. It seemed clear
that he wouldn't take her there just yet, and I still had a good deal of the
journal to transcribe. I took most of a week to finish the task, but as soon as
I had I went to my parents.

They were listening to the week's good cause, an appeal for contributions
to a home for distressed gentlefolk. "Pity their families can't look after them.
That's the way it's going with all this welfare we're supposed to pay for,"
my father said and turned the radio down to silence its solicitation. "Have
you finished your homework at last, son?"

"It wasn't homework." I thought one of my parents might have
enquired further, but when they left my remark unanswered I said "Dad,
can I ask you something?"

"Of course you can." Just the same, he sounded warier than he was
admitting. I suspect he expected the kind of question adolescent boys had
to brave themselves to raise. "Your mother and me," he said, "we're here
whatever you need to ask."

"What happened to Mr Noble?"

"We heard he found himself another job."

"Why, dad? Who got rid of him?"

"I should think your headmaster did, him and the governors at
your school."

"Didn't you do something, though?"

"Quite a few parents had a word with the head," my mother put in.
"Why are you asking all this, Dominic?"

"I was just wondering what anyone said."

"We weren't there when he had his interview," my father said. "No use
asking us if he was told to leave."

It was plain that my parents wanted the subject put to rest, but I said "Don't you think someone should stop him?"

My mother sounded close to leaving her patience behind. "Stop what, son?"

"All the things you said Mrs Norris said he did."

"She ought to be safe where she is. If they don't like what he's up to where he's working now that's for them to deal with. He's no threat to you or your schoolmates any more."

"Dad, he's got a little girl. Do you want him bringing her up to be like him?"

"Where do you think this is, Russia? We don't interfere with families in England even if we don't agree with them. We don't tell other people what they have to think."

"I only thought the way you and the other parents talked to Mr Noble—"

"We did what we had to and that's all. I don't want to hear another word about him in this house, now or ever."

In case this was insufficiently final my father stalked out of the room and stumped upstairs, where he made even the flush of the toilet sound stormy. While he was there my mother murmured "Your father isn't proud of what we had to do, son. You let him forget about it now."

"But mum, do you think you could—"

"No buts. You don't say but to your parents. You heard what your father told you. Not another word."

I could have fancied that his footsteps on the stairs were trampling on any words I had. My words didn't return to me in the night, but too much of Mr Noble's journal did. It felt as if his secrets were eager to take hold of my mind. I no longer wanted to be alone with them. Somebody more equipped to deal with them ought to decide what should be done, and Brother Bentley seemed the obvious choice. He'd praised me and the others for helping rid the school of Mr Noble, after all.

I took the journal with me and kept it in my desk until I had the chance to speak to Brother Bentley after the last class. He'd been teaching us about Henry VIII, whose behaviour he appeared to take as a personal affront, and his sour look didn't relent much when I ventured to his desk. "Sir," I said and cleared my throat louder than my voice had managed to be. "Can I show you something?"

"I presume you are aware of your own capabilities, Sheldrake. If you are asking for permission, please proceed."

When I took the journal out of my desk, he let his eyebrows rise a fraction. "Have you finished your tale?"

"No, sir." Too late I recalled our conversation when he'd previously seen the book. "This isn't one," I had to say.

"I believe you told me it was."

I felt so trapped that I could hardly think. "It's not the same book, sir."

"Kindly bring it here at once."

My progress towards him felt even more ominously inexorable than his approach last time had been. At first he didn't speak, but indicated that I should lay the journal on his desk. "Please don't waste your time and much more importantly mine, Sheldrake," he said at last. "This is the book I saw."

"Sorry, sir."

I could think of nothing more to say as his unfavourable gaze rose from the book to me. "Why are you apologising, Sheldrake?"

"Sir, you're right. I mean, it is. The book, I mean."

"You're confessing that you lied to me."

I felt more trapped than ever. "Sir, I wasn't, I mean, I wasn't sure what it was."

I should think this sounded as desperate to him as it did to me. When his gaze eventually left my face I was able to take a breath. "Then let us see," he said and opened the book with a leathery thump on the desk.

It never had a title. It commenced on the first page with Mr Noble's thoughts about his birth. Brother Bentley scarcely glanced at them before leafing through several pages, and then he shut the book hard enough to rouse a chalky glitter in the air. "Who wrote this, Sheldrake?"

"Sir," I said and felt as if I was leaving all caution behind, "Mr Noble did."

"And how did it come into your hands?"

"I found it, sir."

"You found it." Once he'd left this exposed for a few moments Brother Bentley said "Where?"

"Behind the lockers, sir."

"Behind the lockers." Apparently this also had to be isolated by a silence. At last Brother Bentley said "And why would Mr Noble keep it there?"

"Sir, he didn't." I was unhappily aware that I would be required to say more than "His dad put it there last time he came to the school."

Brother Bentley planted a hand on the book like a priest or a judge. "Please ask your parents to be here tomorrow," he said.

"Sir, when? My dad's working."

"I should hope so, but your mother won't be, will she? Please tell her to be at the school when the final class is finished."

"Sir, why shall I say?"

"That will be made clear at the appropriate time," Brother Bentley said and gazed at me in dismissal.

I grabbed my satchel and trudged out of the classroom, to find Jim waiting near the multitude of empty coat hooks. A solitary mackintosh drooping in a corner reminded me of Mr Norris more than I liked. "What did Bent want now?" Jim said.

"I don't know. Nothing much. Just about something I found." I didn't care how unsatisfactory this was. I shoved the door open and tramped through the sunlight to outdistance any further questions or at least let Jim know they were unwelcome. I felt I'd already said far too much. I was starting to wonder if Brother Bentley was the last person I should have shown the book.

CHAPTER FIFTEEN

A Reappearance

Next day Mr Askew took the last class. He limped around the classroom to rest a hand on each boy's desk while he examined their grammar exercises, humming tunelessly under his breath. "I should think this is second nature to you, Sheldrake," he said over my shoulder. "It's a pity to rein in that imagination of yours."

This kept me happy while I stayed in the classroom, where Brother Bentley had told me to wait. Jim sent me a look that I supposed was meant to be bracing, though it resembled the kind of backwards glance you might leave somebody you'd visited in prison. Other classes passed the room, and then there was silence until the peremptory thump of a fire door announced Brother Bentley's approach. I heard his robes before he appeared in the doorway. "Where are your parents, Sheldrake?"

"I expect they're outside, sir."

"Kindly bring them in," he said as if I'd somehow neglected my duty. "This way, Sheldrake."

As he led the way towards the headmaster's office I could have imagined that I was being made to return to the scene of my crime. I held open the fire door I'd lurked behind, and he strode to the front entrance. When he unlatched the broad door I saw my parents waiting on the drive as if they weren't quite sure where they should be. I'd told them only that I'd found a book Mr Noble had written, which I'd taken to the form master. Brother Bentley beckoned to them without speaking, which provoked my father to remark "Brother Bentley, isn't it? You're looking like a butler."

No doubt this was meant as more of a joke than it ended up, and my mother tried to restore politeness. "Nice to meet you, Brother Bentley."

"Good afternoon, Mrs Sheldrake. Mr Sheldrake. Please follow me."

His briskness made my parents give me an enquiring look I couldn't answer. "Has Dominic been keeping up the good work?" my father wanted to hear.

"I understand from his teachers that he is still applying himself," Brother Bentley said and knocked on the headmaster's door.

I'd expected this no more than my parents could have, and I avoided looking at them. "Enter," Brother Treanor said in a voice high and sharp enough for a drill.

He stood up behind his desk as Brother Bentley led the way into the office, which was so thoroughly panelled in dark oak that it felt like a sombre box. A window overlooked an inner courtyard where I believe the monks would take an evening constitutional, shut off from the world. "Mr and Mrs Sheldrake," Brother Treanor said, and his shiny bulbous tapering head bobbed like a balloon tethered by his celluloid collar. "Please be seated. I'm sorry you've had to be put to this trouble."

"No trouble if it's in a good cause," my father said. "They said that where I work as well."

My parents sat down in front of the desk while Brother Bentley took a seat beside it, leaving me to stand awkwardly next to my mother. "Is it, then?" she said.

Both monks fixed their eyes on me. "Have you informed your parents of the situation, Sheldrake?" Brother Treanor said.

My words weren't too eager to leave my mouth. "I told them what I told Brother Bentley," I mumbled.

"I believe this is the kind of thing I spoke of at yesterday's assembly. Please let us hear exactly what happened in full."

"What do you mean about the assembly?" my mother said.

"I was counselling the school always to tell the whole truth."

"Well, I'm sure he does. You go on, son."

"That's it, Dominic," my father said. "You shame the devil."

Each exhortation felt less helpful, and Brother Treanor added another. "I should like to hear the tale in your own words. From the beginning, Sheldrake."

"Sir, I found a book Mr Noble wrote."

The headmaster held up one hand like a benediction while his face denied the resemblance. He pulled open a drawer of his desk, which emitted a creak that put me in mind of a restless tree. "I take it this is the item concerned."

As he laid the journal in front of him I couldn't help being reminded of a piece of evidence, the sort that so often proved damning in courtroom films. "Yes, sir," I said.

"Where was it found?"

"Stuck behind the gym lockers, sir."

I was hoping my parents wouldn't take this as a cue, but my mother said "Was it on your sports day when you went to find your watch?"

"It wouldn't have been, Mary. He didn't have that book when he came back."

Brother Treanor gazed at the three of us. "May I ask what you're referring to?"

I did my best to head off any threat from that direction. "Sir, I forgot my watch after the race."

"It was just that you were such a long time looking for it in the school," my mother said.

Brother Treanor looked close to pursuing this but said "Let us hear how you went about finding the book, Sheldrake."

"Mr Noble's dad had it when he came in the school the first time, sir, but when he came out he hadn't got it with him."

"I have no idea what you mean, Sheldrake."

"Sir, I don't think you saw him the first time. Didn't anybody else?"

"I have certainly not been informed if they did. Perhaps they were more committed to the sports than you appear to have been."

"Isn't that a bit unfair?" my mother protested. "Dominic was in a race."

"Every boy is required to participate unless he has a medical excuse. We expect boys to show their enthusiasm for the school." As I wished my mother hadn't intervened the headmaster said "It is still not clear to me how you found this book, Sheldrake."

"Sir, I saw his dad go to the gym, and he came back without the book."

"You seem to have spent quite some time not watching the sports. So you searched for what you'd seen."

"Yes, sir. I thought—"

"When did you search?"

It seemed worse than unwise to admit any further lack of interest in the school sports. "The next day, sir."

Brother Bentley raised his head like an unwelcome weight. "The day you told me it was a book of your stories, Sheldrake."

I could barely move my thickened lips when my face felt so swollen with shame. "Sorry, sir."

My mother sounded as if his constant disappointment had infected her. "Why did you tell your teacher such a fib, Dominic?"

I had a desperate inspiration and could think of nothing else to say. "I thought we weren't supposed to talk about Mr Noble any more."

As Brother Bentley made a noise like a summary of his dissatisfaction, my father said "That's pretty much the idea you gave us, Brother Treanor."

Parents seldom dared to challenge teachers in those days, especially head teachers. I was wondering if my father had worsened my situation when Brother Treanor said "Are you saying you communicated it to Sheldrake?"

"We did a bit, didn't we, son?" my mother said.

As I risked agreeing more or less aloud the headmaster said "None of that is an excuse for lying."

"That's rather a strong word, don't you think?" my father objected. "Maybe Dominic didn't know what else to say. Maybe we all confused him."

Brother Treanor gazed at me long enough to let me imagine his sympathy might have been roused, and then he picked up the journal with both hands. "You weren't so confused you didn't know who wrote this, Sheldrake."

"No, sir."

"How?"

As he turned the book to show my parents the covers were blank, I stammered "I saw his writing, Mr Noble's, sir."

"You read his private document."

"Sir, I looked inside to see what it was, sir."

"Brother Treanor," Brother Bentley said, "by his own admission Sheldrake has had the book for the best part of a fortnight."

From the corner of my eye I saw my parents staring at me, but I couldn't look at them even when my father spoke. "There's something I don't understand," he said. "Why would the man's father hide his book?"

"Why do you think," Brother Treanor said, "Sheldrake?"

I thought Mr Noble's father had meant to keep the book away from his granddaughter, but I couldn't say so when it might betray how much I'd read. I was disturbed to think the little girl could read such a book at her age, though if her father read it to her that was at least as bad. "Sir," I pleaded, "don't you know?"

"Please refrain from questioning me, Sheldrake. You have already been told we are concerned with your behaviour. You have yet to answer your form master."

This was too much for my mother. "You're confusing him again. I didn't hear the gentleman ask him anything, so Dominic couldn't have either."

Brother Bentley gazed at her while addressing his disfavour to me. "You need to explain why you took the item home and why you kept it there."

"I didn't know what to do with it, sir." I tried to appeal to the headmaster as well by saying "Sir, I thought you mightn't want it in the school when it was Mr Noble's, sir."

"Very sophisticated, Sheldrake." In case I mistook this for praise Brother Treanor added "Too sophisticated for the good of your soul."

"Cunning is the enemy of truth," Brother Bentley said like a response in church.

This time it was my father who had had enough. "Do you mind if we ask what you're both getting at? It isn't only the lad who's confused. We'd like to hear just what he's supposed to have done that you wanted us to know."

"He lied to his form master," Brother Treanor said, raising his voice both in pitch and volume as my mother made to speak. "He took possession of property which he must have known had been appropriated from its owner, and he read material which the owner may not have wanted to be read. He certainly had no permission to read it. As his parents, perhaps you have a view on how this should be dealt with."

I wasn't listening only to him. I'd heard the thump of a fire door in the corridor, and hoped somebody was on their way to interrupt, even if this might be no more than a postponement. "I don't want him hit," my mother dared to say. "There's too much of that in schools for not enough reason."

"He looked after the book, didn't he?" my father contributed. "He always does with books. And he brought it to you like he should have even if he ought to have sooner. I don't know why you didn't show us first, Dominic."

"Dad, you said I wasn't to mention Mr Noble ever again."

"There, you see," my mother said and turned her eyes on Brother Treanor. "He was just doing what his father told him."

Both monks gazed sadly at her as if they were convicting her of my sin – sophistication that played games with the truth. I could well have thought they were blaming me, and I was trying to think what I or preferably someone else might say to rescue us from condemnation when somebody knocked at the door. Brother Treanor pursed his lips as though to squeeze his voice yet higher and made to bid the person enter, but he'd barely emitted a syllable like a solitary letter before Mr Noble came into the room.

Brother Bentley let out so loud a breath at the sight of him that it felt as though everyone else had as well. Mr Noble lingered over closing the door while his gaze moved from face to face. He might have been deciding whom to stoop towards, and I thought of a snake selecting a victim. "Well, this is quite the gathering," he said. "I feel practically welcomed back."

Brother Treanor cleared his throat like an answer that needed no words. "I didn't expect you so soon, Mr Noble," he said.

"I had a colleague take my last class of the day. They're really quite accommodating where I teach now. Not so bent on regimenting people," Mr Noble said, and then he saw the book on Brother Treanor's desk. His eyes grew so wide that he might have been parodying astonishment as he said "Why, headmaster, have you been reading from my book?"

"I assure you I have done nothing of the kind."

"It makes you look like a priest at his lectern. Doesn't anybody else think so?" When Brother Bentley kept up his habitual expression while my parents and I tried to pretend we hadn't heard, Mr Noble said "So who is my saviour?"

"We pray He is the same as everybody else's here," Brother Bentley retorted.

"Pardon me if I'm being too vague for your taste. I was asking who rescued my book."

"That was Dominic." As if my involvement entitled him to know, my father said "So what is it exactly? Why is it so important to you?"

"Perhaps whoever has read it can say."

When everyone else looked at me I felt worse than accused – more like a victim being given up to his fate. "Mr Sheldrake, of course," Mr Noble said, but his wide eyes were unreadable. "I should have realised you would be the one to know."

"Why should you?" my father said as if he mightn't like the answer.

"We've certain things in common, haven't we, Mr Sheldrake?"

He was speaking to me, but it was my father who demanded "What things?"

"I should think you ought to know your own child's mind." As my father parted his lips hard enough to make a prefatory sound, Mr Noble said "What else but telling tales?"

"You mean," my mother said, "your book is a story like one of Dominic's."

"I don't believe anybody who has read it could think otherwise."

However much this sounded like a challenge, I thought it betrayed exactly the kind of sophistication Brother Treanor didn't care for. I was wondering if he might say as much, not to mention hoping this would distract attention from my own offences, when my mother said "Well, Dominic?"

All I could do was feign incomprehension and will her to realise why. "What, mum?"

"Don't pretend you don't know what I mean. Has Mr Noble been writing stories like yours?"

Desperation found me words that I hoped would satisfy all the listeners. "Not like mine."

"Perhaps yours will grow more like when you have seen more, Mr Sheldrake. We shall see what the future brings you," Mr Noble said and let his gaze stray over the adults. "Is there anything else anyone's anxious to learn?"

"I wouldn't mind knowing one thing," my father said. "If it's just a story, why did your father hide it?"

"I'm afraid his mind isn't what it might be any more. You may have noticed that yourself, Brother Treanor."

"Perhaps you should speak more plainly, Mr Noble."

"When he gave the talk you invited him to give. And more recently I believe he bothered you with some of the notions he's got into his head. I imagine you realise now they were only fiction. I should never have let him read them when he's in the state he's in."

I was beginning to think Mr Noble didn't care what he said so long as it let him retrieve the journal. Brother Treanor laid a hand on it, and I saw Mr Noble grow tense with waiting, especially when the headmaster didn't pass him the book. I thought Brother Treanor was about to open it and enquire into the contents when my mother said "Does that happen to many people you know, Mr Noble?"

His eyes widened as though to fit in more innocence. "What might that be, Mrs Sheldrake?"

"How many of them end up with their minds affected?"

His eyes looked as if he'd stretched them blank. "Only those who can't cope with the truth," he said and turned to the headmaster. "You'd think they ought to, wouldn't you? You'd say it came from God."

Brother Treanor stared at him before pushing the book across the desk with the back of his hand. "Please take your property, Mr Noble. It doesn't belong here."

Mr Noble rested a hand on the book, a gesture that seemed to take possession of a good deal of the room. "I hope we're all as grateful as Mr Sheldrake deserves."

I felt as if the monks were adding weight to each other's frowning silence. It was my mother who said "Why, Mr Noble?"

"Another boy might not have turned the book in." He was still gazing at the headmaster. "I shouldn't like to think he will be punished for it," he said. "You can hardly be surprised if he was afraid to mention me."

How long had he been listening outside? Had he played the trick I previously had with the fire door? As Brother Treanor made to speak Mr Noble said "I should be most unhappy if I thought Mr Sheldrake should suffer for anything connected with me. As unhappy as I was to leave your school."

"That discussion is closed, Mr Noble."

"I'm not so sure that it was ever properly had. I wonder if the reasons you gave me would stand up if I were to take the issue further. Well, perhaps there will be no need," Mr Noble said and weighed his blank gaze on the headmaster. "May I have your undertaking that Mr Sheldrake should expect no worse than a reprimand?"

Brother Bentley might have been emitting his discontented sound on the headmaster's behalf as well. Brother Treanor drew a thin shrill breath on the way to saying "If that is what's required to terminate this interview."

"Thank you for understanding," Mr Noble said, which felt to me like the withdrawal of a threat and a sly gibe too. He cradled his journal in both hands and then hugged it to his chest all the way to the door, where he turned to face the room. "I don't imagine I'll have any further dealings with you," he said and glanced at everyone but me. "Just to ensure there's no misunderstanding, if I thought someone deserved a reminder how to behave I should arrange it myself."

As I wondered whether anyone besides me took this as more than a warning, the door shut behind him. I had no time to judge anyone's reaction before Brother Bentley said "If I catch you in another untruth you will pay doubly for it, Sheldrake."

"I think that will do for now, Brother Bentley," the headmaster said and stood up. "Thank you for attending, Mr and Mrs Sheldrake. I hope our next meeting will be under more auspicious circumstances."

Brother Bentley rose to his feet, but that was all he did. As the monks watched me let my parents out of the office, their robes seemed to darken their silence. Nobody spoke until the fire doors bumped together behind us, and then my mother said "Can't we trust you any more, Dominic?" She sounded as though she hardly wanted to be heard, and her rebuke felt so much worse than any I'd had in Brother Treanor's office that it drove Mr Noble's parting words out of my head.

CHAPTER SIXTEEN

Laughter Needs a Mouth

As we reached the railway bridge Bobby said "Why didn't your teacher's dad just tear up his book?"

Jim halted in the shadow of the arch. "I never thought of that."

"Good job there's a girl to do the thinking, then."

Once Jim and I had finished scoffing at this and rubbing our arms in response to the punches we'd earned I said "You wouldn't say that if you'd seen the book. It wouldn't be like ripping up a magazine, the way our head at school makes people."

"Were they mucky magazines?"

"Girls aren't meant to be interested in those," Jim said like someone older though not wiser. "Anyway, they weren't. The last one was just about films."

"Then whoever's it was should have stood up for it. You don't destroy things just because you're told to. They let us think for ourselves at our school."

Jim looked confused by resentment. "I bet they wouldn't let Nobbly tell you the things in his book."

"I thought you hadn't seen it."

"That's right, Dom never even showed me."

In the hope of giving Bobby no time to feel slighted by his comment I said "I copied it all down, though."

"Then it must be like one of your stories."

"That's what I thought as well," Jim said.

"Well, it isn't one," I retorted. "You ask my mum and dad if you don't believe me."

Vexation was making me thoughtless, since I wouldn't have liked anyone to ask them. I very much wanted my parents to forget about the book and the interview with Brother Treanor in particular. Even if they purported to understand why I'd behaved as I had, too many of their actions betrayed their doubts. Whenever they sent me on a message, the local word for an errand, they would count any change I brought back, though they never previously had. All too often they would ask if I was sure about something I'd just said, another tendency they'd recently developed. Even the increasing number of tasks my mother found me in the summer months – peeling potatoes or turning the mangle, taking loaded flypapers out to the bin, beating rugs on the line, pushing the carpet-sweeper through every room – felt like not just a compensation for distrust but a way of keeping an eye on me. At least my parents hadn't prevented me from seeing Bobby and Jim, perhaps because they had no reason to feel that either of my friends was a pernicious influence. Just now Bobby and Jim were as peeved as only people of our age could be. "I never said you made it up," Bobby protested. "I just meant if you let us read it it'll look like something you wrote."

"When are you going to let us?" Jim said.

"I don't know." For some reason the idea made me nervous. "My mum and dad don't know I've got it," I said. "They'd make me get rid of it if they did."

"You've still not said why your teacher's dad just hid it," Bobby pointed out. "He could have burnt it or chucked it in the bin."

"Maybe he was scared to go too far. Maybe he was frightened what Mr Noble might do if he did, or maybe he was scared of the book."

"Scared of a book." Jim dismissed the notion with a laugh. "Still, he sounded a bit mad when he talked to us," he said and halted under the railway bridge. "Hang on, here's something else I don't get. Why did he bring the book to our school?"

"He must have wanted to show Brother Treanor."

"Then why didn't he?"

"He'd have found out Brother Treanor wouldn't want to know. That's how Brother Treanor was when I brought my mum and dad in."

"But you said Nobbly's dad hid it before Trainwreck saw him."

"Maybe he was afraid someone else would see it. Maybe someone that was mixed up with his son. I'm not saying there was really anybody watching."

"Maybe he thought someone dead was," Bobby said.

She'd borrowed the idea from hearing us talk about Mr Noble, of course. All the same, the remark left me uneasy, and not just because her voice had grown an echo as she joined us in the chill shadow of the bridge

– not even because she'd given me the grotesque image of a dead face peering unnoticed from among the spectators at the sports day. We were in sight of the Norris house, where the rooms looked excessively dark despite the August sunshine, no doubt from dust inside the windows. Did a weed nod at me out of a pot in the narrow garden? A butterfly or a small bird must have weighed it down, though the colourless object that fluttered away from the house looked too tattered for either – a dead leaf, then, which I could no longer locate. "Let's hurry," I blurted, "or the big film will be on."

We'd hardly left the shelter of the bridge when the Norris house was at my back. I found myself listening for Winston and thinking that I hadn't seen the dog for months, not to mention Mrs Norris, who I gathered from my parents' wary references was still in hospital. Was her neighbour looking after the dog? I strained my ears to hear a bark, but none came. I imagined Winston lying in his basket and hoping for company, and then I wondered if he might be cowering there, too afraid to bark, because he had some. I did my best to expel the notion from my mind, because it felt too capable of alerting a presence I wasn't anxious to identify – of bringing it after me from the secretively silent house.

Beneath a blue sky patched with small white clouds a road twice as broad as ours led to the Essoldo cinema. A few more cars were parked beside the kerbs than there would have been last summer. Black bubbles swelled from the surface of the road, and we would have trodden on them to pop them if we hadn't been hurrying to the film. From behind some of the larger houses I heard the murmur of grazing lawnmowers. Otherwise there was silence apart from the flat slap of three sets of sandals on the flagstoned pavement until Bobby said "When are we going to try and get into an X?"

An old lady in a deckchair on her small front lawn flapped her newspaper like a reproof as I said "We did, remember."

"That wasn't proper trying. We never even asked."

At the start of the summer holidays we'd ventured into the Mere Lane Picture House, a local cinema that always smelled of the old gas lamps in the auditorium. It was showing a film in which Kirk Douglas played a detective, apparently so savagely that no-one under sixteen was supposed to watch, and the stare of the woman in the pay box had warned us not to bother trying. "That old cow wasn't going to let us in," Jim said. "She might have told our school if we'd said we were sixteen."

"My dad says if you don't try what you think you can't do you won't try what you can."

This sounded wise, and Jim's confession of cravenness was scarcely worthy of the Tremendous Three. How long would we have to wait before we could bluff our way into some of the films the local paper serialised? I was distracted by a sense that something not much more substantial than a wind was close to touching my neck, but when I glanced back the pavement was deserted. "Some of the girls in my class have got in," Bobby said.

"What did they see?" Jim was impatient to learn.

"The one with the monster ants, and they said you see all the ants get burnt up at the end."

While this sounded irresistible, I was preoccupied with our shadows on the pavement. I had the impression that another shadow, if rather less of one, kept dodging between them as though it was eager to catch hold of them. Or was its source struggling to take hold of theirs? A succession of clouds must be casting a series of shadows, of course, and I refused to look back. "And they saw one where some people find a thing, that's what it's called, under the ice," Bobby said. "They dig it up and the ice melts and the thing gets out and starts drinking people's blood."

I was less taken with the prospect of something disinterred and set free, and I was also troubled by glimpses in the windows of the houses we were passing. Reflected clouds were languidly unfolding in the sky that had settled in some of the bedrooms, while many of the downstairs windows framed temporary tableaus of the Tremendous Three, but I kept feeling that a cloud was about to appear behind our reflections as well – a presence unsure of its shape. Nothing of the kind let itself be seen, and so I had even less reason to glance back. "We're just going to have to look old, that's all," Bobby said.

"You'll need to look like the other girls, then."

We were approaching a post-box that a postman was emptying, and Bobby didn't speak until he drove off in his van. "What do you mean by that, Jim Bailey?" she demanded.

For once Jim's face and hers were vying with mine for redness, if not with the post-box as well. "You know," Jim mumbled, "how girls get. You don't want to hide them is what I'm saying."

She did indeed seem determined to suppress her breasts or at the very least conceal how they were burgeoning. "You don't know what I want," she retorted but stopped short of adding a punch.

"We know you'd like to see those films, don't we, Dom? We can look old enough, so you've got to."

"You think you two look that old." Perhaps Bobby thought better of scoffing, since she didn't quite. "Well, I don't need to now," she declared. "I want to see this film."

We were in sight of the Essoldo, where rakish plastic letters spelled *Knock on Wood* along the edge of the marquee. By myself I wouldn't have bothered with the film. Bobby was the Danny Kaye fan, and would come away from his films gabbling the patter that he sang. This one had a U certificate, which made me think it would be more childish than I liked, although at least we wouldn't have to ask an adult or worse still an older teenager to take us into an A, and we weren't risking the humiliation of being turned away from an X. "Shut up now," Bobby said to spur us onwards and, I suspected, to leave the discussion behind. "It's nearly on."

She was first into the cinema. A manager uniformed like the kind of waiter I'd only ever seen in films was standing by the pay box. "Just starting," he warned us, and we ran to buy our tickets before dashing to the auditorium, where an usherette at least my mother's age brought us to a halt. "You behave yourselves and don't make any noise," she said as she tore our tickets in half.

I liked cinemas with balconies, but this Essoldo didn't have one. Ranks of folding seats sloped down the auditorium to end nearly beneath the screen. The lights went down as the usherette watched us find seats towards the back. The scrape of a match on the side of a box greeted the appearance of the censor's certificate on the screen, and the first puff of someone's cigarette groped into the edge of my vision as a jolly tune accompanied the title of the film.

Danny Kaye played a ventriloquist unhappy with his job. On a flight to London he contrived to trap the leading lady in his seat belt, which was enough to send Bobby and then Jim in the direction of hysterics. I produced a few titters that were lost in the general mirth, but I was beset by a notion that there was something it wouldn't be wise to remember. How could I evade it if I didn't know what it was? If I managed to identify it, wouldn't that lodge the memory in my head?

A spy hid a microfilm inside the ventriloquist's doll to smuggle it to London, where he tried to retrieve the microfilm. As he searched Kaye's room his adversary caught up with him, pinning him to the door with a knife. The sight of the corpse looking like a hat and coat, the hat fallen over its face, reminded me of far too much. I remembered thinking that Mr Norris's coat on the hook in the hall wasn't empty enough. Bobby and Jim and dozens of people around me in the dark were laughing at Danny Kaye's failure to realise it wasn't just a hat and coat, but I was hearing Mr Noble's final words in Brother Treanor's office. Had he meant that I deserved to be reminded how to behave? What sort of reminder might he think I'd earned?

Now I knew why I'd been wary of remembering – in case thinking of it brought it. I was afraid to think of the Norris house too, and for much the same reason. Perhaps they were connected, and I couldn't help flinching as a colourless presence loomed into sight at the edge of my vision, flickering with the unstable light from the screen as it groped to take shape. It was only a cloud of cigarette smoke, but since it reminded me of the glimpses I'd had in the windows of houses on the way to the cinema, it didn't reassure me much.

On the run from the police and the villains as well, the ventriloquist took refuge in an Irish pub, where he had to sing a comic song to pass for an Irishman – the kind of song Bobby would do her best to perform all the way home. The rapid words plucked at my nerves, not least because they seemed to be obscuring another voice. It was surely only in my head, and yet I could have thought it was struggling not merely to form words but to keep hold of them, as if this might help to ground their source somehow. I was both afraid to hear and desperate to be certain what I was hearing, and so anxious for Kaye to finish pattering that I almost shouted aloud.

The song ended at last, but I could no longer hear the thin shaky voice repeating a few blurred words about a boy and pence, if I ever really had. Soon Kaye had to impersonate an English car salesman, rattling off nonsense while systematically mistaking the functions of all the controls, and Jim and Bobby competed with the rest of the audience for the loudest laugh. Was there another – a high giggle so scrawny that, despite its willingness to join in, sounded as if its owner scarcely had a mouth? A pale object in search of a shape nodded close to my shoulder, and I barely managed to swallow a cry before I identified it as another cloud of smoke jittering with light. Just the same, I blurted "What's that? Can you hear?"

Either Bobby couldn't speak for chortling or was unprepared to, but Jim muttered "What, Dom?"

"Someone laughing. Listen, there."

"Everybody's laughing." Jim stared at me, and I saw he resented having to look away from the film. "Everyone but you," he said.

"Not like them," I murmured desperately. "Not like a person. Like someone trying to be one."

"I don't know what you mean."

The shrill giggling was almost lost amid the general mirth, and our discussion made it even harder to hear, but I was starting to think that it sounded like a different species of hysteria, however much it yearned to be amused. I was striving to think how I could bring it to Jim's attention and Bobby's when a woman seated two rows ahead twisted round to glare at us. "Less of the chitchat, you," she said twice as loud as we'd been. "Some of us want to hear."

A flashlight beam poked at us before she'd finished speaking. The usherette who'd warned us about noise was sending a reminder. It and the irate member of the audience silenced me, and I felt more alone than ever, cut off from my friends not just by the admonition but by their unwillingness to listen. The laughter of the audience subsided, isolating a few final chuckles, as Kaye finished clowning with the car, and I couldn't tell when the high scarcely human noise had ceased. I wanted to believe I had never actually heard it, but my panic had left me a symptom that needed relieving. "Just going to the bog," I mumbled.

I was rather hoping Jim would follow so that I wouldn't be on my own, but he was too engrossed in the film even to respond. As I stood up the flashlight beam jabbed at me, and stayed with me all the way to the side aisle before abandoning me in the dimness by the wall. I was heading for the gents when a faceless shape swelled up beside me. Just in time to escape attracting the attention of the usherette I saw the shape was made of light and smoke.

The gents was a tiled white room with cubicles and urinals and a sink beneath a mirror. A fluorescent tube hummed intermittently to itself, jerking at the shadows, so that one of the cubicle doors appeared to keep inching open. I should have been happy not to think this looked as though someone kept peering out, just too surreptitiously to be visible. I hurried to the nearest urinal, above which graffiti had been imperfectly erased, leaving outlines that tried to seem sketchily human. I couldn't stop glancing over my shoulder, which meant that I came close to missing the urinal more than once. The room at my back was deserted and silent apart from my outpouring and a higher sound – a trickle in a pipe. An abrupt shrill stutter like a voice too eager for speech to form words was just a build-up of water that a tap let fall in a sink, and the stealthy movements here and there in the room were the fault of the nervous light. Once I was sure of having dripped my last I shook off a lingering drop and fumbled to button myself up. I was turning to the sink, though I didn't mean to spend much time there, when someone took hold of the back of my neck.

The grasp didn't feel quite like a hand. I thought it hardly could, since nobody was visible behind me in the mirror. While the chill clutch was at least the size of a man's hand, it felt no more substantial than fog. Perhaps the fog had condensed on my skin, because in the time it took me to suck in a shuddering breath it gained some of the substance of water. In a moment it grew still more solid – more like cold unstable gelatin – and I began to see a presence in the mirror. While at this stage it was ominously vague, I had a sense that it was struggling to resemble a man, if with as little success as the graffiti behind it on the wall. It had a pallor rather than a colour, though even this looked more like a notion or a memory of pallidness. For the moment the limb that ended with the object growing firmer on my neck was clearest, but the features on the gibbous bulb of a head were on their way to regaining or at any rate taking a shape. I had the nightmarish notion that the intruder meant to keep hold of me as an aid to assuming some form. I felt my skin crawl, and then I realised this wasn't the whole of the sensation. The substance of the hand was as restless as a multitude of tiny grubs, ranging about my skin as if they were eager to fasten on my flesh.

My whole body convulsed, so instinctively that at first I didn't realise I'd jerked free. I dashed to the exit, skidding on the tiled floor, almost sprawling back into whatever the intruder had for arms. At the door I couldn't help glancing around. The presence hadn't followed me. The naked whitish hulking shape was at the mirror, pressing its hands or the approximation of hands against the glass. While the face was dismayingly incomplete, now it had eyes, which were intent on the reflection – so intent that they were widening to take it in. They would have looked more human if they hadn't been twice as large as any man's eyes – no, bigger. They were swelling bigger still, and even from across the room I thought their substance was growing unsettled, separating into a mass of filaments that twitched with eagerness to grasp the sight in the mirror. Or was that a sign of distress at the spectacle? My panic was enough to send me fleeing into the auditorium.

The flashlight beam blinded me as I ran to my seat with a muffled rumble of floorboards. Jim and Bobby were too busy laughing at Kaye's latest escapade to acknowledge my return. Once I'd blinked my vision clear of the blurred patch the flashlight had left I watched the entrance to the toilets. Whenever shadows shifted there, disturbed by the light from the film, or yet another mass of smoke rose out of the dimness, I was afraid that the malformed unfinished shape with the inhumanly distended eyes was about to come for me. At least I wasn't on my own, and wouldn't my friends have to see what came? Nothing did while the film capered to its end with a succession of routines I was only peripherally aware of, and as the wall lights illuminated the auditorium I determined to be brave. "Jim," I blurted, "come and see something."

"Can't I as well?" Bobby protested.

"It's in the gents."

"Well," she said with enough defiance not to need to add "I'm going to the other one."

We all trooped to the toilets, where I let Jim go ahead of me. The tiled room was deserted. Even the pipes were silent, so that I wondered if I'd ever heard the shrill whisper that I'd thought was coming from the pipes. The shadows were still edging back and forth, but that was all. "What am I supposed to see?" Jim said.

"Maybe it's gone." I nerved myself to shove the cubicle door wide, revealing just the usual. Had I really fancied that an intruder of the kind I'd glimpsed would hide in there? "Something was here," I said, jerking my hand at the room. "Cross my heart there was."

"Well," Jim said with a touch of Bobby's resentment, "if you aren't telling I'm having a slash."

That was a strong word at our age for urinating. I had a token one as well and trudged to wash my hands. I was wary of approaching the mirror, since it was where I'd last seen the intruder. I peered at the glass and leaned gingerly closer. "Jim, look."

He didn't until he'd finished at the urinal, and then he came to squint where I was looking. "What's it meant to be?"

"Can't you see? They're finger marks."

I was sure they were, despite their swollen size and lack of whorls that would have proved they were fingerprints. Two sets of five misshapen blobs discoloured the mirror, just where I'd seen the shape resting or pressing its hands. As Jim stared doubtfully at the marks Bobby called "Can I come in? Can I see?"

"Come in," I shouted, "quick."

As she pushed the door open I indicated the marks, telling myself that despite my parents' admonition it was only rude to point at people. Bobby nudged Jim aside, which he seemed quite to like despite uttering a token protest. She was reaching to touch the marks on the glass when the door swung wide to reveal the usherette. "What do you think you're up to in here?" she said as if she'd caught us all in some intimate activity.

"We—"

This was all I managed to say before she brandished her flashlight like a club. "Get out," she cried. "Right out, the lot of you. Out of this cinema."

"We've seen the film we wanted anyway," Bobby retorted.

This enraged the usherette, who herded us up the aisle and as far as the outer doors. "We'll be watching out for you," she vowed, though the doors trapped her last word with a thud as they shut behind us. I looked back to see her talking to the manager, waving the flashlight for emphasis.

We were tramping defiantly homewards, and I'd begun to let the sunlight reassure me that we weren't being followed, when Bobby said "They were weird, those marks, weren't they?"

"I don't know what was so weird," Jim said, less like a doubt than a denial.

"I do. I touched them." As I grew nervous of hearing what she might have encountered – all at once the sunlight seemed less protective than I'd hoped – Bobby said "They were inside the mirror."

CHAPTER SEVENTEEN

The Call

That night as I tried to take refuge in sleep I heard a dog start to bark, and then another and another. Each one was closer to my house. Whatever had set them off was approaching, and I felt sure it was coming through the graveyard. As I did my best to nerve myself to look, the closest dog fell silent, and the clamour trailed away into the distance. With no lessening of panic I blundered out of bed and stumbled to the window.

A full moon was sharing its pallor with the gravestones. By its muted light I had no more than an impression that some activity had just subsided in the graveyard, perhaps only a feeble stirring of vegetation in the midst of the moonlit stillness. The longer I peered through the window to locate whatever I might have glimpsed, the more the plots in front of the stones appeared to shift as if they were eager to release their tenants. Eventually I retreated to bed, where my nervous thoughts took some time to let me sleep.

I was young enough to hope the worst was over, since nothing had followed me out of the cinema, but it didn't help that I couldn't be sure why I'd suffered the encounter. Had the intruder been a warning to stay clear of Mr Noble and his secrets, or might I have attracted it by feeling apprehensive near the Norris house? If my fears were responsible, could they bring it again? I did my best to stifle them, but they lay in wait each night when I went to bed.

Going on holiday helped me to recover. That year we stayed in a Scarborough hotel on top of a cliff. I still recall the tastes of those English summers – dinners that consisted pretty frequently of cold sliced ham and salad served with triangles of bread and butter alongside the inevitable pots of tea, and then a cornet as a treat down by the fishing boats, the lump of ice cream that you needed to be swift to lick before it dripped down your wrist, the crunch of the cone between your teeth, the last scrap of ice cream that you had to reach with your tongue or else bite off the tip of the cornet to suck it out. At first the cries of gulls above the harbour kept me awake in bed, but they seemed less ominous than the barking of the dogs had. Before our week in Scarborough was over I was sleeping all night without, so far as I could remember, even a dream.

On a day trip to Whitby I bought a paperback of *Dracula* like an unofficial souvenir of the town. I found it comforting to the extent that it reduced the supernatural to a manageable threat, permanently destroyed on the last page. Perhaps the symbols of religion – here and in *The Devil Rides Out*, another lurid paperback my parents let me buy only because it was said to be a classic – had some power after all, at least while you were reading a book. I rather wished the journals in the Stoker novel wouldn't keep reminding me of the material I had yet to show Bobby and Jim, and I was starting to grow critical as well, since I wasn't too impressed with how Wheatley made his characters lecture others on the occult instead of talking like real people. The book that caught my fancy most was *Lucky Jim*, which I found in a second-hand bookshop and which my parents barely approved of my reading. It seemed both to suggest my potential future and to engage with everyday reality in ways I'd never dreamed a book could.

It made me want to write, and to some extent the others did. By the time we returned home I was pregnant with ideas. I'd begun to find my earlier tales childish, and so I sent the three friends to university – Don and Jack and Tommy short for Thomasina, all of them renamed so as not to embarrass Jim. Don was the first to notice oddities about Professor More-Carter, their tutor – the old books whose titles he hid with brown paper covers, the unknown words he sometimes murmured when he thought nobody could hear, the way just a look from his piercing eyes could make students do his bidding. In time Tommy grew suspicious of how students who went to his room for a private tutorial would reappear paler and rubbing their necks. She and Don had to convince Jack that More-Carter was a black magician if not worse, and they'd all sneaked out of the house they shared to follow the tutor wherever midnight took him when they were interrupted. At least, I was, and before long I wished I were still in my tale.

I was at the table in my bedroom, working on *The Devil Wants the Three* while my mother loaded our very first refrigerator. Once she'd finished she would go downtown to the Co-op to collect her dividend, which everybody called a divi, and I was still young enough to relish watching the clerks in the department store on London Road shut bills in metal cylinders to be sucked along vacuum tubes to the office. I was halfway through persuading Jack to wait and see where the tutor was going, since I hadn't much idea myself, when I heard a voice. "Come here," it said.

It was high and small but urgent, and it was in the graveyard. I might not have heard it if my window hadn't been wide open on that first day of September. I told myself that it wasn't meant for me – that someone was calling a dog, because what else would anybody call on such a sunny morning, even in a graveyard? "Come back," the voice pleaded, and I thought I recognised it, which was enough to make me crane over the sill.

Mrs Norris was indeed out there, wandering among the graves. While she was hatless – the first time I'd seen her away from her house in that state – she wore flat shoes and a long summer dress colourful enough for a nursery. She looked as though someone had tidied her up, a condition she was on the way to leaving behind. "Where are you?" she begged. "Come back to me." As she spoke she started forward a few paces, only to falter and head off in a different direction, a performance that put me in mind of a bird searching for food. Then she darted towards the side of the graveyard nearest my house and halted, lifting her head. She might have been straining to listen, but she saw me at the window.

I don't know which of us recoiled further. No doubt a watcher would have found this comical. As I kept Mrs Norris just in sight she turned away and shuffled rapidly across the grass to the nearest path. I ducked my head out of belated politeness and stared at the sentence I'd been writing, but could still hear her pleas. "Aren't you here? Where have you gone? Please come to me..."

Wherever Winston might be now, I was sure she wasn't calling to him, and I was by no means certain that I wanted her appeal to succeed. I found I couldn't write until her voice grew inaudible, whether with distance or because she'd abandoned her desperate quest, and then my words were so clumsy that I crossed them out, a critical approach that it was past time I learned. I'd just written a substitute sentence that seemed to pass muster when someone knocked on the front door, hesitantly and then with some determination. "Can you answer that, Dominic?" my mother called. "I need to put all these in before they go off."

I capped my fountain pen and propped it against the spiral rings of my exercise book, and gave the page a last glance to fix my next thoughts in my head before I ran downstairs two steps at a time. I opened the front door and then bruised my fingers with keeping hold of the latch for want of knowing what else to do. "Oh, Dominic," Mrs Norris said. "Isn't your mother in?"

I wondered how she could have failed to hear, and then I remembered she was deaf. I'd been distracted because now she was closer I could see that she was wearing slippers stained by grass. "Is that Mrs Norris?" my mother called. "Let Mrs Norris in, Dominic."

Stepping back felt like retreating from somebody I was no longer sure I knew. Despite having caught me at my window, Mrs Norris had greeted me as if we hadn't seen each other for a while. Far back in her eyes I seemed to glimpse an appeal, and then it was gone. Did she want me to pretend I hadn't seen her in the cemetery, or had she put the incident out of her mind? She appeared not to realise that the front door needed shutting, and I closed it once I'd stepped aside to let her along the hall. By this time she'd remembered to say "How are you doing at your new school, Dominic?"

"All right, thanks," I mumbled, feeling shorn of more than a year.

Now that we had a refrigerator my mother was convinced that nothing even slightly perishable should remain in the larder. She was busy making room for a pot of lard as Mrs Norris shuffled into the kitchen, keeping her feet on the floor. "Sit down, Mrs Norris," my mother urged. "How are you today?"

"Just like I've always been, Mrs Sheldrake."

Our visitor took a seat at once, hiding her feet under the table. "How long have you been home?" my mother said.

"I'm sorry, Mrs Sheldrake. I should have come round sooner."

I thought this wasn't even a vague answer to the question, but my mother said "So long as you're well in yourself. Will you have a cup?"

"I'd love a real one."

Presumably she meant the tea at the hospital hadn't been to her taste. My mother was about to interrupt her task when I said "I'll make it, mum."

"He's still a good boy, isn't he?" Mrs Norris said, an unwelcome reminder of her husband's catch phrase. In fact my behaviour wasn't much unlike a lie, since it was an excuse to linger so as to hear what she might say. As I stood the kettle on the stove and lit the gas ring before its smell could reach the level my mother would warn me was dangerous, Mrs Norris said "And he's grown such a lot, hasn't he? You've got two men in the house."

She could have been making her voice even louder to hide any wistfulness, but I had an uneasy sense that it was meant for her husband to hear. I tried not to recall my encounter in the cinema or the unnatural marks within the mirror. As the water in the kettle began to grow agitated Mrs Norris seemed to gain awareness of my mother's task. "I'll have to get a fridge one of these days," she said. "And a television now they're on hire purchase."

"I expect it'll be company for you." Apparently my mother felt obliged to add "Dominic's father doesn't believe in buying things on tick. Our parents never did, so he doesn't think we should."

"You've got to let go of the past sooner or later."

I wasn't sure that Mrs Norris had convinced herself. "Forgive me if I carry on with this," my mother said as she shut the refrigerator yet again. "You aren't supposed to keep these open any longer than you have to."

"That's right, you don't want things going bad."

Did her eyes shiver as if they were anxious to avoid a memory? I was glad when the shrilling of the kettle gave me a job. As I let the tea stew in the pot, the way my parents liked it and assumed every visitor did, my mother said "Are you having a drink, Dominic? Would you like some orange now it's cold?"

Perhaps she felt I was sufficiently mature to join in any conversation or at least to listen, but I wondered if she might prefer not to be alone with Mrs Norris until she'd verified that all was well. "Yes please, mum," I said and thought Mrs Norris overstated her coo of approval.

My mother poured me a glass of juice and arranged some of the best china on a tray – two cups and saucers and a plate of biscuits. "Let's all go in the front," she said, politeness having supervened over her task.

The radiogram had a companion now – a wooden stand that held more than a dozen twelve-inch samples of classical music sleeved in flimsy paper. Once she'd sipped her tea and nibbled at a custard cream Mrs Norris examined a few of the records, murmuring over *Liebestraum* and Beethoven's moonlit melody. I wondered if she meant to put in a request, but when she sank back into her armchair without a word I suspected she was trying to prepare to speak. Rather than wait I was anxious to learn "How's Winston?"

Her gaze came back from wherever it had strayed. "I'm sorry, Dominic, he's gone."

I found the word hard to pronounce. "Gone."

"He ran off while I was away. Don't worry, it wasn't your fault even a tiny bit. The lady who was looking after him, she ought to have kept him in her house and not ours."

I was wary of asking why, but I said "Can't you tell the police? I mean, to look for him?"

"Maybe I ought to. Or maybe somebody's adopted him and he's happier with them." She sounded impatient to be done with the subject. "Mr and Mrs Middleton told me he'd gone," she said to my mother. "They came to see me from our church."

"I'm sorry we didn't visit you," my mother said.

"I wasn't expecting you to. I know you had your boy to think of. I'm just saying they told me what was going on."

"About your dog," my mother said, and I sensed that she hoped this was all.

"And the man I was telling you I took to our church. He isn't there any more."

"Oh." It was plain that my mother would have liked to leave it at that, but she said "Will that be a good thing?"

"A lot of them think so. They didn't like what he was doing with the people he brought back."

I saw how little my mother wanted to hear about this. "So long as you're happy with what your church does, Mrs Norris."

"They can't do much." In the same dismayed tone Mrs Norris said "He's started his own church."

My mother seemed to have or want to have no answer. "What's it called?" I said.

"The Trinity Church of the Spirit, Dominic. Don't ask me why."

"Where is it?" I said as my mother made to speak.

"We don't want to know," my mother informed anyone who needed telling. "And I shouldn't think you'd want to go anywhere near it, Mrs Norris."

"I wouldn't if I didn't have to." Mrs Norris took a sip of tea, and the china emitted a shrill jitter as she replaced the cup on the saucer. "I was hoping you could help me," she said.

My mother's lack of zeal was clear before she said a word. "How could we do that, Dominic's father and me?"

"That's true, he's involved as well." If the mention of my father was intended to deter Mrs Norris, it didn't work. "Last time we met," she said, "he was saying he'd be seeing Mr Noble."

"Yes, at the school."

Mrs Norris looked bewildered if not tricked. "Which school?"

"Dominic's." Rather than remind her that she ought to know, my mother said "We hadn't realised till you said his name that your Mr Noble was his teacher."

"He's getting everywhere. Does he want to take over the whole world?" Mrs Norris found a smile that looked not merely nervous but despairing, and then it grew firmer. "Well then," she said, "I should think you'll want to help me deal with him."

"You still aren't saying how."

"The school can as well. They'll have to when you tell them what I'm going to tell you."

"Mrs Norris, he isn't there any more."

Mrs Norris sounded as if she'd been promised a treat only to have it rescinded. "Where is he, then?"

"I'm afraid I've really no idea. I'm sorry, but we were just concerned that he shouldn't influence our son."

"We'll have to find out where he's gone. Is it another school?"

"I believe so, but I'm afraid we won't be—"

"You mustn't let it go like that, Mrs Sheldrake. People who know about him have to stop him while we can. He's doing worse things than he used to do."

My mother wouldn't let herself be prompted, but I was. "What things?"

"He's taken my Herbert away and I can't get him back."

I thought of the version of a hand that had clutched at my neck and the shape I'd seen groping at the mirror, and remembered the street party, where Mrs Norris had been desperate to avoid the touch of an unseen companion. "I thought you didn't like him any more," I blurted.

"Dominic," my mother cried. "Think what you're saying."

"He's right, though, Mrs Sheldrake. Don't stop him telling the truth."

As my mother parted her lips in a wordless rejoinder Mrs Norris said "I don't like what your Mr Noble's made him into, Dominic, but he's still my Herbert and I want him back."

"Has Mr Noble done it to anyone else?"

"I couldn't say. I've been away, you know."

I was aiming to suggest that she and his other victims ought to get together. "Isn't that why they didn't like him at your church?"

"They just didn't like how he'd started talking to their loved ones." With a visible effort Mrs Norris recalled "Like they belonged to him. Like they had to say what he wanted them to say, and if you got on the wrong side of him he wouldn't let them talk to you."

"But where have they gone now he's gone?"

"That will do, Dominic," my mother said, putting her cup down almost hard enough to crack the saucer. "Mrs Norris, you say you want help."

"Any you can give me, Mrs Sheldrake."

"Then just you come with us to our church."

Mrs Norris looked as though she hoped she didn't understand. "How can they bring my Herbert back to me? Can they make him how he was?"

"Maybe praying can." My mother went that far only to retreat. "If you speak to our priest," she said, "maybe he can bring you something better."

Somewhere between protesting and pleading Mrs Norris said "What's better than my Herbert used to be?"

"Peace, Mrs Norris. If you'll just let Father Kelly talk to you about your loss—"

"You don't understand what's happening. You do, don't you, Dominic? You're starting to."

"Please don't involve him, Mrs Norris. That really isn't fair. Dominic, weren't you busy in your room?"

As I made to stand up, Mrs Norris beat me to it, brushing crumbs off her lap onto the tray. "Don't trouble," she said. "I've bothered you long enough. Thank you for your hospitality and everything else you've done."

The reversion to normalcy seemed to abash my mother. "I do wish you'd give Father Kelly a chance," she said. "He won't mind that you aren't with the church, I'm certain."

"I don't think I'll risk it, thanks. I'll have to find someone else."

Mrs Norris didn't make too fast for the hall, but the sight of her stubborn back deterred any further conversation. By the time my mother and I followed her she was opening the front door. She strode onto the path, only to falter and start to turn back. "Why, Judith, there you are," a woman called across the road.

She was with a man who looked just as parental, though they were both decades younger than Mrs Norris. As she hesitated on the path they crossed the road at not much less than a march and opened our gate wide. "Judith, that will never do," the man said. "You've come out without your shoes."

"You come back with us now," his companion said, "and we'll find them."

As the man sidled behind Mrs Norris while the other nurse took her arm to lead her on the path, he gave my mother a concerned look. "Has Judith been disturbing you?" he murmured.

"Not a bit," my mother said, but her composure wavered at the sight of the nurses ushering Mrs Norris to a discreetly white vehicle near the railway bridge. "Come inside, Dominic," she said like a denial that she had been watching as well, and once the front door was shut she rounded on me. "Just you forget all that nonsense. She still isn't right in her head. I hope you didn't make her worse," she said, and I felt more alone than I'd ever felt in my life.

CHAPTER EIGHTEEN
Mother and Child

Every church is a mask which hides the truth. All religions are lies told to control the ignorant, but some of them embody codes which the enlightened may decipher. The Christians are given feeble hints of the ancient rite of the three, and the Mohammedans come trailing after them, desperate to pretend there is a solitary god. Perhaps their insistence on converting the world to their view betrays a secret fear that the world is poised to regain its primal state. The multitude of spiritualists never glimpsed the path on which they shone their tiny uncertain light, and mistook for truth the scraps of life which their efforts brought back. The likes of Conan Doyle were deluded into thinking that only the dead live in the farther dark. As the days of Daoloth draw near and the future grows ever hungrier for incarnation, perhaps the time is ripe for a religion which may speak to the enlightened while it herds its worshippers. Tina, while our minds grow equal to the unmasked truth, we shall continue to send explorers voyaging on our behalf. However weak they prove to be, their transformed shapes bring us hints of reality. Perhaps we should found a church to which they can be sacrificed in the service of the truth...

"Dom, you ought to show someone what he wrote about his church."

"They'd only think Dom wrote it," Jim said. "That's how it looks."

"You're never thinking I did," I protested.

"I'm saying anybody else would. We believe you if you say Nobbly did."

I could only hope that my friends weren't simply humouring me. Arranging for them to read my transcription of the journal had been hard enough. We'd had to pretend that Jim was helping me with homework in my room and then that Bobby had happened to come looking for us. It felt like one of the games we'd outgrown years ago, when somebody would tell the other two what to pretend – most often Bobby had been the director, since I'd been shy of proposing ideas and Jim's tended to earn him a punch.

I still disliked lying to my parents, but only because it would give them further reason to distrust me. Like quite a few of the ways I'd started to behave, I no longer felt it was much of a sin, particularly since it seemed to be in an honourable cause. "If nobody's going to believe us," I said, "we'll have to stop him by ourselves."

We were in the park opposite the graveyard. That Saturday in late September we'd gone to the Essoldo in the hope of being let into an X, only to retreat when we saw that the usherette who'd previously chased us out was standing by the pay box. We'd loitered on the swings in the playground until some children half our age wanted a turn, which made me and very probably my friends feel more childish than ever. Now we were on a park bench near the playground. "Stop what?" Jim said.

"You read all the stuff he wrote. He's using people even when they're dead."

"You said he told old Trainwreck it was just a story he'd written."

As Bobby snorted at his name for the headmaster now that she was too grown-up to giggle, I said "That's only what he wanted everyone to think. You saw what he did to Mrs Norris."

"Maybe that's how you end up if you believe all his rot."

"That's not all." I might have reminded Jim of the field in France and the prints within the mirror, but he would only have rationalised them, growing more stubborn if Bobby had sided with me. "She wants us to help," I said.

"She never asked me. Did she ask you, Bobs?"

"Give up calling me that," Bobby said, which sounded like a substitute for an answer.

"She asked me. I told you what she said and how she was. She needs us," I insisted and felt driven to add "Aren't we still the Tremendous Three?"

"Maybe we're getting a bit old for it," Jim said.

I tried not to let my silence seem too wounded, but a swing gave a squeal that might almost have been protesting on my behalf. "I'm not yet," Bobby said and looked uncertain who if anyone to touch.

"Well, maybe I'm not quite," Jim mumbled, looking variously embarrassed, and regained distinctness to say "You still aren't saying what we're supposed to stop."

"Whatever he's up to at this church of his," Bobby said.

"How are three kids meant to do that?"

"Maybe we'll know when we see what he's doing."

"So where's the church, Dom?"

"I don't know yet. I looked it up in the phone box but it wasn't in the book, and the operator said it isn't on the phone."

"Tell us how we're going to find it, then."

"We could watch his house and follow him," Bobby said, "if we knew where he lives."

"I do know," I said and jerked my thumb over my shoulder. "Opposite the graveyard."

"Couldn't be anywhere else," Jim said as if he'd forgotten we lived near it too. "How long are we going to have to watch?"

"There's three of us," Bobby said, which felt loyal to me. "We can take turns."

"Suppose he goes to his church while we're at ours?"

"I don't go any more. We never went that much."

Jim gave her a dismayed look. "Aren't you scared what may happen to you?"

"Nothing's going to. My dad says religion is the opium of the people."

"That wasn't him talking." As Bobby readied a punch Jim told her "It's what someone said who my parents don't like."

"Doesn't matter who says it if it's true, and if my dad says it is I know it is."

"And I know what mine says is."

I was trying to think how to head off the argument when I saw a woman wheeling a toddler in a pushchair towards the playground. "Look, both of you," I whispered. "That's Mr Noble's wife."

Her broad face looked determined to be placid or at any rate expressionless, but the lines stacked on her forehead didn't help. I wondered whether she'd pulled her headscarf low on her brow in a bid to cover them up. When she glanced towards us I raised a hand in a gesture even more timid than the one I used to make in class, but she looked away at once. "She'll know where his church is, won't she?" Bobby murmured.

"She's never going to tell us," Jim said under his breath.

"She might," I realised. "I don't think she'd like it very much."

As the Nobles reached the playground I heard Tina call out "Swing." Her voice was far stronger and clearer than it had been last year. I took her to be enthusing about the swings, though the word had sounded vigorous enough for a command. I could easily have fancied that her mother was flustering to obey, undoing the straps of the pushchair so that Tina could step out and march to the smaller swings like a child at least twice her age. She turned to gaze at her mother while she waited to be lifted in, and even from where I was watching across a lawn I thought her attitude looked little short of dictatorial. Her mother strapped her into a swing, and as Mrs Noble gave it a tentative push Bobby said "Well, are you going to ask her?"

"Maybe Jim better had. She won't know him."

"Who cares if she does?" Jim said, and not too quietly either.

"We don't want her telling Mr Noble we found out, do we?"

In fact I didn't want her telling him that I had, in case this brought a visit from the presence I'd encountered in the cinema. "Don't ask her where the church is," Bobby said as if she were organising us in a game. "Just ask what he's doing now he isn't at your school."

"I know what to do," Jim said but sounded close to abandoning caution. "I don't need anyone to tell me."

He shoved himself off the bench hard enough to be ready for a confrontation, and we hurried after him across the grass. Mrs Noble was pushing the swing at arms' length now, but let it start to lose momentum as she frowned at the three of us. While most of her auburn hair was tucked under the headscarf, I thought the strands she hadn't hidden were paler than last year. "I know you," she said, focusing her frown on me. "You're... "

"Sheldrake," Tina said.

I didn't know if I was more disconcerted to be named or because of who'd done so. She inched her long smooth oval face at me, which intensified its similarity to her father's. "She's right, Mrs Noble," I had to say. "She's good."

As Mrs Noble hid whatever expression she'd almost betrayed, Bobby said "Shall I push the baby so you can have a rest?"

"I'm not a baby," Tina said. "I'm Tina."

"You're not one, are you?" For longer than a breath Bobby seemed to be held by the toddler's gaze. "I can still push you," she said, "if your mummy likes."

"I don't mind," Mrs Noble said and then seemed to recollect the situation in some way. "It's up to her."

"You can push me," Tina told Bobby. "Push me past the sky."

"You like going high, do you?"

Tina raised her gaze from Bobby's face. "See past the sky," she said.

It might have been an invitation, and I glanced up as Bobby did. Perhaps not just the pale blue of the sky made it look thin as a shell. I wondered if Mr Noble had told Tina any of the things he'd written in his journal; I could easily have thought her words showed he had. As Bobby moved behind the swing to give it a first push, Mrs Noble said "How are you getting on at school, Sheldrake?"

"My name's Dominic." There was no longer any point in hiding my identity, but I wasn't about to be called by my last name when she wasn't even a teacher. It wasn't just how her question recalled one of Mrs Norris's that made me feel she was similarly anxious to pretend everything was normal, and it seemed I had to play the game as well. "I'm getting decent marks," I said.

"Yes, my husband used to say he could rely on you."

At once I was nervous of learning how much she knew. Might she have the incident with his journal in mind? Or if she was thinking of how I'd helped to put him out of a job, Jim had been involved too. I hadn't thought of a response when Tina swung down from the height of a moderate push to gaze at her mother, which looked as if she was bringing her attention down to Mrs Noble's level. "What does that mean, mother?"

Perhaps the last word was disconcerting just because it sounded too mature in such a young mouth, but I could have thought it hid some implication not too far from sarcasm. "What are you asking me?" Mrs Noble said.

She might have been taken for a parent patiently indulging a small child, and yet it seemed less than appropriate. I could have fancied that Tina resented having to descend from her next flight in the air to explain. "What does rely mean?"

"It means you can know that somebody will always do what you'd hope they would."

Tina sent her a look from the height of the swing. "You mean like father."

"Oh, yes," Mrs Noble said and returned the stare. "You can rely on him."

Was I alone in hearing more in her words than they owned up to saying? I had a sense that Tina might be meant to, but my friends seemed unaware of any of this. "What's he doing now?" Jim said.

Mrs Noble stared at him as if he hadn't understood her last remark, and Tina kept her eyes on him while she sailed down from on high. "What's your name?"

It was Tina who asked, and not very much like a child. "I'm Jim," he said.

"And I'm Bobby," Bobby said with all the breath she had left from dealing a vigorous push.

"Is that for Roberta?" At least it was Tina's mother who asked, not the toddler. When Bobby nodded with a scowl that suggested she would like to dislodge the name, Mrs Noble said "Please don't push her too high, Roberta."

"Father sends me higher. He sends me past the clouds."

"I'm sure even he wouldn't want you hurt, Tina."

Within this was a word that I wasn't sure I grasped or cared to grasp. "Can I push her this high?" Bobby said.

"Yes."

While Tina and her mother both said so, Tina's voice was stronger. I had the uneasy notion that Mrs Noble was echoing her, and not too willingly either. As Bobby gave the swing a shove Jim said "So what's Mr Noble doing?"

"No need to repeat yourself, James. I don't forget what's been said." Mrs Noble looked as though she would have used his surname if she'd known it. "He's doing what he's always done," she said.

"What's that?"

Before Jim could ask this Tina did. If she had been considerably older I would have said it sounded less like a question than a warning. "As he likes," her mother said.

How defiant was this meant to be? I was disturbed to think we were glimpsing hints of her relationship with her child and perhaps with her husband as well. If this was how mother and infant behaved in public, what might their home life be like? I saw my friends were determined to ignore the situation, and as Bobby dealt the swing another push Jim said doggedly "Isn't he still a teacher?"

"Oh, he likes to think he's much more than that." For a moment Mrs Noble looked provoked to add something other than "If you're asking about school, that's what he's doing."

"We wouldn't mind still having him, would we, Dom?"

I took Jim to be assuring her of our good intentions. "No," I said as unambiguously as I could.

"Where is he now, Mrs Noble?"

Her eyes flickered, and I sensed her nervousness. "May I ask why you want to know?"

"We're only interested," I tried protesting. "Like Jim says, we miss him."

"I should tell him, should I? Perhaps you'd like him to get in touch."

She'd narrowed her eyes as if this might hide how she was scrutinising both of us. I was wondering how closely she might think we were involved with him and his beliefs, and searching for a way to reassure her without admitting any of the issues that underlay the wary conversation, when Bobby said "What else does he do?"

She must have lost patience with our tentative attempts to learn the truth, but she left Mrs Noble yet more suspicious. "Just what are you thinking of?"

"These told me he helped people at a church."

No doubt Bobby thought this sounded innocent enough, but Mrs Noble's eyes became slits that might have been trying to shut out the world. "Helped people," she said.

"Yes, when they were—" I saw Bobby realise she was close to saying too much. "When they were sad."

"That's what they were. That's what they all are," Mrs Noble said but plainly had a stronger word in mind. "And yes, he's still up to his tricks."

This was surely our cue, but neither Jim nor Bobby seemed to know how to respond, any more than I did. Mrs Noble opened her eyes wide to gaze hard at us. "I hope none of you or your families are mixed up with them," she said.

"We aren't," Bobby said and gave the swing another push. "So where—"

"That's enough now."

The voice started on high and seemed to grow louder as it descended – loud enough to be addressing everyone below. The gesture Tina made might have been embracing us as well, unless her outthrown arms were miming flight, though surely not mimicking a crucifixion. This wasn't the whole of her movement. The top half of her body strained forward against the strap of the swing in a miniature version of her father's habitual posture, and I couldn't help thinking of a baby snake. I wondered how much of this Mrs Noble was attempting to ignore as she said "Mother's talking, Tina."

"I want to go home now. I want to wait for father."

I couldn't judge how ironic Mrs Noble meant to be by saying "Wouldn't you like to stay with your new friends?"

Tina didn't even glance at us. While the swing subsided to a halt she kept her gaze on her mother. "He doesn't want you talking about him," she said.

I don't know which daunted me more – the fancy that Mr Noble was speaking through his infant daughter or the alternative, that she was speaking for him. After a silence that felt reluctant to acknowledge its cause Mrs Noble said "I won't discuss my husband with children. Come along, Tina."

I think we all realised that she was determined to pretend she was in control. She unstrapped Tina from the swing and waited while her daughter climbed into the pushchair. As she strapped the toddler in I noticed that her hands were trembling, and I could have thought she was doing her best not to touch her child. We were loitering out of confusion and embarrassment when she turned on us. "Haven't you anything better to do except gawp?"

Bobby stepped forward. "Can I help you, Mrs Noble?"

"Of course you can't," Mrs Noble cried. "There's nothing any of you can do except leave us alone, so please do that at once."

My face grew hot enough to sum up everyone's embarrassment. As we stumbled away from the playground – Jim and I did, while Bobby marched – Tina called "Thank you for being my helper."

Perhaps she meant Bobby and the swing, but I could have thought she was contradicting her mother. I glanced back to see Mrs Noble pushing the chair towards the park gates so fast that she might almost have been following it, drawn in its wake. "Bloody hell," Jim said, the strongest words he used even when there were no adults to overhear. "That's the weirdest kid I've ever seen."

"Maybe she's how girls need to be," Bobby said.

This silenced Jim and me, and disturbed me more than I understood. "I don't care what Mrs Noble says," I declared, which felt like a bid to reunite the three of us. "We can help. We can watch the house."

CHAPTER NINETEEN
The Price of Information

"How long are we going to have to carry on with this?" Jim said.

We were crouched behind the hedge between the graveyard and the main road. As a solitary lorry passed the Noble house with a clatter of its tailgate Bobby said "How long do you think, Dom?"

"Can't it be as long as we have to?"

I was reflecting that none of the Tremendous Three would have asked Jim's question in any of their adventures when he made the difference plainer by saying "I've got footy practice later."

"Well," Bobby said as if they were competing to demonstrate the extent of their lives outside our little gang, "Elaine's coming to mine to give me a perm."

I found this so unexpectedly female that it seemed not much less than a betrayal of my assumptions about her, but then I'd taken Jim to be more committed to our mission than he was proving to be. "I can watch by myself," I said, "if you want."

"Don't make it sound like we've let you down," Jim complained. "It doesn't need us all to stay here. Just one of us can follow Nobbly if we ever get the chance."

"We weren't saying we were leaving you right now, Dom. Just there's other things we could be doing."

This only made me feel that the Tremendous Three were in danger of drifting apart, at least in the form we'd clung to for so many elongated youthful years that it felt like our entire lives – mine, at any rate. "Do we want to stop being the Three?" I blurted.

Bobby's lower lip shrank inwards, giving me a glimpse of her small not quite even teeth. "We never said that, did we, Jim?"

"We won't stop being friends, will we? Let's vow we won't for as long as we live."

I could see that Bobby realised this wasn't what I'd had in mind, but she said "We're meant to swap our blood."

"That's just in stories, Bobs. We aren't in one of them."

"We're in something like one, aren't we? Like one of Dom's."

"If we're still pretending we can pretend we've swapped blood."

I didn't know which of them made me feel more childish for wanting to preserve our bond. "All right then, let's vow," Bobby said. "Only it's got to be real, not a pretend."

"Tell us what to say, then," Jim said.

"We've got to hold hands at least."

We both took hers, and I felt an unfamiliar thrill that I couldn't quite admit to locating as her small soft cool fingers closed around mine. "We'll always be friends and we'll always look out for each other," she said. "Go on, Jim."

"Always friends," Jim mumbled as though he was determined not to be told exactly what to say, "and we'll always look out for each other."

"Dom," Bobby said and gave my hand a gentle squeeze that roused a new sensation in the pit of my stomach.

"We're always going to be friends and we'll never stop looking out for one another."

Bobby let go of my hand at once, and I was disconcerted to feel jealous because she was still holding Jim's. In a moment she released his, and I saw that she'd relinquished mine to peer through the hedge. "Someone's coming out," she whispered.

The front door of the house was inching open. I thought someone might be spying on us, and I crouched so that my eyes were just above the wall beyond the spiky hedge. I was about to grab Bobby's hand to tug her down when she copied me, and Jim did. We stayed low as the door swung inwards, revealing Mr Noble's father, who limped with his stick along the short path to the gate, making way for Tina in her pushchair. As Mrs Noble tilted it to ease the wheels over the doorstep, I could have fancied she was raising the child's face to watch the colourless October sky. Indeed, Tina declared "There's no sky" loud enough for us to hear across the road.

At first I thought that Mr Noble must be elsewhere – that we'd missed him. The rest of the family was past the gate by the time he appeared, rubbing his hands together as if he'd just washed them. I supposed he might have been writing, though I saw no trace of ink, but I couldn't help thinking of earth. "I'll finish that later," he called as he shut the door.

"Lots of time."

Though the response was surely innocent enough, it was Tina who answered. Before I had much of a chance to be disconcerted by this or to decide if her mother and grandfather were, Bobby said "Where's he taking them?"

Mr Noble had moved to the head of the party and was leading the way towards the intersection where park gates faced an entrance to the graveyard. "We'll find out," I said and started after them, keeping close to the hedge.

"His wife didn't look as if she likes it much."

"Maybe he's making her go," Jim said as though this was the way of the world.

"Maybe she should tell him he can't tell her what to do." Fiercely enough for her whisper to grow intermittent Bobby said "How can she let him make her take their little girl somewhere like that?"

This silenced us all until we came to a wary halt, because the Nobles had stopped opposite the football ground. "Maybe they're going to the footy," Bobby said.

Jim gave her a look that stayed just short of incredulous. "There's no match on."

In a moment Mr Noble turned his back on us and led his family up the nearest side street. We waited until they were out of sight and dashed out of the graveyard. We couldn't cross the main road until we'd looked both ways as we were forever being reminded to do and then loitered for an unnecessary number of cars to pass – at least half a dozen. We sprinted through an oily cloud of petrol fumes and peered around the corner of the side street. The Nobles were nowhere to be seen.

For a distracted moment I wondered if the Nobles had taken Tina to the junior school that occupied one side of the road. Of course the school was shut on Saturday, and in any case she was surely years too young. Unless they'd gone into a house they must be in a side street, two of which crossed this one. We ran to the first and saw it was deserted. We were about to make for the next one when the Nobles reappeared ahead.

Tina was leading the procession. I could easily have fancied she was directing it from her pushchair. The item she was hugging like a tribute was a bag of groceries. Her mother was wheeling the pushchair, while the men were empty-handed except for the stick Mr Noble's father seemed to need more than ever. This was all I had time to see before we dodged into the side street, trying to look casual but nearly tripping over one another. Once we were out of sight we raced to the end and around the corner. "That's it," I gasped. "You're right, we're too old for this crap."

It was the strongest word I'd ever used. It appeared to impress Jim, unless he was simply regaining his breath. When Bobby looked about to disagree I said "It's just stupid. Even if we found this church of his we'd be no use."

"Hey, hang," Jim said before he found much breath, "on. If we find, it we can fig, ure out what to, do."

"And it wasn't a waste just now, Dom," Bobby insisted. "Didn't you think it was a bit strange?"

"No." In an attempt to be less sullen I said "What?"

"Why did it need them all to go out for just that little bit of shopping?"

"Maybe they like going," Jim said, "out with the whole, family."

"Mrs Noble didn't seem to very much," I said. "Maybe his dad wouldn't either."

"Maybe they wish they, did. Maybe they're, trying."

"Or maybe someone doesn't want to leave someone on their own at home," Bobby said. "Maybe they don't trust them."

At once I was sure of it, and it persuaded Jim. "That's pathetic," he said. "I'll bet it's worst for the little girl, specially when she's so smart."

"Got to be." Jim paused, not for breath but as a mark of concern. "We'll watch tomorrow then, shall we?" he said.

"I will while you're at church," Bobby promised.

I ought to have been pleased with their renewed commitment, but I couldn't help feeling that Tina could take care of herself. Wasn't that a ridiculous notion to have about a two-year-old child? In ordinary circumstances it might well have been dangerous. We made our way homewards by a devious route through the side streets and parted at the railway bridge. "You're home early," my mother called as I let myself into the house. "How were your films?"

"I don't like cowie serials so much any more."

She came to the door of the kitchen to give me a wistful look, and a soapy smell of Omo followed her. "I expect you're growing up, Dominic."

In that case it entailed letting her think the three of us had been at the cinema. On a scale of seriousness the deception scarcely merited a mark, and I no longer thought it was a sin, but I still felt guilty for tricking my parents. I spent the afternoon in my room, reading tales based on the three laws of robotics. The number seemed to figure a good deal in my life, and next day at church I was aware how it kept occurring in the prayers and hymns – indeed, how it underlay the entire ritual. Mr Noble referred to this in his journal – "the rite which is older than humanity and which the Bible seeks to veil, both in the myth of the three persons and in its fable of the garden, though the allegory hints how man descends from the trinity who performed the ceremony of the tree, the couple and their sire born of light and chaos" – but I was still wary of recalling this while I was in church, where it felt too close to blasphemous.

Jim was waiting for me outside the porch. "Ready," he said as if we were playing hide and seek, unless it was a question.

His mother seemed to speak for all our parents. "Where are you two running off to again?"

"Just meeting Bobby," I said.

"Maybe you should both go home first."

Just then anything unexplained felt ominous. "Why?" Jim said before I could.

"To get changed," my mother said as though nobody should need to be told.

"Maybe the lads want her to see them in their Sunday best," my father said with a wink at Jim's.

Jim's father had other concerns on his mind. "Where does she go on Sundays, then?"

Jim and I risked a glance at each other, which didn't help us to respond. When we made our confusion plain his father said "I'm asking you which church."

"We don't know," Jim said as I tried saying "We never talk about it."

"Maybe you should." Jim's father frowned at us while he said "Don't go picking up any ideas of her dad's."

"Dad," Jim protested. "We know they're rubbish."

"Just so you do," my father said to both of us.

I could have done without Jim speaking for me, especially since I wasn't sure that I wholly agreed with him, but I mustn't argue right now. "Jim said," I said.

We were so relieved to escape that we almost made straight for the graveyard. Instead I headed down our road and under the railway bridge. Reflected clouds stirred in the uncurtained dusty windows of the Norris house, and I tried not to be reminded of a presence groping for a shape. Beyond the graveyard arch we tramped across the grass alongside the wall by the railway line. As we reached the expanse of lawn that the main road bordered we saw Bobby crouching at the hedge opposite the Noble house.

We were picking our way between the graves when she glanced back at us. She shook her outstretched hands in our direction and then jerked them at the house before using them to indicate that we should hunch low if not hide. I took her to mean that we might be too visible from the house, and thought of dodging from tree to tree, but much of the space between the hedge and us offered only headstones for cover. Instead I ran towards the nearest section of the hedge, belatedly slowing down to a walk in case this was less conspicuous. I saw no need to crouch by the hedge, and walked swiftly to Bobby with Jim at my back. "Didn't you see what I told you?" she demanded as soon as we were close enough for her to whisper. "Someone's watching."

"Who?" I said as Jim said "Where?"

"Up at the window. Don't let them see."

By now we were doing our best to improve on her crouch. Through the hedge I saw a curtain at the upstairs window subside into place, closing a gap. "I think they've gone," I muttered. "Maybe they didn't spot us."

We were straightening up when the front door opened to reveal Mr Noble's father. He leaned on his stick while he eased the door shut, and then he limped at speed out of the garden gate. Though a car was approaching, he clattered his stick against the kerb and lurched off the pavement towards us. The car slowed with a screech of brakes, but he ignored it while he limped across the road. "Who's in there?" he demanded fiercely though not loud.

Jim retreated from the hedge at once, halting to stare at Bobby and me. "What are you waiting for?"

"It's only Mr Noble's dad," I hissed. "Maybe he knows where the church is."

"Think he's going to tell us?"

"He might. I don't think he likes it much."

"But won't he tell Mr Noble he saw us?" Bobby murmured.

"She's right. Is that what you want, Dom?"

"No," I admitted and turned away from the hedge, beyond which Mr Noble was calling "Who is it? I know you're there." I would have led a dash across the grass, but there were people in the graveyard. "Come on, then," I urged, "only don't run."

Perhaps we were too concerned with staying inconspicuous. We weren't even halfway to anywhere to hide when I heard the peremptory rap of a stick on a path. "Don't bother trying to run off," Mr Noble's father shouted. "I saw you."

Several people who were tending graves stared at us. He'd made us sound like criminals, and my face blazed with the unfairness. Why were we fleeing? Given how he'd treated his son's journal, mustn't the old man be as uneasy about him as I was? "Wait," I mumbled as I swung around. "Let's see if we can talk to him."

He was limping fast along the path from the gate to head us off. At every other step his stick clacked on the compacted gravel. With its loose lips drooping low his flat squarish snub-nosed face might have been striving to look even less like his son's. When I crossed the grass to meet him Jim and Bobby followed me with rather less enthusiasm. As we reached the path he peered hard at Jim and me. "Where do I know you from?"

"You talked to our school about the war," I said. "You told us about the place in France Mr Noble took us to."

The old man swayed as if I'd robbed him of balance. "Which place?"

"The field where you thought somebody was waiting to be dug up."

He gripped his stick with both hands for support. "You're telling me he took you boys there."

"We went past it," Jim said. "We stayed near."

I nearly rounded on him. I'd hoped dismay might prompt the old man to reveal more about his son, but now I had to say "He went there by himself one night. We saw him."

His father's mouth shrank inwards as though he wished he needn't speak. "How close did you go?"

"We were on the road that goes past." As the old man's mouth relaxed to an extent I said "He looked like he was digging something up."

"God help us, I knew it."

He hardly seemed to be speaking to any of us or even seeing us. "What do you think he was doing?" I said.

"I need to sit down." The old man stared around him until he located a bench beside a nearby path. "Come along if you want," he said, not very much like an invitation, and made for the bench with a series of raps of his stick.

Jim and Bobby glanced at me as we trailed after him, but there was no opportunity for discussion. He sank onto the bench, which was smudged with faint shade by the doggedly evergreen foliage of a tree at his back. "Room for some of you," he said once he'd finished leaning on his stick. "Room for the young lady at least."

"I'm all right," Bobby said and stayed with me and Jim.

"Do as you like. That's what you all do these days." The old man looked sufficiently offended to have finished speaking, and when he relented we didn't gain much. "I don't want to talk about that place any more," he said. "Just be thankful you didn't go too close."

Frustration made me reckless. "Has it got something to do with his church?"

The old man clasped his shaky hands around the stick, which gave a faint nervous rattle on the path. "What do you know about the church?"

"A lady told my mum about it. She was at the spiritualist one when Mr Noble was. The lady, not my mum."

"She's a spiritualist," Jim contributed, "but she thinks this new one ought to be shut down."

For a breath that I found hard to take I thought he'd said too much, and then Mr Noble said "She's not wrong there."

"Where is it, then?" Bobby said.

"You shouldn't go anywhere near it. None of you, ever."

"Why, what's the matter with it?"

"It's just a front for what he's planning." The old man stared not so much at us as through. "You don't need to know any more," he said. "If I can't stop him, you've no chance."

"Our dads could, though," Jim said, and as Bobby glared at him "Our mums as well."

The old man's gaze focused on us but seemed to find no reassurance. "Why should they?"

"They got Mr Noble fired from our school."

"It was them, was it?" Without betraying how he felt about it Mr Noble's father said "What for?"

"For things he was saying that weren't Christian. And Dom, that's him, he found Mr Noble's book and gave it to our teacher."

If I'd known Jim meant to say this I would have done my best to stop him. It wasn't a subject I wanted to address, especially since I didn't see how it could help, but I didn't manage to hush Bobby either. "Why did you hide it?" she asked Mr Noble's father.

"You'd wonder why I bothered. It doesn't want to be got rid of, that thing." Not much less despairingly he said "I didn't want it making anybody else like him."

However little of an explanation this was, I didn't feel eager for more. "So do you want us to tell our parents?" I said.

"I don't suppose it can hurt if they spread the right word. Maybe more people can do more than me." The old man squeezed his eyes shut, gathering wrinkles around them, and closed his hands together on the stick as if he were about to pray. "It's in Joseph Street off Kensington," he said. "I just hope they'll be quick."

"Why," Bobby said, "what's going to happen?"

"Pray you never find out." More to himself the old man said "I don't know how much time I've got. I won't have him using me after I'm gone."

While Jim was as reluctant to speak as I felt, Bobby said "How do you mean?"

The old man's eyes fluttered open as though the right lid had to overcome a droop. He might have been wakening to the situation, because he gave us all a searching look that plainly failed to satisfy him. "Well," he said, "are you going to tell your parents?"

My answer wasn't quite a lie. "We'll see what they say."

"Come on, then," Jim said, catching the spirit of the deception. "I expect they'll be at home."

We were turning away from the bench when Mr Noble's father said "You don't know what to tell them. I haven't told you enough."

Bobby grabbed Jim's arm and mine, having swung around. "Tell us now, then."

"No," the old man said, levering himself to his feet. "I'll tell them."

For a number of reasons this struck me as inadvisable. "We can," I said. "We'll make them see."

"They need someone to show them how serious it is. Just take me to them."

"We aren't going home yet," Jim said at once.

"I thought you told me you were. Yes," the old man said as if the effort to remember enraged him as much our deceitfulness, "I know you did."

"Come on, you two," Bobby said and turned her back on him. "We've got to be somewhere else."

"Don't you walk away from me while I'm talking," the old man said louder. "Just you wait for me."

We could only ignore him. We were making to retrace our route when I muttered "Don't go straight home or he might see."

We veered towards the allotments, not quite running. I felt as if the clacks of the stick on the path were driving us onwards. "Don't try and run away from me," the old man shouted. "I'll find you, don't you fear."

Most of the people at the graves were watching us now. Some of them gestured as though we needed our attention drawn to our pursuer. Bobby pointed at her head and twirled her finger, a mime that didn't seem to please them. They were the reason we were trying to appear guiltless by not breaking into a run, though I was more afraid that Jim's parents and mine might hear the old man's shouts and look for the cause. When we reached the gates the rapid clatter of the stick was still keeping pace with us. "Don't go home yet," I muttered. "Let's not stay on this side of the road."

The main road was deserted except for the occasional passing car. All the shops were closed on Sunday, and most of the local folk would be at home or in the park, where I was more than wishing we'd gone instead of rousing Mr Noble's father. As we ran across the tram tracks in the middle of the carriageway I heard the stick rap the pavement and then the tarmac of the road. "I'm still here," Mr Noble's father shouted. "You won't get away from me."

We trooped along the pavement on the far side of the road, still miming innocence for the benefit of anyone who might be watching. The determined clatter of the stick was following us along the middle of the road, beside the tracks. How far did Mr Noble's father mean to chase us? Wouldn't he ever grow tired? I'd begun to feel desperate to bring the pursuit to an end, and then I saw the railway bridge that crossed the road ahead. "Let's go round the bridge," I urged. "Maybe we can lose him."

The insistent knocking of the stick gathered speed while we hurried to the arch. The bridge greeted us with a wide-mouthed squeal of metal as a tram swung around a bend ahead. We were almost at the bridge when I heard a cry of rage behind us. I thought Mr Noble's father had realised the tram might hide us from him, but his stick had lodged in a tram track, and he was struggling to free it. "Come out," he snarled.

The tram sped under the bridge, and a spark turned the stonework a hellish red. The old man stared at the oncoming vehicle but didn't relinquish the stick. He looked as if he thought his infirmity meant the tram had to give way to him. We might have dashed to save him – all three of us started towards him, not even watching out for traffic – but the tram was already closer to him than we were. "Get out of the way," I yelled.

"Leave it," Jim shouted.

"Let it go," Bobby begged loudest of all.

We were all shouting at once, and I never knew how much the old man might have heard. "My wife gave it to me," he protested, turning away to throw his weight into a last yank at the stick.

His words were almost blotted out by an agonised screech of brakes. As the stick jerked free, he staggered sideways. One foot caught the track, and he fell face up across the path of the tram. Jim and I shared the same unspoken instinct. While I suspect we would never have looked away if we'd been on our own, we spun Bobby around and turned our own backs on the old man's fate. We couldn't avoid hearing, and the sound of the wheels had never reminded me so much of a bacon slicer. Did I hear another piercing noise amid the shriek of brakes? It fell silent before they did.

Once there was silence except for the cries of passengers I risked glancing over my shoulder. I still wish I never had. I looked away at once, shaken by a convulsion that made Bobby squeeze my arm. Mr Noble's father was in far too many pieces behind the tram, but I wasn't sure whether the bulk of him had just finished twitching like a decapitated chicken – a bird shorn of its entire head, not just the upper half.

CHAPTER TWENTY

Visitors

That night was the next time I saw Mr Noble's father. My mother had urged me to go to bed early, since despite witnessing the old man's death I'd insisted that I didn't need to see the doctor. A large mug of Horlicks was designed to help me sleep. To my surprise it must have, since the clamour of my fears and other thoughts eventually subsided and left me alone, abruptly unaware of the dark.

I didn't know how soon I heard the barking. The dog was somewhere in the distance, and at once I hoped there would be no closer sound. When a second animal began to yap I did my best to think it was at least as far away, but once a third dog joined in I couldn't pretend that they weren't increasingly nearer. Did they have to mean that something was on its way to my house? While I dreaded finding out, waiting to learn might be worse. Though the bedclothes seemed eager to keep me where I was, I struggled free and stumbled to the window.

Clouds like faded skeins of the October moon patched the black sky. Though the moon wasn't quite full, it appeared to have grown brighter to compensate, driving all the stars into the far dark. It blanched the grass in the cemetery, which looked as if the earth were sprouting slivers of stone. Or perhaps the headstones were draining the grass of colour if not life to aid their own kind of growth. I found I was thinking all this to avoid looking for activity in the graveyard, where the shadows beneath the trees seemed unnecessarily black. With a good deal of reluctance I grasped the edges of the table and leaned closer to the window, and glimpsed movement within a shadow on a path.

Before I could retreat, having decided that I really didn't want to see, Mr Noble's father emerged into the dead light. Although he was limping – indeed, lurching as if he no longer quite knew how to use his legs – he didn't have his stick. Apparently he needed both hands to keep hold of whatever headgear he was wearing, even though the night was windless. Then I saw what I was desperate to avoid seeing: that he wasn't wearing a hat after all. The item he was trying to hold in place was the upper section of his head, and now it slipped askew. It was sliced diagonally, and I watched the fleshy corner that contained the left eye slide down the cheek and off the head. I couldn't entirely choke back a scream, but although it wasn't much of a sound it made the intruder in the graveyard aware of me. One hand clutched at the scalp and lifted the portion of the head, extending it in my direction like a ghastly lantern kindled by the moonlight. Its solitary eye blinked at me, and behind it the rest of the head opened its mouth. "Dominic," it said, "help me," and as the figure hitched itself towards me at a speed that suggested it needed to keep up with the section of the head it was brandishing by the hair, I did my utmost to let go of the table and shove myself back from the window. I couldn't move, and so I put a dismaying amount of energy into a feeble scream.

"Dominic." The voice was growing higher. "Look at me."

"Won't." I was straining to pronounce the childish word when I realised that my eyes were shut. Just a single dog was barking, but why couldn't it chase away the figure that was tottering across the graveyard as though its legs were about to collapse into fragments? "Make him go away," I mumbled by no means as loud as I meant to.

"Dominic, there's nobody. There's just me."

As I tried to find some reassurance in this I saw the figure leave more than its feet behind, only to land on the unequal stumps of its legs and sway wildly from side to side as it hobbled with appalling determination towards me. No part of me except my mouth would move, and so I concentrated on producing another enervated scream. "Dominic, wake up," the voice urged. "We're both here now. Here's your father."

My eyes took quite a time to open while the barking somewhere near the graveyard faltered into silence. My mother was kneeling by my bed, and my father was silhouetted against the light above the stairs. "Are you awake now, son?" my mother pleaded. "Talk to us."

"Mall rye." With an extra effort I succeeded in pronouncing "Own lead ream."

"Who was leading something, son? I can't understand you. Wake up properly, there's a good boy."

The echo of Mr Norris's old phrase jerked at my consciousness and seemed to bring my body into focus. "I said I knew it was a dream, mum."

"Are you sure? You didn't sound as if you did."

She might almost have been asking if it had been real. I was certain that it hadn't now, but I wished I didn't know the reason. "I do now," I said.

"Well, don't go having it again." I saw her realise this sounded unreasonable and turn her anxiousness on my father. "I said we should have taken him to the doctor," she complained.

"Don't make him worse, Mary." As she gave him a look that foretold an argument my father said "Do you want us to stay till you're asleep, son?"

I imagined struggling to lose awareness while they watched or pretending to sleep so that they wouldn't keep me awake. "I'll be all right knowing you're in your room," I said.

"You keep telling yourself that," my mother said. "And tomorrow we'll see about the doctor."

She plainly thought I'd been traumatised – upset, she would have said, or shaken up – by the old man's death, though I'd let my parents think I had seen no details. I didn't understand how a doctor could cure me of dreaming, since the dream was just a substitute for worse. I knew it was a dream because I feared the old man would return not in that form but as something like the presence I'd encountered in the cinema. I was afraid he might visit me because I'd caused his death by trying to elude him. In that case, wouldn't he come back to Jim and Bobby too? The thought failed to comfort me once my parents left me with it in the dark.

I must have slept again, since I woke up. When I stumbled down to breakfast, almost missing at least one stair, I saw that my parents were waiting to speak. My mother was sprinkling a second layer of sugar on a bowl of cornflakes while my father poured a glass of chilled milk. "You look as if you've hardly slept, son," my mother said. "Would you like to stay off school?"

"No, I'll go." Mr Askew was our form master this year, and I'd lent him my latest tale when he'd asked what I was writing now. "I need to," I said.

"Don't put him off school, Mary. We don't want him falling behind."

"I wasn't trying to," my mother said and turned to me. "What about your friends? Will they have been to the doctor?"

"I don't know, mum. They didn't see any more than me."

"I'll be finding out. Eat up or you'll be late for school."

I wanted to foil her plan, but I couldn't think how or even precisely why. At least I should warn Jim and Bobby, and I downed my breakfast so enthusiastically that I was told not to gobble and not to make myself sick. The instant I'd finished I hurried to stuff myself into my coat and grab my satchel.

Autumn was heaped around the trees, where people had brushed leaves from the pavement in front of their houses. A few rusting leaves clung to the flagstones, and I skidded on some as I made for Jim's house. I couldn't see or hear him anywhere, and was wondering if I should knock when he and Bobby appeared on the corner of the main road. They had their backs to me, but Jim lifted a cupped hand in my direction, and then Bobby threw her arms wide in an outspread shrug. A pang in my guts sent me forward, but I wasn't close enough to hear my friends by the time they noticed me. "What were you talking about?" I demanded.

Jim grimaced at the subject or at me. "What do you think?"

"It isn't like a story any more, Dom," Bobby said.

"Not a story we ought to be in, anyway," Jim said.

"We are though, aren't we?" More like my fictitious character than the irrationally jealous adolescent I'd just been, I said "We don't want Mr Noble's dad to have died for nothing."

"I don't know why he had to die like that at all," Bobby said, rubbing the shadows under her eyes with a finger.

"It wasn't our fault," Jim protested. "He shouldn't have kept coming after us."

"You remember why he did, though," I said. "If we fix that we'll be helping him."

"We'd have to pray to help him now," Jim said, though not to Bobby. "He's gone wherever he's gone."

Bobby looked as embarrassed as this kind of talk had begun to make me. "Fix what, Dom?"

"See our parents do what he wanted them to do. That way he won't have died in vain."

I thought my friends didn't care for my writerly choice of words until Jim admitted "I didn't tell mine what he said. I just told them he got run over."

"I didn't even tell mine what we saw," Bobby said. "My dad's got enough to bother him at work. He thinks they want to fire him for getting people to join the union."

I felt unnecessarily confessional for saying "I think my mum's going to talk to yours and Jim's."

"What about?" Bobby said more fiercely than I understood.

"About what we saw. I had a bad dream in the night and woke them up."

"I didn't," Bobby said with defiance if not pride.

"Me neither," Jim said.

Bobby stared at me as if she thought I'd let the team down. "I've got to go to school," she said and stalked across the road.

Jim raised his eyebrows and wriggled them like a comedian. "Girls," he declared.

"Bobby's Bobby," I objected. "She's not girls."

"She's one, or haven't you been noticing? I've noticed quite a bit lately, me."

I felt uncomfortable with him as I never previously had. "We shouldn't talk like that when she isn't even here."

"If she was we'd get a punch," Jim said and watched her step onto the platform of a bus, baring a glimpse of leg. "Or maybe we wouldn't," he said more to himself than to me. "Maybe she wouldn't mind."

"I want to keep her as a friend."

"She can still be that, can't she? Maybe she'll be more of one."

Since we'd gone this far I had to learn "Are you going to ask her out, then?"

At once Jim looked as awkward as his size sometimes made him. "Bit soon for that," he muttered.

I wasn't sure if he meant our and Bobby's age or his relationship with her. At least he seemed to have no intentions that I needed to be jealous of, not that I was entitled to be or would have had a reason I could bear admitting to myself. I think Jim was as relieved as I was that he could end the discussion by saying "Here's the bus."

Brother Treanor had some words on health for the school that day – how sins would rot our souls just as too many sweets would rot our teeth. I found myself wondering if there was a spiritual equivalent of chewing gum, which advertisements assured us would clean the sugar off our teeth. Perhaps prayers were meant to be the gum, not least since both ended up in your mouth. Until recently I wouldn't have dared to indulge in such thoughts, but now I was tempted to write them. Since they would feel out of place in a tale of the Tremendous Three, perhaps it was time I wrote something else.

Just the same, I was eager to learn what Mr Askew thought of my new story, where Don and Jack and Tommy destroyed Professor More-Carter's occult powers by burning all his books. I suspect that as well as Mr Noble's journal I had Ray Bradbury's new book in mind. Mr Askew took our class for the second lesson of the day, and when he limped over to my desk I did my best not to be reminded of Mr Noble's father and his dogged uneven pursuit. "Sheldrake, I haven't had time to give your work the perusal it deserves," he said. "I promise you it is on top of my heap to read."

This felt like a hole in my day, even though I could look forward to his comments. It left space in my mind for thoughts of my mother and Bobby's and Jim's. As Jim and I made for home in a twilight that smelled like a ghost of smoke I was hoping that the situation might be resolved without involving us too much. The Three had had their latest adventure, after all. But as we crossed the carriageway while the policeman mimed our safety I saw Bobby and her mother heading for our road.

Mrs Parkin looked readier than Bobby to wait for us. I blamed my talk with Jim for making me wonder if Bobby's breasts would grow to match her mother's, which were so generously prominent inside her tautly buttoned overcoat that they seemed capable of unbalancing her small wiry frame. I felt my face turn red, but Mrs Parkin ignored whatever guilt it might have been betraying. "That's handy," she said. "We'll just pick up your mother, Jim, and go along to Dominic's. We've been having a word and now we want another."

"What about?" I had to ask.

"Roberta's already asked me that. We'll talk about it when we're all together."

As she bustled along the street she kept glancing back to urge us onwards if not to make sure we weren't having a surreptitious discussion. We waited beneath a tree tattered by October while she rapped on Jim's front door, which Mrs Bailey opened so nearly instantly that she might have been waiting for the signal. As she saw Jim her placid padded face snatched at a frown. "You're there," she said as if he'd strayed. "Hurry up and come along."

She followed us while Mrs Parkin led the way, and I suspect I wasn't alone in feeling like an escorted prisoner. I wanted to run ahead of Bobby's mother so that I could at least let everyone into my house, but she was first at the door. She had to knock twice before my mother opened it. "Here you all are," my mother said, not entirely like a greeting. "Well, come in."

She showed everyone into the front room, which I saw she'd tidied for the occasion. As Jim's and Bobby's mothers left a space between them on the couch she said "Would anyone like something to drink?"

"I've had enough tea for one afternoon," Mrs Parkin said. "And Roberta doesn't need anything."

Perhaps Bobby had already had a drink at home, but it sounded punitive. Out of loyalty I said "I don't either."

"Nor me," said Jim.

"You three can sit down at least," my mother said, perching on the edge of the chair by the radiogram.

Mrs Parkin slapped the space in the middle of the couch to summon Bobby, where she looked like a prisoner flanked by warders. Once I'd sat on the remaining armchair and Jim took the arm Mrs Parkin said "So what haven't you told me, Roberta?"

"I didn't want to worry you or dad. He said he isn't sleeping."

"Never mind him just now. He's not here. What should you be telling your mother?"

As Bobby sucked her lower lip in and gripped it with the upper one, Mrs Bailey said "Shall we go a bit gently? We don't want anybody more upset than they have to be."

"It won't help to keep it in," Bobby's mother said. "Talking, that'll help."

Bobby released her lip with a small empty sound. "We saw their teacher's dad get run over."

"We didn't really see," Jim said. "We didn't want you seeing."

"I could take it just as much as you, Jim Bailey."

"Nobody's saying you're not strong," Bobby's mother told her. "That's how we've brought you up, so get on with the truth."

"I just did."

Mrs Bailey's face stiffened into composure. "We've heard that wasn't everything that happened."

I don't know how accused my friends felt, but I was loath to speak. "It was, though," Bobby said.

As Mrs Parkin let out a breath ferocious enough to shake a lock of Bobby's hair, my mother said "Miss Mottram saw you from her shop. She says the gentleman was chasing all of you."

Bobby gazed at Jim and then at me, and I saw they both felt it was my responsibility to answer. Why had Miss Mottram needed to be in her shop on Sunday when you weren't meant to work on the Sabbath, even hang out washing? "Assertive," I mumbled.

"What was that, Dominic?" Mrs Parkin said. "We didn't hear."

"He was sort of," I said again, though with more consonants. "After us, I mean."

"Why," Mrs Bailey said, "what had you been doing?"

"He wanted somebody to hear about Mr Noble's church. Mrs Norris said about it, mum, remember."

My mother wasn't letting this placate her. "Why would he want any of you?"

Jim shifted uncomfortably on the arm of the chair, cramping my space. "He knew Dom and me from when he gave a talk at school."

"Mrs Sheldrake's asking why he'd think you three could help," Mrs Bailey said.

"He didn't," I said before anybody else could speak. "He thought all of you and our dads could."

"Then why were you running away from him?" Mrs Parkin said.

My face was growing hot with my efforts to manufacture an answer when Bobby found one. "Like I said, we didn't want him bothering my dad. He was trying to follow us home because we wouldn't tell him where we lived."

Mrs Parkin stared at her and then shut her eyes for the duration of a weary nod. "Fair play, Roberta, we believe you. Don't we, ladies?"

"It looked worse than it was," Mrs Bailey said and hastened to explain "Not the poor man's passing. Your side of it, the three of you."

"It was tragic but it was an accident," my mother said. "Try and forget about it now, all of you. It wasn't any of your doing."

This seemed to end the discussion, which I thought had achieved nothing at all. As Jim's and Bobby's mothers set about standing up I said in desperation "He told us where the church is."

Mrs Bailey frowned at Jim. "Why would he want to tell you?"

"Because he wanted everyone to know, mum."

She and Mrs Parkin were on their feet, and I did my best to delay them by saying "It's in Joseph Street off Kensington. It's the Trinity Church of the Spirit, like Mrs Norris said."

"Well, I don't know what we're supposed to do about it," Mrs Parkin said.

"You saw how Mrs Norris was at the coronation party. She's got worse, hasn't she, mum, and Mr Noble's father was like that as well."

"You're saying he wasn't quite right in the head," Mrs Bailey decided. "All the more reason why we shouldn't get involved."

"We don't want anyone like that telling us what to do," Bobby's mother told Jim's and mine.

"Mum," I protested, "Mr Noble made them like that, didn't he? Maybe he's doing it to other people too. Don't you think somebody should stop him?"

"They saw how he was at the other church and sent him packing. I expect they will at this one if he's still up to his tricks."

"How can they? It's his church."

"Come along, Roberta," Mrs Parkin said and turned towards the hall. Bobby didn't stand up until she'd asked "Are you going to tell dad?"

"I'll tell him what you should have told us. I don't fancy he'll be too concerned about this church."

"That's us as well," Mrs Bailey said and waited for Jim to follow her. "We may not agree with what someone believes, but if it's not against the law it isn't up to us to interfere. There are too many people wanting to tell others what to think."

I felt left behind with my useless thoughts, and not just by my friends. Bobby sent me a wave as she went out of the gate, but the gesture looked too feeble to be meaningful. "See you tomorrow," Jim called from the street, but I didn't feel this promised much either. As my mother shut the front door I said "Will you say to dad?"

"I'll tell him what we had to find out, yes."

"I mean will you say what Mr Noble's dad wanted?" When she opened her mouth to show me her silence I said "He wanted it so much he got run over."

"Don't you try to force me, Dominic. Just you remember you're the child here. You don't tell your parents what to do." As I wondered how much of her anger was embarrassment left over from the mothers' meeting she said "Now make yourself scarce. Go and write one of your stories," and I trudged upstairs past "Thou God See All", feeling more alone and misunderstood than ever.

CHAPTER TWENTY-ONE

At the Window

"Your mother's right," my father said. "It's up to them at the church to sort him out."

We were at dinner, and my mother had relented, even if it came with an unspoken warning not to argue. She'd given me the second biggest lamb chop and kept the smallest for herself. No doubt she would have said I needed feeding to help me grow up, but it felt like an apology for her having been unreasonable earlier. It let me risk saying "But he's the one who made the church."

"If he's made it up it oughtn't to last long."

"Don't you think he could fool people? You met him."

"I told you before, Dominic," my mother said. "If the people there can't see through him that shows them up for what they are."

"It's not their fault," I pleaded, "is it, mum?"

"Just pray God shows them the right road," my father said and applied himself to chewing a mouthful of his chop.

I was tempted to tell my parents everything about Mr Noble that I'd kept from them, but they would just have been dismayed that I'd grown so credulous if not dangerously deluded. Perhaps I could have shown them my copy of his journal, but what would this have achieved beyond demonstrating how devious I was? My father's last remark had sounded as unanswerable as the final words of a sermon. He and my mother had made up their minds, and I hardly needed to ask Jim or Bobby if their parents had. I did need to learn if my friends had been visited by anything unwelcome, not to mention dead, but they hadn't even dreamed they had.

Did this mean I'd been singled out for visiting? I was afraid our failure to make our parents intervene might bring Mr Noble's father back in whatever shape he'd taken. I lay awake for nights, fearing that my very fears about him might attract him. When he repeatedly neglected to put in any kind of an appearance I managed to start catching up on my sleep, if only to stop my mother scrutinising my face for signs of insomnia every day at breakfast. More than once a dog wakened me in the night, but I managed to convince myself that the barking didn't herald Mr Noble's father, and was able to take refuge in sleep.

I have to admit that from feeling pitifully grateful to be spared any nocturnal visits I began growing less concerned about Mr Noble's church. Perhaps my parents were right, and once its members realised they were being used it would destroy itself. Meanwhile I had distractions in my life, and Mr Askew's comments weren't the least of them. He'd kept his word about my story, returning it to me the next day. "So, Sheldrake," he said, tapping the cover with a swarthy nicotined forefinger. "I see you've been reading trash."

My face grew so hot that it made my lips awkwardly stiff. "Which, sir?"

"The wretched Wheatley. Christian doesn't always mean worthwhile, you know, not when it comes to the arts. Find yourself Charles Williams if you want to see that kind of thing done at a higher level. Or if you're ready for more realistic fare, search out Graham Greene."

This seemed sufficiently encouraging to let me blurt "Was the story any good, sir?"

"I believe it shows promise." Mr Askew grimaced, but only at his leg as he took a step away from my desk. "Study better models," he said, "and you'll improve as a writer."

His words took their time over making themselves felt, but when Jim and I encountered Bobby on our way home I couldn't help announcing "Our form master says I might be a writer."

"We already knew you were," Bobby said and halted on the corner of her road. "Why'd he say?"

"I gave him my new story to read."

"Can we see?"

I feigned reluctance, which was how I thought a writer would behave, while extracting the book from my satchel. I opened it at the tale and handed it to Bobby, who took hold of it so delicately that she might have thought it was as fragile as my feelings. As she began to read, Jim glanced at the page and away. "You're still writing about us."

I heard the objection he didn't need to make clearer. "Maybe I'll stop," I said, "when I've read the writers Mr Askew said I ought to read."

"You don't have to stop for me," Bobby said.

I saw Jim decide not to start an argument. "See ya round," he said like someone in a film I couldn't place.

"See ya tomorrow," I called after him.

Bobby was too engrossed in my tale to contribute. When she turned the book towards the nearest streetlamp to catch more of the misty light I said "Do you want to take it home?"

"We don't want it getting wet, do we?" Bobby said and shut the book to place it with some care in her schoolbag. "It's good. I'll bring it back tomorrow."

I was belatedly aware that we were alone together. I felt awkward enough to flee and yet eager to prolong the togetherness. Having fumbled for some words, I let loose the first that came to mind. "Have you heard about the film about the girls' school, what's it called, St Trinian's?"

"Some of my friends went. They said it's tops."

"So do you want to go and see it sometime?"

"We can on Saturday if it's on. Maybe there's a cowie on with it somewhere so Jim won't feel done out of a film."

It wasn't long since he'd decided only Westerns were worth watching, or at least films with guns in. Bobby had given me the best cue to speak that I was likely to get, but my words felt like a lump that was clogging my mouth, and my face had grown painfully hot before I managed to dislodge any of them. "I meant," I mumbled, "what I mean, I mean shall just us two go so he won't think we've made him?"

Bobby faced me, and the streetlight glinted in her eyes. "Are you asking me out, Dom?"

"Er." I followed this with "I mean, if you like."

"I don't, then."

I didn't realise how much of me had been clenched around hoping for a different answer until I felt how hollow I'd become. "Right," I said, and with even less conviction "Okay."

"Don't you want us to stay friends, Dom?"

I grew conscious that Miss Mottram was watching me between booklets in the window of her knitting shop near the streetlamp. "I didn't say I didn't," I said with little sense of how this sounded, or concern about it either.

"If we try and be more we might end up not even that. I know girls it's happened to."

The clutter of my emotions didn't let me appreciate the sense of this. "See you when I see you," I said in a bid to flee.

I hadn't turned away when she reached into her schoolbag. "Do you want this back?"

"I wasn't giving it you to keep."

"No," Bobby said as if I'd threatened to retrieve more than the book, "do you want it now?"

This felt far too close to ending our friendship. "You can have it till you've read it," I mumbled, "if you still want."

I must have been infecting her with clumsiness. Miss Mottram watched us turn our awkward backs on each other without finding any more words. Once Bobby was out of sight I tramped home too fast to think, even of how I might look to my mother. I'd eased the front door shut and was sneaking upstairs, hoping not to be accosted, when she came into the hall. "Dominic, what's the matter now?"

I could only voice the thought that came to my rescue. "Mr Askew says I ought to read different books."

"Well, I'm sure your teacher must know best. You try doing as he says."

I escaped up the stairs to begin my homework, and by dinnertime I was able to pretend all was well. That night, however, thoughts of Bobby – quite a few of which would have earned Brother Treanor's wrath – rather than of unwelcome visitors made it hard for me to sleep. I didn't see her in the morning, and on my way home I couldn't decide whether I was hoping to meet her or the opposite. She was waiting on her corner with her schoolbag in her arms, and produced my book at once. "It was good," she said and immediately made for home.

Jim blinked at me. "Have you two had a fight?"

"Ask her," I said and instantly panicked. "No, don't say anything, all right? We just had a bit of an argument. It wasn't about you."

Another blink left his eyes narrow. "Why's it going to be about me?"

"I'm saying it wasn't. That's why you needn't ask."

He was plainly less than satisfied, but I wasn't going to explain. I'd alienated both my closest friends, and I didn't know what to do. At least by next morning he appeared to have forgotten our exchange, unless he was somehow biding his time, but Bobby was another matter. If my parents had an argument while I wasn't there I could always tell by how they behaved afterwards, treating each other so politely that it made the house feel starved of air. Now Bobby and I were acting like that, and Jim didn't help. As we set about planning our Saturday, which felt more like an obligation now, Bobby's dutiful enthusiasm and my token zeal provoked him to demand "What's up with you two?"

"It was nothing. It's been sorted," Bobby said. "Just be here tomorrow."

It was Friday evening, in our usual place for meetings and farewells, beneath the streetlamp on the corner of her road. Jim and I were back there well before noon, the time we'd all agreed. I think it was Jim who first looked at his wristwatch, whose face boasted more dials than my watch did. By ten past twelve we were competing at timekeeping, and Jim said "We'd better see what's kept her."

I wasn't sure I wanted to find out, but I trailed after him. Mrs Parkin opened the front door, a slab of oak with a lion-headed knocker and ambitions to confer seniority on the house. "Isn't Bobby coming to the film?" Jim said.

Mrs Parkin frowned and spoke low. "Not this week."

"Why," Jim said while I sensed that he was avoiding my eyes, "what's... "

"Nothing boys should talk about." Mrs Parkin's scowl might almost have been weighing her voice down. "Or know about either," she said.

Jim's face turned practically as red as mine must have. "Sorry," he mumbled. "Didn't know."

"Tell her," I blurted, "we hope she gets well soon."

This was a bid to regain Bobby's friendship, but her mother's unrelenting frown suggested it was inappropriate. "Make sure you don't mention it when you see her," Mrs Parkin muttered and shut the door.

I felt close to disloyal for going to the film. Having seen from the list of cinemas that occupied an entire column on the expansive front page of the *Echo* that the giant ants had flown to the Essoldo cinema opposite the Co-op in London Road, we'd determined to bluff our way in. The girl in the pay box gave us searching looks but took our half-crowns for a seat each in the circle. Though the ants looked a little like colossal soft toys to me, the idea of giant toys on the rampage was disturbing enough, especially since the film began with a little girl whose mind was damaged by what she'd seen. I couldn't help thinking of Tina Noble, which brought me back to Bobby and how she'd formed an almost maternal or certainly sisterly bond with the toddler. It felt as though too much in my life was eager to converge, though I could never have foreseen how it would.

On Monday Bobby was back at school. When we met her on the main road I tried not to imagine what she was feeling like, however fanciful my version would have been. "How was your film?" she said.

"It was fab," Jim said. "We'll see it again if you like, won't we, Dom?"

As I agreed so vigorously it might have sounded fake, Bobby said "I'll see how I feel at the weekend."

This reminded Jim and me what we were forbidden to discuss, and it seemed to infect with wariness anything we said to her. That was how it felt to me until the middle of the week, when I had to tell her and Jim "I can't come out on Saturday."

"Why, what's wrong with you?" As Bobby stared at Jim he attempted to take back his stress on the last word by saying "What's wrong with you now?"

"The school nurse's sent me to the dentist." In a sally at bravado I said "Just some fillings."

"You poor bastard," Jim said, another of the words we'd begun to use when adults couldn't hear.

"I've had one," Bobby said and pointed at a greyish lump embedded in a back tooth. "Nothing to cry about."

"I won't be crying," I retorted and saw her thinking I'd rebuffed the bluff sympathy she'd meant to offer. I didn't understand girls, especially her now she was growing more like one. "We don't cry," I said in case she could take this as including her, but I couldn't tell whether she did, and she hadn't much else to say before she made for home.

I thought of her when I was in the dentist's chair, and it didn't help at all. Either she'd been trying to lend me some bravery or her dentist was considerably gentler. Mine was a Polish Catholic who blamed the end of sweet rationing for the state of children's teeth and apparently regarded treatment as a penance for the patient. No doubt he believed toothache was sent by God. The first time the hook he was using to pluck at my teeth dug into a nerve, I fought to think of Bobby's words in case they could blot out some of the pain, and when they failed I gave myself up to praying. That didn't work either. Even before it touched me I thought the drill sounded like agony refined to a penetrating squeal, and when the bit set about piercing my tooth, no amount of supplicating God prevented it from finding a nerve. I squeezed my eyes shut and strained helplessly to concentrate on the prayers my gaping mouth was unable to pronounce, but Jesus didn't intervene to protect or anaesthetise the nerve, and Mary didn't even deal with the sweat that was breaking out all over me as I dug my nails into the arms of the chair. I suppose the session lasted less than half an hour, but the virtually unrelenting pain rendered time endless. I felt I was learning what hell might be like, and if anything of the sort was the result of believing in sin, I'd had enough of religion. God shouldn't let anybody like the dentist get away with his behaviour, especially since I was sure the man thought it was somehow justified by the crucifix that I saw on the wall whenever my eyes winced open in the hope that the drill wasn't coming back. I was already on the way to leaving behind the beliefs I'd been taught, and now I could see no reason to keep hold of any of them.

I was growing more convinced of this as I trudged home when I met Jim and Bobby on the main road. "What was the film like?" I said as best I could with my aching jaw.

"Just as good," Jim said, and Bobby confirmed "It was gear."

The pain in my face gave my jealousy a keener edge. Even if they'd been keeping up our Saturday tradition in my absence, Bobby had gone to the cinema with Jim although she wouldn't just with me. I was close to confronting both of them when Bobby said "Were you all right at the dentist?"

"Why shouldn't I be?" Since this persuaded them no more than me, I found the strongest word I could risk uttering. "It was a sod."

"Oh, Dom," Bobby said as if we'd never had our disagreement. "What was it like?"

"What do you think? It hurt a lot. Hurt like a bugger."

"You mean the needle did."

"He never gave me one."

"Well, he ought to have. You should have asked. You want to tell your mum and dad or he'll keep getting away with it. My dad says too many of the wrong people have got too much power."

"Telling about Nobbly didn't fix him, did it?" Jim said.

Though I would have liked to take my pains home, I couldn't miss the chance to say "Then it's up to us again."

"We can't do anything if our mums and dads won't help."

This sounded like the ignominious end of the Tremendous Three, an admission that we weren't really any use. As I wondered if it was even worth discussing – all at once our little gang seemed as ineffectual as religion – Bobby said "Like my mum says, it's up to the people at his church."

Pain lanced my jaw, and I no longer felt like arguing. "I'm going home," I said and did so without waiting for Jim.

For a change my parents didn't immediately greet me as I let myself in. Perhaps they didn't want to seem too anxious. I was attempting to compose my face when my mother came out of the kitchen. "Dominic, was it that bad?"

My father appeared from the front room, flapping the evening paper. "Have an omelette then, son. You can whip it if you like."

He'd recently been demonstrating a new device at Cooper's, a plastic plunger with a porous disc for a head, which would turn an egg in a tall glass into the makings of an omelette if you pushed it up and down vigorously enough. The action took my mind off my aches to an extent, not least because it couldn't help recalling an activity I'd begun to practice in the bathroom. My mother cooked the omelette, which left me ravenous for more, but I didn't like to ask. After dinner I stayed up until *Variety Playhouse* on the radio was over – comedians, pianists, women singing arias, a chorus performing an Italian favourite – and then my mother said "You take that face to bed, Dominic. Shall we give him a Phensic?"

"It won't hurt a big lad like him." As if this was insufficient compensation for my woes, my father said "We can all have a walk in the park tomorrow."

Just then I didn't care much what we did. Once I was in bed the throbbing of my jaw drove away any night fears, and when the painkiller eventually took hold I fell into an exhausted sleep. In the morning the dental aftermath had subsided to a dull ache that breakfast didn't aggravate. The ache accompanied me to church, where it felt not much worse than tedium. "Ite, missa est," the priest said at long last, and when everyone responded "Deo gratias" I did so with enthusiasm. I felt close to having made a sly joke, thanking God that the mass was finally over. It was only what everyone else said, and I had no sense that God minded one way or the other.

I couldn't think God cared how we dressed either, but we kept our respectful togs on for the park. The October afternoon was recalling summer with a blaze of sunshine, and the leaves on every tree glowed like mosaics made of shades of amber. At the end of a polite muted stroll suitable for Sunday we sat on a bench opposite the playground, where a few small children were sending cries of pleasure up to the uncomplicated sky. Now I wonder if my parents were sharing silent memories of when I was young enough to be pushed on a swing, but that Sunday I was put in mind of Tina Noble and her nervous mother. I remembered the toddler demanding to be sent higher than the sky, a memory that invoked the darkness masked by the unbroken blue expanse. I was finding other thoughts, whatever they may have been, when my mother nudged my father. "Don't look."

He gave her a frown and a sample of a grimace. "What are you saying, love?"

"Don't look or he'll see us. It's that teacher of Dominic's."

I glanced past them to see Mr Noble striding fast along the path from the gate closest to his house. He looked so preoccupied that I thought he mightn't notice us, but as he glared towards the playground he recognised my parents. I glimpsed contempt flickering on his face, to be replaced by indifference and then by an emotion not far short of loathing. He must have detested feeling forced to approach my parents, but as he made for us I saw him leave all expression behind, apart from a faint smile gracious enough for a Sunday. "Why," he said, "it's Mr and Mrs Sheldrake."

For once I didn't resent feeling excluded by adults. My parents turned to face him as though they hadn't realised he was there and wished they'd stayed ignorant. "Mr Noble," my father said.

"And how is Mr Sheldrake?"

"I'm quite well, thank you."

"No," Mr Noble said and stooped snakelike in my direction. "The forthcoming generation."

"They're happy with him at his school," my mother said.

In case this was insufficiently pointed my father said "They're still teaching him what's right."

"So long as you believe that." As Mr Noble's smile shrank he said "Just tell me, have you seen my daughter?"

"I don't think we ever have," my mother told him.

"Not you." Courtesy was deserting him. "Mr Sheldrake," he said and stared at me.

"I haven't today, sir." I wondered if my parents would have rebuked me if I'd omitted the last word. "Not for weeks," I said.

"How old is she?" my father asked him.

"She's two," Mr Noble said with an emphasis I didn't understand. "She's much older than her age."

My mother was concerned now. "Has she run off? What does she look like? What's her name?"

"It's Tina, and she's very much like me." Before he'd finished speaking Mr Noble swung around to survey the park. "Tina," he called at the top of his voice. "Tina."

Everybody in the playground stared at him, and so did people further off, but these were the only responses I could see. "When did you lose her?" my father said.

"When I was about some business and she was meant to be asleep." With enough resentment to be aiming some of it at us for learning of the situation, Mr Noble said "I'm looking for her and her mother."

I could see my parents wished he hadn't told them, but my father said "Why, what's happening?"

"My wife," Mr Noble said, visibly restraining his answer. "She's been in something of a state since my father left us."

My mother gave a sympathetic murmur while she and my father crossed themselves. I didn't know whether they glimpsed the disdain in Mr Noble's eyes, which made my hasty version of the gesture feel even less meaningful. "Please accept our condolences for your loss," my father said.

"It's no loss."

My mother parted her lips so sharply that the noise was a comment in itself. "How can you say that about your own father?"

"No," Mr Noble said. "I mean I haven't lost him."

I saw my parents were reluctant to argue with his beliefs under the circumstances, but my father said "Is that why your wife's in a state?"

"I think you've hit upon it," Mr Noble said as if he were praising a minor effort by a pupil. "So many people aren't equipped to see the truth."

Before my father could respond my mother said "Are you saying she's run away with your daughter?"

"I fear she may have. She has no appreciation of how I'm bringing Tina up. I know what's best for my own child, and I won't be hindered by ignorance."

I saw that my parents felt bound to let the subject go, and I made a desperate bid to rescue it. I was remembering his journal as I said "Mr Noble, what did your dad think?"

"I won't discuss my private matters with you any further."

This could have been aimed at my parents as well, since he was gazing at us all. In a last attempt to prompt them I said "You heard what happened to Mr Noble's dad."

"We did." My mother gazed at Mr Noble. "It seemed so unnecessary," she said.

"That's the word for it." Perhaps my father was close to confronting Mr Noble too. "Was he on your wife's side?" he said.

"This doesn't concern my father," Mr Noble said so coldly that I for one knew it did. "If you can't help you must excuse me. Sheldrake, if you see Tina or her mother, kindly let me know at once."

He'd abandoned his old pretence of respect, and my mother seemed offended on my behalf. "How is Dominic supposed to do that? Are you on the telephone?"

"I've felt no need for one, and nobody else has." As I wondered if this could be a way of hindering his wife from speaking to her friends, Mr Noble said "I trust you won't object if your son comes to my house."

"To be honest, Mr Noble," my father said, "we'd prefer him not to."

"Then I hope you realise you may be putting my daughter in danger."

"Of what?" my mother protested.

"Of leaving her at the mercy of a woman who's unbalanced," Mr Noble said and turned his back to stride away along the path.

My parents exchanged an unhappy look. "We don't really know, do we?" my mother said.

"Maybe their neighbours would."

"You're never saying we should talk to them."

I saw the outrageousness of the proposal catch up with my father. "I don't see what else we can do," he said.

I was hoping this expressed determination rather than defeat when my father muttered "Watch out, he's coming back."

My mother followed his gaze past me, and I saw Mr Noble marching towards us even more purposefully than he'd left us. I was afraid he'd overheard my parents until I realised he was staring past them at a black car on the main road alongside the park. While it put me in mind of a funeral, the unlit sign on the roof showed it was a police car. As it passed the park gates I saw a woman and a toddler in the back. The car slowed as it approached the Noble house, and Mr Noble broke into a run. "It's Tina and her mum," I said. "They've brought them back."

My mother stood up. "Let's walk home that way."

"We don't want to get too involved," my father said.

"I'd just like to see all's as it should be. No harm in that, Desmond."

Mr Noble was already past the gates and sprinting across the road with little regard for the traffic. By the time we trotted at some speed to the gates, the police car had halted outside the Noble house. "Stay on this side at least," my father hissed.

He led the way along the pavement bordering the graveyard as the driver climbed out of the police car and opened the kerbside door. I saw Mr Noble slow down to a purposeful stride as his wife emerged from the car. Her broad face tied up in a headscarf that was failing to contain a good deal of her hair looked not so much placid as slumped into dullness. Tina came next, helped onto the pavement by a policeman who'd been sitting with them in the back. Mrs Noble glanced at her husband and stooped to their daughter, lifting her in a hug that even from across the road I could see was fierce. She turned away from Mr Noble and began to retreat along the pavement not quite at a run. She hadn't reached the nearest side street when the long-legged driver easily overtook her and held up a hand. "One moment, madam," he said and called to Mr Noble "Is that your house there?"

Mr Noble pointed with both hands as if he was celebrating its existence. "Our family home."

"That's what your little girl told us. You aren't going the right way, madam. You need to go home."

"You don't understand," Mrs Noble said in a voice that shivered with the effort to stay calm and reasonable. "They shouldn't be together."

"Didn't this young lady say your husband teaches at St Cuthbert's?"

"That's where I'm employed," Mr Noble called. "I'm in charge of their history."

"I'm sure the gentleman can't be any kind of danger to children, madam, or he wouldn't be in such a trusted position. Be a good lady and don't give us any more trouble. You don't want your neighbours to see you making a scene."

I willed my parents to point out how Mr Noble had been fired from his job at my school, but they would have had to shout across the road, and

I knew they never would. As Mrs Noble turned, still clutching Tina, and trudged back to the house, Mr Noble said "Please let me apologise for any inconvenience. My wife has been upset since my father died."

Surely this was another cue for my parents, but we still weren't close enough. "Will that be affecting your little girl?" the other policeman said.

"Not in any way I wouldn't want. Truth helps her grow."

"You don't think she's a bit young for that kind of truth."

I was urging the policeman to pursue the issue, but Mr Noble's silence seemed to win him over. "I expect as a teacher you'll know if she is," he conceded. "She's certainly a credit to you. She told them at the railway station that she was being taken away without your consent. She didn't make a fuss, but she was so convincing that the ticket office called us."

"Mummy," Tina said, "that's too tight. You're hurting."

"You can put her down," Mr Noble said. "She won't run away."

As both policemen moved towards his wife, she planted Tina on the pavement and opened her hands in a mime of despair before clawing at the emptiness between them. The little girl marched to her father purposefully enough for someone several times her age, and I saw the policemen take this as resolving any doubts they might have had. Mr Noble swept Tina up in his arms as if he meant to launch her towards the sky, and the policeman who was lifting out the contents of the car boot – the pushchair but no luggage – watched with an approving smile. Something distracted his attention, and he said "Is someone in your house?"

Mr Noble followed his gaze to the window above the front door. "Just the wind."

As he turned back to the policeman he saw us across the road. Disdain pinched his face so briefly that it seemed we weren't worthy even of contempt. "In you come, Tina," he said, slipping his key into the lock. "Dear, you bring the pushchair."

"Will you need us any further, sir?" the driver said.

"I'm sure I can deal with any situation now. If I may I'll write to your chief constable commending your professionalism."

Couldn't the policemen sense his sarcasm? Wasn't it their job to see through deception and disguise? I watched helplessly as Tina ran into the house and swung around to smile at the police. "Thank you for bringing me home," she said out of the dimness of the hall.

The police stayed close behind Mrs Noble until she plodded along the path, which she made seem considerably longer than its few feet, and tipped up the pushchair to send it into the house. Her husband stepped aside for it and her before sending us a last scornful look as he shut the front door. When the policemen noticed us they seemed to share his view. No doubt they took us for idle spectators, and they plainly made my father feel that way. "I hope you're happy now," he told my mother. "I'm for home."

"So long as the little girl was happy I am."

I could only follow them, though not without more than one backwards glance. I didn't know whether they'd seen what I had, but I knew they would dismiss it, just as the policeman had. He'd been right to question Mr Noble, but too ready to accept the answer. The curtains at the upstairs window had been more agitated than the breeze along the main road could have made them. While it had swayed a few branches in the cemetery, it couldn't have produced the glimpse of an unpleasantly lopsided shape blundering like an enormous moth against the curtains and fumbling at the pallid fabric – a shape with little in the way of hands but, to judge from the asymmetrical mass that was pressed against the inside of the curtains, altogether too large a face.

CHAPTER TWENTY-TWO

A Shape in the Fog

"I don't understand my mum. It's like she doesn't care about Tina and her mother."

"How about your dad?" Jim said.

"I don't think he does either. Him and my mum won't do anything. They say leave well alone."

"Maybe they're right and that's how they care. Our dads and mums aren't always wrong."

Under the circumstances I found his defence of my parents close to disloyal. "They couldn't see what was really going on," I protested. "You two ought to have, though."

"Sounds like Nobbly's wife has flipped her lid a bit more," Jim said. "So the kid's best off back with him."

"But it's him that's done it to his wife just like he did to Mrs Norris and his dad."

"It won't be him, will it? It's the stuff he believes. I'm not saying it's right or anything like, but it hasn't driven him mad either."

"Do you want him teaching it to that little girl?"

"He's her dad. It's up to him, don't you think, Bobs?"

We were on the corner of her road again, where it was darker than last time we'd met. Some of the traffic confronted the dusk with lights, and some cars left their headlamps dead. "If it's what she wants," Bobby said.

"She's too young to say," I objected.

"She says a lot. I thought she was amazing. She's what girls ought to be."

"She's only two."

"You're saying her dad taught her, are you, Dom? Sounds like it wasn't her mum."

I had a sense of losing the argument before it was even articulated. "Suppose, if it wasn't his dad."

"It wouldn't be him when he was crazy, would it? So maybe what her dad's teaching her is good for her mind."

"It isn't for her mum's, is it?"

"Then it's good Tina's like she is. She must have seen something was wrong with her mum, but you said she sorted it all out and didn't even make a scene."

In a final effort to persuade at least one of my friends I said "Don't you think she's in danger with her mum in the house?"

"Not when her dad's there as well."

"He won't be when he's teaching. She might be alone with her mum."

I almost blurted what I'd actually come to think, except that I knew they wouldn't be convinced – that one reason Tina had run back into the house was the presence of the tenant I'd glimpsed at the upstairs window. Had she been impatient to meet her grandfather, whatever form he took? Her father seemed eager to accustom her to encounters of the kind. If her mother sensed the presence, would she try to take the little girl away again? Perhaps this was why she had, but I suspected her failure had left her defeated. I was gazing at Bobby, hoping my doubts had reached her, when Jim said "I expect he'll make arrangements if he's got to."

To my dismay, this satisfied Bobby as well. "I'm going to watch their house," I declared.

"I've got footy training," Jim said – he was in the school team now – "and then I've got homework."

"We've started rehearsing for the Christmas play," Bobby said.

Though I'd had an inkling they would find excuses, I felt let down. "Do you want me to tell you if anything happens?"

"You ought to know we do," Bobby said and only just withheld a punch. "We're still friends."

"You won't mind if I let my mum and dad think I'm meeting you, then."

"Just don't say you are," Jim said.

At home I stayed upstairs with my schoolwork until dinner, for which my father had provided a treat. Sometimes he brought home jars of chicken breast in jelly, but today's extravagance was tinned salmon, a favourite my mother celebrated by adding brown bread and butter. I'd always enjoyed chewing the bones that the canning process softened, but just then I didn't need to be put in mind of transformations death might bring. "Why are you leaving those?" my mother said, and inevitably "Aren't you feeling well?"

"I'm fine, mum. It was lovely. I've just had enough."

"Don't start getting faddy with your food." My father sounded more insulted than he was admitting. "We eat up what we're given in this house," he said.

"Honestly, I'm full. Someone else can have my bones."

He gave me a look that offered a glimpse of the distrust I'd earned over Mr Noble's journal. "Growing up, are we, son?" he said. "There aren't two men in the house yet. There's only me."

"There's me as well," my mother said, scraping the remains of my dinner onto her plate. "So you two see about getting on with each other."

My father didn't seem too pleased with her exhortation or her action. He stared towards the hall as if he would rather hear the radiogram, where Ronnie Aldrich was playing the piano, than us. While I helped my mother wash up after dinner he adjourned to the front room to listen to *What Do You Know?*, shouting his answers to the quiz to ensure we caught them. "I've done my homework," I told my mother. "I'm just going out for a bit."

"Where are you going, Dominic?"

I felt under pressure from Bobby and Jim as well as my mother. "Just to see," I said and found a guilty ruse, "you know, them."

Beyond the kitchen window mist was smudging treetops in the graveyard. "I don't like you being out on a night like this," my mother said.

"I'll be fine, mum." Had I said that already, too recently? In a bid to forestall any more objections I protested "I said I'd see them."

This silenced her, though visibly unhappily, while I rinsed the last dish. As I grabbed my coat from the hook in the hall and buttoned myself up she came to the kitchen doorway, wiping her hands on a towel. "I wish we all had telephones," she said, "then you could tell them you're staying in."

I'd opened the front door when my father left off competing with the *Brain of Britain* contestants long enough to ask where I was going. "Mum knows," I called and shut them in.

From the gate I saw the mist was turning into fog. As the trees in the street grew more distant they faded and turned vague, while those closest to the main road looked like paralysed columns of smoke. Beyond them a shoal of rectangular lights crawled by, smearing the murk with their glow – the windows of a bus. Away from the main road the night was as silent as the fog that loitered on the far side of the railway arch. I no longer felt so eager to make my way to the Noble house, and even thought of using my mother's concern as an excuse to postpone the adventure. Surely the fog would help me spy on the house unobserved, and was I really going to prove unworthy of the mission just because I was on my own? I shut the cold wet gate behind me and strode to the railway bridge.

A moist chill wind met me, and so did a surge of fog. It wavered on the far side of the road beyond the arch, where pallid haloes swelled around the streetlights. I was past the bridge when the fog faltered backwards, and a pale mass glimmered at the downstairs window of the Norris house. As it shrank into the dimness I told myself that it had been the reflection of a streetlamp fattened by the fog. All the same, I wasn't slow in making for the nearest exit from the road.

I hadn't previously noticed the figures carved above the massive iron gates. A shield was flanked by a knight with a porous mossy face and a man whose lower half was a serpentine tail. Perhaps I should have known he was meant to be Neptune, but the pair of figures and the stone bird glistening with moisture on the shield seemed to conceal a meaning, however unintentional. What would Mr Noble have found in them? The bird might have put him in mind of the Holy Ghost, and perhaps the knight could have symbolised the son of God, leaving the half-human presence to play the creator, all of this just another inadvertent echo of an infinitely older truth. I could easily have fancied I was entering Mr Noble's territory as I ventured under the arch.

The side entrance for pedestrians led onto a pavement bordering the road that stretched past half a dozen broad stone columns beneath the deep archway. As I hurried past each column in the dripping murk, the fog dragged itself back from the next ahead, and I had the unwelcome impression that something more substantial than a shadow had withdrawn out of sight to wait for me. I was less than halfway through the arch when it found a voice, a thunderous open-mouthed roar that grew louder and found echoes to make it more overwhelming still, so loud that I thought the columns quivered. When I dashed out of the far side of the arch I heard a skeletal clicking recede into the night until the train was out of earshot down the line.

The road and the twin pavements merged into a path that disappeared into the murk, where trees and headstones looked decomposed by fog. I turned away across a sodden lawn, which was as grey as the unstable walls that closed around me, lowering the sky. For a time that felt slowed down by my wary footsteps the murk was my only companion. Its chill gathered underfoot as the wet grass turned my shoes blacker. At last I saw pale silhouettes ahead, and the corroded figures set about reclaiming their shapes from the fog as it started to absorb light beyond them. By the time I reached the memorials I could see the source of the glow – the blurred lamps on Walton Lane, where the Nobles lived.

I tramped across the grass to the hedge and sidled along it until I was opposite the house. A car crept past with a protracted hiss of tyres on tarmac, and then the road was as still as the drops of condensation dangling from spikes of the hedge. A pair of murky side streets framed the block of houses across the road, and a streetlamp lent them the look of a theatrical set ready for a performance. I watched my breaths drift through the hedge to grow indistinguishable from the fog and waited for the play to begin.

I waited long enough that I began to shiver. Though it was only the chill of the night, it felt absurdly like nervousness. All three front windows of the Noble house were curtained, and a thin unsteady veil of fog added to its secretive appearance, so that I risked jogging on the spot and thumping my chest with my arms. However surreptitious they were, the noises I made might have prevented me from hearing some activity in the house. I was wondering if the fog would let me venture closer, though I didn't know whether I could trust it not to retreat, when I heard Tina's mother.

She was somewhere in the house. Her voice was shriller than I'd ever heard it, but I couldn't make out any words. I leaned so close to the hedge that my breath set a beaded cobweb quivering, and the spider darted out of its thorny lair in search of prey. As I strained my ears, aggravating the ache the chilly night had laid on them, Mrs Noble's voice grew louder, but I heard no words until she threw the front door open. "You get on with playing your horrible games," she cried. "I'm off to see my friends. I've still got some, whatever you tell them."

She sounded distressed – not least, I've come to think, by her own behaviour – and helplessly desperate. Beyond her I saw her husband standing hand in hand with Tina, and it disturbed me to wonder which of them she was haranguing, if not both. She turned her back on them and slammed the door, its thud rendered duller by the fog. She marched away in the direction of the park, vanishing into the fog before her rapid footsteps did.

She'd made one point obvious to me: that if something happened in the house, I had no chance of hearing it from where I was. I hurried alongside the hedge fast enough to splash my trouser cuffs and emerged from the cemetery opposite the gateway to the park. I wouldn't be able to hear if I stayed by the graveyard, and so I dashed across the road. The fog flapped ahead of me, urged by a bitter breeze, to reveal block after block of houses flanked by side streets. When it unveiled the Noble house I was still on the corner of the street at the far end of the block – not close enough to hear. I took a breath that tasted like soot and catarrh, and then I sprinted as quietly as I could along the block to dodge around the windowless side of the Noble house. I barely managed not to falter in front of the building, because I could hear Mr Noble and his daughter.

Their words weren't so clear where I was now, and I edged my face around the corner of the house. I could only hope that if any neighbours saw me they would think I was playing some kind of hide and seek, ignominiously childish as that would seem. I'd closed my fingers around the edge of the house as if this might concentrate my senses, though it mostly made me aware of the cold rough bricks under my fingertips, when I began to understand what I could hear. "Remember the first words I spoke to you," Mr Noble was urging.

He was in the room above the front door – the room where I'd seen movement at the window when Tina had been brought home. His voice sounded deliberate, close to a chant or at any rate some kind of ritual. "Remember the first time you held me in your arms," Tina said.

Was she answering him? Her voice seemed ritualistic too, and very little like a two-year-old's despite its childish pitch. "Remember how I told you truths you never knew," her father said, "and you didn't think I should."

"Remember how I used to when you took me for a walk."

Could those even be a two-year-old's words? Why did she and her father want to share these memories in that room? I couldn't help wishing someone else were there to hear, and as I peered at the sluggish clumsy dance of the fog in the wind I might have been hoping it would produce them. Then Mr Noble said "Remember the field where you found my father."

I was appalled to think he'd taken her to the French site, and then the truth caught up with me. Mr Noble and his infant child weren't talking to each other at all. I'd been right to think that their deliberate almost hypnotic speech was a ritual, but they were trying to use the memories to entice the person they belonged to – Tina's grandfather. All at once I didn't want to have my thoughts confirmed, but they were, by a third voice in the upstairs room. It was excessively large and yet feeble, not to say unrecognisably shapeless, more like an uneven gust of wind than any sound produced by a mouth I'd call human. Nevertheless it managed to pronounce words, however loosely. "Leave me dead."

"You are," Mr Noble said. "You always will be. All you can do now is help us."

I thought and very much hoped I'd heard the worst, and certainly enough that I wasn't tempted to linger. I deeply regretted failing to wait until Bobby and Jim were free to help me watch the house. I was shoving myself away from it when I heard worse still: Tina's giggles. They sounded a little hysterical, and she had to be reacting to whatever had joined her and her father in the room. This shocked me so badly that I hadn't managed to move when I heard something blunder against the upstairs window.

It sounded like a moth, if far larger and yet less substantial. It made me stumble around the front of the house to look. There was something in the curtains, not so much entangled as struggling to borrow more of a shape from them. Apart from the ill-defined appendages that were fumbling at them, I could see a gibbous mass identifiable as a face only because it consisted largely of a mouth, gaping in a cry that it seemed unable to utter. Then a version of a pair of eyes swelled above it, both of them uncertain of their size and shape. They pressed against the window so hard that they spread distressingly wide, and then the presence let the curtains sag and was gone. When it spoke again it sounded more pleading than ever. "Out there," it said like a child finding someone else to blame.

"Out where?" Mr Noble said, and his voice grew sharper. "Outside?"

The sound of footsteps crossing the room released me from my paralysis, but I barely had time to retreat around the side of the house before I heard the sash of the window thrown high. "Hello?" Mr Noble called. "No point in lying low. We know you're there."

As I fought not to breathe I saw a wisp of breath escape me. I clamped my hands over my nose and mouth until I heard the sash clump down. I thought I'd managed to escape notice until I realised Mr Noble didn't need to locate me. "Find them, then," he said, and Tina giggled. "Find something even you won't be afraid of."

For a desperate moment I was able to pretend I'd misunderstood, and then I fled. I dashed across the road, even though this brought me closer to the graveyard. Glancing back, I saw that the fog was swelling towards me, but only from in front of the Noble house. Was there a faint restless outline on the fog, like a pallid shadow cast by nothing I could see? I wasn't anxious to know, and I turned and ran.

I couldn't help praying to meet people on the road, but the fog had driven everyone indoors; there wasn't even any traffic. The only sound was the panicky clatter of my footsteps on the flagstones. I wanted to be reassured by the lack of any noise behind me, but I'd sprinted just a few yards when the silence made me look back. My gasp filled my mouth with fog. The mass of murk that was following me along the road was no longer featureless. In its midst a blurred figure was floundering after me. While its swollen unequal limbs were squirming in a parody of pursuit, as if it wasn't certain how to move, it was coming as fast as the fog – as fast as I could run.

I fled past the corner of the graveyard, into the side street that led to the railway bridge. Along here the streetlamps were fewer and dimmer, and the fog looked close to dousing them. If I'd seen someone in any of the houses opposite the cemetery I might have sought refuge, but all the houses were curtained or dark if not both. I'd added panting to the exhausted clatter of my footsteps, and fog rasped my nostrils with every breath. From the second streetlamp I glanced over my shoulder, and almost stumbled against the wall that hid the railway alongside the graveyard. The pursuer was already at the first lamp, which showed me far too much – showed the figure blundering out of the glow of the lamp, waving all its malformed pallid limbs in the air as if miming the capture it anticipated. It appeared to be incapable of keeping its size or its shape, which it was borrowing from the fog, but the features on the misshapen bloated head were dismayingly clear. While I couldn't judge whether the greyish blobs of eyes were blind, one of them was almost as large as the wavering lopsided mouth.

I sucked in a breath that came near to choking me with fog, and dashed past the next lamp. When I risked looking back I saw that the pursuer was no closer than it had been. I was able to think that the fog wouldn't let it reach me, since the fog to which it owed its substance could never come so close, and I succeeded in turning my back on the shape that was wallowing after me through the dimness. Then a sooty breath reminded me how close the fog was, even if it wasn't visible, and I put on a desperate burst of speed. I was within a few strides of the railway bridge when the fog seemed to condense on the nape of my neck, and I felt how solid it had grown – solid enough for a version of fingers, however boneless.

I cried out and flinched away, staggering across the road. Too late I realised that I'd veered away from the bridge. I was lurching towards it when I glimpsed movement in the dark beneath the arch, and the figure bulged towards me, all its limbs outstretched like a spider's, its eyes and mouth fluctuating with eagerness. I stumbled backwards, almost sprawling on the road, until my shoulders thumped the window of a corner shop as dark as all the houses. "Go away," I begged like someone nowhere near my age.

The figure emerged from its lair as if it had grasped how to control the fog, and I had a dreadful notion that it was about to grow taller than the bridge. Then it faltered as though the fog had, thrusting its approximation of a face at me. I was struggling to retreat further when I saw that the spasmodic eyes were intent not on me but on the reflection in the window. "Not me," it pleaded, and in a moment it was gone like fog dispersed by a wind.

I was daring to breathe again, despite how foggy this tasted – I was wondering how I'd heard the distorted shaky voice, more in my head than anywhere else – when I became aware of rapid footsteps under the bridge. In a moment Bobby appeared and hurried to me. "Dom, where have you been?" she demanded. "I was just coming home. I thought I'd go to yours to see what you were doing."

"I've been watching Mr Noble's house." I stared about at the fog, which was as featureless as fog should be. "Did you see?" I hoped aloud. "Did you hear?"

"I didn't hear anything, but—" She shivered before saying "What was it, Dom?"

"You've got to believe me now. It was Tina's grandfather," I said, and saw how to win Bobby over at last. "Mr Noble makes her call him."

CHAPTER TWENTY-THREE

The Whispering Church

"Jim, he's making their little girl think she can call back the dead."

"He is," I insisted in case Bobby didn't sound forceful enough. "I heard him."

"So what's her mother doing about it?"

"She's given up, Dom says," Bobby told him in disgust. "She just goes out and leaves them."

"Maybe she knows it isn't that serious. She must know it doesn't work."

"That doesn't matter, does it?" I said, because I was afraid Bobby might try to make Jim accept more than he would. "He'll still be affecting her mind. Look what happened to his dad."

"And suppose they're doing it to other children at his church?" Bobby said.

"We don't know if they are," Jim said. "Anyway, I thought you thought Tina couldn't do anything wrong."

"Don't put words in my mouth, Jim Bailey." As I wondered how much Bobby still believed what I'd told her she'd seen at the railway bridge, she said "She's already got more to her than her mother."

"Doesn't sound like it if they both do what Nobbly says."

"So do you want to let that happen? Want her to grow up doing just what men tell her to do?"

I had a nervous sense that Jim mightn't find the prospect disagreeable enough for Bobby's taste. I was about to assure her how little I would welcome the development when Jim let the argument lapse. "Dom, have you told your parents about her?"

"They wouldn't want to know. They're glad she's back with him."

"Well, if she's a genius like Bobs says, shouldn't it be her choice?"

"Don't keep saying I said things I never." Though Bobby looked ready to follow this up with a punch, she restrained herself to saying "We aren't talking about getting her away from him, are we, Dom? We want to find out what's happening first and then we can tell our parents."

I saw Miss Mottram watching us from behind the counter in her shop. No doubt she thought we were having a typical teenage conversation, however she envisioned one of those. Now I wonder how safe she felt in her soft lair full of knitting patterns and balls of wool, or how threatened by the future we might have seemed to represent. "Find out how?" Jim said.

"Let's try seeing what's at his church," I said. "We can on Saturday before we go to the flicks."

I thought Jim was about to raise yet another objection until he gave a grimace like a facial shrug. "Don't know what good that's going to do, but fair enough, I wouldn't mind seeing."

It felt as if we were the Tremendous Three again, or the best we could counterfeit at our advanced age. I left Bobby at the corner and Jim outside his house, and strode home through the distantly befogged October dusk, feeling almost sufficiently heartened not to look for an apparition taking shape in the remote murk. However awful the thought was in more ways than I cared to define, I suspected that Mr Noble had other uses for the presence he'd brought back than to send it after me a second time. I only hoped he hadn't learned who had been spying on his house.

Wouldn't spying on the church increase that risk? Just the same, I was eager to see it now that the three of us would. The rest of the week felt as if it was holding back the future, which I was still young enough to yearn for without knowing what it might be. I couldn't even predict the outcome of taking a book into school.

It was *Brighton Rock*, which I'd found on the second-hand bookstall in St John's Market downtown. Usually I bought science fiction books, but I'd remembered Mr Askew's recommendation. Before I'd finished the first chapter I was excited and flattered that he'd told me to read so relentlessly adult an author. Besides the seedy truthfulness that I hadn't realised books were able to convey, the vivid details – observations of behaviour, impressions of the seaside resort and the darker aspects it couldn't contain – felt as lifelike as memories, even if they weren't mine. I was so eager to show Mr Askew I'd taken his advice that I took the novel into school despite having several chapters still to read.

Mr Askew was talking to Brother Treanor at the gates, but as Jim and I left the bus he headed for the school. Unusually for him, the headmaster was on gate duty, no doubt to emphasise his warning that everyone represented the school wherever we wore the Holy Ghost uniform. "Good morning, sir," Jim and I said, raising our caps just as much in unison, none of which we meant as the joke we were immediately aware of. We were hurrying away to keep any mirth at a distance from him, and I was removing the book from my satchel, when Brother Treanor called "Sheldrake."

I didn't know why I should be singled out, and Jim turned around as well. "Sir," I had to say.

"What book have you brought here now?"

"It's Graham Greene, sir."

"It should not be." As I wondered what he was trying to deny, Brother Treanor said "Bring it here to me at once."

I thought the paperback looked respectable enough – the cover bore no picture, just the title and the author's name politely lettered in a white rectangle stacked between two orange ones, the lower one declaring that the book was complete and unabridged, a phrase that used a penguin for an ampersand – but he glowered at the book. "He has no place at Holy Ghost," he said loud enough to blot out the good mornings of the boys who'd just come through the gates. "Especially not that shilling shocker."

"But sir, Mr—"

"Give it here immediately." His voice was growing higher and more strangled, and I could have fancied that his mottled face was ballooning out of the constricted collar. "Sensational filth," he cried. "Heresy as well, I shouldn't wonder. Do your parents know you read such stuff?"

I was afraid he meant to rip the book apart or, worse, make me do so on the stage. "Sir," I protested, "Mr Askew said I ought to read it."

Brother Treanor's face quivered with rage, and I thought the convulsion was about to spread to his grip on the book he was leafing through when Mr Askew said behind me "Did I hear my name?"

Brother Treanor shut the book and brandished it at him. "Here's what this boy from your class has brought into the school."

"Sir, it's one of the ones you told me to read."

"Is it one I lent you?" Before I could risk answering on the assumption that I'd understood, Mr Askew said "Very well, Sheldrake, leave it to me. I am indeed the proud owner of that book, headmaster."

"You feel it's an occasion for pride," Brother Treanor said as if he was accusing Mr Askew of the sin.

"I think fine writing is, and I'll make that claim for Mr Greene. And if you'll permit my saying so, I believe Sheldrake has the intelligence to read the book as it should be read."

"The boy has a mind all right," Brother Treanor said, though not too favourably. "May I ask how you're saying he should read?"

"Critically, headmaster. That should always be the way. It'll stand him in good stead when we've qualified him for university, and he's more than ready to learn."

Brother Treanor gazed at him before handing him the book. "This is yours," he said, not entirely unlike a question. "You might take care how much trust you put in your pupils, Mr Askew."

Jim was waiting for me on the drive, but Mr Askew waved him away with his stick. "Walk with me, Sheldrake," he said and no more until he'd limped halfway to the school. "You'll find this in your desk. Please keep it there until it's time to go home, and don't fall into the habit of fibbing."

I thought this was unfair: he'd told the lie or at any rate implied one, while I'd simply been his mute accomplice. "As the headmaster said," he murmured, "I'm trusting your intelligence. Please don't let me down."

The novel was indeed hidden under several books in my desk when I reached the classroom. Throughout the English lesson I felt as if Mr Askew's behaviour was disclaiming its presence and our conversation. When home time came I transferred the book between two others into my satchel. Jim and I were on the drive when I saw Brother Treanor standing guard. If he asked about the book, what could I say? Mr Askew wasn't there to help, and would I be able to play with the truth as deftly as he had? I felt my face turn red, and my mouth grew parched of words as we made for the gates, where the headmaster stared at me. "So then, Sheldrake," he said.

I managed to say a word I hoped was neutral. "Sir?"

"No doubt you imagine you've had a lucky escape." As I searched for a response I could risk giving, he said "Too much of a burden?"

I felt trapped and childish for having to repeat "Sir?"

"Your schoolbag. Is it weighing on you for some reason?"

I'd shrugged it higher on my shoulder while he was musing about my escape. "Just homework, sir," I mumbled.

"You must expect that if you've set your sights on a university." He paused long enough to make me wonder if he'd asked a question, and then he said "Best hurry home and make a start on it, then."

I never knew how much he suspected. Perhaps at some stage of the confrontation he decided against learning whether Mr Askew had given me the book. I resented the panic he'd caused me to suffer, particularly since it had proved to be needless, and I vowed I wouldn't panic over anything connected with Mr Noble or his church. "Let's meet as early as we can tomorrow," I urged Jim and Bobby as we parted at the corner of her road.

On Saturday morning I was there before ten. I'd called at Jim's, only to find he'd been sent on an errand. Bobby was next to arrive, and we rediscovered how awkward we'd grown with each other. Whenever she grinned mutely at me, which was often, I grinned back. We'd spent some minutes working on this routine by the time Jim showed up, and I couldn't help saying the first words that came into my head. "Are we ready for everything?"

It used to be the rallying cry of the Tremendous Three, and Bobby made the first response. "Ready for anything."

"Ready," Jim gave in to saying, though even in my latest tale his character declared "Ready as can be."

Our route took us through the railway bridge and past the Norris house. I kept my eye on it in case there was something I could point out to my friends, but although the air in the front room looked dim with dust even from across the road, it didn't adopt any shape. The bus we caught on the main road passed the Noble residence, but the curtained window over the front door showed no signs of life, and I couldn't see any activity in the house. I hoped Tina and her parents were all together somewhere, which I didn't think would be at the church.

When the bus left us on Everton Brow we turned away from the view across the city – buildings that grew paler and flatter with mist as they receded towards a skein of fog the length of the visible river – and headed along Kensington to the Grafton ballroom. Jim and I knew boys met girls there and danced with them, not to mention more than dancing, and I was surprised Brother Treanor hadn't warned the school against this famous occasion of sin by now. As we followed the road that forked away from Kensington behind the ballroom I heard a faint waltz from within, presumably a rehearsal. The music faded and was gone as the road led us into a wasteland.

Though the Liverpool blitz had ended before I was born, all the bombed streets on this side of Kensington lay in ruins. Every roadway was strewn with fragments of houses, and the smell of stale fire caught in my throat. Apart from the infrequent shrill clink of bricks as our footsteps disturbed a stray dog or cat in the rubble, ours were the only sounds for miles of devastation. Here and there a street or at least a block of houses appeared to have survived intact, until you saw how empty the windows were, bereft of glass and the rooms they'd belonged to. Some solitary houses were framed by the remains of their neighbours, where jagged bricks sprouted weeds. Crutches of fallen timber propped up crumbling frontages, and everywhere we saw remnants of bedrooms, their floors bitten off in mid-air. We'd been picking our way through the streets for some time when Jim said "So where's this church?"

"It's in Joseph Street, isn't it, Dom?"

"I know that," Jim complained. "Where's that supposed to be?"

None of us knew. Quite a few of the streets we'd passed had lost their signs, either buried under rubble or carried off as souvenirs, but I assumed none of them had been Joseph Street, since we hadn't seen a church. Despite the gaps everywhere, the wasteland seldom let us see very far, and was proving to be more of a maze than it had looked. By now I would have welcomed someone we could ask for directions, but it was plain that nobody lived here, and the streets seemed even more lifeless because of the utter absence of shops. The shattered roadway we were following ended at a high wall fanged with broken glass, alongside which we had to make our way around chunks of exploded houses before we came to a collapsed section of the wall, where the opening gave us a view across the devastated land. "Is that going to be it?" Bobby said.

Beyond several streets we could see a church. "It doesn't look like much," Jim said.

I had an odd sense that it was trying to look less than itself. It was the only church in sight, a long low red-brick building with a blunt spire at one end. Even at that distance I could see it had been rebuilt, new bricks filling gaps in the original frontage beneath a new slate roof. As we made our way through the rubbly streets I saw the spire was incomplete, lacking the point it must once have had, which had been replaced with a cap of incongruously bright red bricks. A couple of stained-glass windows were intact, undistinguished images of angels gazing up at Mary with her baby in her arms and of the disciples with a radiant bird above their heads. The rest of the windows were new, with perfunctory arches rendered secretive by frosted glass. We were nearly at the entrance to the church at the far end from the crippled spire before we were able to read the noticeboard that stood on two poles to the left of the shallow porch. The poles and the board had been painted black as if to disguise the newness of the wood. Cheap plastic capitals spelled out TRINITY CHURCH OF THE SPIRIT – SERVICES BY APPOINTMENT, and I wondered if the sign was meant to look uninviting so as not to attract the uninitiated. We'd taken care to make no noise as we approached the church, and now we gazed at each other while we listened for noises within. At last Bobby whispered "Aren't we going in?"

"You bet we are," Jim said by no means as low, "I don't think it's even a church any more," and strode into the porch to twist the brass ring of the latch.

In those days you could expect a church to be open to the public even when nobody was there to keep an eye on them, but I wondered if Mr Noble mightn't like the ordinary person to see inside. Apparently he didn't care, since the thick door rumbled inwards readily enough. Jim was first into the building, and as I followed Bobby in he halted, slapping his hips in a mime of disgust. "Did this use to be a Catholic church?"

At first I couldn't see why he would think so, even if the surviving stained-glass images were Christian. Beneath the peaked rafters, most of which were new, some of the old pews had been retained, while the rest of the space on either side of the nave was occupied by folding seats that would have looked more at home in a school hall. At the far end of the church an altar or at any rate a lengthy table was bare except for the white cloth it was draped in. Pale sunlight through the pair of pointed whitish windows beyond the altar helped it look emptier still. I was about to ask Jim what had made him raise the question when I saw a solitary confessional booth by the left-hand wall near the altar. "Maybe it was," I said.

"Then he's got a damned cheek," Jim said loud enough for his final syllable to drop on us from beneath the roof. "What else do you think he's done?"

"We're here to find out, aren't we?" Bobby said like herself in my tales, and made for the altar.

I peered about as Jim and I went after her. All I could see were bare pews and seats – no hymnbooks or missals, which suggested Mr Noble mightn't want anyone unconnected with his church to read what they believed. We climbed the token steps up to the altar – Jim stalked up as if to demonstrate how stripped of holiness he thought the place was – and I saw that the cloth it bore wasn't as white as it had looked. It was faintly stained in places, and sprinkled with black soil. "What's he been doing here?" Jim demanded.

"Was it a harvest festival?" Bobby said, and I was agreeing with the idea when we heard voices near the church.

We knew they would be coming in, because we recognised them. "Here we are," Tina was saying, and her father said "She knows our place." My friends and I exchanged panicky glances, and Bobby spun around. "Quick," she said, "in there."

She was pointing at the confessional, and made for it at once. "I don't like that," Jim said. "It's disrespectful."

"It's stopped being what it used to be. Where else are we going to hide?"

I couldn't pretend I shared Jim's scruples any longer. I'd grown impatient with the trivia you were meant to confess to the priest, and the prayers he gave you as penance felt like lines you had to write in detention, surely not how praying ought to feel. "You go in that side," I urged Bobby. "We'll go in the other."

She opened the left-hand door at once and dodged into the booth. Jim hesitated until we heard scattered bricks rattling close to the church, and then he shrugged unhappily and snatched the other door open. A penitential kneeler of bare wood was the only item in this half of the booth. Jim sidled past it and stood with his back to the wall of the church, and I faced him, having shut the door. Although we were close enough to feel each other's breath, I could barely make out his dim face, and beyond the mesh that separated sinners from their confessor I could only just distinguish Bobby seated in the priest's half. Jim shifted his feet, rapping the kneeler against the wooden floor of the booth, and I was jerking a finger to my lips when we heard the door open in the porch.

It let in a faint squeak of wheels – the noise of a pushchair – and then small footsteps trotted towards the altar. "She looks as if she wants to give a sermon," a woman said with a determined laugh.

Until then I hadn't realised that a pulpit was among the items missing from the church. "Perhaps it's in her future, Mrs Richards," Mr Noble said.

It was a man who asked "Does she attend your services?"

"Of course, Mr Wharton," Mr Noble said as if the question was unnecessary. "She's of the faith."

"I see she is," the man said, and I wondered how Tina was behaving near the altar. "It was good of you to let me come along with you. When I saw you all I thought you must be on your way here."

"There's nowhere else round here to go, is there?" the woman said. "So what do you think of our church?"

"I'll admit it isn't quite what I expected."

"It hardly looks like one inside, does it? That's what I thought at first, but it's how they used to be."

I didn't need Jim's grimace in the dimness to make me think she was reproducing Mr Noble's thoughts. "Not just the building either," she said. "Everything it stands for."

"You mean how Mr Noble says—" The man stopped his words with a cough that sounded flattened by a knuckle. "Pardon me," he said, "should I be calling you Father Noble?"

A giggle that I knew too well echoed through the church. "I will," Tina called.

"You know that's not appropriate." As I wondered how the man and woman felt about his speaking like this to a toddler, Mr Noble said "We've no need of titles here, Mr Wharton. Words that restrict have no place in our faith. They've always been designed to obscure the truth."

"And you say it's true that you can bring my father's mother back to us."

"I believe I told you so. You asked what kind of church this was." Lightly enough for slyness Mr Noble said "Can I do it, Mrs Richards?"

"He brought my Tom back. I can speak to him whenever Mr Noble brings him. I have twice."

I looked away from Jim, not least because he couldn't be sharing my fear that the woman might soon find her husband dreadfully transformed. "So what would I have to do?" the man said. "Are donations involved?"

"Just a tribute," the woman said.

"A tribute, then. How much might that be?"

"Not money. Mr Noble never asks for that," the woman said with another resolute laugh. "One like this."

They were nearly abreast of the confessional, and I had to resist an impulse to retreat from the door, crowding Jim. He looked close to pondering aloud what the woman meant, but then the man helped us guess. "Any special kind of flower?" he said.

"One that's grown on your loved one's grave," the woman told him. "Mr Noble says it's an old tradition."

"It's why flowers are still placed on graves," Mr Noble said. "It's like so much about religion, an old truth that's been changed to suit the new beliefs. In more enlightened times the living never left flowers for the dead. Flowers were messages the dead sent."

He and his companions were past the confessional by now. Footsteps ascended the steps, and a dull thud let me deduce that the woman had placed a flowerpot on the altar. The idea seemed banal enough, not too remote from Bobby's notion of a harvest festival, but I felt as though the action had darkened the box in which I was trapped with my friends. I could have fancied it had summoned a chill from under the floor of the booth, and I wasn't wholly comfortable with hearing the man ask "What else do you believe?"

"You say we're the oldest church of all, don't you, Mr Noble?"

"I believe I've said something of the kind."

"Is that why you called it the Trinity Church?" the man said.

"The three have always been with us. What are they, Tina?"

"The past and the present and the future."

As the woman gave a gasp of awed delight Mr Noble said "They're the three which are one, the three which have to be made flesh. That's the oldest truth behind the Bible and the newest too."

"You showed us in the windows, didn't you?" the woman said.

"So I did," Mr Noble said, and I realised he meant the stained glass – the woman cradling her baby, the luminous dove. "There's the infant which is also its own father, and there's the ghost it already was. Everything is metaphor, a veil over the truth."

"I'd like to hear you say more about the Bible," the man said.

"Do come to our next meeting. I told you when it is." As I willed him to repeat the information, Mr Noble said "Or ask me anything you want me to make clear."

"I was wondering where you get these ideas from."

"A very few of us are able to remember. It's in our bones, or if you like, our souls. We can reach back through all the memories that made us."

"I'm afraid you've left me behind, Mr Noble. Can this lady do it too?"

The woman gave a nervous laugh that was almost blotted out by Tina's giggle. "I think I'd be scared to," the woman said.

"Then can I?"

"You'd like to see through the Bible, would you?" When the man gave no response that I could hear, Mr Noble said "Let me put you on the path. Do you remember your genesis?"

"The book of the Bible, you mean."

"I wouldn't expect you to remember your conception. Most people don't," Mr Noble said with a laugh not wholly unlike Tina's giggle. "That's right, the book."

"I think I know it pretty well."

"You'll recall the first parents, then. Adam and Eve, who had to forego knowledge because they were only human, and then they ate the tribute that would bring it to them."

"I wouldn't put it quite like that, but—"

"Indulge me a moment. God was supposed to have transformed the serpent for sharing knowledge with them, yes? He made it crawl on its belly, isn't that what the Bible says?"

Jim was growing impatient with the conversation, and I was afraid he might make some inadvertent sound. Bobby looked intent on the questioning, so that I felt isolated with my sense of an underlying darkness, a furtive presence that might be the essential substance of the church. "I believe that's so," the man said.

"If it was a serpent, wouldn't it already have been crawling? Why do you think we aren't told what it was like before?"

This felt like a threat that too much was unstable and no longer to be trusted, if it ever had been. "I've no idea," the man admitted.

"See if you can think it out for our next meeting. Or perhaps you can dream it, Mr Wharton. Will you both excuse us now?" Mr Noble's voice had grown brisk. "Thank you for the tribute, Mrs Richards," he said. "We'll look forward to seeing you both next week."

I was urging someone to be more specific about the occasion, but all I heard were footsteps returning from the front of the church. Some of them halted uncomfortably close to us, and the man said "Do you hear confessions, Mr Noble?"

"Why, have you something you'd like to confess?"

"I'm simply asking why that booth is here."

To my dismay I heard him advancing towards us, and almost flinched against Jim. "Like those windows, it was a feature of the church," Mr Noble said. "We've kept them because our follower who did the building work thought it was respectful."

"Didn't you, Mr Noble?"

The voice and the footsteps were closer, and I stared at Jim as if this could hold him as still as I was striving to remain. "The building was deconsecrated after it was bombed," Mr Noble said. "Our spirit fills it now."

I didn't think this would satisfy his questioner, and as the footsteps kept coming I held my breath so hard my chest began to throb. "Forgive me, are we keeping you?" the man said, though not as if he cared much.

"You are rather."

"I wouldn't want to overstay my welcome." The man's voice sounded closer than an arm's length to my back. "I'll wait for the demonstration," he said.

His voice had turned aside at last, but I couldn't begin to relax until his footsteps moved away, and then I had to muffle the breath I'd expelled in relief. I was afraid it had been all too audible until I heard his footsteps and the woman's recede along the aisle. The church door shut with a thud and a clank of the latch, and Tina giggled again. "Serpent," she said.

"Sir Pent, that's what they tried to make him. The third person in the garden. The one who could be anything till religion tried to fix him in a shape. The bringer of all truth. His old name was Daoloth if anyone needed a word for him, and they even tried to take that away from him."

I saw Jim press his lips together as if he had to lock an angry outburst in. "They're afraid of anything that's too big for their minds," Mr Noble said, "but we aren't, are we? Let's take the new one down."

We heard them moving away from the altar, and then a key turned in a lock. "Let your father go first," Mr Noble said. "I know you want to see." A door laboured open, dragging across the stone floor, and their footsteps began to descend. I'd counted more than a dozen when Jim muttered "Better get out while we can."

"We mightn't have time," Bobby whispered. "I'm staying here."

"Quiet," I murmured urgently. "Listen."

Our voices had obscured the sound I was straining to hear. It had greeted Mr Noble as his footfalls stopped descending – a vast soft surreptitious restlessness. I thought the noise had resembled a feeble chorus, however vague and wordless. Now there was nothing to hear except a distant thud like the one the woman had made by planting her tribute on the altar. After that came a silence that could have been respectful or watchful or otherwise significant in a way I mightn't even have wanted to grasp, and then Tina giggled. "Good night," she said like a secret joke. "Sleep well."

"They never sleep, Tina," Mr Noble said, "but they dream."

Jim and I stared at each other while Bobby gazed at us through the confessional mesh. I heard a faint click at the foot of the steps, and realised I'd failed to notice it earlier – the sound of a light switch. Tina scampered up the steps while her father followed more deliberately, locking the door and shaking it to confirm it was secure. "Home now," he said. "We don't want Mrs Noble drawing more attention to us, do we?"

"When will we come back?"

"Soon enough, I promise." He seemed a little disconcerted by her eagerness. "Give them time to gather from the dark," he said.

We listened as the two of them left the church. The pushchair receded with a faint squeak of wheels, and as soon as the noise grew inaudible Bobby stepped out of the booth. I fumbled the other door open, and Jim lurched out after me. "God," he said, an imprecation I would never have expected him to use. "I know you said, but I didn't realise he was teaching her that stuff. Something's got to be done."

He strode past the altar as if he didn't believe it was anything like one, and shook the door in the right-hand corner of the walls more vigorously than Mr Noble had. I was afraid of what he might disturb, not having overheard it as I was sure I had, but apart from the rattling of the locked door there was silence. "What do you think they were talking about down there?" Bobby said.

"Some rubbish he believes," Jim said before I could speak. "All that matters is he's putting it in her head. Shouldn't her mother know?"

"We ought to tell her, you mean."

"She'd be on our side. I don't know who else would."

I saw that Jim didn't think too much of the idea now that it had been made specific. I wasn't anxious to linger while we talked, because the empty almost unadorned church felt more than ever like a shell concealing a presence I preferred not to imagine. "We'll need to watch for people coming here," I said. "If we know what they do at their services we'll have more to tell."

I wasn't sure how workable the plan was, but I was growing desperate to leave the church. Unless the sky outside had turned cloudier, I could have fancied that darkness was seeping up from beneath the church to enfeeble the light within. I hurried to ease the door open, struggling to hush its sounds, and we lingered in the porch until we were certain Tina and her father were nowhere to be seen or heard. As we crossed the weedy desolation I glanced back. I was tempted to draw Jim's attention to the detail that had caught my eye, but I didn't want to risk provoking disagreement now that he was committed to dealing with Mr Noble. Even if I'd reminded him about the field in France, he mightn't have found the resemblance as significant as I did – the way that all around the building the weeds crouched almost flat, as though they were striving to grow away from the church.

CHAPTER TWENTY-FOUR

Lies

That Sunday the priest warned us about false prophets. Scientists had invented bombs that could destroy the world, and now they'd dreamed up an idea that was destroying some people's faith in God. However big a bang they came up with, they wouldn't blow God away, and Father Kelly paused to await an appreciative laugh, though not too much mirth. However impermanent the world might seem, this should remind us God was constant – only God. Let the scientists try to shape the future in their own image as much as they liked, but they were going to learn that it belonged to God. They were false prophets masquerading as authorities, and the faithful needed to beware of them. We should always remember how knowledge had led to every sin in the world, and by this point I'd begun to doubt everything the priest said. That was the end of his sermon, and eventually the mass finished too, though not before I'd taken communion alongside my parents at the altar rail. I felt hypocritical, even if I was joining in so that my unbelief wouldn't distress them, and the wafer had never seemed so scrawny and desiccated in my mouth. Its faint oddly undefinable taste lingered as the congregation thanked God for releasing us, and was still on my tongue when we emerged from the church.

Miniature rainbows gleamed in beads of dew on the grass in the small churchyard. Misty sunlight laid a soft glow on the eroded headstones, where the etched messages put me in mind of telegrams from the past. My parents exchanged a few polite words with Father Kelly in the porch, and we were almost at the gates when I saw Jim and his parents waiting beyond them.

Jim looked too embarrassed to meet my eyes, and I had a sense that his parents' composure had grown ponderous, turning them into obstacles that blocked our way out of the gates. "Can we have a word?" Mr Bailey murmured.

"Have as many as you like," my father said. "No charge."

"Shall we walk along a little first?" Mrs Bailey suggested.

Though it was plain that they didn't want to be overheard, my mother said "Are we going anywhere in particular?"

"Home to ours if you like."

I wondered if they meant to postpone discussion until then. Our route was leading us towards the railway bridge where Mr Noble's father had been run down by the tram, and a stale taste of the wafer returned to my mouth. We hadn't reached the bridge when the Baileys must have noticed we were alone on the pavement. "Do you know where these two and their friend were yesterday?" Mr Bailey said.

"At the flicks," my father said. "Weren't you, Dominic?"

I was mumbling confirmation when Mrs Bailey said "As well as there, Kevin means."

Before I could reply beyond opening my mouth Mr Bailey said "They went to another church."

My parents halted in unison to stare at me. "What church?" my father demanded.

There seemed to be no point in mumbling. "The new one Mr Noble built," I said and gazed at Jim.

He looked at me, but not for long. "I thought mum and dad ought to know what it was like."

"We'd have liked to be told as well," my mother said. "So is someone going to?"

My hot face made it clear that she meant me. "It isn't like a church," I said.

"It looks like it's pretending it's one," Jim said.

My father wasn't satisfied with the answers or with us. "What is it like, then?"

"It doesn't feel holy."

"I'm asking Dominic."

"It feels dead," I told my parents and tried to be more specific. "As dead as a graveyard but like it's pretending not to be alive."

"You aren't writing one of your stories now." My father frowned at me. "Maybe that's the trouble," he said. "You think you're in one."

"I don't, dad. We all know it's real. We wanted to see if Mr Noble takes his little girl to the church."

"Why's that any of your business?" my father objected as my mother said "Did he?"

"Yes, and he's telling her things like he told Mrs Norris. Maybe worse." "He's telling her he knows better than the Bible," Jim said.

We were heading for the bridge again, and the wafery taste was back in my mouth. "And how did you manage to hear all that?" Mr Bailey said.

"We just did."

"I don't like you spying." Mr Bailey had lowered his voice, but not so that the rest of us couldn't hear. "That isn't how this family behaves," he said.

"Dominic's father is right," Mrs Bailey said. "You're acting as if you think you're in one of those stories of his."

While I didn't know how fiercely Jim might refute the accusation, I was provoked to interrupt "Doesn't anybody care about the little girl?"

"Certainly we do." Before I could respond to my mother she added "But it's not your place to ask. Just remember who the parents are."

"See you do." Having given my face time to grow hotter still, my father said "And maybe you can try and realise the police cared, and they took her back to him."

"Maybe," Jim protested, "they didn't know about his church."

"What difference do you think that would make?" Mr Bailey retorted. "We don't like all the nonsense he believes, but it's not against the law."

"Even if it should be," my father said.

"We don't live in that kind of country, do we, Desmond? I didn't think we lived in one where people spy on people either."

"Our homes are still supposed to be our castles," Mrs Bailey said.

"As far as we're concerned it's past time you left this Noble fellow alone," Mr Bailey said, and the bridge muttered in agreement. "If you can't stay away from him, stay away from each other."

"Which is it going to be?" my mother said as if she was trying to outdo him for severity.

I felt devious and in danger of being exposed while I said "We'll do what you're making us do."

"It's for your own good," Mrs Bailey said. "Forget about anyone else's. We know you mean well."

Her husband wasn't too patient with this. "Jim?" he said like a warning.

"Mum's right. Honestly, we did."

Mr Bailey scowled with the whole of his face. "I'm asking how you're going to behave."

"Like Dom said."

Although I couldn't tell whether Jim had understood my ruse, I was afraid he'd given it away until his father said "No need to let him do your talking for you. You're a bit too influenced by him."

"I'm not, dad," Jim complained. "I was after Mr Noble because I've seen what he's like."

"Don't talk to your father like that," Mrs Bailey said. "You're both too obsessed with that man, you and Dominic. Just try to remember he's nothing to do with you any more. He's been dealt with."

I saw Jim was as provoked to argue as I was, but neither of us did. At least my slyness appeared to have been overlooked, and nobody spoke again until we were passing Bobby's road. "We'll be having a word with your friend's parents," Mr Bailey promised, which followed us in silence all the way to the Bailey house. "Will you come in for a cuppa?" Mrs Bailey said as if she thought or hoped life had reverted to normal.

"Will you excuse us if we don't just now?" my mother said. "I think we'll be taking this one home."

As soon as the Baileys' front door shut behind them she said "Dominic, can't we trust you any more at all?"

"What do you mean, mum?"

"I think you know." My father seemed less angry than disappointed, which I felt was worse. "It started with this Noble fellow and his book."

"Dad, I never—"

"We don't want to hear it." He was closer to anger now. "You took something that didn't belong to you," he said. "That isn't how we brought you up."

"It's all to do with this Mr Noble of yours. It's as if he's turning you as bad as him."

"Mum, I'm not. How can you say—"

"You're letting us think half the truth. They should have told you at your school that's as bad as lying."

My face blazed, but I had to ask "Half of what, mum?"

"You told us you were going to the pictures," my father said with angry weariness, "when all the time you were going to that church as well."

"So in future," my mother said, "you can say exactly where you're going before we let you go."

"If we do."

"All right," I mumbled, knowing I would have to be more of a liar than ever: even my answer was a lie.

I felt everything was false and perhaps had always been – our formally attired stroll in the park that afternoon, where I wondered how my parents would react if we met the Noble family; our politely muted Sunday tea, yet another ritual and a denial of any concern about Mr Noble's behaviour; the Sunday evening variety shows and the mirth that the comedy interludes were meant to prompt, when my parents competed at joining in with the audience and glanced at me to incite participation, a gesture I took as a conditional pardon for my sins. They couldn't pardon any that they didn't know about, and I doubted they would if they learned of the disobedience I already had in mind.

As I chortled dutifully at quips and jokes, even some I failed to grasp, I was worrying about Bobby and her parents. in the morning I made sure I was in time to meet her on the way to school, having picked up Jim as I hurried along our road. For a moment she looked ready to avoid us, so that I was afraid she'd been warned not to speak to us and, worse, was obeying. Then she confronted Jim, too somberly even to indulge in a punch. "Why'd you tell?"

"I thought they'd have to do something now it's got so serious."

"Mine have. They've made me promise not to go anywhere near your Mr Noble or I won't be able to stay friends with you and Dom."

I couldn't bring myself to ask if this was just what her parents had said or what she intended. The most I felt able to risk saying was "So what are we going to do?"

Jim stared at me as though he didn't understand or didn't want to. "Maybe leave it for a bit at least," Bobby said. "My dad's organising the union at work, so I expect him and my mum will forget about us if we don't remind them."

I saw the idea didn't please Jim any more than it satisfied me. We were on the bus to Holy Ghost when he admitted "I don't know if I want to do what I said I wouldn't."

By now I knew better than to bring up the Tremendous Three. Far from persuading him, it might have aggravated his aversion, and in any case our exploits were too far removed from the ones we used to have, too characterised by banal subterfuge, deceiving people we never had to in my tales. "I've got to," I said.

I couldn't tell whether he admired me for it or was dismayed by my untrustworthiness. "I'll wait and see like Bobby says," he said.

I suspect he was hoping the Noble situation would resolve itself without involving us, and I'd started to wish that myself. I couldn't do anything until Saturday – I didn't think I would be able to delude my parents that I was meeting my friends after dark – and when the weekend came I gave in to doing only what I said I would, going to the cinema with Bobby and Jim. If the adults wouldn't intervene over Mr Noble and his daughter, was it really up to us? The trouble was that the excuse felt worse than a lie – it felt like cowardice.

A week later it still did. I wasn't due to meet my friends until noon, and I ended up trying to write a new tale, which didn't work at all. Thinking up a fresh adventure for the trio felt like a lie I was struggling to tell myself. I was tempted to write about Mr Noble and his family, not to mention the Trinity Church, but suppose my parents asked to see it? They often read my stories, giving them exactly the same praise they'd bestowed when I started to write, indulgent then, embarrassingly patronising now. If I wrote about the Noble business they would only think it proved I was obsessed. I felt bereft of experiences to draw upon – I wouldn't have dared to write about my relationship with Bobby, not least because it was so unresolved – and I was sitting with my unproductive pen poised above a page that was bare except for a drip of blue ink when my mother called "Dominic, come down here."

Her voice sounded close to ominous, and I wondered what I'd done. When I ventured to the stairs I saw her in the hall, the morning paper open in both hands. "What is it, mum?"

"Have you been talking to someone?"

"Talking to who about what?"

She gazed up at me and then relaxed. "I don't suppose you would have, or your friends," she said. "Well then, come and see. It looks as if you're all getting your wish."

CHAPTER TWENTY-FIVE

The Power of the Press

WHARTON'S WAY

Good morning, one and all! I hope you've breakfasted well. But let me warn you, some of what I have to say in today's column may turn your stomach.

You know Mrs. Malone, the Irish lass who comes in to do my rooms. I've shared her wisdom with you often enough. Just the other day, as she was dusting my trophies, she cried, "Oh, Mr. Wharton, 'tis a sin all by itself, this world we're after making."

I tore the page out of my Remington and screwed it up to chuck it in the bin, the way photoplays have taught us scribblers to behave. "What's troubling you, Kitty?" I enquired.

"How some of the churches are getting to be," she wailed, "they're the real sin."

Summing up the theological chat we had, she thinks too many modern clerics are giving out their own gloss on the Bible rather than the word of God. When I probed a little deeper (we journalists can be detectives too, you know), she told me she was "discombobulated" most of all by a new church she'd heard of from a friend at the washhouse. Its leader sells it as the oldest church, which, as Kitty says, ought to mean it speaks the truest word of God. "But oh, Mr. Wharton," she cried, "may the good Lord strike me dead if I don't think it's the work of the Devil."

When she told me all she'd heard I undertook to investigate. I met the man who runs the church and attended what he presumes to call a service, and it is my considered view that Mrs. Malone's old-fashioned words may not be so short of the truth.

The Trinity Church of the Spirit stands in Joseph Street near Kensington. It is housed in a building which was deconsecrated after being damaged in the blitz and which has been rebuilt by a disciple of a new belief. Christian Noble, the leader of the church, was unwilling to explain whether it has been consecrated afresh. He insists that he is not a priest, and resists the use of a religious term for himself. Perchance this betrays more about the nature of his organisation than he would prefer.

Many folk would think his church is based on Spiritualism. However this belief may appeal to the credulous, it cannot compare with our home-grown British faith, soul of the nation. How much less so is Noble's church, which is more akin to a reversion to savagery than any revival of the Christian verities which its name seeks to evoke. Its services involve what he describes as spiritual tributes, which are grown upon the family graves of members of the church. He claims that our harvest festivals are based on the ritual whereby these tributes are placed upon his un-Christian altar. One member of the congregation informed me that the rite which follows was (according to the leader of the cult) the origin of Holy Communion. Say rather that it is a blasphemous parody, in which participants consume a portion of the tribute they have brought and then believe they hear the deceased speak. Why, if I had believed hard enough, I too could have imagined I heard whispers. Many mediums offer as much, and most have been exposed as the frauds they are.

Are we not a tolerant nation? I hear some of my readers ask. Should our countrymen not be allowed their beliefs, however abhorrent we may find them, so long as they do no harm? I leave aside how such a cult may prey upon the vulnerable. Let me say only that of all the spectacles I witnessed at the Trinity Church, I was most appalled to see its leader's two-year-old child at the rite. While she was not made to participate, I shrank from asking how soon she would be involved, but I pose that question now. I will further say that the Trinity Church of the Spirit is neither spiritual in any healthy sense nor a true church, and that Christian Noble is very far from living up to either of his names. If he wishes to respond, I shall make space in my column for him.

Let me end by quoting Dennis Wheatley, our leading authority on the occult and Satanic, who graciously made time to hear my account of the church. "Beware the evil in our midst," he advised me. "Remember Crowley was an Englishman. We should always be on the alert for an invasion of our shores, but we should never let that make us overlook corruption that is growing from our own soil."

"My dad says he wasn't praying but thank God that's all over," Bobby said.

Jim looked pained by the profanity but let it go under the circumstances. "My mum said Nobbly deserves all he gets."

"I shouldn't reckon she called him that, did she?" Bobby said with a laugh that sounded like abandoning nervousness. "Mine says that now it's done with she doesn't mind admitting she was worried."

"They aren't saying, but I think my mum and dad feel a bit like that too."

We were walking to the bus stop into town, and I halted in front of the tobacconist's to ask "Why aren't they still worried? Aren't we?"

The tobacconist watched us through the glass door, quite possibly assuming the discussion was about which brand of cigarettes to buy. "Why, Dom?" Bobby said.

"The story in the paper won't save Tina, will it? She'll still be with him."

"Maybe she won't be now so many people know about him. Their neighbours will, so maybe they'll do something. Maybe they'll get her adopted, or somebody will."

I thought her hopes for Tina were as unreal as any of my tales of the Tremendous Three. "You haven't told us what your mum and dad thought," Jim reminded me as if this had some importance.

"My dad's at work. I expect he'll think what my mum does and everyone, it's all finished with or it will be soon and they can forget about it, and we can. Look, I thought that too at first." Reading Eric Wharton's column in the newspaper had come as such a relief that I'd let myself imagine everything was resolved; I'd almost told my mother that we'd overheard the journalist investigating the church. "It doesn't matter what they think," I said.

"Maybe you don't care what yours think," Jim said, "but we aren't all like you, Dom."

"I mean they can't be right when they've never been to that church."

"We have and I think they are. Don't you, Bobs?"

As Bobby set about agreeing with him I said "Then what do you think he'll have to do about it?"

"I expect he'll move away if he's got any sense," Jim said. "The further the better."

"About what's underneath his church. Don't you think he's going to be worried somebody might look?"

"At what, Dom?" Bobby said too much like someone talking down.

"At whatever he's keeping there. You heard it, didn't you? You'd both have heard."

"It was a flower or something like that the woman brought in, wasn't it? I heard him and Tina take it down."

"That's what I heard too," Jim said. "Can we get a move on? We don't want to miss the start of the film."

As he strode away from the disappointed tobacconist's I hurried to overtake him. "There was something else. Did you honestly not hear?"

"Honest," Jim said, and in case I didn't catch his meaning "That's what I am."

"I heard Tina laughing," Bobby admitted. "I don't know what she'd find to laugh at in a crypt, if that's what it is."

"You've got it. There's something there that shouldn't be."

"Well, it's someone else's job to find out now," Jim said, though not as if he thought there would be much if anything to unearth. "Like you say, somebody probably will."

I hadn't said that, and I was unsure whether it would happen; I'd no reason to suppose it would immediately or even soon. "We ought to see what he does now he's in the paper."

"Dom," Bobby said, "we shouldn't go anywhere near him."

I felt betrayed or about to be. "Why not?"

"Suppose he thinks we made Eric Wharton write about him? If he even sees us he might blame us."

"Anyway," Jim said, "we're going to see *Apache.*"

"There's more important things than films," I said before I could catch up with him.

I was hoping this might slow him down, but he didn't even bother looking back. "Bobs wants to see it too," he said. "It's got Burt Lancaster."

"It can wait till next time, can't it? It'll be on somewhere else."

Jim might have been trying to outrun my scrutiny as he said "I've told my mum and dad I'm going."

"I told mine I was too. Well," I said and felt inspired, "I was."

He stopped at last and turned with a frown. "I don't like not telling them the truth."

"I don't really either. Dom," Bobby said, "when you read about the film you said you'd like to go."

"Yes, but not till we've seen what Mr Noble's doing."

"Why do you think we'd even be able to?" As I stayed where I was she took a step after Jim. "Aren't you coming with us?" she said.

Just then all I could hear was her and Jim raising every objection they could think of, but now I realise she was trying to persuade me not to take risks on my own. "You go if you want," I said. "Someone's got to keep an eye on him."

I was hoping this might bring them back, but Bobby turned away, twitching one shoulder in an unadmitted shrug, to follow Jim. I felt as if I'd wasted all the time I'd spent in trying to convince them. I hurried down the nearest side street that wasn't mine or Bobby's – I couldn't chance being seen by any of our parents – and made for the Noble house.

The streets smelled of a fog that had faded away hours ago. A thin shrunken sun was the only item in a sky as pale as mist, and lent a weak glow to the twisted brownish leaves the trees still held. As I passed the Norris house, where the empty rooms looked drained not just of life but colour, I felt vaguely guilty that nobody I knew had visited Mrs Norris in hospital. I came to a stop by the entrance to the graveyard, wondering if I should watch the Noble residence from behind the hedge. Suppose Mr Noble was already at the church or on his way there? The bus that would take me closest passed his house first, which seemed like a plan.

I dashed past the railway alongside the graveyard, and as I reached the main road I saw a bus approaching the nearest stop. I put on a final sprint, shoving my hand out so far that my arm ached with stretching. I was afraid the bus would sail by – they often did when people of my age or younger tried to flag them down, even if we were waiting at the stop – but this one slowed to arrive at the stop as I did. I'd hardly clattered panting upstairs and fallen onto the right-hand front seat when the conductor came after me. "Where are you going, sonny?"

"Brow." Having regained more breath, I said "Everton Brow."

He hadn't been smiling – with the NO SPITTING sign above his head he looked as if he was warning me against the offence – and now he found even less of a reason. "Everton Brow please, I think you mean."

"Yes." I was growing afraid that even if he didn't put me off the bus for impoliteness, he would distract me from watching Mr Noble's house. "Everton Brow please," I gabbled, snatching out the fare so hastily that I almost scattered it across the floor.

The conductor looked at the very least dissatisfied, whether with my speeded-up courtesy or because I hadn't given him the correct change. He lingered over snapping coins out of the holder he wore, and accompanied them with a scowl before winding my ticket out of the machine. I don't suppose he approved of my turning away as soon as I'd taken the ticket from him. I remembered to mumble my thanks, but I was mostly aware that the Noble house had come in sight ahead. The conductor was tramping downstairs deliberately enough to make each step a comment when Mr Noble strode out of the house.

I could see the bus had brought him out, but he turned to call "Look after her or someone else will." Even if the front hall had amplified his shout, for me to catch it at that distance he plainly didn't care who heard. It occurred to me that he'd left Tina behind so that she wouldn't slow him down. He slammed the front door and marched across the road, brandishing a rolled-up newspaper to stop the bus. I had to hide, and I slid off the seat so fast that the metal under the front window scraped my knees. At least there was nobody upstairs to see my behaviour. As I crouched out of sight the bus halted abruptly, bumping the top of my head against the metal, and Mr Noble came on board.

I heard his footsteps on the stairs and tried to hush my breaths. If he made for the unoccupied front seat he would see me at once. I was both afraid of that and dismayed by how ridiculous I would look. His footsteps hesitated as they reached the top deck, and my breath caught in my throat like stale tobacco smoke. Then his steps receded along the aisle, and I was starting to relax as much as I could in my cramped posture when I heard the conductor set about following him.

The man knew I was there. He would want to know what I was doing, and even if I pretended to have lost something on the floor, Mr Noble would hear my voice. I couldn't tell whether I was holding my breath or unable to breathe. When I heard the conductor halt at the top of the stairs I was certain he was staring towards me. In a moment Mr Noble said impatiently if not with pique "Yes, here I am."

The conductor tramped halfway down the bus to him. "Thank you," Mr Noble said, "the Brow."

So he was going to the church. At once I was afraid that the conductor might make some remark, perhaps that the Brow seemed to be a popular stop, but he said nothing at all. Change clicked out of the holder, and the whir of the ticket machine was followed by a silence that I feared might mean the conductor was about to come and find me. Then I heard a juvenile commotion on the lower deck, several boys competing at how loud they could fart with their mouths once they'd finished laughing at each performance. The conductor's footsteps clattered fast along the aisle and down the stairs. "Any more of that," he said loud enough to be heard throughout the vehicle, "and you'll be off this bus."

The storm of mirth subsided into a lingering drizzle of giggles, which let me hear faint sounds on the upper deck. They seemed familiar from somewhere else – from the stage at my school. I'd grasped that Mr Noble was tearing paper into shreds when the conductor came upstairs again. As I strove to crouch lower and smaller, every one of my joints felt eager to ache if not to flare with pain. From the top of the stairs the conductor demanded "What do you think you're doing there?"

Rather than answer I sucked in a breath. I wasn't going to speak until he came to look at me, and perhaps then I could whisper low enough for Mr Noble not to hear. While I couldn't judge how far the bus had travelled, surely we must be close to his stop. I didn't realise that I hadn't been addressed until Mr Noble said "Just dealing with some rubbish."

"We don't want it on our buses, thank you. Will you kindly pick it up and take it with you."

"I can promise you want it more than I do."

The conductor paused, whether in disbelief or for emphasis. "Sir, I must ask you to clear your litter up."

"You've already asked and you've had your answer."

I was shocked by the pettiness the situation had exposed – Mr Noble's need to exert power in even so trivial a fashion. "Sir," the conductor said, "for the third time—"

"All good things come in threes, is that the thing? Pick all this up, you're saying, or you'll throw me off your bus. Don't bother fancying you can. Here's my stop."

The bell clanged once as Mr Noble set it off, and I heard him march to the stairs. I could only assume that something about him had daunted the conductor, who made no attempt to detain him that I heard. The bus coasted to a halt, and I hauled myself up to risk a glance out of the window. Mr Noble was already striding towards the Grafton and the devastated streets beyond, so purposefully that his top half was inclined forward in the way that increasingly put me in mind of a snake.

As I rose to my feet my eyes met the conductor's. He was stooping to collect torn fragments of the newspaper, and turned his rage at them on me. "What were you playing at, sonny?"

"Dropped my money. Got it now." I was hardly even aware of lying. "Missed my stop," I said and made for the stairs.

He looked ready to delay me, having failed to arrest Mr Noble for littering. Perhaps he meant to demand an extra fare, though I was certain it cost the same to the next stop. Then he heard a burst of mirth downstairs, which he plainly took as a preamble to more mischief. "Go on," he told me, less like a release than a warning.

I jumped off the platform before the bus had quite halted and hurried uphill to the ridge overlooking downtown Liverpool. In less than five minutes I reached the ruined streets beyond the ballroom. Besides smoke and brick dust they smelled of fog, which was loitering among the smashed houses, too far away to help me hide if I needed to. I couldn't see Mr Noble or hear him, and had no idea how close he might be. Surely he must be well on his way to the church, but I was taking care not to make any unnecessary noise as I picked my way through the rubble in the streets when I heard him.

He was several streets away, at the church or very near. I don't know if he said a word; all I caught was a bellow of rage or anguish that resounded through the derelict streets. For a moment I thought he'd injured himself – his cry had sounded agonised enough – and then I wondered if the issue was something he'd seen. I dodged between the collapsed houses, taking care to stay out of his sight, until I heard the church door slam.

I made for the church so fast that I came near to tripping over bricks. Their shrill clink slowed me down, but it didn't take me long to reach a two-storey remnant of a housefront from behind which I could spy on the church. Though I was hundreds of yards away, I made out that every window on this side of the church had been shattered, while the signboard for the Trinity Church of the Spirit lay in pieces beside the porch. In a moment Mr Noble's voice resounded through the church. From his tone I could have thought he was praying, but even if I hadn't known him too well to come to that conclusion, the name he was calling had more syllables than God.

After those three syllables he fell silent, and I was waiting for sounds when he emerged from the church. He slammed the door and stalked towards me. He looked ready to strike down anyone he suspected of having vandalised his church, and as I flinched out of sight I was sure he'd seen me. I heard him kick rubble out of his way so viciously that it shattered against a wall. I was staring around me, desperate to find somewhere I might be less visible, when he tramped past my hiding place and away down the devastated road.

At least he was making plenty of noise, but I didn't risk stirring until I couldn't hear him. Even then I peered around the wasteland to reassure myself that he wasn't on his way back, and then I headed for the church. As I'd assumed, every window was broken, leaving the apertures toothy with glass. Having made a circuit of the church, which looked as though it had set about reverting to the ruinousness around it, I let myself in.

Inside was worse. Not a single item had survived. The pews and the other seats had been hacked to bits, and the confessional where my friends and I had hidden was reduced to splintered chunks of wood. Whoever was responsible must have devoted quite some time to the altar, which was strewn in bits across the broad ledge at the top of the steps, while the drapery lay crumpled in a corner. I guessed that the vandal or vandals had been provoked by Eric Wharton's newspaper column. I was gazing about, trying to decide how the destruction made me feel, when I saw that the job wasn't finished. While the wood around the lock on the door to the crypt had been gouged with an axe, the tool had been abandoned among the fragments of the altar.

I felt worse than an intruder – unreasonably like a vandal – as I ventured along the aisle between the wrecked seats to pick up the axe. Just the same, I had to find out what Mr Noble was keeping beneath the church. Someone had to see, and wasn't I entitled if anybody was? I gripped the shaft of the axe as firmly as I could and swung it at the deepest gouge beside the lock.

The blade bit deep into the stout wood, and the impact shuddered through my arms. At the second blow they began to ache. At the third, chips of wood flew out of the panel, and I was firming my grasp for another blow when I heard a sound beyond the door. It wasn't quite a voice, though I could have fancied that it was attempting to become one. Since it was audible through the door, its source had to be unappealingly large or else numerous. Neither possibility encouraged me to renew my efforts to break into the crypt. Retreating at some speed, I hid the axe under the altar cloth in the corner, and then I hurried out of the church.

I was making for the bus stop when a glimpse of crimson showed me a phone box on the main road. Surely I had sufficient reason now to call the police. I pressed button B in the hope that the slot would yield up a coin, as they often did, but the mechanism was keeping all its money to itself. I dialled one 9 and faltered as the dial returned to zero with a sluggish whir. Was this really an emergency? I looked up the number of the nearest police station in the dog-eared floppy book and fed pennies into the

A slot, but I'd only dialled three digits before I lost confidence. When the police heard how young I was, they would never believe the kind of thing I had to say; they'd think it was a prank. I poked button B to retrieve my coins, and the phone box let out a cigarette breath as I ran for a bus. I was going back to the church, but first I had to find Bobby and Jim.

CHAPTER TWENTY-SIX

Farming the Dead

"Hey, look, it's Dom. Couldn't you find Nobbly? You've missed the big film."

"It was good even though it was a cowie. We can sit it round again if you want to see it."

"No, you've got to help me, both of you. He went to the church and he's in a rage. Somebody's smashed up the church."

"Well, nobody we know would have, but maybe you ought to just be glad someone did."

"They haven't smashed it all, Jim. They've left the door that goes down."

"Still ought to teach him a lesson, though. Maybe he'll stop what he's been doing now he knows how people feel."

"You know he won't. He doesn't care what anybody thinks except him and Tina. He'll just start up somewhere else."

"I expect the same thing will happen then, Dom."

"Bobby, you don't understand. Neither of you do. Whatever he's keeping under the church, we need to find out what it is before he moves it. We need to go now."

"The other film's on in a few minutes. It's a gangster."

"We can see it another time, Jim. I'll pay for us all if you like."

"You're really serious about it, aren't you, Dom?"

"Cross my heart, Bobby, I heard something down there. On the Bible I did, Jim, something alive. I mean I did while you were watching your film."

"You followed Mr Noble in there all by yourself."

"I had to, didn't I? Only I waited till he'd gone. I'm certain he'll be coming back. We need to see before he does."

"And then what are we supposed to do?"

"When we know what's there we can show people. They'll have to believe us then, and maybe someone will do more about him than just wreck his church."

"But won't he know it was us that told?"

"We can make an anonymous phone call. I know, we could phone Eric Wharton."

"Jim, the lights are going down. We can't talk any more or we'll get thrown out."

"Jim, I need you to help me break the door down."

"Never mind leaving me out, Dominic Sheldrake. I can do it just as much as him. You've felt how strong I am. I'm coming with you."

"Then I am as well. Just make sure our parents never know."

If the conversation had gone along those lines, what difference would it have made? Probably none to the world, but a great deal to me. It was the kind of thing I rehearsed in my head on the bus into town – a tale of the Tremendous Three I was telling myself. Would Jim have referred to our parents, or was he still calling them our mums and dads? I can't even say if all of us were less mature than we thought we were, or if I was alone in that as well.

I jumped off the bus outside Lewis's department store, on the front of which a stone giant trained his penis on Saturday shoppers and strollers through town. I sprinted along Lime Street, past a pair of cinemas to the third of the trio, the Forum. Beyond it, opposite a frieze of pigeons on the colonnade of St George's Hall, a horde of football supporters red-necked with scarves emerged chanting from the railway station. Do I honestly remember all these details? How much am I inventing? At least it helps to fix my memories and bring them to life. At least they feel as if they're only mine.

The pigeons took flight as the football fans flooded towards them, and I hurried into the cinema. I hadn't taken out my cash by the time I crossed the tiled lobby, and the woman in the pay box gave me a guarded look. "Can I just go in and find my friends?" I said.

"Don't try that on, son." Her face made it clear I'd confirmed her initial suspicion. "Nothing's free in here," she said.

I hadn't time to argue. I shoved enough money under the window for a seat in the front stalls, remembering barely in time to pay for an adult ticket. For a moment I thought she was going to refuse to admit me, even though the film only had an A certificate, unless I found an adult to take me in. She took her time over counting my pennies and threepences and sixpences before releasing a ticket from one of the metal slots in front of her. No doubt she disapproved of how I snatched the ticket and dashed to the entrance to the auditorium.

An usherette tore the ticket, and her flashlight beam set about guiding me as I strode fast down the aisle, but I knew where I was going. Jim and Bobby and I always sat on the front row, so close to the screen that we had to lean back in our seats with our legs stuck out in front of us and gaze up at the film. Just now Burt Lancaster was naked from the waist up, which I suspected might please Bobby a good deal, and hiding from pursuers in a field. I could see this was the climax of the film, and it seemed best to let my friends enjoy it before I told them about the church. Surely that wouldn't lose us too much time – but then I saw they weren't on the front row after all.

I swung around beneath the screen to peer at the auditorium. Dozens of scattered faces flared up and grew dim with the shifting light from the screen, but none of them belonged to Bobby or Jim. Someone shouted at me to sit down, though my head couldn't have been bigger than a seed in the field. I sprinted up the aisle, earning stares and frowns, and found the usherette watching the film from beside the doors. "I'm supposed to meet my friends," I whispered. "They must be upstairs. Can I go and look?"

She said nothing while she followed me into the lobby, and I was afraid she meant to eject me from the cinema until she called to a young man wearing the male version of her uniform. "Just take this lad up to the balcony to see if he can find his friends," she said and told me "Five minutes and then you've got to go back where you paid for, and don't go making any noise."

The usher led me up several flights of carpeted marble stairs. I'd never been up here before, and I wondered why Jim and Bobby had now. Why would they have made it a special occasion when I wasn't with them? An usherette was standing by the doors to the circle, and her colleague sauntered over to her, indicating me with his flashlight. "He's stalls," he said, "but Judy says he can go in to look for someone."

The usherette narrowed her eyes at me but shrugged off her doubts – responsibility, at any rate. As she let me into the circle I saw that the film was coming to an end. Despite how it had looked downstairs, Burt Lancaster hadn't been killed after all. Music swelled up as I took my first steps down the stairs of the aisle, and I saw Jim and Bobby at once. They were three rows back from the edge of the balcony, silhouetted against names that were crawling up the screen. I recognised their profiles as they separated, and I saw the thread of saliva that linked them.

I twisted around and stumbled blindly up the aisle. I felt sick and very possibly about to be. I was so desperate to be gone before the lights came up and the lovers could notice me that I tripped over the top step. I blundered against the doors and fell into the upstairs lobby, almost colliding with the pair of uniformed staff. "What's wrong?" the usherette cried. "What's wrong with you?"

By the time I thought of an answer, not that I cared how she and her colleague took it, I was too furious to feel sick any longer. "Somewhere else," I blurted and ran downstairs to stalk out of the cinema.

The enervated sun was sneaking its cold light over the roofs, a glow that seemed too fierce to me. While my rage made it hard to think, I knew that I didn't need Bobby and Jim any longer, and that they must never learn I'd caught them at their business in the dark. As I headed for the bus I loathed everybody in the crowd I was dodging through – loathed them for seeing however I must look and dismissing it as adolescent self-indulgence. When it occurred to me that they probably weren't even aware of me, I began to detest myself for believing I mattered. I certainly didn't to Bobby and Jim.

I was going to matter. I shouldn't have wasted time in trying to involve the pair who used to be my friends. The Tremendous Three showed how childish my view of Bobby and Jim had been. I was tempted to go straight home and tear up all my stories, but I had a more important mission, and they would have to wait. The bus came within minutes, even if those provoked me to grimace like an oldster at every bus I didn't need. I hauled myself onto the platform with the pole, earning a frown from the conductor – a frown of recognition. He'd been on the bus that had brought me downtown.

I tramped upstairs to the front seat, where I tried to be ready to restrain my anger no matter what he might say. Though I felt capable of walking to Everton Brow, I didn't want to be turned off the bus and waste even more time than my former friends had robbed me of. I heard him mount the stairs behind me, and then he loomed at my side. I was counting out the correct change when he said "Do you think I look out of shape, sonny?"

I couldn't very well not meet his eyes, which were as unfriendly as his voice. "No?" I said, far more of a question than one word.

"I was thinking you might fancy I'm needing the exercise, making me shinny up here every time."

I was sure he was eager for an excuse to put me off the bus. "I just like sitting at the front," I said and was enraged by how infantile I sounded.

"Your sort always does, and hang everybody else." Having apparently exhausted the objections he could make, he said "Off to do more mischief?"

"I haven't done any yet." All at once I couldn't hold my rage in. "I won't, either," I declared, clenching my fists hard enough for the coins to bruise my palm.

"You're a rare one, then." This might have resembled praise until he said "It won't buy you a free ride."

The implication that I was trying to cheat him made me nearly unable to contain my rage. I only just managed to thank him once he'd wound the ticket out of his machine. None too soon he left me alone to watch the streets grow less crowded and then close to empty as the bus laboured up Everton Brow. As I hurried downstairs, having rung the bell, he said "Off home, are we?"

"I don't live here."

"You'd wonder what the appeal is, then."

I stared straight into his eyes as the bus slowed. "I'm going to church."

In a sense it wasn't a lie, although the way he must have heard it was. It felt like a summation of the person I was becoming, and expressed my ire as well. As I strode fast towards the streets beyond the ballroom I wouldn't have minded encountering Mr Noble. He was as good a target for my rage as any, and I imagined I was capable of dealing face to face with him.

The shrunken sun hung low above the wrecked streets. It looked as if the devastation had dragged it down the pallid greyish sky to drain its light, lending the broken houses a muffled lifeless glow. The skeletal buildings that still clung to bits of their rooms looked as dead as my friendship with Bobby and Jim, and so the wasteland felt like the most appropriate place for my teenage self to be. Better yet, I had a reason to be there – a reason that no longer involved them.

I met nobody as I tramped through the ruined streets to the church. I'd guessed that Mr Noble would need a vehicle to transport whatever he planned to house elsewhere, but there was no sign of one so far. When I came close enough to see the weeds crouching away from the church, I was tempted to go back to the phone box without investigating the vault myself. Was I too scared to venture there without Bobby and Jim? The idea infuriated me so much that I strode through the debris to the church and flung the door open, almost slamming it against the inner wall.

So far as I could tell, the place was exactly as I'd left it. As I tramped along the aisle between the chopped-up pews and seats I glimpsed movement to my left, near the wall, and faltered while my mouth grew dry as ash until I realised I'd seen my own fragmentary reflection in a shard of broken window. The moment of panic renewed my fury, and I stalked past the demolished altar, having retrieved the axe from where I'd hidden it beneath the cloth. Gripping the shaft of the axe in my fists, I vowed that I wouldn't give up before I'd broken into the room under the church.

It took more than a dozen blows to dislodge the lock, by which time my arms were shivering. The last efforts sent an ache all the way from my fingertips to my shoulders, and I couldn't help cursing Jim – I even said bloody and bastard. The blows had grown clumsily inaccurate, and the very last clanged against the lock instead of wood. The block of metal sagged inwards, and a shaky push with the head of the axe sent it clattering down the steps beyond the door.

The door swung open, revealing the steps. The feeble rays of sunlight slanting into the church came nowhere near them, so that I couldn't even see the step where the dislodged lock had ended up. I wanted to believe I was hesitating only to let my eyes adjust to the dimness beyond the door, but I was also listening for any hint of the sound I'd heard last time I was there. The basement was as quiet as the miles of devastation surrounding the church. As soon as I was able to distinguish the lock, which had lodged against the wall on the seventh step down, I shoved the door wide in the hope of admitting more light. This made no difference that I could see, but I made myself venture onto the steps. I'd heard one of the Nobles switch a light off down there, after all.

The steps were barely wide enough for two people. I was enraged by wondering who would have gone first if I'd been with Bobby and Jim. However they were behaving now, I hoped bitterly that that they were having a good time, not really a hope at all. As I stepped down past the fallen lock I saw where the stone stairs ended, in a darkness larger than I could define. It was as silent as it appeared to be still. Six more steps took me to the bottom, where I was just able to make out a switch on the wall to my right. I didn't realise how shaky my hands were from hacking at the door until I fumbled to switch the light on. The shivering felt like a symptom of fear, which infuriated me so much that I seized my wrist to steady the hand. When my unwieldy fingers snagged the switch, three bare bulbs lit up beneath the subterranean roof, and I stared at the sight they'd revealed.

I couldn't have said how the vault had originally been used. It was a room as long and broad as the church, with unadorned stone walls and a floor set with large flagstones. A dozen token pillars were embedded in the walls, pairing to form rudimentary arches beneath the low stone roof. There were cracks in the ceiling and some of the pillars, no doubt from the blitz. I remember all this, but just then I was preoccupied with the contents of the vault – four trestle tables that you might have seen at a church fête, and the items on them reminded me of that kind of stall. They were plants in pots, perhaps a hundred of them.

Though I suppose I must have expected something of the kind, the sight struck me as worse than grotesque: disappointing, frustrating, not worth all my nervousness, even less worth having lost my friends for. So these were the tributes Mr Noble exacted from his congregation, and presumably he chewed them to give himself visions, the way I'd read shamans did. As for the noise I thought I'd heard, no doubt that had been the wind through a ventilation system. I'd begun to feel childish again for imagining that I could have found some secret in the vault that would impress adults with my skills as an investigator – my search was just a last pathetic exploit of the paltry remnant of the Tremendous Three – when I noticed that the contents of the tables weren't quite as banal as I'd originally thought. While I recognised some herbs as species that were grown in the more enterprising of the allotments near my house – sage, mint, rosemary – several of the growths in pots further from the steps weren't quite or even very much like any that I'd seen.

My shadow ventured between the nearest tables before I did. They were halfway down the crypt, presumably leaving space for more. As I went forward, dropping the axe beside the steps, I might have been challenging the place to reveal more than it had, since it appeared to have so little to offer. The herbs I'd identified were closest to the entrance to the vault, and beyond them were some of the same, except not quite. Their growth was more profuse, and that wasn't all. The stems that spilled over the rims of the pots and rose towards the roof were entwined in patterns so elaborate that my vision couldn't disentangle them. Somehow they put me in mind of algebra, of equations far too complex for me even to begin to grasp, and yet I felt as though I had to decipher their secrets before I could move on.

I loitered until I began to feel as though the unreadably intricate structures of the scrawny stems were imprinting themselves on my brain. Perhaps they were rooting themselves there as I lost awareness of anything except them. I no longer knew where I was, but I felt as though I were about to be somewhere else – somewhere vast and dark and unimaginably inhabited. My sense of it was less than a glimpse, just an impression that I was in danger of rousing a presence somehow even vaster than the dark, but it was enough to send me fleeing back to ordinary consciousness. As I grew aware of the vault again I felt as if I were lurching awake from a dream that had swallowed my mind.

Having lost so much awareness brought me close to panic, but I wasn't about to retreat. I needed evidence, not least to show my one-time friends that I'd braved the crypt. Once I'd shown them, I might have nothing more to do with them. I could let them believe that their refusal to help me investigate the crypt was why – the death of the Tremendous Three, and I didn't care how childish they might think I was being. That would just be another excuse – no, a reason, and a good one – to avoid them.

My thoughts were distracting me as much as the patterns of the stems had, and I made myself focus on the situation. I ought to be quick, since I had no idea when Mr Noble might return to the church. As I stepped forward my shadow shrank back, having met the light from the second naked bulb. The further I advanced, the more elaborate the plants on either side of me appeared to have grown, the stalks so intricately entwined above each pot that I avoided looking directly at them for fear of becoming entranced again. Instead I stopped between the pair of tables furthest from the steps.

At first the items on the tables didn't seem as disconcerting as the herbs. Each pot contained a flower, some of them in bloom. If I was unable to identify any of them, I wasn't a florist or even a botanist; we didn't learn about flowers at school. Perhaps one was a species of rose, although the petals were unusually plump, and infused with a bluish glare that made it impossible to judge what colour they should be. Was that a daffodil across the aisle? An unhealthy greenish tint had invaded the irregularly swollen petals, which looked as though the contorted stem was infecting the blossom. Those were the only two plants I came anywhere near identifying, because those beyond them were more distorted still.

I thought it would make sense to take one of the worst away with me, but I wasn't prepared for how malformed the flowers closest to the back wall of the crypt would prove to be. Some had adopted shapes that I felt should never have belonged to flowers: more than one exposed set of roots resembled a miniature hand clenched in the soil, and one bloom the colour of pale flesh contained a swelling that reminded me of a somnolent lidded eye, while next to it a set of greyish petals cupped like stubby fingers surrounded a slit like a tiny fat-lipped mouth. By now I was under the bulb at the far end of the crypt, where my shadow looked desperate to hide beneath my feet. The stillness of the plants around me, not to mention between me and the steps to the outside world, had begun to feel ominously unnatural, and the journal I'd copied put an idea into my head. Perhaps the herbs and flowers were hinting at the shapes of whatever they were meant to body forth, while the ones with human traits had been deformed by the efforts of the dead to regain substance wherever they could find it. I didn't want to examine the notion until I was out of the crypt – indeed, well away from the church. I grabbed the nearest plant pot, which contained the greyish growth. With its malformed bloom and its moist obese glistening leaves, nobody was going to mistake it for a natural flower.

My fingers were clumsier than I expected, still unwieldy from using the axe. The pot wobbled in my grasp, and I seized it with my other hand as well. I couldn't understand how I'd failed to steady it – some kind of movement was continuing in my hands – until I realised they were still. It was the article they held that was moving. The greyish flower was nodding towards me, parting its plump lips in the middle of the greyish bloom. Before I could react, a bunch of swollen leaves groped to close around my wrist. They felt as I imagined a cluster of slugs would feel, cold and slick and uncertain of their shape. I cried out with disgust and stumbled backwards, dropping the object that was squirming in my hands. As the pot smashed on the floor I blundered against the table behind me and knocked it over. Pot after pot shattered on the floor or against the wall, and the crypt came awake.

It was the sound I'd heard when Mr Noble had brought Tina down here, and later when I'd been outside the door. I'd been right to think it resembled a chorus of voices without words. Now I saw it was an aberrant attempt at speech, since even those plants that hadn't developed anything like mouths were opening and closing their petals in a grotesque mimicry of lips. The fallen plants squirmed like crippled worms amid the debris of their pots, and the contents of the table opposite were writhing too, while the herbs wove new patterns with their restless stems, adding to the wordless whispers and inhuman murmurs growing more articulate beneath the vaulted roof.

The oppressive clamour and the sight of all that monstrous restlessness left me almost unable to think. I staggered towards the steps, frantically rubbing my wrist, where the feel of swollen groping leaves still lingered. I caught sight of the axe, and my loathing found a focus. Grabbing the axe, I stalked back through the crypt to chop every herb and plant to pieces, flooring the tables as well. Mixed with my abhorrence was disgust at how I'd caught Bobby and Jim. Wherever I saw a growth still moving – some of them tried to hump like grubs out of reach of my fury – I hacked at it until it was in bits too small to move any more. I was so intent on destroying even the slightest sign of life that I didn't notice the shadows until I heard them.

At first I thought the sounds were the last wordless pleas of plants that weren't just plants, and then I realised the noise was more like the swarming of insects. It was all around me, and I was almost too afraid to look. Shadows not unlike the outlines of the plants I'd chopped to bits but considerably larger and to a dismaying extent more human were streaming over the walls of the crypt with a concerted murmur that was only just substantial. They appeared to be searching for a way out, and as I watched they found the junction of the walls and floor, and lost shape as they vanished into the earth.

I let myself believe I'd liberated whatever had been tethered to the vegetation. Perhaps I'd achieved more than I'd meant to, even if I had nothing to show for it. The flight of the shadows had mesmerised me, but now I found I was exhausted, my arms throbbing from wielding the axe. I dropped it between the splintered remains of the tables and lurched towards the steps. Even my mind was tired out, because as I took the first step upwards I automatically did what my parents had trained me to do at home: switch off the light whenever I left an empty room. The instant I did so, a presence that might have been waiting for the darkness to let it take shape clutched at my back.

I twisted to face it, almost falling backwards on the steps. Though I could see nothing, I felt far too much – a distended body at least twice my size but with far less of a shape. It had lost its imprecise hold on me, but now it fumbled at me with hands that felt plump as tripe, yet insubstantial. They seemed to be trying to separate their wads of flimsy boneless flesh into fingers, altogether too many of them. Worse still was the sense of an unseen face about to press itself against mine – perhaps even into my head, given the unnatural nature of its substance. The prospect drove me beyond panic, and I thrust a flinching hand at the face. I felt its huge features not just writhe but relocate themselves, and my fingers dug into two of the eyes. I felt the eyes retreat deep into the sockets, which closed around my fingers, fastening masses of tendrils on them.

I don't know what kind of cry I uttered. Flinging myself backwards, I flailed my arm to find the light switch. Despite my clumsiness, my free hand encountered the switch, and the bulbs lit up. Apart from all the destruction I'd caused, the crypt was empty. I floundered up the steps into the church. I could still feel how the innumerable fleshy tendrils had seized my fingers, but nothing followed me. Perhaps the light kept it back, unless it was still tethered to some item I'd failed to rob of life.

I stumbled down the aisle and out of the church. The sun looked as if it wouldn't need to grow much weaker to succumb to the dark. I was trudging shakily through the demolished streets, feeling as if my mind was too damaged to risk thoughts, when I saw a vehicle chugging across the opposite side of the wasteland towards the church. It was a jeep or some kind of army truck, and I guessed Mr Noble was driving. I lingered out of sight until I heard the vehicle halt and the distant church door open, and then I held my breath. All at once I heard a muffled roar of rage that sounded capable of shaking the foundations of the church, and I managed an unsteady grin as I turned my back on him.

CHAPTER TWENTY-SEVEN

Something Like a Sky

"So what was your film like?"

"Good, except he ought to have died at the end. Bobs thought so too."

"You both of you wished he was out of the way, did you? I didn't know that was like you."

"We just thought it'd have made more sense if he'd died. I expect they couldn't let him because he's the star."

"That's someone else's trick, keeping people alive when they ought to be dead."

"You're in a funny mood, Dom. It was still good, though. You should have seen it. Maybe we can go again."

"You'd have wanted me to come, would you, Bobby?"

"Why wouldn't we? What's the mood for?"

"I think he's mad because we didn't find out what Nobbly was up to. Did you go and watch his house, Dom?"

"I followed him to his church."

"You didn't let him see you, did you?"

"Don't bother worrying about me, Bobby. He never knew I was there."

"What happened, then? Did anything?"

"Someone smashed up all the church, even the stuff underneath. I went in when he'd gone off in a fit."

"I'll bet he was. His church was all wrong, but who'd do something like that?"

"Must have been someone who read what Eric Wharton wrote. Somebody who cared."

"I expect they were religious, the way our school makes people, Bobs. Only what did you mean, Dom, the stuff underneath?"

"Just a lot of plants, that's all. Plants in pots on tables."

"You look like you think they weren't just plants."

"The ones people brought him that they'd grown on graves. Maybe now they won't be so eager to trust him."

"What do you think he'll do? Do you think he'll give up now everybody knows about him?"

"I've stopped caring what he does since you two don't. Just so long as he stays away from me and all his stuff does."

It would have been truer to say that I'd stopped wanting to talk. I'd sensed Jim's eagerness to question me after mass on Sunday, but our parents hadn't given us the chance. At least meeting Bobby on our way to school meant I only had to tell my sly lies once. Did she notice that I'd just said me rather than us? She seemed less than happy as she said "I've got to catch my bus."

Jim and I caught ours, and I set about rejoining everyday life as best I could, even to the extent of treating him as if I hadn't seen the two of them necking in the cinema. Just now this seemed insignificant, however much it nagged at me, compared to the other things I had to come to terms with.

I don't know how long I wandered through the devastated streets after I'd fled the church. I kept rubbing my fingers on my sleeve in a frantic attempt to rid them of the memory of tendrils clinging to them in sockets vacated by eyes. The end of daylight drove me home to pretend the day had been normal. Telling my mother that the film had been all right let me escape to my room. At least my father didn't quiz me during dinner, but afterwards I was required to enjoy the Saturday evening radio variety show as visibly and vociferously as my parents thought I should. I was all too aware that it only postponed my having to lie in bed in the dark.

I would have left the bedroom light on if this wouldn't have called for more of an explanation than I could provide. As soon as I switched it off I remembered how darkness seemed to have summoned or let loose the presence under the Trinity Church. I could only squeeze my eyes shut and pray even more fervently than I had in the dentist's chair. Did I still retain enough of my lost beliefs for prayers to work? I knew only that I wasn't visited before I succumbed to exhaustion and sleep. After that I prayed every night in bed and devoted most of Sunday mass to repeating the same silent prayer, though the communion wafer still tasted flat as an absence. I might have been reassured by an entire week of nights in which I was left alone if it hadn't been for the encounter in the park.

It was the weekend after I'd been under the Trinity Church. On Saturday I had indeed gone to see *Apache* with the others, though I'd felt they were offering me compensation they might not even recognise as such. For whatever reason, Bobby sat between Jim and me, and I couldn't help growing tense every time they turned to each other. Now that the film had migrated to the Majestic at the top of London Road it had acquired a different second feature, which meant I could tell my parents I'd wanted to see that without lying too much. When we went for our Sunday stroll in the park I didn't feel unduly nervous, even of meeting Mr Noble and his family while I was with my parents – but it was a small wide woman in a fur coat and matching brimless hat who bustled up to us. "Excuse me," she said, "weren't you friends with Mrs Norris?"

"We still are," my father said, I thought more from duty than conviction.

"Oh, then you haven't heard. I'm afraid she passed away last week."

My parents crossed themselves, and I tapped four points on my chest. "That's sad news for a Sunday," my mother said. "We'll pray for her."

"We'll do that," my father declared. "Was she ever discharged from the hospital?"

"She never was," the woman said and turned to my mother. "You brought me her dog. I'm only sorry it ran away."

"Of course, you're Mrs, please don't tell me." Once the woman had refrained from doing so for some moments my mother said triumphantly "Mrs Brough."

"I hope Mrs Norris had a peaceful passing, Mrs Brough," my father said.

"She was calling her hubby's name, they said."

"Well, let's pray they'll be together," my mother said, "and at peace."

"I don't think she was calling quite like that," Mrs Brough said and glanced at me. "Is it all right to speak?"

"Dominic has to grow up," my father said. "He'll be a young man soon enough."

"Well, they said—" Mrs Brough lowered her voice as a family came towards us from the playground. "Supposedly she wasn't calling for her husband so much as about him."

"What about him?"

"Dominic," my mother said, and I thought she'd hushed Mrs Brough as well until the woman murmured "She didn't seem to like what she thought she was going to find."

"That's that Noble fellow's doing," my father said. "The character who ran that travesty of a church she was mixed up with."

"I read about it in the paper. I wish it had been exposed sooner. Let's hope something is done about it," Mrs Brough said, pinching her fur collar tight as if she'd been assailed by a chill.

I nearly betrayed that I knew something had been done, but I needed to learn "When did she die?"

"Last Saturday afternoon. A week yesterday." As though my parents had asked her a pointed question Mrs Brough said "I'd have let you know sooner but I'd no idea where you lived."

I hadn't meant to imply that she'd been remiss in telling us. I'd been hoping that my fears weren't true – that Mrs Norris hadn't died about the time I'd destroyed the contents of the crypt or shortly after. I had an anguished sense that I'd released whatever had stopped Mrs Norris's heart, and that far from calling to her husband, she had been trying to drive him away. When I mumbled "I'm sorry, I didn't mean..." I could have been apologising to her at least as much as I was to Mrs Brough.

"It's all right, son," Mrs Brough said. "I know you cared. I saw how you looked after her dog."

This only made me feel I'd failed there too. "Well, I'll leave you to your constitutional," Mrs Brough said to my parents. "I just wanted you to know you needn't worry any more."

Once she'd ambled away my father said "God help anyone who dies believing what Mrs Norris did."

"That man has a lot to answer for," my mother said, "and God help him."

I no longer had much faith that God helped anyone. I was still hearing Mrs Brough contend that there was no more need to worry when in fact she'd given me an extra reason. Was the creature that had once been Mr Norris on the loose now? That night in bed I prayed more fervently than ever to be left alone, and kept my eyes tight shut so as not to see if I wasn't, a stratagem that very belatedly let me sleep. My fervour decreased as the weeks passed, but I didn't quite dare to stop praying. It felt like abandoning too much.

Guy Fawkes Night brought weeks of ripraps hopping about the streets – fireworks that leapt in every direction, spraying sparks and emitting bangs as they challenged you to avoid them, and made even Bobby scream. On the night itself bonfires and rockets were everywhere, not to mention fire engines and the clangour of their bells. As I watched distant tardy fireworks from my bedroom window I forgot to be afraid of the dark. Some days later I thought I had another reason to forget, which my father found in the morning paper. "Here's an early Christmas present for us all," he said.

He passed it across the marmalade jar for my mother to read. I still recall how the breakfast smell of toast seemed to celebrate our owning our first toaster. When I'd finished my sugary cereal they let me read the item, which was a single paragraph in Eric Wharton's latest column. I've kept the page, along with his other column and the copy I made of Christian Noble's journal and the rest of the evidence. I no longer know what difference I imagined keeping all this would make, if I ever did.

Loyal readers of my ramblings may remember how some weeks ago I wrote about the Trinity Church of the Spirit, a local cult which travestied Christianity and even Spiritualism. At the time I challenged its founder, who is pleased to call himself Christian Noble, to respond to my comments and offered him space in this very column, but apparently he prefers to up sticks and skedaddle. He and his family have moved away from our part of the world, and I fancy many of my readers will join me in wishing him a considerable journey. I gather that the church in Joseph Street has been destroyed by persons unknown. My readers may decide for themselves why this has not been reported to the police. "O, Mr. Eric, sure and you're not responsible," Kitty Malone assures me, "but" (here's some Irish logic for us all) "you ought to be proud if you are."

I didn't quite believe that the Nobles had gone until our Sunday stroll let me see the distant house, outside which a board said SOLD. At first I felt pathetically relieved, and then my thoughts began to swarm. Mr Noble might have moved away from anyone who knew him, but I very much doubted this meant he would change. Oughtn't I just to be glad that I wasn't responsible for dealing with him? I saw this was how my parents felt, and on Monday I found out how Bobby and Jim did. "Hope you read the paper," Jim said. "Nobbly's gone for good and we didn't have to do anything after all."

This might have provoked me to tell them the truth, but I didn't feel they'd earned it, given how they'd behaved when they thought I was investigating him. "You don't think he's going to stop what he does," I protested. "And he's still got his daughter."

"She'll have her mum as well," Bobby said. "Mrs Noble will be able to tell people if she doesn't like what he does now he's been in the paper."

"Bobs is right," Jim said. "Now she'll have evidence."

I tried to find this reassuring, and to an extent I succeeded. At least I felt safe to stop praying at night, and embarrassed by how craven my pleas had been. While I couldn't think I'd destroyed all the presences Mr Noble had summoned, surely he would have taken them with him. That night I slept more soundly than I had for weeks, and it occurred to me that praying had kept me awake.

My doubts hadn't finished with me, however. Not many nights later I was wakened by a dream that felt composed of thoughts. Now that Mrs Norris was dead and Mr Noble had no doubt moved well away, suppose I was the only way Mr Norris could anchor himself to the familiar world, to the image of himself he yearned to have? "Good boy," I could almost hear him whispering, which made me think of a dog. It wouldn't be a penny he was proffering this time, and I preferred not to imagine what the gift might be. The whisper was so close that I dreamed his face was only inches from mine. I lurched awake to avoid seeing what it had become, and opened my eyes before I had time to feel afraid to look.

It wasn't far from dawn. A greyish twilight lay beside me on the pillow, and so did a face. I was able to believe it was an illusion until it moved. The larger of the eyes widened, swelling out of the lopsided head, and beneath the flat patch where a nose should have been, the lips that occupied just the left side of the face writhed like worms. Even if it was composed of an uneven section of the pillowcase, it had a body too, which resembled a snake except for an uneven pair of armless hands, not even opposite each other on the elongated torso that stretched into the dimness of my room. Despite all this, I recognised the intruder from its voice, even though I heard it only in my head. It was indeed repeating "Good boy" as if the words might revive a memory it could grasp.

I think the worst thing might have been the hands, which were waving in a feeble mime of unutterable helplessness. I couldn't move, and panic had cleared all thoughts out of my head. The solitary instinct I still had – childish if not primitive – was to squeeze my eyes tight shut and pray that my visitor would disappear. For a time during which I couldn't breathe I thought the face was crawling closer to mine. Certainly in some way it came so close that I shared a little of the contents of its invaded mind.

It felt like having a nightmare while I was awake – like the effect of a hallucinogenic, as I would learn later in my life. I was watching an unkempt wild-haired man dash through a maze of derelict streets beneath an ominously solid sky the colour of raw liver. He dodged from ruined house to house, peering from behind the incomplete frontages in preparation for his next sprint. He looked desperate to hide but worse than uncertain where he could. Over this spectacle hung a sense of dreadful watchfulness, as if he was being observed with inhuman amusement that felt close to a vast unconcern. He faltered short of an open space that might have been a square, and as he broke cover I saw what was watching him, and cowered within myself.

The raw sky was indeed solid: so substantial that it was able to open a colossal bulging eye that had been peering through a slit I'd taken for a gap in clouds. It was more than an eye, that pupilless gibbous protrusion, for it stretched down from its socket to fasten on its prey. By the time it reached him, the tip was no more than a scrawny pointed tendril that thrust deep into his skull. I saw him jerk in a helpless dance, flailing all his limbs, as it drained him of whatever it craved. When the tendril withdrew into the mass that occupied the sky miles overhead, he was no more than a withered remnant that pranced away through the devastated streets, giggling in a shrill voice that no longer even sounded human. The noise was almost blotted out by another: a rumbling that might have been the preamble to an earthquake. In a moment I recognised it as a monstrous chuckling, a gargantuan utterance of satisfaction after feeding. It was so gigantic that it seemed to swell past definition, so that it might have come from many mouths or from a single unimaginable orifice.

The spectacle appalled me so much that I couldn't keep my eyes shut. The room was brighter now, and there was no face beside me on the pillow, just a crumpled patch of the pillowcase that I dared to rub smooth with my forearm. I lay watching more light gather in the room, and tried to get ready for the day – to maintain my pretence that everything was normal, even banal. In time, when I'd gone through another series of desperately prayerful nights without suffering a second visit, I managed to persuade myself that the incident had been wholly a dream brought on by thoughts of Mr Norris. As for the ruined streets, of course they were based on the wasteland beyond the Grafton. Just a nightmare, I managed to think, but now I know better, that ironic word. I was being treated to a glimpse of a future that was hungry to be born.

ACKNOWLEDGEMENTS

Jenny was there first, as ever. I've a special thank you to Tony Snell and his Radio Merseyside show, on which he reminisced about starting at a new school and brought back all sorts of memories I lent to Dominic Sheldrake. And my profoundest gratitude goes to my old friend Pete Crowther, who gently but persistently suggested I should write a trilogy of supernatural terror until at last I found sufficient reason.

The climax of the novel was written over two weeks at a favourite accommodation of ours, the Matina Apartments in Pefkos on the island of Rhodes.

My old friend Keith Ravenscroft kept me supplied with good things, not least the fine French Blu-ray of my favourite horror film. "Maybe it's better not to know... "

FLAME TREE PRESS
FICTION WITHOUT FRONTIERS
Award-Winning Authors & Original Voices

Flame Tree Press is the trade fiction imprint of Flame Tree Publishing, focusing on excellent writing in horror and the supernatural, crime and mystery, science fiction and fantasy. Our aim is to explore beyond the boundaries of the everyday, with tales from both award-winning authors and original voices.

•